LAST COMES FATE

BOOK 3 OF THE SILVER SPOON TRILOGY

NICOLE FRENCH

raglan

PROLOGUE

Xavier

I was becoming something of an expert on funerals.

This one was rather nice, so far as they go. Smaller than the grand procession organized for my father, but there was still a line of cars that snaked through the village following the chapel service. Henry was buried in the old churchyard on the day autumn arrived. A chilly breeze skimmed off the lake, forcing us into overcoats, but the remnants of summer flowers still floated about the air, reminding everyone of better days. The estate hosted a wake afterward for the peers and MPs and other aristocratic fools who were there more to hobnob with each other than to bid farewell to a man they only ever knew as the brother, then uncle, to much more influential people.

In other words, they were there to see me.

I ignored every one of them.

The service was short. Henry was never much for a lot of words. He preferred a brief, dry joke and a stiff upper lip, as they say. So I offered a few quick remembrances without meeting the eyes of a single supposed mourner. Listed, with the help of Elsie and Frederick's notes, a few of his accomplishments and other contributions to his community.

I actually found out a lot about him. That his favorite food was cook's roasted lamb, and when he was a boy, he dreamed of being a chef himself. Like me. I learned he took particular pride in the little sheep herd we maintained at Kendal and submitted them from time to time to local fairs or shows. He even took first place ribbon at Findon when he was a boy.

What was more than clear was the way he loved Kendal like nothing else. Despite being the second son, he'd been the estate's caretaker for nearly his entire life, since my grandparents both passed when he and Rupert were still just lads. But while Rupert had been more interested in polo and parties, Henry had quietly revolutionized Kendal's means of income over the past thirty-five years. He had seamlessly translated the estate's holdings into a digital economy, yet somehow maintained its status as a modernized country dukedom, complete with farms and tenants that others thought belonged to a different age. A truly hybrid operation that was much more innovative than I'd ever given him credit for when he was alive.

It was understandable, then, why he'd never had children. Kendal was his family. It was the only thing that had ever mattered to him.

The love was clearly returned. The village church was small but packed with locals who cried genuine tears on his behalf. Remaining tenants too. Various businesspeople who had conducted affairs with him outside the ranks of the House of Lords. Friends, family. Even some extended cousins who, yes, included my stepmother, her sister, and the other distant Parkers waiting for my imminent demise as the reluctant Duke of Kendal.

Gone was the only person who'd ever believed I could actually fill the shoes of this ridiculous title.

I couldn't look at any of them. Couldn't fathom this entire congregation who had known and appreciated my uncle, and by extension my father, and therefore me—someone who knew so little about what they had done and was now forced to take it on or let their hard work wither on the vine.

Henry deserved better than that. He deserved better than me.

By the end of the service, I had the outright shakes as I escaped to the garden. I yearned for a drink in peace without a thousand people wondering about the future plans for the estate. It was maybe a little early for brandy, but I was past caring. Anything to quiet the storm that was threatening to split me into pieces.

Unfortunately, the garden was anything but a refuge. The camellia bush at the southeast end was starting to bloom. Amid the browns and yellow and burnt siennas of autumn, the bright pink stood out like a herald.

The color of deepest longing.

The color of my utter regret.

The color of Francesca.

It was everything I could do not to call her after Henry passed and beg her to come back. I did everything through the service to keep her from my mind, knowing I'd have smashed my fist through the lectern if it had come to that.

But with that pink flashing like a strobe through the falling leaves and garden greenery, the memories of her sweet scent, the soft warmth of her body, the mischievous curve of her smile—each one cut through me like one of the rapiers mounted in the library.

She should be here. She'd know exactly what to say to put my head right. But more than that, she'd be grounding, a safe place for me to go when the rest of the world was pressing in, demanding their pound of flesh.

But now she was gone.

Because I'd cocked it all up.

"All right, mate?"

I turned to find Jagger and Elsie—otherwise known as the only other people in the world I could trust—approaching slowly, as if I were a wild animal. Elsie, my mother's best friend and my executive assistant, wore a black version of her typical jumper, wool skirt, and Balmorals—the same uniform she'd had since first meeting my mum in a library nearly thirty years ago. The consistency was, as always, a particular comfort.

Meanwhile, between a designer suit, diamond-encrusted cuff-links, and a manicured goatee, Jagger, my best friend and business partner, was a bit too flash for a gentry funeral. It was something I loved about him, though. You could take the boy out of Croydon, but never Croydon out of the boy. Like me, there was a side of Jag that would always indulge no matter how successful our empire of restaurants became—the part of him that still remembered what it was like to have nothing. Maybe had a hole, deep down, that could never be filled.

They were a bit of an odd pair, standing there in the middle of the garden. But right now, they were everything I had in the whole fucking world.

I yanked at the lapel of my morning suit. To be honest, I was quite annoyed that I had to wear this thing at all. Henry hated fuss, but he did like propriety. Georgina insisted that as the head of the family, I'd be expected to dress like it. And so, to the tailor I went to make my very best impression of an emperor penguin.

Elsie offered a rueful smile as she popped onto her toes to adjust my collar. "Only a bit longer, dear, and then you can leave."

I glanced toward the sky-high windows of the library, where guests hovered around the books in their black and gray finery, some of the women in hats that nearly grazed the ceiling. Shadowy peacocks, all of them.

I snorted. "Leave for where? The nearest pub? I wouldn't mind getting pissed."

"You're not going back to America?" Jagger frowned at my brandy glass, then Elsie, then back at me. "I still have the Paris projects on hold, but if you're game to get them started again..."

I shook my head. "No, don't do that. I've enough to keep me occupied here until we can find another steward."

"You can't be serious, boy."

My mouth fell open. "I—Els—"

"I mean, *really*," she continued. "I raised you better than that. Your dear mum and I taught you right."

I gawked. "Isn't that what Henry would have wanted? Stay here, keep things going?"

"And do exactly what your father did to you? Abandon your child? Make them feel unwanted, uncertain of their place in the world, just like you were?" She shook her head. "Xavier Parker, I have *never* been so ashamed."

I stared into my brandy snifter, cheeks turning the color of the autumn leaves. First the camellia, now Els. I was trying *not* to go there. "It's not abandoning them if I'm giving them a better life, Els."

Neither she nor Jagger looked convinced.

I closed my eyes, inhaled, then exhaled forcefully. I did it another four times, just like Dr. Hazelwood taught me when I started seeing her a few weeks ago. I didn't want to see a therapist. But it was that or tear my fucking flat apart.

My heart rate did calm down, just like she always said it would. I was still angry. Still *so* angry and sad, above all. But I didn't want to rip anyone's heads off anymore. Shockingly simple. I did sometimes wonder why I was paying five hundred quid a session to learn how to breathe. But whatever. If it helped, it helped.

"Boy," Elsie started again.

"I'm not a boy, Els," I cut in. "I haven't been since I was sixteen years old."

Her harsh gaze softened at the mention of that age. When Mum died, and I was on my own for the first time. When Elsie used to bring over stews every few days just to make sure I was at least eating properly.

"Ah, sweetheart. That's where you're wrong. You'll always be my boy."

One of her small hands cupped my face, and the hell if I didn't want to bury my nose in her jumper and cry until my eyes were dry as the Sahara. Dry as my dirty, empty heart.

"Fuck," I muttered. "Oh, *fuck*."

"That's right," Elsie said as she continued to stroke my cheek. "You know what you have to do. Find Francesca and make things right. Henry's at rest now, so you go get your babies, love. Jagger will manage the Parker Group just like he has been, and the estate will keep itself. I'll help Frederick, and whatever we need from you, well, you're only one ring away."

"Babies?" Jagger said, a bemused expression bouncing between us. "Did I miss something?"

Elsie preened. "Did you not know? Our Francesca is expecting. We've got another darling baby Parker on the way."

I took another slug of brandy. "Els, have you been snooping through my emails again?"

She didn't look the slightest bit remorseful. "It's not snooping if it's my job. And no one told you to leave Francesca's missive open in your inbox for all the world to see." She cocked her head. "It was a very nice letter, if I do say so."

I closed my eyes. I'd probably read that email at least a hundred times since it arrived just after Henry's death. It had come as a picture of a handwritten note, one where Francesca's struggle with me, with *us*, with the choices ahead of her, were scrawled through her neat script and multiple cross-outs.

At the end, though, her message was clear: she didn't want to repeat the mistakes of the past. And so, she was telling me this time outright.

And staying exactly where she was. An ocean away.

"She's pregnant again? Blimey, Xav, what were you trying to do?" Jagger was still gaping like a boy watching fireworks.

I wanted to tell him to shut his mouth—he wasn't the one who'd been slapped in the face—twice—by a surprise baby. "It was an accident, just like the last time."

"More like a Freudian slip," Jagger joked. "It was a mistake the first time, so you'd think you'd both be more careful the second go. Happens again..." He shook his head. "Come on. How hard it is to wear a Johnny?"

I opened my mouth to argue but found I couldn't. It was true—Francesca and I had been playing with fire all summer. She was on the pill, yeah, but she'd forgotten it plenty of times over the course of chaos—not to mention it was a complete ball-ache to get a refill while on a waiting list for a GP. Meanwhile, I had a box of Durex in my nightstand I hadn't even opened. Best intentions flew out the bloody window the second I saw that woman naked and willing.

And maybe Jagger was right, too. Maybe there was a part of me that wanted it. Wanted more with her. Wanted everything. I'd bought a ring after all—the pink diamond cluster I'd carried it everywhere, even after she'd left.

Fuck me. I still had it even now in my jacket pocket, a sad talisman of my complete and utter failure.

"She's only a few hours away right now, you know," Elsie prodded.

I turned. "What?"

"Italy. For her brother's wedding, remember? She sent you her schedule last week so you could keep up your FaceTime dates with Miss Sofia."

I blinked. All the communication with Francesca, since she had fled England last month, was a blur between too much drinking, mourning my uncle, and bruising my knuckles nightly on my heavy bag. I hadn't missed a FaceTime with my little girl, but only with Elsie's help.

"She's in Italy?" I repeated.

Elsie nodded. "A quick plane ride away. And I happen to know the Parker jet is available at the Kendal airstrip just now."

Jagger lifted one brow expectantly and helpfully took my near-empty brandy glass out of my hand. "Go on, Xav. We can entertain the suits. Go get your girls."

I was moving before I even realized my decision, jogging through the garden and up around to the front of the estate to avoid the crowd. There were things that needed to be done. Papers to sign, deals to make, projects to finish that Henry had started.

They could rot in the lake for all I cared.

"Xavier! Where in the world are you going?"

I stopped at the great entry to face Georgina. The dowager duchess—my father's widow who had been a thorn in my side for years—stood at the bottom of the front steps in her funerary finest, including a hat approximately the size of Germany on her perfectly set, light brown hair. Her pearl earrings dangled softly in the breeze, but her face was pinched sharp as an arrowhead.

I took another deep breath and held it long enough for my fists to unclench before I faced her.

"You can't leave," she said. "We've still guests here. You're expected to welcome them properly, as the duke."

For now, her tone suggested clearly as if she'd said it aloud.

After all, wasn't that what she wanted?

"I have to go, Georgie," I said. "I've some business with my family, and now that the funeral is over, I need to tend to it."

There. Short and sweet, and I'd even managed not to rip her head clean off.

I turned to leave, but she hurried up the stairs to catch me by one of the coat tails, like a spoiled little girl grabbing her kitty's tail.

"What is it, Georgina?" I practically roared after she jerked me backward. "What the fuck do you want from me?"

So much for sweet. Deep breathing could only go so far when it came to this one.

"How dare you speak to me that way. I demand respect!"

"You," I said, thrusting a finger in her face, "can fuck right off. How's that for respect?"

"Xavier!"

"Don't Xavier me, *Duchess,*" I snapped. "I'm leaving now to fix the mess you made. Do you think I don't know it was you who sent Ces and Sofia home? Do you think I don't know you've been working for months to have my title stripped in the House of Lords? Do you think I don't know all of it?"

It came out like a waterfall of bitterness, and just like that, my fists were clenched back up, tight as rocks. God, when I thought of what she'd done, I wanted to burn the place down. And her with it, like the witches of the old days. In my frame of mind, I really thought she deserved it.

Heartless, I know. But I never claimed to be a good man. I wasn't going to start now.

Georgina's overly plump mouth fell open as she took another step backward, like she sensed the pending threat. "I—it doesn't matter now. This family has appearances to keep up. You can't just *leave*."

"I can, and I fucking will."

I turned then and started back up the stairs, taking two at a time in a hurry to retrieve my things and be gone.

"If you leave, you'll lose it all."

I froze at the top as her voice echoed through the foyer.

"You're right," she said evenly, glancing to the side to make sure we weren't to be interrupted by any guests. "Caroline and I *have* been working to overturn the entail. It's absurd that you ever became the heir, when by rights it should have been Henry, and then Frederick, considering *his* father was the next male heir in line. Rupert was *my* husband. I knew him better than anyone. And there was no way he would have ever married a kitchen maid, much less in a Buddhist temple. I *will* find the proof, Xavier. That is a promise."

I stared at her for a long time. Long enough for her brown-eyed gaze to waver and for her set jaw to tremble. I took one step down, then another, and another until I was back on the landing, staring down at her from my considerable height.

"The next time you address me, you will use my title or Your Grace, as custom demands," I said in a low voice that shook with suppressed rage. "In the meantime, you will vacate the premises immediately after the wake or else be escorted by every Bobbie in the area. Squatting rights *don't* apply to the likes of you, you despicable piece of shite."

Her mouth fell open. "How *dare* you—"

"Now," I interrupted, waving away her weak admonishments. "I'm going to Italy to get the mother of my children. And I may not be back for a very long time, depending on how badly you've fucked things up. So, until then, your behavior will determine your fortunes when I do return. And you do not want to be on the receiving end of my rage, Georgina. You won't like what comes of it when properly simmered."

ONE

Francesca

"**I** do."

The pair of words couldn't be said enough on this trip, apparently. Which made sense. It was a wedding, after all.

But since my brother, Matthew, and his new wife, Nina, had declared their intentions not two hours ago in a fourteenth-century Italian church, they seemed to be using that particular phrase for just about everything.

Would you care for a refreshment, *signore?*

I do.

Nina, do you want someone to save your bouquet to dry for the future?

Why yes, *I do.*

Matthew, do you want to dance with your new bride?

Yes, I fuckin' do.

Every time, the crowd went even more wild. Like right now, when approximately fifty people were laughing like hyenas after Matthew shouted it, profanities and all, across the *Piazza Guglielmo*

Marconi, this time in reply to the bandleader of the jazz quartet who'd asked him if he wanted them to start playing so he and Nina could dance later. Every person at the party cheered as my brother then leaned down and delivered yet another long, drawn-out kiss to his bride.

I should have been happy for them. A perfect little family that had fought for so long to come together this way. Matthew was ecstatic. His wife was aglow. Her daughter, Olivia, was practically a sunbeam.

And I was the rainiest rain cloud there ever was.

A Mary Bennett compared to the rest of her vivacious sisters, antisocial and irritable. My kinship with Elizabeth and her Darcy was long gone.

It was a lovely autumn night. The forty or so of us who had made it to the destination wedding indulged in wine, pasta, hand-pulled mozzarella, and the last of the season's tomatoes beneath a canopy of strung lights, courtesy of the trattoria hired to cater this lovely affair. The little band kicked off a selection of jazz standards that only added to the overall ambience, especially when some of the locals and other tourists made use of the dance floor hastily erected atop the cobbled square. No one seemed to mind—if anything, the impromptu dancers lent even more romance to what was already a near-elopement.

The sunset gleamed off the Mediterranean waves.

Plates of trofie noodles steamed in front of every carefully set place.

Guests joked and chatted while enjoying the bountiful food and wine.

And I was heartbroken, lonely, and sick as a freaking dog.

"God, just *look* at them," my sister Kate muttered. "Disgusting, aren't they?"

Matthew swept Nina up from her chair, abandoning their food to start waltzing in the middle of the square. My brother was old-school in ways that included a penchant for vintage suits and our grandparents' dance moves, but he never cared for propriety. Not when it came to his Nina. It shouldn't have been a surprise that he was abandoning tradition to dance with his new wife just as soon as he damn well pleased. And if Nina's glowing smile was any indication, she liked that impulse just fine.

I couldn't help staring as the nausea in my belly was temporarily replaced by envy. They were elegant together, yes. Nina was possibly an even better dancer than Matthew, an impressive feat given the fact that all of us had been subject to Nonna's "lessons" when we were growing up. The two of them moved so naturally to a jazz version of "Someday My Prince Will Come" that they could have been doubles for Fred Astaire and Ginger Rogers, especially when his dark head touched her bright blond hair.

But mostly, it was their closeness that made jealousy gnaw at my empty stomach. Nina had changed from her couture wedding gown into a simpler off-white dress that fluttered around her calves, and Matthew had long since eschewed his tie and jacket, making do in shirtsleeves while he wrapped one arm around Nina's waist and used the other to tuck her hand against his chest so that they were truly dancing cheek to cheek.

His lips moved, whispering some silent, sweet nothing into her ear. Nina only nuzzled him further, then allowed him to engage her with yet another kiss in which they were obviously the only two in the entire town, guests and villagers be damned.

It made me want to retch.

Or sob.

Maybe both.

"Hey, you two, the first dance is supposed to be *after* dinner," Marie, one of my younger sisters, called from the other side of the table.

"Let them be," I chided, even though watching them was so painful, I wanted to shriek.

That was supposed to be me.

Or maybe it could have been.

For one short summer, I had been so, *so* close. Eight weeks ago, I'd been in love too. I had a man to dance with, and my daughter, Sofia, had a father at last. When Xavier Parker, dashing London restauranteur and prodigal duke, had strode back into my life with the force of a gale, I certainly hadn't intended to fall in love with him all over again. Honestly, I'd barely expected him to like me after what I did. Hiding the fact that you had a man's baby and not telling him for five years isn't exactly a direct path to his good side.

But somehow, the love and attraction and, well, the outright passion we'd shared all those years before had prevailed. Which was how Sofia and I had come to spend the summer in England with Xavier—both so she could continue building her new relationship with her daddy and so he and I could determine whether what we thought we had between us was real.

Spoiler alert: it wasn't.

They say love conquers all.

"They" would be dirty rotten liars.

It took all of two months for the pressures of Xavier's job, title, and uptight conniving family to rip our tenuous bonds to shreds and decorate them with tinsel. I had left almost as suddenly as I'd arrived, chased back to Brooklyn with every intent of returning to my simple life as a third-grade teacher and single mom.

Life, however, had other plans.

Specifically in the form of a positive pregnancy test.

Again.

"God, this is so good." Kate inhaled from her bowl of *trofie al pesto* and couldn't help but moan. "Nonna, don't kill me, but I think this might be better than yours."

Our grandmother just turned from the next table where she was enjoying a fifty-years-in-the-making cigarette with her sister and several cousins. She held her fingertips together as she gave a little shake of her hand, then went right back to gossiping with her family.

"That's how you know she's had one too many," Kate joked in my ear. "Won't even argue with critiques of her cooking."

I offered a weak smile. The twists of pasta were famous in this town, but to me, they looked like someone had lost their lunch on my plate.

"Look at her," Kate continued. "The cigarette, the wine, the big, big hair. She's so Italian right now it hurts. It's like watching a salmon return to its spawning grounds after the long migration."

I was supposed to laugh, but suddenly all I could sense was the flavor of Kate's breath, tinged with red wine, basil, and garlic.

"Jesus, Katie," I gasped, trying and failing to breathe only through my mouth.

"What?"

I pushed back from the table and made a beeline for the restaurant, weaving in and out of the crowd, flapping my hands at stray relatives who wanted yet another kiss to the cheek, and barely finding my way to the tiny bathroom in time to lose every bite I had just taken into the toilet.

I retched again.

And again.

To the point I thought it might actually turn my body inside out.

But eventually, the nausea faded away, leaving me sweaty-faced, clammy, and exhausted when I emerged from the stall, only to find Kate leaning against the sink with her arms crossed over her chest.

"Thought you might need one of these," she said, offering me one of the hand towels. "And also someone to talk to."

My stomach dropped again, and this time it wasn't because of too many aromatics.

"What's going on?" Kate demanded.

I leaned over to wash my hands and splash my face with water. "I don't know what you mean."

"Frankie, come on. You were about as green as a lima bean out there. I thought you were going to hurl all over the table."

I gazed at my reflection in the mirror. Sweat gleamed around my brow line, and deep circles were pressed under my eyes, but my makeup wasn't too badly ruined. My green eyes were a bit brighter than before, but at least they matched the color of my dress.

"I almost did," I admitted.

"Yeah, I can see that." Kate checked her updo in the mirror, then her sleek black dress, which was almost certainly vintage, as if making sure I hadn't splattered on it through the door. "That's the third time I've seen you sprint for the bathroom today. Please tell me it's just a virus. Or maybe food poisoning. Because the last time you were like this, you were..." She trailed off, clearly cut off by the look on my face. "Ah, shit."

I gulped and managed to stand up straight so I could look myself over. There was no use hiding it from her. Not when she knew me better than anyone else. Unfortunately, this also meant the cat was out of the bag. Kate was reasonably discreet, but there was no way this was going to stay a secret for long now.

I turned from side to side. I wasn't showing yet. Not really. The hunter-green dress I wore wasn't exactly form-fitting, and the only other discernible difference was my boobs, which were more than filling out the bust. Before, I could write it off as weight gain in Europe. Too many scones, not enough fresh air.

I sighed, then grabbed one of the complimentary bottles of water on the counter to swish around and cleanse my mouth. "Don't tell anyone, Kate. Please. I don't want to mess up Mattie and Nina's special day."

My sister just looked me over, pity written across her delicate features. We looked so much alike, but Kate was always the stronger of the two of us. Taller, of course, but it was more than that. She had the no-nonsense sensibility of someone who had never lived in the throes of an existential crisis. She'd always known exactly who she was.

I sank onto an upholstered bench in the corner to wait for my face to return to a normal hue. Kate sat down with me and rubbed my leg.

"Is it bad?" she wondered.

I shrugged. "About like last time. My boobs are pretty tender, and the nausea comes and goes throughout the day. Most of the time it's all right, but now and then, it hits me, and…"

I trailed off. No need to explain *that*.

Kate glanced down, obviously looking for a bump. "Does he know?"

I didn't have to ask whom she was talking about.

I sighed. "I sent Xavier an email a few days ago. He hasn't responded yet. He must have read it, though. He checks his email like once an hour. Or at least Elsie does. His assistant, I mean."

My chest squeezed again at the thought of the kind, middle-aged woman who had taken Sofia and me under her wing all summer. In a way, she'd become a part of our little family too. England hadn't been all bad…

And for maybe the hundredth time since I'd gotten on that plane, I wondered again if I'd left too soon.

Right before I remembered Xavier's lips on someone else's.

Nausea struck again for an entirely different reason.

Kate grimaced, like she knew exactly how hard this was for me. Life was certainly repeating itself in the worst possible ways.

Once again, I'd fallen deeply in love with Xavier Parker over the course of a few weeks.

Once again, he'd broken my heart with his involvement with another woman.

Once again, I was left single and pregnant.

Fate certainly had a funny sense of humor. Stupid cow.

This time, however, the father knew. He just hadn't said a word. And it was killing me anyway, as if he'd never known in the first place.

"Everyone's going to flip when you tell them," Kate remarked.

I looked at her. "Why do you think I want you to be quiet? I'm not really interested in every Zola on the continent gossiping about how I'm going to hell while my brother is basking in marital bliss."

She blinked like she was surprised just imagining it. "I don't mean like that. We all know you're a good person, babe, not to mention a killer mom. I just mean, they are going to flip the fuck out at Xavier. Mattie's probably going to fly to England to kick that posh Brit's ass. Joni will post all about him on social media, which you know will blow up. And since the press over there seems to think you two are a tasty treat, I'm sure you'll have them at your door in no time, which means—"

"Which means you and everyone else need to keep your mouths shut," I said sharply. "And not say anything before the wedding is over. I'm not kidding, Katie. Shut it."

She mimed zipping her mouth with a lock and throwing away the key. I quieted with her. Kate was the one Zola kid I knew could keep a secret. With the others, I might as well just send a press release to the *New York Post*. When Nonna found out, she'd be dragging me to confession for days.

Kate looked down at my hand resting on my belly. "I assume you're keeping it. Again, I mean."

I gave her a look. "Are you really asking me that?"

"How can I not? Don't get me wrong, Frankie. A woman's got a right to choose and all that. Of course. But can we take a second to really think about this choice? Raising Sofia on your own has been hard enough. You're a third-grade teacher who's been broke all her life and sleeps in a stairwell. I know Mattie gave you the house, but what are you going to do to support two kids alone? How are you going to take care of yourself?"

"It will be different this time," I replied stubbornly. "For one, I'm *not* doing it completely alone."

"I thought you said he hasn't responded."

I sulked at my hands. "He hasn't. Yet."

"So how do you know he will?"

My scowl literally hurt my face, it ran so deep. "I just...do."

Kate did not appear convinced. I wish I could say I was.

"Mattie's gone," she reiterated. "And I know I'm not moving to Brooklyn. I love you, but I can't. Marie's in Paris, Lea's got her own henhouse to attend to. So that leaves, what, Joni? You want ADHD Tinker Bell taking care of your littles?"

I just sighed. She was right. I knew she was right. With Xavier living in the UK, it wasn't like we'd be able to trade custody nights or anything like that. If he ever did respond to my letter, the most he was probably going to do would be to send some money. Not unhelpful. But not the same as actually being around.

"I've thought about it," I admitted. "A lot. But here's the deal: I always wanted a family. A sister or brother for Sofia. Maybe not this way, but it seems to be what fate has in store. Better my kids have the same father than get pulled between three different households, you know?"

I sighed, shoving a hand into my hair, which was already noticeably thicker. One of the lesser benefits of pregnancy, I supposed.

"Besides, this time Xavier knows," I insisted. "Or will know. Or something. We might not have worked out, but he's not a deadbeat dad. Once he gets his head around this little surprise, he'll support his kids. We won't be destitute. Not even close."

"I sure as shit hope not. The guy has more money than God." Kate looked at me for a long time and tapped her fingers on her knee. "What about your heart, though? Is that going to be destitute?"

That part I didn't like thinking about. "Maybe I'm not destined for some great love affair, Katie. Most people never get a happily ever after, and that's okay, you know? I may not be someone's perfect match, but I can be a great mom. I can have a family on my own terms, this time. Maybe that's good enough."

We watched each other in the mirror for a few minutes, our twin green eyes and dark hair speaking to the generations of other Zola sisters who had come before us, maybe not even that far from where we were sitting.

They'd gotten through times like these.

So would I.

Kate pursed her red-stained lips and sighed. "Okay. But when we get home, you have to spill the beans to everyone. You might be living on your own, but you still have your family to support you. We can, I don't know, get a babysitting train going or something. I could give you a few Friday nights a month so you can do a yoga class. Or get laid."

"You're the best," I told her honestly. "I don't know what I would do without any of you."

I pulled her into a tight embrace, but just as we released, the bathroom door opened, and Marie and Joni came bouncing in. It was quite a feat, considering Joni was on crutches after having surgery to fix a knee injury. It had been almost two months since Marie had left for culinary school in Paris, but they were as inexplicably inseparable and as different as ever. Even in their choice of dresses—Marie wore a plain blue frock that brushed her toes and completely covered her arms and shoulders, while Joni's bright pink confection pushed the limits on what was socially appropriate with a neckline cut halfway to her navel and a lace skirt that barely covered her butt.

"What did we miss?" Marie asked, looking between the two of us as she pushed her glasses up her nose.

"Nothing," I said with a warning glance at Kate. "Absolutely nothing. Just, you know, overcome by all the wedding joy."

"Well, nothing is about to become something," Joni said eagerly. "We came to find you, Frankie, because there is a super hot-as-frick man asking for you outside. One Sofia just called Dad. Yes, *please*, by the way. I remember him being yummy, but dayum, Daddy!"

"Ew, Joni, that's Sofia's father," Marie said, elbowing her in the ribs.

"Doesn't mean he can't be Frankie's daddy too," Joni said with a wink.

I reared. "Xavier's *here*?"

Marie nodded but elbowed Joni again. "Yes. And don't be gross."

"Don't be celibate," Joni retorted, then hobbled forward with a conspiratorial grin. "Seriously, though, sis. Do we need to go out there and kick his ass for you? I might have a bum knee right now, but I still got thighs of steel. I could squeeze the life out of him, then kick him across the square if you want. Or we could just sic Mattie on him. He's so wound up with sexual tension, he'd probably tear Xavier a new one for cheating on you the way he did."

Kate just gave me another look, this one of the distinct *I told you so* variety.

I stood up, checked myself in the mirror, then turned toward the door.

"Thanks, but I don't think that's necessary," I told my sisters. "When it comes to Xavier, I can take care of myself."

Maybe if I said it enough, I'd really learn to believe it.

TWO

I found Xavier pacing impatiently at the periphery of the party, rendering a tall and admittedly intimidating shadow by the lights hanging above. Kate left to distract Lea and Nonna, but I'd been unable to shake my two younger sisters, who insisted on escorting me to the "sexy gargoyle," as Joni called him.

He wasn't dressed for a wedding, but more for travel, in jeans, an Arsenal T-shirt, and a black jacket that hugged his broad shoulders and trim waist, plus a pair of colorful sneakers from the collection I happened to know took up a full wall in his London closet.

Chef.

Duke.

Sneaker addict.

I loved every iteration of this man.

But right now, I was furious no matter what form he took.

And terrified of what he must be thinking of me.

"Holy smokes, I forgot how hot he is." I heard Joni's heated whisper to Marie as we all approached.

"You've already said that like ten times. And he's not hot," Marie replied, though she didn't sound very convinced. "And don't be gross. That's Frankie's man, not yours."

I whirled around. "He is not my man."

Both my sisters gave me the same expressions they wore whenever they said "Okay, boomer" to Nonna.

"He's here, isn't he?" Marie countered.

Joni was back to eyeballing Xavier over my shoulder. "Didn't you say he has a brother?"

"Stepbrother," I hissed, horrified that this conversation might be overheard. "They're only very distantly related, and they look nothing alike."

"Still." Joni licked her lips as if Frederick was the equivalent of a slice of Nonna's cheesecake. "If he's got half your man's attitude, I'd climb that baby duke like a damn tree."

"He is *not* my man!"

"Francesca?" Xavier called. He was waving a big hand, trying to get my attention.

I waved back, then turned to my sisters.

"Ooooh, Franc*esc*a," they tittered at each other. "Fancy!"

"Do you mind?" I snapped. The two of them really were as bratty at twenty-four and twenty-five as they had been as toddlers. "This is kind of important. Take the peanut gallery somewhere else."

Joni gave me a quick salute and then somehow managed, with Marie's help, to skitter back to the party on crutches.

I needed to get out of here. The festivities were slightly derailed by more than a few cousins whispering about "Frankie's man." I could already see Kate talking to Lea and Lea pointing my way. Sofia was with her cousins, all of them dancing around Matthew and Nina while they were still wrapped in each other's arms. But that wouldn't last long.

Then I caught Xavier's hypnotically blue gaze fixed squarely on me and nearly forgot to breathe. I had to admit, Joni was right. Six weeks apart hadn't exactly dimmed Xavier's inherent shine, which would only make him that much more attractive to the gossip fiends around us.

"Ces," he said, reaching out as I exited the cordoned-off wedding area. "I found you."

How could three simple words speak so deeply? Even his frank, open expression made me stumble. It had been so long since I'd seen that expression. Well before all the drama with his family, before he'd transformed from a charming, tattooed chef into the Duke of Kendal.

My heart squeezed at the thought. Lord, I missed that Xavier. I wasn't necessarily looking for the carefree twenty-something cook I'd met five and a half years ago, but the man who'd welcomed me to London in July would do just fine. He was still richer than Croesus, but that Xavier loved jeans better than suits. His idea of a perfect evening was dinner with his family, snuggling on the couch while he watched a soccer match, then sweeping me off to bed to score a goal of his own. He was a far cry from the besuited aristocrat I'd left in August, who was more concerned with wealth and politics than the mental health of his own family. Who went around kissing the local viscount's daughter when he was sad.

The familiar knot of anger and nausea tightened in my belly again at *that* particular memory. I grabbed it like an apple and held fast. Yes, that was what I needed to remember here. Not the way I wanted to swim in those deep blue eyes or how that growl turned me into a different kind of animal.

I needed to remember that Xavier Parker was a liar. A cheat. A complete and utter thief of my heart. And no matter how charmingly bereft he looked, how long he searched for me, how many times he found me, he couldn't have it back again. Ever.

"Here I am," I said shortly. "What are you doing here?"

"Well, I got your email."

When I didn't respond, he gave me a look, which I didn't need to be Sherlock Holmes to decipher. It was a very clear "What the fuck, Frankie?" kind of expression. I got it a lot from my siblings.

I sighed, then glanced behind me, where even more people were taking note of the appearance of a six-five, half-Japanese Englishman glowering at me. My audience now included Nonna and the rest of my siblings on the far side of the piazza, and even Matthew and Nina had stopped dancing to look our way. Sofia had yet to stop playing ring-around-the-rosy with a bunch of other children, but when she saw her daddy again, it would all be over.

We needed to have this conversation in a private place, or this wedding was going to turn into the "Frankie and the Duke" show real quick.

"Come with me," I said, grabbing Xavier's hand, ignoring the little pricks of electricity that flew through my skin at his warm, solid touch. The black tattoo that wound around his torso, shoulder, and left arm was peeking over his wrist, threatening to lick my fingers.

No. I wasn't going to think of that now.

His fingers curled around mine and squeezed, and I ignored the way my heart seemed to do the same in response.

I pulled him through the smaller crowds of tourists at a few other restaurants until we reached the road traversing the other side of the harbor. Xavier followed my brisk steps down *Via Visconti* until we had passed the village and were striding by boats tied to the jetty. When we could walk no farther and were primarily surrounded by the winds and water of the Mediterranean, I turned to face the shadow who had come to call at last.

"So," I said.

But Xavier did not speak, simply folded his arms across his broad chest and waited.

I pressed my lips together. "I know you didn't stalk me all the way to Italy just to stare at me, Xavi."

The divot between his brows grew deeper. "I didn't stalk you. You and Sof both told me about the trip last week when she and I FaceTimed. And you sent me a note about the time change too."

I opened my mouth to argue but found I couldn't. "Fine. Okay. But you didn't want to have whatever conversation this is by phone? You had to come here and disrupt my brother's wedding? Put on a show for the whole family? You're not exactly someone who blends in, and now there is an entire piazza full of Zolas ready to eat up this gossip like it's the world's best tiramisu."

He tipped his head like a raven. "It seemed...important to do it in person."

For a moment, I imagined this wasn't about the bomb I'd dropped on him via email only three days earlier. I imagined he was here for a completely different reason. That maybe he was about to beg for my forgiveness, declare his undying love, maybe even get down on one knee under this starry sky with the music playing in the distance...

I shook my head violently. No. Those fantasies were silly girlish ideas that had earned me this broken heart and dashed dreams in the first place.

No more silly fantasies for this girl. No more unreasonable expectations.

It was time for me to come to terms with who Xavier Parker really was. A cad. A rake. My children's father, yes, but never again would he be the master of my heart.

Xavier took a step forward and captured my hand with his. "So, it's true, then?"

I blinked down at my hand, engulfed by his broad, warm palm. "I—"

"We're going to have another baby?"

I looked up, and the vulnerability I saw in his sapphire eyes nearly sent me to my knees. Was it possible he *wasn't* angry?

I knew that expression well. It was the same one I'd seen in the mirror both times I ended up with a positive pregnancy test. The same one that haunted me whenever I got a call from Sofia's school or heard that *particular* scream when she scraped her knee.

Pure. Parental. Terror.

Honestly. You don't really know the meaning of fear until you love someone more than you love yourself. Parenthood is like walking a bridge without a guardrail. You're always a little bit certain someone might fall to their death.

"Yes," I said quietly, squeezing his hand, if only to let him know he wasn't alone in that feeling. "Yes, I'm pregnant."

His eyes flew over me, a man taking stock. "You know, I think I can see it."

I yanked my hand away. "You cannot. I'm only eight weeks along. Not showing at all."

Xavier's wide mouth curved into that wicked smirk I loved so much. "Maybe not to other people. But *I* know that body, Ces."

I *hated* the way my skin warmed at the reminder. As if said body knew that to be true, even if I mentally insisted it was not.

"It's different," Xavier continued. "Your cheeks are fuller, a bit more pink in the apples. Curves just a bit more distinct, 'specially round the backside."

"You cannot possibly see that in a dress," I argued, though I was already twirling around like a puppy chasing its tail to see if I could spot the difference he mentioned.

"And your breasts, babe. Come on. Obviously I'd notice when they're *that* big." Xavier chewed on his lower lip appreciatively in a way that made my stomach flip. "All in all, you look like an impossibly ripe peach, ready to be picked from the tree."

His eyes drifted over each body part as he spoke, and by the time he was finished, goose bumps covered my skin. There was no hint of nausea anymore, just the distant taste of peach juice in the back of my mouth. And a distinct desire to be plucked, as promised.

Dammit. Yes, *that* was another pregnancy side effect I was really hoping to skip this time around. With Sofia, I had worn out *two* vibrators for want of a partner. One partner in particular, who was standing in front of me, looking like I was something he wanted to eat.

Oh, *lord*.

Xavier blinked, and when his gaze met mine again, his desire vanished, replaced by concern.

My heart gave a strong thump. When I'd sent that email, it was only out of the desperate knowledge that this time, I couldn't make the same mistake. I might have been angry at Xavier, but I wasn't going to rob him of his child's birth all over again. Nor could I rob this child of their father. Not when I knew what a wonderful one he could really be.

"So...what now?" I asked. "I know it's not exactly convenient. Especially after how we left things in Kendal."

"You mean after *you* left things in Kendal."

Something flashed in his eyes, and it was clear Xavier's famous temper wanted to rear its ugly head. Yell, insult, maybe break something while he did it. It was a good reminder that his poor time management and wandering lips weren't the only reasons I was better off without him.

Besides, we'd done enough fighting after I'd returned to New York in August. Shouted at each other from across the Atlantic and traded angry texts while Sofia slept. I'd thought initially—maybe even hoped—that he would have gotten on a plane to follow us. But things with his family were too difficult. And now that his uncle had finally passed, I couldn't imagine they were any easier. Xavier was basically a lone mouse in a pit full of snakes.

And so, eventually, the shouting had stopped. We'd come to an uneasy ceasefire, if not full acceptance.

"I might regret a lot of things when it comes to us, Ces," Xavier said heavily. "But I could never regret our children."

Again, my heart squeezed when he said "children." As in, not just the one, but both, including the little cluster of cells multiplying inside me. Xavier felt the same way I did, that already this little being was a part of our family.

It gave me no end of relief.

"Anyway, we can grapple through what you did when you come back."

My brows flew up. "Come back?"

Xavier paced back and forth in a tight formation while he spoke. "Well, obviously you're returning to London. We've got better hospitals. We'll go private, of course, but NHS is still there if you need it.

Sof can do her last year of nursery in London, and meanwhile, we'll get her into the best primary school the year after. No need for you to work or do much of anything unless you want. But there's loads more to get done—set up a new nursery at the flat, to start. I'll call Elsie, have her get in touch with the decorator. Ces, what is it?"

He stopped moving to inspect me with interest. I must have looked like a ghost, because with every item he listed, it genuinely felt like a pint of blood drained from my face. By the time he was finished speaking, my mouth was fully agape, and I had grabbed hold of a post to steady myself.

"Ces, what's wrong?" Xavier scanned my body again, this time in a completely un-lascivious manner. "Are you all right?"

"I'm—I'm fine." I finally managed to regain control of my features and stand up straight. "I'm just wondering what fairyland you're living in right now where you think any of that is actually going to happen."

All the hope on Xavier's handsome face was immediately replaced by his trademark scowl. "Come again?"

I took a deep breath, then gave a great sigh, counting to ten as I did. This was not the place to lose my temper with him. "Xavi, I hate to disappoint you, but we're not moving back to the UK. You can be a part of this child's life as much as you like, same as with Sofia, but none of us are leaving New York."

A storm was brewing on his face, the same as it might off this very coastline. His fists curled into tight mallets at his sides.

"That's absurd," he said through his teeth. "You can't just make that decision on your own."

"What, like you just did?" I countered. "That was a lot of planning you made without consulting me."

"Ces, I realize you have connections in New York—"

"If you call living there *my entire life* 'connections,' then sure." If he hadn't been blocking my path down the jetty, I would have marched back to said connections right then, gossip fest be damned. "I have 'connections.' Personally, I would call it a family. Friends.

Literally everything that makes me happy. People who don't abandon me with strangers and run around behind my back and break my heart. But, sure, 'connections.'"

Xavier looked like he'd been slapped.

"I have an entire business to run," he continued as if I hadn't even spoken. "Two, actually, if you count the dukedom and Parker holdings. Not to mention my uncle just died—"

"Yes, and I am sorry for that, but—"

"Leaving me to manage a thousand-year-old estate without anyone else to replace him," he finished. "Even if I wanted to, I can't just uproot everything for you. It's bloody unreasonable!"

He couldn't have hurt me worse if he'd tried.

I wasn't being unreasonable. Some things had to matter more than money. Things like my kids. My family. My job, even if it wasn't the one I wanted right now.

I knew I had already pledged not to take Xavier back, but there was obviously still some part of me that wanted Xavier to put me first in a meaningful way, just once. Otherwise, hearing him so clearly do the opposite wouldn't hurt so damn much.

Why was I the only person who understood these priorities? Why was I the only one expected to be flexible and mold my life around my family's needs instead of taking care of my own? Why was he allowed to prioritize his job and businesses and career while I was supposed to leave everything important to me?

I wasn't asking for anything out of the ordinary.

Scratch that. I wasn't asking at all.

Besides, we weren't that couple anymore. The one that would do anything for each other. If we ever were. I might have been carrying his baby, but that didn't mean my life belonged to Xavier Parker. That didn't mean I had to put his personal interests before my own.

Not anymore.

And the truth was, I couldn't wait for a man to put me first anymore. Kate was right. I needed to take care of myself. And that did not mean leaving everyone I loved for someone who had already proven he did not have the ability to put anyone first but his stupid, gorgeous self.

"That's all up to you," I said between my teeth. "But I'm not leaving my support system. Not after what happened this summer."

"Are you fucking kidding me? After *what* happened this summer, exactly?" The storm clouds in his eyes flashed as if struck through with lightning. "Are you talking about how I provided for you and Sofia completely while I managed a family crisis? Or where I introduced you to every part of my life without asking a thing in return?"

"I am not doing this with you again," I informed him, though my jaw was grinding, holding back a shout. "We've had this fight too many times to count already."

"Maybe it's the moment you walked out on me without a word that you're referring to?" Xavier rambled on. "Maybe that's what you're trying to avoid, eh? Actually owning your own mistakes. Taking real accountability."

"You can't tell me what to do anymore, Xavi!" I cried. Lord, the tears were coming fast, thanks to the fact that I had fully transformed into a Francesca-shaped ball of hormones. "We're over! I'm sorry, but that's the truth. So you don't have the right to dictate my life—not that you ever did!"

"Well, I *do* have a right to be there when my child is born!" Xavier thundered right back. "And you're not going to take that away from me again either!"

"No one is saying that." I swiped viciously at my face. It wasn't nausea, though this was almost worse. "But I'm not willing to uproot everything because you say so. Sofia and I have friends in New York. Family we actually love, who have been there for us since the beginning. I have a job. She already has a school. We have a *life*, Xavi. You don't get to come in here with your wads of money and your arrogant grin and take our world away just because you knocked me up again!"

"He *what*?"

Xavier and I both jumped at the sound of my brother's voice, then turned to find him, plus the rest of my family, striding down the boardwalk toward us.

"Dammit," I muttered.

"Fuck," Xavier spat.

Matthew approached with a face as black as the night sky. "Frankie, is it true?" He turned to Xavier. "Did you get my sister pregnant *again?*"

THREE

Matthew didn't wait for an answer, just hurtled down the marina, followed by Lea, Kate, Joni, and Marie, all jogging in their heels and dresses to keep up with him like a row of ducklings.

"Mattie, don't," I started but had to turn away from them all so I could wipe tears and smudged makeup off my face.

Not that it would hide a freaking thing. But really, this was the last thing we needed right now.

"Fucking hell," Xavier said, not even bothering to censor himself for my family's benefit.

"Is this true?" Matthew repeated, already rolling up his sleeves in preparation for a fight. "Frankie, are you actually pregnant?"

I sighed and looked up at the stars, which twinkled brightly overhead. So much for not stealing his day. "I—I wasn't going to say anything until after Italy. But...yes. I am."

Matthew's eyes darkened toward Xavier. "So this asshole left you high and dry for another woman? When you're gonna have his kid? *Again?*"

"Well, to be accurate, I left him," I pointed out. "Not to mention—"

"What the fuck did he just say?" Xavier demanded, taking a few menacing steps in Matthew's direction. "What is he talking about, 'other woman'?"

Right. Yeah. We'd had plenty of fights about the fact that I'd left England in such a hurry...but I hadn't had the guts to tell him that final reason why.

Tears pricked at the fleeting memory of Imogene Douglas, Xavier's beautiful blonde neighbor, leaning over his desk as her lips met his.

This was why I couldn't talk about it. Because recalling her stupidly perfect face for even a second crumpled mine like a piece of paper and made my throat seize with trapped sobs. And the idea of saying "you kissed Imogene Douglas" out loud had the same effect on my insides as my stomach's current reaction to meat and cream products.

Plus, I didn't want to feel more pathetic than I already was.

"You limey mother*fucker*."

Before I knew it, my brother strode to where Xavier stood, wound his arm back, and punched him clean in the face.

Xavier stumbled backward, perilously close to the edge of the dock. He stood up straight again, hand to a bleeding lip. "Try that again, mate. I fucking dare you."

Matthew took three more steps, so they were chest to chest, despite the fact that Xavier topped him by at least three inches. He shoved him hard right in the sternum.

To his credit, Xavier didn't move this time.

Matthew tipped his chin up. "How's that...*mate?*"

And that was all it took.

All at once, the two of them were grappling on the pier, caring little for splinters or pebbles, or the fact that if they moved more than six inches, both of them were going to end up in the Mediterranean. Xavier landed several punches that seemed to attack

Matthew's kidneys, though my brother was no slouch as he managed a solid blow to Xavier's gut and kneed him in the hamstring.

"Oh my God!" I shouted at them. "Get off the ground! This is insane. Matthew, this is your *wedding day!*"

"Clock him in the ear, Mattie," Lea called behind me. "He's not guarding his right side."

"Lea, shut up!" I flapped my hands around like an excited penguin. "Mattie, Nina's going to wonder where her groom disappeared to. Come on, you look like animals down there. "

"He looks like he's kicking the crap out of him," Marie remarked with a bit too much satisfaction.

"I don't know," Joni replied. "Sexy gargoyle is getting in a lot of punches too. Come on, Keanu, don't stop now!"

"Keanu?" I asked, unable to help myself.

Joni just grinned and shook her head, causing her oversized earrings to swing like wind chimes. "We watched *The Matrix* dubbed in Italian last night. Marie thinks Xavier looks like Keanu Reeves."

"I do not," Marie countered, though her cheeks were red.

"Do too. You said he would make a good Neo."

"I see it," Kate said evenly like she was judging a contest, not an amateur wrestling match.

"Nah, he's too tall," Lea put in. "More like the wolf guy from *True Blood*. But Asian."

"Oooh, the werewolf? Yeah, he was hot!" Joni exclaimed. "Remember the shower scene?"

"I liked Bill better myself," Lea said. "But yes, Alcide was very attractive."

"Please. Everyone knows Eric is the hot one on that show," Kate put in. "Give me a brooding androgynous vampire any time of day."

"Oh my God, shut it!" I snapped at all four of them, though they continued to debate the merits of sex with vampires, werewolves, and other fantasy characters on HBO.

It didn't matter. Neither man appeared to have heard us, anyway.

"Think you can fuck around on my sister and get away with it?" Matthew demanded as he drove an elbow into Xavier's gut.

"Keep. Your. Fucking. Nose. Out of it!" Xavier flipped Matthew over and shoved a fist directly into his kidney.

"Never," Matthew gasped. "Nobody cheats on my sisters. Fucking *nobody*."

"What?" Xavier paused, popped his head up, and looked at me. "Who cheated on you, Ces?"

And that was all it took for Matthew to pile-drive right into his waist, forcing them both into a rolling ball of angry men that tumbled over backward. They fell straight into the water between two sailboats beneath the row of Zola women in their wedding finery.

"Well, that's a terrific way to ruin a nice tux," Lea remarked as we watched them flounder in the water. She picked a piece of lint off the mauve dress she'd gotten on sale at TJ Maxx.

"I know," Kate agreed. "It was couture Givenchy too." She sniffed, almost as if she was about to cry. "He was going to let me resell it after the wedding. I already had a buyer lined up and everything. Man, that suit would have paid my mortgage for two months."

"Yeah, but it's a hell of a wet T-shirt contest," Joni said, only to receive a nudge from Marie as they both watched Xavier stand up fully in water that barely came to his waist.

"Don't be nasty. One of them is our *brother*, and the other is Frankie's man," said Marie, though she didn't seem particularly convinced while she stared at Xavier too.

"He is not my man."

I could barely get the words out, though. Xavier wasn't making it easy on any of us. That's what happens when six feet, five inches of supernaturally cut man-muscle is dripping wet. His T-shirt was plastered to his body, leaving even less to the imagination when he stripped off his jacket in disgust and abandoned it to the water.

"What in the *fuck* are you talking about, cheating?" Xavier demanded as he rounded on Matthew, who stood himself, eyes narrowed, clearly trying to map out his next ambush. "And don't even think about it unless you want to drown in three feet of water. I don't care if you're her brother."

Only with a glance at me did Matthew relent. "Just say the word, Frankie. Say it, and his ass is fuckin' grass."

Xavier snorted at the idea, but his attention was fully on me as well. "I didn't cheat on you, Ces. For fuck's sake, is that why you left? Why would you even think that?"

"BECAUSE I SAW YOU!" I shrieked, no longer able to keep my tears from flowing freely.

"Jerk," Kate murmured as she reached around Lea to rub my shoulder.

"Dick," Joni concurred.

"Lowlife," Marie added.

"Jackass," Lea declared.

"What?" Xavier's reply was immediate. "When? Fucking where?"

"In Kendal," I told him while I swiped at my face with curled fists. "That last day. After you left me and Sofia in the kitchen, I decided the conversation wasn't done. So I went upstairs to find you, got waylaid by your stepmonster, and by the time I made it back to your office, you were there with *her*."

"I was with *who*?" Xavier demanded with utter disbelief.

"That snooty neighbor," Marie offered helpfully. "The viscount's daughter, right? Or is it just count? I don't really understand titles."

"What was her name, again?" Joni asked. "It was super old-fashioned. Like a grandma name."

"Imelda, I think," Lea said as she folded her arms, looking like she wanted a shot at Xavier herself alongside Matthew.

"No, it was Imogene," Kate corrected her. "And I think the name is pretty."

I exhaled through my nose and massaged my temples. I loved my sisters, but I desperately wished they would disappear right now. It was like a Greek chorus had mated with the cast of *Mean Girls*.

Xavier's brow furrowed as he gaped at me. "*Imogene?*" he

repeated as if they'd suggested he'd slept with his own mother. "You think I cheated on you with Imogene bloody Douglas?"

"You said—" I rubbed my eyes, begging the tears to stop. "I heard you, Xavi. She said I couldn't be happy with you. And you agreed with her. That I was the type of person who couldn't be happy anyway. So why—why even bother with me, right? Why even try?"

I hiccupped back a gut-churning sob. God, I hated even thinking of the whole thing. For weeks, every time the memory had reappeared, I'd shoved it away, wanting only to forget how I'd felt outside that office door.

Small. Inconsequential.

A complete and total burden.

Kate rounded Lea and pulled me into her shoulder as I finished speaking.

"You said that?" she asked like she didn't want to believe it.

Xavier's eyes were rounder than the moon above us. "I—I didn't—"

But his words faltered, stained with something akin to shame, and I could tell the memory was coming back to him.

"And then she said..." I continued. "She said you deserved something better. And then she kissed you. Don't try to deny it, Xavi—I saw you! She kissed you *and you let her!*"

A hush fell over the boardwalk as my sisters all processed the moment with me, this time with a waterlogged Xavier watching us. They'd heard the story before, of course, though perhaps not in so much detail. Right now, however, Xavier didn't just have one Zola who wanted to kick his ass. He had an entire army.

"What a fuckboy," Joni pronounced with a curling lip.

"Two-timing snake." Lea's hand balled into a fist.

"Jerk," Marie murmured like she was watching an episode of *Judge Judy* with Nonna.

Kate just shook her head while she stroked my hair. "You complete and utter *ass.*"

"Fucking prick," Matthew said as he swung around with obvious intent.

His fist, however, was caught like a hardball in Xavier's hand, and Matthew was forced a step back in the water as Xavier rounded on him like a bull seeing red.

"Touch me again, you lose a fucking eye," Xavier gritted through his teeth as he took an equally rough handful of Matthew's collar and lifted him a solid inch out of the water. "You're not the only one who grew up street fighting, mate. And I'm primed right now, I *really* am."

He released him roughly, and the two men eyed each other much like two wolves vying for leadership of a pack. A solid minute passed before Matthew exhaled, then took his fist back. Xavier watched him a moment more to make sure he was truly relenting, then turned back to me.

"Imogene kissed me, yes. Just like you said, babe, she. Kissed. Me. And for a moment, I was caught by surprise, frozen, as it were. But I'm guessing you didn't stay for the next part, because as soon as I realized what was happening, I pushed her off, told her to get the fuck out of my office, and we've barely spoken since. That's it, Ces. That's all that happened." He took a deep breath, his dark eyes never wandering from my face, keeping contact the entire time. Begging me to see whatever truth he was trying to impart. "I swear to God, Francesca. I swear on our daughter. *I did not kiss Imogene Douglas.*"

We stared at each other for a long time, and my entire family remained so still I could hear the water dripping off Xavier's and Matthew's soaked clothes back into the sea. Matthew tensed, clearly ready to pounce again. My sisters looked like a set of colorful statues dressed in silk and poly-blend.

But Xavier's expression never wavered from me. He never even blinked. Those blue eyes held mine in a grip so tight I couldn't move a single muscle, though I was several feet away.

The tension was too much to endure. I sucked in a breath, squeezed my eyes shut, and exhaled.

"I don't know," I croaked. "I don't know what happened. Not anymore."

Kate pulled me into her arms, and I sensed a few of my other sisters offering comfort. A hand on my back, another stroking my hair. Warmth and murmured kindness. They might have driven me crazy, but they knew the meaning of support.

This was why I had really gone back to New York. I had never been more glad for it than right now.

Eventually, there was the sound of someone getting out of the water and the slap of wet shoes on the decking until a shadow fell over all five of us. My sisters released me, and I turned to find Xavier dripping on the dock, wearing an expression of such sorrow and disbelief.

For the first time that night, he looked truly vulnerable under the vicious stares of the Zola family.

He chewed his lip a moment, eyes darting between each of us, then fixed his expression on me and spoke again.

"I'm not always a good man," he said. "I know that. *God*, I know that. But I promise you with everything I am, Francesca. On Sofia, my mother's memory, on everything I hold sacred on this earth. I would *never* hurt you or our child"—he gulped with a quick glance down at my still-flat belly—"*children* that way. Not ever."

He dropped to one knee, and every woman on that dock sucked in an audible breath.

"Oh, for fuck's sake," Matthew muttered as he swatted at the water by his hips for lack of anything else to hit.

"He is *not*," Joni murmured.

"Hush," Marie said. "He might be."

"Oh my God, he wouldn't," Lea hummed under her breath.

"Holy crap, I hope not," Kate agreed.

I couldn't speak. He wasn't doing this. Not here. He *wouldn't* ask me that question now, would he?

He had to know better than that.

Didn't he?

"Francesca," Xavier whispered as he took both my hands.

"Y-yes?" I was shivering with nerves.

"I'm on my knees. Begging. Will you—"

I gasped. Oh, God, it was really happening.

"Will you *please*...believe me?"

I closed my eyes as my entire body deflated. I couldn't even look at my siblings. Didn't even want to know one iota of what they were thinking when that question emerged instead of the other one that had clearly crossed all our minds.

What a difference a single word could make.

"Please say you will," Xavier continued with a squeeze of my fingers. "I will do anything to make you believe. I swear it."

Gently, I extricated one of my hands from his and pressed my fingertips to my mouth, unsure how to respond. What exactly was he asking me to say here? Yes? I do? What? Maybe this excused the kiss, a little.

But what about the rest of the summer?

"*Scusa.*"

"Matthew!"

We turned to find Nonna and Nina ambling down the dock together, though Nina looked like she was moving slowly out of respect for Nonna while her gray eyes flew wildly to Matthew's sopping wet form.

My grandmother, on the other hand, was taking her sweet time, carrying her wineglass and a cigarette, though her dark eyes were no less sharp than they had been hours before. She wore a pretty beaded black dress befitting a grandmother of the groom, dainty gold earrings swinging from her earlobes, and a sash tied through her teased black hair that took her straight back to the nineteen-sixties. She was obviously having fun, but as she took us all in, her gaze was sharp as ever as it drifted between Matthew in the water and the row of Zola sisters standing like attendants in their dresses. Then to a dripping Xavier on one knee, one of my hands still clasped in his, while tears ran down my face.

"Huh," was all she said. "Oh, my."

"Oh, Matthew," Nina said again in a voice that made my brother flush bright red.

And while I happened to know Matthew had a special talent for torturing himself with guilt, I had a feeling no one else made him feel as embarrassed as his name when Nina said it like that.

He held his hands out, though water still dripped loudly from his shirtsleeves. "I had to, duchess."

At the nickname, both Xavier and I straightened. It didn't mean anything. Nina was no more a duchess than I was.

But after the events of the summer, my heart ached with something akin to jealousy. Hearing it now, with that sweet tone of voice, I wondered for the first time if *that* love and kindness wasn't what the prospective title had been missing all along.

Then, in her brisk way, Nonna clicked her tongue and started giving everyone directions.

"Matthew, your wife needs you," she said to my brother in the Neapolitan accent that had grown considerably thicker on this trip. "Nina, take him back to change his clothes, okay? And Lea, the babies need you, too. Michael, he wants help with the children."

Shooting twin arrows of disgust toward Xavier, Matthew and Lea both nodded, then obediently left to tend to matters more important than their little sister's melodrama.

As it should be.

"Katie, Joni, Marie, go help with the party. Not enough people are dancing yet. Ask your cousins."

"But, Nonna, I can't dance—" Joni started to argue as she held out a crutch.

"*Go,*" Nonna ordered, gesturing with her wineglass.

Not a peep was uttered as the three of them left, Kate with a squeeze to my elbow.

Nonna approached Xavier and me, taking in our compromising positions. She sighed and shook her head, muttering, "*Mammàma*" under her breath. "You. Get up. You're gonna ruin your pants."

Eyes wary, Xavier did as he was told, though he didn't let go of my hand.

Nonna muttered something more to herself in Italian that I didn't understand, but I would have bet translated roughly to "these idiot kids."

"Frankie, you take him back to the house," she ordered. "Dry his clothes. I will watch Sofia for the night."

"Oh, Nonna, that's all right. I can come back—"

"No," she said brusquely. "You have a family, Francesca." Her penetrating gaze dropped to my stomach, then back to my face, revealing she had noticed a lot more than I realized. "You take care of them now."

FOUR

I could hear the drip of Xavier's clothing on Vernazza's cobbled streets all the way back to the three-story house where I was staying with my family. It was one of uncountable, slightly crooked, pastel-colored buildings carved into the rocky cliffs of the Ligurian coast, draped now with the shadows of night, a sopping gargoyle, and my own personal dread.

He was here. Xavier was here.

Wet. Angry. And still probably shell-shocked by my recent disclosure, but more importantly, also still as reeling from our last conversation as I was.

I didn't know what to make of his insistence that he had not kissed Imogene Douglas. It was so at odds with the scene that had played on repeat in my mind for the last six weeks. I had seen them kiss. I had *seen* it. Which meant she had kissed him, and then he had kissed her back.

Didn't it?

True, I ran away almost immediately after seeing her mouth touch his. If he had pushed her away, if I hadn't been witness.

If he had told her off in his signature, rough Xavier way, I hadn't heard it.

And knowing Xavier—knowing at that moment, he had been desperate for connection with *me*, and when he was like that, he wasn't particularly forgiving to anyone who got in his way—well, part of me was inclined to believe him.

After all, a man wouldn't fly nearly a thousand miles if he was cheating.

Would he?

The house Matthew and Nina had rented for the family was located about four streets up the hill from the piazza, up the main avenue of Vernazza, then down a much narrower street that ended on the other side of a cliff towering over the tiny village and the sea below. Xavier followed me there like a big wet dog, shoulders hunched while he breathed heavily from the cool night air. When we reached the threshold, I unlocked the door and led Xavier inside after he had removed his shoes on the front stoop.

"I'll see if I can find some newspaper for those," I said as I slipped off my heels and padded through the little living room in my bare feet.

"Don't bother," Xavier said as he stripped off his socks and tossed them onto the shoes. "They're ruined now, and I've got a change at my *pensione*. It's just a block or two from here anyway."

I didn't know why it hurt that he had gotten himself a hotel, but for some reason, it cut like a knife. Maybe on some level, I'd wanted him to barge into my bedroom and plant a flag like a conqueror, family and propriety be damned.

I'd wanted him to fight for one small part of me, even if it was just a corner of my bed. My stairwell. Wherever I ended up.

"Would you like some tea?" I asked as I walked into the kitchen to make myself a cup.

I still felt rather lightheaded despite not having any champagne at the reception. Not to mention exhausted from being, well, knocked up. A cup of tea and a book sounded like the perfect antidote for the evening. I'd have to settle for just one of them.

"Sure. Green if you have it."

"We brought some."

I puttered around quietly as Xavier proceeded to strip off his shirt. I turned just as he was unbuttoning his pants and nearly dropped the kettle.

"What are you doing?

He looked up. "Well, I'm not going to sit around in wet clothes. Is there a dryer in the house?"

I gulped, then nodded. "There—yes, actually. Here, give me those."

I tried not to notice him, but it was kind of impossible, given his size and the amount of space he took up. Xavier smirked as he peeled off the denim, then handed me his pants along with his soaked T-shirt. His jacket, retrieved from the harbor, had been squeezed out on the walk home and now lay drying over the back of one of the chairs.

I looked away, but not before I caught a glimpse of the way his drenched boxer briefs were clinging to *every* part of him like wet tissue, and how the serpentine tattoo—an homage to Kiyohime, the serpentine woman who avenged her broken heart—climbed like a vine up his torso and down his left arm, gleaming black and red and gray.

"Oh, for Pete's sake," I muttered as I whirled around.

"Something wrong?"

The sly lilt in his voice told me he knew *exactly* what was wrong. It also told me he thought he could play that to his advantage.

"I'll just get you a towel," I said shortly, then darted out of the room before he could respond.

When I came back, features controlled, I thrust a striped beach towel I had swiped from the laundry room at him.

"Here."

He took it with a cheeky half grin, then tossed it onto the sofa before reaching down and tugging off his boxer briefs. Well, crap.

Now I was exquisitely aware that Xavier Parker was standing naked in the middle of the room, seawater glinting where the light danced everywhere across his golden skin, carved muscles, and the tattoo.

And I do mean *everywhere*.

I wanted to lick off every drop.

Yeah, this baby *really* wasn't going to make it easy to be around him.

Was it possible he had gotten bigger in the last few weeks?

"Er, I'll just, um, pop your clothes in the dryer," I mumbled.

Xavier chuckled as I swiftly gathered his things and studiously avoided his gaze—or his other parts, for that matter. When I returned, I found (somewhat to my disappointment) that he had wrapped the towel around his waist. He had already fixed us both tea and set our mugs on a side table between two armchairs in the living room. I took mine and curled into the seat, eager to be more than a few feet from him. I caught his telltale scent of soap, fire, and salt, accentuated further by the briny Mediterranean drying on his body. Even in nothing but a towel, he looked so regal in his chair with his straight posture, broad chest, and black hair inky as an oil slick.

It reminded me of who he really was.

Not just a smart-mouthed chef from South London.

A duke, holder of one of the oldest titles in Britain.

And that was why I'd had to leave him.

"I didn't kiss her, Ces," he said again after taking a long sip of his tea. "Tell me you believe me."

I sighed and tucked the edges of my dress around my knees, wishing I'd had the forethought to change into something more comfortable. "I—fine. I guess I can believe that. Even though I saw you."

I wished I sounded more confident. I wished I were.

"She kissed me," Xavier pressed again.

"So you say. But even if you did stop her, it wasn't right away."

"Because I was stunned by it, like I said."

"You were surprised?" I snorted. "Xavi, she was all over you from the second she knew you were back. I watched her all summer, plastering herself on you like a corsage wanting to be pinned to your lapel. Just like every other aristocrat in the country, descending like vultures at all those stupid events. She just happened to live next door."

"It wasn't like that." His frown created two strong lines between his brows. I resisted the urge to rub them away with my thumb. "You heard the conversation, babe. You knew I was talking about *you*. Worried about you and me. I didn't exactly expect Imogene to make a move." He shook his head. "But maybe I should have."

I scoffed. "You think?"

He gave me a long look.

I gave him one back. "Jagger and Elsie filled me in on her little crush on you. And the fact that you were expected to marry her at one point. You didn't think to tell me about that?"

Xavier opened his mouth as if to argue but then seemed to give up. "Honestly, I didn't think it mattered. I love *you*, Ces. How could you have thought I would do something like that to you?"

It didn't escape me that he spoke in the present. Love, not loved.

But there was no use getting caught up in things like tenses.

"Maybe because it wasn't just that," I said honestly. "The whole betrayal wasn't only her. In a lot of ways, it felt like the whole summer was leading up to that point. The kiss was just my breaking point."

He looked at me hard. "Explain."

"What is there to explain that I haven't a million times already?" I took another sip of tea, if only to calm myself. Just the thought of rehashing this conversation made my blood boil. "From the moment Sofia and I arrived in the UK, literally no one wanted us there."

"I wanted you there," Xavier said. "And I was the only one who should have mattered."

"The papers printed lies about us from the get-go," I continued as if he hadn't said a word. "Even took interviews from my turncoat of a mother. Your family, of course, hopped right on board and proceeded to badmouth us to every person within forty square miles. By the time we had to attend the Season events, every rich person in England was looking out for your American chit and child and wondering out loud in public if Sofia even belonged to you."

"And what was I supposed to do about it?" he demanded. "Did you want me to fight every person in England? Sue every paper out there?" Xavier set his teacup down on the side table with a clatter.

"I wanted you to be on *our side!*" I blustered. "You acted like none of it mattered, Xavi. You brushed it off, told me to ignore it. I wanted you to tell your stepmother where to shove it, tell Imogene to stop petting you like a pony, and stop punching people just because you were a little jealous. I wanted you to be mad *with* me instead of at me! I wanted us to be a team, but you left us alone every chance you got!"

His mouth dropped like he couldn't believe what I'd just said. "That's—that's how you really felt?"

"That's how I *feel*," I confirmed. "Present tense. And that's why I had to go. I need to be in New York. I need to be around family."

He mulled on that for a minute, then leaned forward so his knees almost touched my toes where they peeked from under the hem of my dress. "And what about *our* family, Ces? What about us?"

"A two-month vacation and some mean rich people do not make a family," I told him, though it felt like I was lying through my teeth.

Flashes of the three of us in his London apartment skipped through my mind. Xavier making us dinner. Sofia playing in her room. The three of us cuddled on the couch while I read a book, Xavier watched soccer, and Sofia yammered to one of her dolls.

"I'm sorry," I said, my voice suddenly weak. "But they just don't."

"And being Sofia's father doesn't?"

"That takes more than blood too."

I scooted farther into my chair and looked out the window, searching for some reprieve. Maybe a bit of guidance. Then I caught the lights of the wedding party in the square below us.

"See those people down there?" I said. "The ones who chased us to the dock? *That's* family. They're messy and snarky and have way too many opinions about my life, to be sure. But every one of them is there for each other, no matter what. Why do you think my brother tried to beat you up, or my sisters were so quick to call you names? Because family stands up for one other. Families have each other's backs. We fight, just like you do, but it's not when someone personally insults us. It's because we defend our own."

"Oh, I am aware of that," Xavier said dryly, touching the blooming bruise under his left eye. "Your brother has made that very clear."

"Say what you want about them, but my siblings would never let anyone else call me trash or denigrate me in any way." I swallowed hard, suddenly realizing the truth. And this time, there was no uncertainty left. "But you did, Xavi. You did, again and again. It wasn't about Imogene Douglas. It was about everyone in that world. You left us to the wolves and insisted they were only puppies. *That's* why I left. I was tired of being hunted and eaten alive while you stood by and told me each bite was only a scratch."

Xavier's blue eyes darted between me and the window several times while his mouth worked silently. But then he stilled. Recognition straightening every part of his body.

"I—I see," he said quietly. "I understand."

He looked so forlorn, so immediately heartbroken, that I almost got off my chair and went to him. Pure loneliness emanated from him in waves, and I wanted only to crawl into his lap, accept the shelter of his warm body, and give him the shelter of mine.

But I had to stick to my guns here. Now that I finally knew what was right.

"I hope you know how lucky you are," he said. "I never had family like that."

I frowned. "But your mom—"

"Mum wasn't a fighter," he cut me off. "She made it alone, sure. But her own family was ashamed of her, so she shut them out too. Taught me to do the same, I suppose."

"You fought," I said. "I know you did. You still do."

He shrugged. "I probably get that from my dad. Rupert was a fighter, right? Fought with me plenty. But it was only when his own bloody pride was damaged. He didn't stand up for me either. No one did." He shook his head. "Fuck. I never knew."

I bit my lip, gripping the chair to keep from taking his hand. He had everything it took. I knew he did.

But for my own sake and Sofia's, I couldn't keep waiting for him to figure out how to be the kind of support we really needed. Not when we already had it out there.

Xavier rubbed a big hand over his face and sighed as he sank back into his chair. "All I've ever wanted is for us to be a family, Ces." His eyes blinked large and blue in the night. "I can learn. I know I can."

I stood, picking up my teacup to return to the kitchen. "Xavi, it's not that easy."

"Would this help?"

I turned and found him following me through the living room. He bent down to retrieve something from his drying jacket pocket. Then he turned to me, somehow managed to keep his towel in place, and sank to one knee all over again, just like he had on the dock.

And this time, he held out a box.

A very small, very square velvet box.

I sucked a sharp breath through my teeth. "Is that—"

"An engagement ring, yeah?" Xavier smiled shyly. "You want a secret? I've been carrying it around all summer in my jacket pocket. Waiting for the right time." He shook his head with something like regret. "Never seemed to be one, right? Stupid man, I am."

He opened it to reveal the most beautiful piece of jewelry I'd ever seen.

A simple white gold band framed a cluster of pink diamonds against the black velvet. There had to be at least fifty in all, each tiny and perfect, looking for all the world like a bouquet of English roses. Perfect, pink, and sparkling.

I couldn't breathe.

I'd anticipated this all summer. Hoped for it. Maybe even in my heart of hearts prayed for it.

I'd never actually imagined what the ring itself would look like. Or how it could be so perfect.

Nor had I imagined it would happen at a time like this.

"So, what do you say, Ces?" Xavier's deep voice rumbled. His large hands shook where they held the box, the only sign he was nervous at all. "Want to get married? Want to make a family with me for real?"

Lord, in some ways, he knew me so well. But in others, not at all.

"Oh, Xavi," I breathed, still unable to take my eyes from the gems.

"I'll take that as a yes."

I floated a hand over the ring nestled in its box. Part of me wanted to accept it. See how the pink would shimmer against my fair skin. Hold it out in the light to watch the facets sparkle.

But he wasn't asking out of love, but guilt. Yes, he had said he loved me, but that was in the middle of a fight. Even over the summer, he'd said it, what, once? Twice?

He was asking out of obligation. And if there was anything I knew about Xavier Parker after this summer, it was that his sense of duty ran deeper than anything else.

Even love.

"I—I'm so sorry," I said in a voice I barely recognized as my own. "But my answer is no."

Heartbreak scrawled across his handsome face in harsh, blatant lines like one of Sofia's preschool drawings. My heart cracked right along with his.

Oh God, what had I just done?

"Your answer—you don't—" He pushed off his knee and sat back into one of the dining room chairs, then looked up at me with two pools of sadness so deep I thought I might drown in them. "All I want is for you to come back with me, Ces. You don't want to marry me, well, fine. I'll deal with that. But please, I'm begging you. Come *home.*"

"I did go home," I whispered, though I was unable to help the twin streams of new tears running down my cheeks all over again. "I went back to New York. And that's where I'm staying. After all, England was only ever supposed to be for the summer, right?"

I waited for him to say no. I waited for him to say again he wanted us to stay permanently. Beg me more, give me reasons to stay, promises of change, tell me he'd fix everything with the press, his family, all of them.

I wasn't even sure if I wanted him to, but I had a feeling if he did...I wouldn't find the strength to say no again.

For a moment, I thought he might.

But there had been too many moments like this. Times I'd seen the right thing play across his lips like a symphony.

And just like all the others, he remained quiet.

"Does it matter that I love you?" he asked, not without some bitterness. "That I'll never love anyone the way I love you? Fuck, does any of it matter at all?"

Something inside me cracked as the ring box snapped shut.

Hadn't I just been dying to hear him say that?

But not like this. Not out of resentment, like it was a favor he was extending and expected to be repaid.

Now it was too late.

"I love you too," I said honestly as my vision clouded. Oh, God, the tears really were back. "But sometimes love isn't enough, is it?" I looked down, refusing the urge to stroke my belly, where I knew this little person was growing. "We have more to think about than just ourselves. We have to figure out how to be a family together in another way. I think maybe that is easier when we are apart."

Xavier gave me a look then that was full of such hunger and yearning, I very nearly broke down. But instead of fighting or snapping or lashing out like he once would have done so easily, he seemed to take several deep breaths, and eventually reached for my hand.

"If that's really what you think is best." He shook his head, the damp hair fluttering back and forth. "God knows I can't figure it the fuck out."

"I—it is."

It had to be.

Xavier sighed long and low from the back of his throat, like a lion. "I suppose that's that." He stood suddenly, taking his jacket with him. "Can you get my clothes from the dryer? I don't care if they're done. I'd rather not stay."

Numbly, I nodded, then went downstairs to fetch his things. He pulled on his half-dry things while I brought the dishes to the sink. When I came back, he was dressed, already moving to the door to find his wet shoes. Every movement was settled, but sad, like a dog that had just been beaten in a race.

Every inch of me wanted to embrace him. Pull him back to me.

But I'd made my decision.

He stopped at the bottom of the stoop when I walked him outside. "When's your next scan? I'd like to be there."

I blinked. "You want to go to the doctor with me?"

He just nodded solemnly. "I'm not missing a thing this time, Ces. Can I come?"

Maybe I should have said no. I could have said the doctor was a safe place for me, and I didn't need him there.

But I'd already shut him down enough tonight. I couldn't inflict that sadness in his big eyes anymore.

I nodded. "Two weeks. I'll send you the information."

He reached out and took my left hand in his, rubbing a thumb over my knuckles. It lingered over the empty ring finger. "I—I don't want to get lawyers involved, but I think we should make an agreement. For Sofia. And the little one, when it arrives." He nodded toward my stomach. "I think moving forward...we should have it all down. In writing. Solid, you know?"

I gulped. It was scary, maybe. But nothing he was saying sounded like a threat. "All—all right."

He nodded again. "Okay. We'll talk in two weeks, then." His half-smile, so forlorn, nearly broke my heart in two.

"'When pain is over, the remembrance of it often becomes a pleasure,'" I muttered to myself.

"What's that from, then?"

I jerked, realizing I'd spoken my thought aloud.

Xavier was peering down at me, curiosity blended now with a sad, sweet almost smile. "Who are you now, babe? I know that look."

I swallowed tightly. Oh, God, this hurt.

But there was no use lying to him. There never had been.

"Anne Elliot," I said. "She's the main character in *Persuasion*."

"Saying goodbye to her love?" he ventured.

It was meant as a joke, but he had no idea. That was essentially the whole plot of the book—saying goodbye and the torment it caused.

I flushed, blinking hard so I could see. "In a manner of speaking," I admitted.

Xavier's half-smile grew even more lopsided. "Does he ever say anything back?"

I sighed. "Xavi..."

"If it helps you, maybe it would help me too."

I sighed, then finally recalled what was probably the most famous line from *Persuasion*—a sentence written in a letter when Captain Wentworth confesses how he feels at last.

"He writes to her, yeah. He says, 'I am half agony, half hope,'" I whispered.

I squeezed my eyes shut. I couldn't see Xavier's face just then. I honestly couldn't bear it.

He was quiet for a long time.

Then, at last: "Fitting."

I opened my eyes again, and before I could stop him, he dropped my hand and used his to weave his fingers into my hair, pulling me down for a kiss. His lips as soft and sweet and salty as they had ever been. And just as I started to sink into them, he pulled away.

"What—what was that for?" I wondered as I touched my lips.

A bit of slyness stole into his overall sadness. "Had to sneak a goodbye kiss, didn't I?"

"I suppose..."

"I'll see you in two weeks," Xavier said, then turned and left.

And I stood there long after he was gone, feeling that, despite the fact that our words had clearly ended whatever had been between us, nothing was finished at all.

Half agony, half hope, indeed.

I just wasn't sure which side would win.

FIVE

"*O*h my *God*, I need coffee."

With a catlike stretch of her lithe arms, Joni padded down the stairs exactly ten minutes before we needed to leave that morning.

After partying hard with some friends in Brooklyn the night before, she had opted to crash on my old bed on the landing rather than schlep all the way back to the Bronx at four in the morning. Unfortunately, both Sofia and I had woken up just a few hours later to get ready for school. By the time Joni joined us, Sofia was already done with breakfast and was deep into multiple princess costume changes in her room while I filled her lunchbox in the kitchen.

"How was the landing?" I asked Joni, knowing full well that the mattress sagged in the middle and was creaky when you moved. Given that I slept like an eggbeater, twisting and turning throughout my slumber, it had always woken me several times a night.

Two weeks after the wedding and nearly six since Matthew had moved to Boston with Nina, I'd taken over his old room with aplomb and was finally getting used to a bit of privacy. And a queen-sized bed. And a door that I could shut or even lock.

Not that I really had anything to keep particularly private. My new bed was irritatingly large, quiet, and annoyingly empty. Still, I was planning to enjoy every second of the next seven months until little no-name burst onto the scene.

I poured a mug from the pot I'd brewed as soon as I came down and pushed it across the counter to where she sat, acutely aware of how Matthew used to do the exact same thing for me just a few months ago.

"Since your bed came without a nosy nonna poking her head in every six minutes, it was fantastic," Joni pronounced as she yanked on a messy black bun that still managed to look chic and shook her head so her oversized hoops danced from her ears.

It really wasn't fair. Even with barely any sleep, zero exercise for two months while she'd been hobbling on crutches, and a reported hangover the size of Connecticut, my youngest sister still looked like she had walked off a runway. Joni was the family beauty, and she absolutely knew it. Meanwhile, I was still waiting for chilled gel pads to shrink the suitcases under my eyes.

"Well, I made a pot, so help yourself to more if you need," I said as I placed a satsuma and some carrot sticks into Sofia's lunch box. "You have PT today, right?"

She checked the time behind me on the oven clock. "At two, yeah. First day, and I'm gonna kill it. You watch, I'll be back on Broadway in six weeks."

She gave me a grin, though I could tell she was nervous.

Two months ago, Joni received a call to be an understudy, then a full-cast member in *Chicago*. For someone who had never really succeeded at anything in her life besides dancing, it was beyond a big break. It meant she was actually good at something. It meant that at twenty-four, she was more than just a three-time college dropout, cosmetology school failure, GED-recipient, part-time go-go dancer, and resident family mess. A pretty face and life of the party, sure, but generally treated like nothing else.

Less than two months into rehearsals, though, her brief success ended with a bad fall on stage, a trip to the ER, two surgeries, and a recovery period that had reportedly been driving everyone in the Bronx up the wall.

Call me crazy, but I felt a little guilty, having missed it all when I was in England. Well, I could make up for it now with some coffee and a place to crash here and there.

I reached across the counter to rub her shoulder. "You'll do great, Jo. Just be disciplined and consistent, and you'll be back on stage in no time."

Joni's face fell at the phrase "disciplined and consistent." I didn't remark—we both knew neither trait was a strength of hers. Dance was the only exception—for what reason, I never knew.

Still, she managed to pull out another sweet smile. "Well, even if I can't, there's always the bar."

I did my best to mask a cringe. "You want to go back to serving shots off your ass?"

She scoffed. "It's off a tray, not my ass. Not unless they gave me a huge tip, anyway." She avoided my gaze. "But the manager said he would teach me to tend bar one day if I came back so I won't always have to be a shot girl. Promotion! I hope."

I tipped my head. "Sure you can remember all the drink recipes?"

I hated to ask, but we both knew the truth; memorizing things wasn't exactly Joni's strong suit either.

"If I do it, I can remember it," she said with more confidence than I knew she had. "Plus, maybe I can teach ballet at the rec center to the littles like Sofia. Those who can't do, teach, right, sis?"

Maybe I deserved that after doubting her ability to mix drinks. I knew it was only a joke, but I couldn't help but flinch. I might have made it mid-way through my master's degree, but I was just as much a dropout as she was. Not really one to judge, honestly.

"How long is Marie in Paris again?" I asked.

Fine. It was another cheap shot.

Given everything she was struggling with, Joni wouldn't appreciate being reminded that Marie hadn't come home to New York after the wedding but had returned to Paris, where she was currently living her best life attending culinary school courtesy of her super rich employers.

Heck, that would make anyone jealous.

"I don't freaking know," she said, sounding closer to fourteen than twenty-four. "But I guarantee she won't enjoy anything but the dumb kitchen school. Especially not any hot Frenchmen. She wouldn't recognize someone flirting if they smacked her in the face with their coc—"

"Language!" I interrupted with a stifled giggle. "Sofia doesn't need to hear that."

Joni just smirked and sipped her coffee from a cup that aptly read "Sly Bish" on the side. "Plus, Mimi's too obsessed with her boss to do anything anyway."

"Come again?" I asked as I put together a sunflower butter and jelly sandwich. "Marie's in love with who?"

Joni wasn't totally wrong in her assessment of Marie's social skills. The idea that she had any sort of life was news to me. Then again, I hadn't been involved enough in either of their lives over the past year to know, had I? I'd been too invested in my own drama.

Joni's eyes gleamed over her coffee cup, clearly eager to be the bearer of juicy gossip. "He's the younger son of the super-rich family she works for in Westchester. Have you ever heard of Daniel Lyons?"

I frowned. "Oh, you mean the younger son she's had a thing for since she was sixteen?" I chuckled. "For a second, I thought you meant one of her teachers."

Joni's mischievous grin told me everything I needed to know. "Daniel Lyons is more out of reach than any stuffy French chef. He's in *Page Six* more than the Kardashians."

I set down the butter knife. "Joni, you know every time you read that crap, you are giving those shitty sites more reasons to invade people's privacy and print lies, right?"

She shrugged, making her hoops bounce again. "Eh, they're rich. They can deal with it."

"Nina was in *Page Six*, you know. They reported on every little drama with her first marriage, not to mention her ex-husband's criminal activities. They persecuted her for years, not to mention all summer and last year. Do you think Matthew would like the fact that you're supporting them?"

Joni's smile faded a bit, but she chose to take a large gulp of coffee instead of answering my question. Or meet my eyes, for that matter.

"What about me and Sofia, huh?" I pressed as I smacked my knife over the jelly side of the bread. "We were in the London tabloids too, because of our association with Xavier. They printed lie after lie about us. Even interviewed Mami, remember?"

By the time I was pulling up my phone to demonstrate my point, Joni's grin had fully morphed into a frown.

"Shit," she said. "I forgot about that."

"It *just* happened."

"And you *just* told me how crappy my memory is!" she retorted. "I can be dumb or I can be cruel, Frankie. You can't have it both ways. I just didn't think about it, all right?"

"That's kind of the issue, Jo. You don't really think."

Immediately, I knew I'd gone one too far.

Maybe I'd been gone for several months and out of the house much longer, but I still remembered the way Joni would cry whenever her report cards came home or the teachers called Nonna in for a school conference. Just like I remembered the way those tears eventually morphed into the expression she was wearing now—a blank, practically porcelain face that bore no signs of emotion one way or another besides the tiny divot that appeared just above her perfectly plucked brows.

When that mask went on, Joni's ears turned off.

There was no use talking to her now. Especially when I was acting like a bully.

I sighed and set down my knife. "I'm sorry. I'm being a jerk."

She clutched her mug, but eventually, her green eyes met mine. "Yeah. You are."

"Hey," I said, reaching across to set my hand on hers. "It was uncalled for. You do think. I'm just stressed because Xavier's coming in tonight for the ultrasound. I haven't seen him since the wedding, and...yeah."

Joni grimaced sympathetically. She stared at my hand atop her knuckles for a moment, then turned hers over and squeezed my fingers.

"Are you worried he's going to bring up...you know?"

"His horrible proposal?" I filled in. "That would be a no. We've both just kind of decided to pretend it never happened."

Yes, I'd told my sisters. If anything, that night had made it clear that secrets were not the order of the day.

Joni grimaced with what looked like sympathy. "It's okay. I sort of deserved that comment anyway. I need to be more considerate, I know."

"Those articles just really hurt." I packed Sofia's sandwich in her lunchbox, along with a granola bar. "Especially Mami's article. Did you ever read it?"

Joni shook her head. I wasn't surprised—not even hurt, really. My sister had never been much of a reader, which partially explained her issues in school. Even now, when she looked at the tabloids, she was mostly interested in the pictures, headlines, and fashion. I had regular updates on whatever Karlie Kloss or Bella Hadid were wearing that week, but she could never really tell me any of the actual gossip.

"It was awful," I said. "She called me a terrible mother. Said I was a liar and irresponsible and all sorts of things. And the paper didn't bother to find out the fact that she barely raised us because *she* was the one in jail and everything for, you know, *killing our dad.*"

The more I talked, the more uncomfortable Joni clearly felt. She rotated her now-empty coffee cup around and around in her hands, chewing on her upper lip most of the time. She barely knew our mother at all, having been just a baby when the accident happened that killed our father and sent our mom to prison for vehicular manslaughter while driving under the influence.

Eager to avoid that particular memory, I did a quick search for the article I was discussing on my phone so I could send it to Joni. I wasn't sure why I felt so strongly that she know. Maybe I wanted her to be on my side. Or maybe I just wanted someone to feel as enraged about the whole situation as I was.

I'd dealt with enough apathy over the last three months to last me a lifetime.

Instead, however, I found something else that shocked me completely.

"Holy shit," I muttered as the search results loaded.

"What?" Joni asked, as if she didn't want to know. "What's wrong now?"

"It's...holy crap...*Page Six* interviewed her, too. Mami, I mean. This article is from yesterday."

I flipped the phone around to show Joni the site as it loaded. She took it while I turned, my body shaking, to put away the various lunch materials. I checked my watch to find that school started in an hour. I had to leave, drop Sofia at school, and somehow manage to keep my cool with a bunch of third graders for the next six hours while this garbage was floating around out there.

Crap, crap, crap.

"'Watch out for my daughter, the Red Hook Gold Digger,'" Joni read from the headline. "Oh my God, that's a picture of Mami. And Xavier. And *you!*"

She looked up, green eyes bugging.

"You could sound a little less excited," I said, taking my phone back and tucking it into my coat pocket.

"I'm not—it's just shocking. Holy crap, my sister made *Page Six!*"

"And it very well might ruin my whole life," I snapped at her. "I showed you that so you'd understand why these sites are absolute junk. I would hope you'd be on my side."

"Of course I'm on your side," Joni said. "I'm just surprised, that's all. I'm just—my God, I can't believe Mami would say that about you!"

"She's mad because I wouldn't let her see Sofia last spring. I didn't trust her then, and I sure don't trust her now." I rubbed a hand over my face. "God. I have to get to school. Hopefully no one shows up in the neighborhood. She basically told them all where I live! And Xavier's coming today too...if the cameras see him, they won't leave him alone."

"Red Hook is a big enough neighborhood they won't be able to find you," Joni assured me with her signature careless optimism.

She was the only person I knew who always genuinely believed things would work out no matter what.

I wished I felt as self-assured.

"Don't answer the door if you don't know who it is." I swiped my keys from the counter and got ready to gather Sofia from upstairs. "Put your mug in the dishwasher when you're done. Are you heading home tonight or planning to stay here again?"

"Um...I might stay another night if that's okay. My friend Charlie wants to try this club downtown, and your place is closer. But I'll probably go back tomorrow. No offense, Frankie. Nonna's a snoop, but she's a way better cook than you."

She held up her coffee mug as if to demonstrate.

I smirked but took zero offense. Even my coffee was weak. After six weeks of living without the benefits of Xavier's cooking or Matthew's, I was getting pretty sick of my mediocre kitchen skills myself. Sofia was nearly in full mutiny.

"No worries," I told her. "I'm tempted to move back myself just for that."

"You should. It's lonely there without anyone else."

I smiled. By "anyone else," Joni clearly meant Marie, even if she didn't want to admit to missing her sister/nemesis.

"Want me to pick up Sofia after PT?" she asked. "Then you don't have to rush her over after school, and you could meet Xavier wherever."

I brightened. "That would be great if you could get the kiddo. I'll bring home a pizza so we don't

have to eat grilled cheese."

"Nah, we'll pick up something so you can have a few minutes to yourself," she replied.

I smiled. It was unlike Joni to be that thoughtful. Maybe she was growing up a little after all.

"Maybe freshen up?" she continued. "Or get fresh with your big sexy Englishman?"

Maybe not.

Joni winked, and I reddened. She couldn't know that the last two weeks had only made my libido go even *more* nuts, particularly since the morning sickness was starting to subside. It didn't help that since seeing him in Italy, a wet Xavier emerging from the Mediterranean had appeared in my dreams almost nightly to do extremely dirty things to me on that dock. The idea that I was going to see him in person in a matter of hours wasn't exactly helping.

"It's not like that anymore," I insisted.

"If you say so. But you kind of look like a lollipop right now. Your cheeks are so pink."

I tossed a balled-up paper towel at her, grinning at Joni's infectious laughter. "Good luck at PT, you brat. I'll see you tonight."

"Good luck at, I don't know, life," Joni called as I walked out of the kitchen to find Sofia. "It'll all be fine!"

I only wished I could believe her.

SIX

After dropping off Sofia, I arrived at P.S. 058—otherwise known as Carroll Elementary—to find a covey of photographers outside the front entrance. The volunteer crossing guards were working a little harder than usual to clear the road for early arrivals. Dolores, a fifth-grade mom and head of the PTA, did not look pleased.

"Shoot," I muttered, stopping a full block away and ducking behind a big hydrangea bush.

They hadn't spotted me. Yet. But it was pretty obvious whom they were looking for.

"I'd take the back entrance if I were you."

I turned to find Adam Klein standing behind me.

My stomach dropped another inch.

The last time I'd seen Adam, only days after getting into a fist-fight with Xavier at a major event of the London Season, he'd appeared on the grounds of Kendal and announced that he and his mother were working with Georgina Parker to strip Xavier of his inheritance and title. His mother and Georgina were sisters, both divorced or widowed, both with sons from first husbands with distant claims to the Kendal dukedom, both with obsessive desires to wrest that title away from the half-breed upstart who, in their lofty opinions, had no rights to the title that should belong to either Frederick or Adam. According to them, the Buddhist marriage certificate produced when Xavier was nineteen (and rendering him a legitimate heir rather than the bastard he'd always been called) was a fraud, and they would stop at nothing to prove it.

All of this made the fact that Adam and I worked together exceedingly awkward, to say the least.

But at least we were back on familiar footing. He'd traded his posh clothes from the summer for the more familiar uniform of an art teacher: paint-stained overalls, horn-rimmed glasses, and the tweed driver's cap I'd always associated with him—a scrappy look that matched my own leggings and secondhand red tunic to hide any signs of pregnancy, my long hair tossed up into its messy bun where it would be relatively safe from glitter and glue. No more comparing my borrowed clothes to his designer duds. We both looked like the teachers I'd always thought we were.

Adam glanced at the photographers, then back to me with a bit of sympathy. "Carrie said they've been camped out there all morning. They asked about you as soon as she got in."

I grimaced. Our principal couldn't have been happy to start her day this way.

"I asked John, the day custodian, to put a brick in one of the emergency exits when I got in," Adam said. "Figured I'd catch you before you got in. Come on, I'll show you where it is."

I shook his hand off my elbow, but another glance at the paparazzi had me convinced. "Fine. But no funny business, all right?"

And then there was the fact that Adam had been trying diligently to steal me away from Xavier for the better part of a year. At this point, I didn't know how or if his interest in me overlapped with his interest in the Kendal title, but I wasn't interested in finding out.

Adam held his hands up in defeat. "Nothing at all. Just helping a friend over here."

Friend. Right.

Begrudgingly, I allowed him to steer me around under the cover of a bunch of red and orange maple trees toward the back gate of the school, where we dashed through the playground before anyone saw us. Adam pushed the heavy fire door open and helped me inside, then shoved the brick away to let the door slam behind us.

The echo clanged around us for a solid ten seconds once we were alone in an empty corridor.

"Thanks," I said shortly. "But to be extremely clear, I'm not your friend. Not after the crap you pulled this summer."

Adam cocked his head, then irritatingly walked with me in the direction of my classroom. "Really? I think I deserve a little more credit. After all, we've known each other for years."

"We've been coworkers for years," I corrected him shortly. "Which, to be frank, I'm surprised we still are. You made your goals apparent in Kendal. Why is a hopeful heir settling for working at a Brooklyn elementary school?"

"I'm not the heir yet. And did you ever think maybe I just like it here?" He smiled as a passing kid waved at him on his way back to the morning care room from the bathrooms. "Hey, Armie. What's up, man?" He leaned closer to me after the child had passed. "Did you ever think I just like my 'coworkers'?"

I veered away as we rounded a corner. I had liked Adam once. Maybe even thought he was cute. But even then, something had been off, and now I wanted to put the entire island of Manhattan between us. At least.

Not a couple of classrooms.

I stopped short outside mine. "Well. Thank you for helping me inside, but I'm going to make things super clear for you. We're not friends. Things are too complicated. We can work together and be courteous if you absolutely have to stay at Carroll, but otherwise, that's it for us socially. I can't really be friends with someone who is actively trying to screw over my family."

Adam scoffed. "Xavier's your family now? Is that why you ran off in Kendal? Why do you even care about the future of a man you left?"

"Because we share chil—a child together, and I care about *her* future, you pompous jerk," I said, only too aware of how close I'd come to saying "children."

I didn't know what stopped me. It wasn't like I needed to hide my condition anymore now that Xavier and my family knew. But something told me not to reveal to Adam that I was pregnant. Not yet.

He tipped his head to the side, like he was evaluating a piece of art. "Maybe that's because you still don't really know what kind of person he actually is."

"Why, because I don't share your petty high school grudges?" I snapped. "I have to get ready for class now."

But Adam reached around me to grab the door handle and keep me from opening it, effectively pinning me against the door. "You don't understand. You weren't there."

"Yeah, but look at where we work. Do you really think I don't have the experience or wherewithal to understand schoolyard politics?" I gestured around us to the actual school we were standing in. "I get that Eton College isn't exactly a public elementary school, but come on, Adam. Kids are kids. So Xavier was a little mean to you when you were teenagers. So what?"

"It was more than just a little mean. He made my life a living hell."

I rolled my eyes. "Please. By all accounts, you barely knew each other."

Adam's eyes narrowed through his glasses, and his jaw clenched beneath the layer of well-trimmed scruff. He glanced down the hall where a few other teachers were entering their rooms. I checked my watch. We had about forty-five minutes before the rest of the kids arrived for the day, and I had prep to do.

But before I could excuse myself, Adam grabbed my elbow and shepherded me into my own classroom, then shut the door and turned to me.

"I was fourteen when I started at Eton," he said before I could protest. "Dad got transferred to London, yeah, but it was always the plan for me to attend Eton College because of my mother's family. That was the compromise, right? Travel with Dad, then go home to be a proper Englishman. Because at that point, I was still in the running to be the next Duke of Kendal. Mom and Georgina had been arguing about the entail for years since both Frederick and I share a common ancestor with Xavier."

"Yes, I know about that," I said. "But last I checked, it goes to the next oldest, doesn't it? I don't think your mothers being twins affects that."

"They're not the only twins in the Parker family," Adam said. "Frederick and I both share a great-grandfather who was also a twin— born one minute later than the eleventh Duke of Kendal. Xavier's great-grandfather. He might have been a jackass who was stripped of his own minor title, but he was still a legitimate Parker. So, you see, with Rupert gone, and Henry on his way, it seemed like I might have as much claim as Frederick. So I was supposed to be ready, just in case."

I probably should have told him to leave right then, but nothing came out.

After all, I was always a sucker for a good story.

"The thing was, you can't just *become* an aristocrat when you're also an American," Adam continued bitterly while he paced around some of the quads of student desks. "Not when you talk like we do or act like we do. You understand this now, Frankie. You know what they're all like."

I opened my mouth to argue but found I couldn't. I'd known from the moment I landed in Kendal that I could never belong in that world.

Adam approached my teacher's desk, then leaned across it and grabbed my wrist. I didn't pull away, sensing his intensity.

"Can you imagine how hard I had to work for one grain of acceptance in that place?" he asked. "You tried for a summer. Me, it was years. I did everything I could to make the sons of dukes, prime ministers, lords and ladies, if not *like* me, then at least accept me a little. I had to work at everything. My manners, my speech, my clothes—it was all a struggle. Everything that came so damn easily to *him*."

Xavier. He couldn't mean anyone else.

I frowned. "That's not true. They weren't nice to him either. He told me. He—he was bullied too—"

"For maybe a second," Adam said with a snarl. "But you don't understand—Xavier Parker never knew it, but he was everything those rich prats at Eton wanted to be. Ever heard of street credibility? They called him a bastard to his face, but deep down, every one of them wished they were as cool as the new tall kid from South London."

By the time he was done, my jaw was practically on the floor. While I could understand how some of it might have seemed this way from Adam's perspective, I also knew Xavier's story—that particular period of his life had been marked by a ridiculous amount of cruelty and social alienation. Eton had never been anything but torture for him, particularly since it was well before he had been acknowledged as the heir to Kendal. I was acutely familiar with the scars those years had left. There was just no way it matched Adam's description.

"They wanted to be like him?" I wondered. "Or was it just you?"

"It was *everyone*," Adam insisted. "He wanted a spot on the polo team? Done. Wanted to shag the hottest girls at Wycombe? All he had to do was give them one stupid, brooding stare. Everything came so fucking easy to him—and he *never* appreciated it!"

"I don't get it. You hate Xavier because, what, he took your place on the polo team and girls liked him fifteen years ago?"

"I hate that prick because he has taken every fucking thing I have ever wanted!" Adam exploded. "My school, my friends, my title. And then the girl of my dreams!"

I stepped back, pulled my wrist out of his grasp, and skittered to the other side of a cluster of child-sized desks. "Adam..."

He moved like he was going to follow me but seemed to realize it would be a mistake.

"I don't mean to pressure you," he said carefully. "I know I've blown it too many times to count. But I couldn't just let you push me away without knowing the truth. I'm in love with you, Frankie. I've been in love with you for years. Ever since you started at Carroll and I saw what a real, genuine, kind person you are. And it *killed* me that just when I got up the nerve to make a move, I found out that asshole was back in your life—"

"Back?" I jerked against a stack of cubbies. "What do you mean 'back'?"

Adam's eyes popped open. "I...er—"

"Did you *know* who Sofia's father was before Xavier came back to New York?" My voice started to tremble—with rage or fear, I wasn't sure. "Adam, did you *know the whole time?*"

"I—yes." The word expelled from his body like a blast of wind. "Yes, I knew."

My eyes goggled. "But—what—*how?*"

For once, he had nothing to say. He just stood there, one thumb hooked into a paint-splattered pocket, thin lips worrying under a short, regrown beard that he couldn't stop tugging on.

"You're obsessed," I whispered. "Not with me, but with him. That's what this is about, isn't it? You were stalking him—through me —or, or something."

"Frankie, please," Adam said in the same voice every adult in the building used to soothe a hysterical child. "Listen to yourself. I never stalked anyone. That sounds ridiculous."

"Ridiculous, but you're not denying either. You are completely obsessed with Xavier."

"I am not obsessed with Xavier Parker." Only a slight edge to his voice said any differently. "Curious, maybe. Who wouldn't be curious about the guy who literally stole his inheritance, huh? Show me a single person who's never looked up their childhood nemesis on Instagram. It's totally normal."

"It must have been more than that. You must have watched him for years, maybe. Followed him from afar. Watched *us*. Even back then—it's the only way you could have seen us together." My eyes popped open as icy-cold waves of awareness continued to wash over me. "And then you stalked me, didn't you?"

I clapped a hand over my mouth. Every hair on my body was standing up straight.

"Frankie," Adam said, hands up like a lion tamer approaching a new wild cat. "It wasn't like that. I promise. Yes, I saw him once with you, back when I'd just moved to the city. It was an accident, I swear." He shook his head. "You were so beautiful back then, do you know that? So brave. He never deserved you."

"No one knew," I whispered. "That I was pregnant. He left before I even knew. I didn't even tell my family until I was almost six months along. Which means after he was gone...you kept following... me?" I cringed. "What was that about? Some sick *Black Swan* action to take over Xavier's life? What the hell, Adam?"

His brown eyes brightened with something akin to rage, though he didn't shout. Only because he couldn't. Outside the door, we could both hear the increased pitter-patter of tiny feet in the hallway. At any moment, that door was going to open, and my day was going to begin. Meanwhile, I was going to have to work just a few doors down from an honest-to-God stalker.

"I am not obsessed with Xavier Parker," Adam said again. "The only person I care about anymore is *you*. I'll get you to believe me somehow, I promise. Maybe not today. Maybe not tomorrow. But one day you'll forgive me for any wrongs you think I've done, and I'll have my chance again. Because you're finished with that guy at last, right?"

I gulped. "I will *never* be finished with Xavier, Adam."

For whatever reason, Xavier's kiss tingled on my lips—meant to be an homage to the past, it still felt like a promise for the future.

How messed up was I?

Adam just smirked as he checked his watch. "Pick up and drop offs don't make a relationship, Frankie."

"No, but having his baby all over again does," I retorted, then clapped my palm over my mouth as I realized my mistake.

All the good-natured ease and feigned kindness had been erased by that one small sentence, revealing a monster of an expression that was as different as Frodo from Gollum.

I might as well have threatened his "precious."

Oh, *God*.

"His—*what*?" he demanded.

"Get out." My voice was a knife, subtle and low, but no less menacing. "Get away from me, get out of my classroom. If you're smart, you'll turn in your notice today. But in the meantime, you need to stay away from me and mine. Starting right this freaking second."

"Ms. Zola!"

Before I could answer, we both turned to find the door opening as my first student of the day walked in. I exhaled heavily, never so glad to see an eight-year-old girl in my life.

"Ms. Zola," said Esther Tompkins, "My mom said I couldn't bring peanuts to school anymore because we are a nut-free classroom this year, and I just want to say, that is totally unfair! Oh, hi, Mr. Klein!"

I smiled at her, but before replying, I looked back at Adam, who had only just managed to school his features back to something presentable.

"Go," I told Adam quietly. "Now. We have class."

His light brown eyes bore into me so intensely, I thought I might literally see a mark on my forehead had I glanced in a mirror. "I can't believe it. That you would—"

"*Go*," I interrupted.

Defeat finally slumped over his shoulders. "Fine. But Frankie, we will finish this discussion later."

No, we will not, I thought mentally as he finally turned to leave.

But even then, I couldn't believe myself. Even then, I knew that wouldn't be the last thing Adam Klein had to say about Xavier Parker.

———

IT WAS, however, the last thing I had to say to him that day. After receiving a couple of irritated, but mostly sympathetic comments from other teachers and the school principal, I was allowed to skip a faculty meeting and leave early when my kids went to PE.

Finding myself with an extra hour before I was due to meet Xavier at his hotel at three, I decided to go home so I didn't have to confront him in clothes littered with marker stains. The weather was nice as I meandered down Van Brunt, even taking a half hour to check out the latest art installations at Pioneer Works.

I couldn't remember the last time I'd had even thirty minutes to myself like this. Even with the help of a nanny in England, all my spare time had seemed to go toward, well, if not Xavier, then doing something to help him, whether it was researching his family or getting dressed up for some silly event.

I could buy *myself* flowers or coffee or whatever else I needed, as I did just that at a little bodega. I wasn't rich, but I didn't need to wait for a man to take care of me anymore.

Not my brother.

Not Xavier.

Not anyone.

I could demand enough of Xavier's money to give Sofia and little no-name-on-the-way what they needed so I could prioritize my own needs for once.

In my mind, and with an extra spring in my step, I rehearsed exactly how I would inform Xavier of that until I rounded the corner toward my house. I immediately stopped short when I clapped eyes on a familiar long-legged figure seated on my little brick stoop like he'd been waiting for me for years.

Dressed in his favorite dark jeans, brightly colored sneakers, and a bright turquoise hoodie to ward against the mild fall breeze sweeping off the river, Xavier didn't even notice as I approached.

How could he when he was deep in conversation with my mother?

SEVEN

"What are you doing here?"

The question flew out of my mouth sharper than one of Nonna's kitchen knives. My mother and Xavier twisted toward me with twin expressions of confusion.

Confusion and guilt.

I hadn't seen my mother in nearly six months, but she looked a lot better than when I'd run into her at the little bodega where she worked in Hunt's Point. Instead of ill-fitting jeans and over-bleached hair, she looked much more refreshed, maybe even younger than a woman in her late fifties. Her mottled skin had been plumped, tightened, and painted, her nails covered with two-inch, hot pink acrylics, and her caramel hair reconditioned, professionally highlighted, and almost certainly lengthened with extensions.

Even her clothes looked new. The too-tight black pants, frilly green sweater, and high-heeled booties had nary a scuff nor a pulled thread. That bag looked like real Chanel, not just a street-table knockoff.

Xavier, of course, looked dashing as ever, but unlike my mother, he didn't exactly look refreshed. Dark circles under his blue eyes told me the man hadn't been sleeping well. And the tight line of his mouth and furrow between his brows showed that he wasn't happy either. With my mother or with me, I didn't know.

"My flight arrived early," he said. "Thought I'd meet you here instead of the hotel to see the peanut." He looked behind me, and his frown deepened. "Where is she?"

"Not you," I said, completely ignoring his question. "*Her.*" I pointed at my mother. "Mami, what are you doing here?"

My mother threaded a few fingers through her hair and gave me an indecipherable look with green eyes that were irritatingly like my own. In fact, the more I peered at her, the more surreal it all became.

My siblings and I all took after our dad's side with our coloring— fair, if lightly tanned skin, dark brown-black hair, and the fine-boned stature of Zola genetics. But we all shared our mother's green eyes, and now that I was looking, I could see other things she'd given me. The lips that were a little fuller than most of my sisters'. High cheek- bones and a heart-shaped jaw. And my short, curvy shape. That was definitely hers as well.

But for all the similarities, her face was utterly indecipherable. I found myself wishing I knew her better, if only to understand what in the world she was thinking.

Or planning to do.

"*Mamita*, are you telling me your mother isn't welcome at your home?" she asked through a thick Bronx accent as she tucked a few sun-kissed strands behind her ear, from which a thick gold hoop swung.

The guilt trip yanked me out of my stupor.

"Correct," I said sharply. "She is not. You need to go."

"Ces, come on. She's your mum. She has a lot to tell you—"

"Why are you taking her side?" I demanded, turning my ire on him. "You know what she's said about us in the papers. Or are you forgetting?"

Xavier pressed his broad mouth into a thin line. "I remember perfectly."

He shot my mother a narrow blue glance I found oddly comforting. It was the same expression he gave his chefs when they misbehaved. The same one that was meant to tell them they risked being literally thrown out by their shirt collars.

That was when most of them did exactly what he said.

Mami, however, had no idea what that expression meant. She unwisely chose to ignore it. "Thank you, Xavier. Such a gentleman, Frankie. You have a good one here."

"She came to apologize, Ces," Xavier said. "At least, she's been apologizing to me for the last half hour. The *Daily Mail* cornered her for that interview and printed lies. She didn't have the money to sue, and you know the libel laws in England are weak. They can basically print whatever they want."

"I don't want to hear it," I snapped. "She has nothing to say that interests me anymore. And please spare me the bullshit about libel laws. Not when she's been spouting off to American publications *this morning.*"

Xavier reared, his head pivoting to my mother so fast it was as if a rubber band snapped. "What?"

I glared at her, pleased at least a little color had risen in her cheeks. "Check the *New York Post.* Joni was very proud of the fact that she made *Page Six,* like a bona fide New York socialite. Too bad she's so broke, Mami. She'd be your perfect target."

Xavier took his phone out of his jacket pocket and pulled up the site I'd seen earlier that day. Immediately, his blue eyes lost all reflection of the sky and turned to storm clouds.

Mami just sighed. "Frankie, it was taken completely out of context. I said so many nice things about you they didn't even print!"

"Things like 'there was something wrong with her from the beginning'?" Xavier read with disgust as he thumbed through the article. "'Same as the little girl. My husband wasn't good for much, and the apple doesn't fall far from the tree.'" He looked up. "The papers in the US can't print things like this without confirmed quotes. There are strict laws about it. My lawyers told me."

"Exactly," I spat. "Everything in there is on record." I tipped my head at my mother. "How much did they give you? Enough for a little nip and tuck, I see. Nice new bag. Get your hair and nails done, huh?"

Just the idea disgusted me. My stomach roiled, and it was from a hell of a lot more than morning sickness. Even as the smug look on her face started to fade, I wanted to be sick.

Xavier finished scanning the article and looked up with that blue flickering dangerously in his eyes. He stood up and joined me on the sidewalk to face her. I crossed my arms with satisfaction. Xavier and I might have ended our romantic relationship, but I couldn't lie—it felt good for him to have my back at last.

"Tell me, Mrs. Zola—" he started.

"It's Ortiz," I cut in through my teeth. "She never took Daddy's name."

I'd never been gladder for it.

"Ortiz," Xavier repeated in a voice with a whole lot more lurking beneath its even surface. "What's your end game here? Spit salacious shit about your daughter and me for what? A few extra quid? Fifteen minutes of fame?" He cocked his head. "That's barely worked for the Markles, you know. And I'm certainly no Duke of Sussex. The papers won't be interested in you forever, and meanwhile you'll alienate Francesca completely. Honestly, I think you've done a good enough job of that over the years without the help of the press."

My mother stood slowly, picking up her Chanel handbag from the steps. As if she could see the disdain in our eyes as we looked at the designer label, she thrust it guiltily behind her back.

"I didn't mean any of it," she insisted. "Obviously. They were willing to pay more if I said things like that. They promised."

While I had essentially already known that, it hurt to hear her say it so willingly. As if she didn't really need to feel bad. As if I was the one who ought to understand.

"You don't realize how hard it is," she said, her Bronx accent growing thicker with every syllable. "Every day. I live in this terrible apartment with four other women just like me, fresh out of the joint. Tracy, she lasted two months before jumping off the wagon. We all got minimum wage jobs because no one hires anyone with a record. My hair looked like it had been washed in garbage, all my friends were gone, and then none of my kids would see me—"

"Lea said—"

"Lea cut me out after you shared that interview from the summer," my mother spat. "Ungrateful. I couldn't believe her."

I pursed my lips. "I hope they paid you well."

Mami shrugged. "It was enough to cover my rent for a few months, but..."

"But you wanted more, so you turned to the *Post* instead," Xavier continued for her. "Did they pay better?"

She shot him a glare. "I just need a little more. Just enough to get back on my feet."

"Or pay for Botox?" I asked as Xavier muttered something like "for fuck's sake" under his breath.

"The article did well today," Mami said, as if that was supposed to make me feel better. "People are interested in you, baby. They want more. Another magazine said they'd pay for a video. A group interview with you, Frankie. More, if the duke here does it too." She swallowed. "Five hundred thou for all three of us. We can split it fifty-fifty if you want, even though *his highness* doesn't exactly need the cash, does he? You let me take it all—enough to get an apartment of my own somewhere, you know?—and that's the last, I promise. Who knows, they'd probably pay you for an exclusive of your own. Get a little something to help fix this place up for you and Sofia. I'm on your side here, Frankie. I'm your mother. This could be a good thing for all of us."

It was impossible to miss the glee that passed over her face as she considered that amount of money. It was fleeting, but she couldn't hide it completely.

Which told me one thing only—this would never be the last thing she'd ask of me. And because she was even asking, she wasn't a mother at all.

I swallowed thickly, counted to ten, then finally managed to look at her without wanting to tear her eyes out.

"I'm going to go inside," I said quietly. "And you're going to leave. And then I'm going to ask Matthew to file a restraining order against you. It's what he's wanted to do from the beginning."

"Don't bother him," Xavier said as he pressed a button on his phone and tucked it back inside his back pocket. "I've already texted one of my lawyers." His gaze flashed at my mother, the color of steel knives. "You'll be receiving the notice within a few days, Ms. Ortiz. I suggest you don't ignore it."

He took three strides so that even in her heels, he was towering over Guadalupe Ortiz like a vulture peering over its carrion.

It fit, really. She was dead to me already.

"You'll stay away from my family," he said in an eerie half-whisper that somehow could have been heard over the roar of an ocean, much less the occasional car passing down Van Brunt. "You'll leave Francesca alone. Sofia will never see you again. And if I ever hear a *whisper* of their names from your mouth in so much as a neighborhood pamphlet, I'll lock you up in so much litigation, you'll wish you'd never been born." He cocked his head. "I let things slide in England, but let me be very clear, madam. You do not want to fuck with me or mine. And your daughter *definitely* qualifies as mine. Understand?"

Goose bumps had rippled all over my body by the time he was finished. Maybe I should have corrected him right then. I could have mentioned that he did not have the right to be possessive of me anymore. That I did not, in fact, belong to him, nor was I his to protect any longer.

But the simple truth was, I *wanted* to hear him say just that. For months, I'd watched his anger rise in defense of his restaurants, his uncle, really everything but his own family, and a piece of me had been dying for him to care about us at least that much.

Part of me wanted the white knight.

Even if he had a black heart.

My mother took an unsteady step down one stair, then another, and the last until she was able to slink around Xavier's imposing form like a cat escaping down an alley.

"I—okay," she said softly. "Okay. But Frankie—"

"Don't," I said sharply, unable to look at her anymore. "You heard him. Go."

With another quick glance between us, she finally seemed to take the hint.

"All right," she said as she moved down the sidewalk. "I'll go. But Frankie, I do love you. I'm your mother, right? Mothers always love their babies. Please remember that."

I just shook my head, unable to answer. Inside, a small part of me shattered for good, unable to be swept up at all until the woman was gone.

I took several deep breaths, waiting until I could no longer hear the clip of her heels on the uneven pavement. My eyes squeezed shut while I waited for the twist of my gut to loosen so I could find a way to maneuver myself inside.

But, as it turned out, I didn't have to. Gently, Xavier took the keys I hadn't realized I'd been holding, then wrapped a muscled arm around my shoulders and shepherded me up the stairs to the front door, which he quickly unlocked to guide me inside. A few seconds later, the door shut, the lights were turned on, and before I knew it, Xavier had pulled me securely into his big body while I cried, nose tucked into his chest as he gently stroked my hair.

"Fuck," he whispered. "I'm so fucking sorry, babe. Fuck her. Fuck all of it. I've got you."

My heart ached as tears slid down my cheeks. Only Xavier could make the dirtiest of words sound like endearments. The complete and utter tenderness in his voice broke me.

"She's—I—God*dammit*!" I cried into his soft cotton shirt.

I couldn't explain this pain completely. How could someone I barely knew have such power to hurt me?

But she did. She really did.

Xavier's warm, fiery scent engulfed me completely, and despite how angry I still was with him, something in me relaxed. No matter what we'd been through, no matter how he'd hurt me, some part of me still registered him as a safe place.

Safe, yet still painful.

Half agony, half hope indeed.

How messed up was that?

Mine, he'd told her. *Your daughter is mine.*

God, part of me so deeply wanted to be.

"I'm so fucking sorry, Ces," he repeated as his large hand continued to pet my hair.

The scrunchie holding it up fell out under his ministrations, and he took advantage of it, weaving his fingers through the unruly waves, giving me more of that sweet comfort I needed.

"I should have paid more attention to what she was doing. I didn't know." He sighed. "Maybe I didn't want to know."

"Why?" I sniffled into his shirt. "Why look away from what I was trying to show you?"

He sighed. The hand in my hair paused for a moment before it continued its soothing strokes.

"I think I was a coward. I couldn't bear the thought of someone hurting you like that. I wanted to believe it wasn't anything."

His hand left my hair, and then both of his palms traveled to cup my cheeks and gently raised my gaze to his. One thumb stroked my cheekbone. Tracing the outlines of my face.

"So beautiful," he murmured.

His gaze adored. His heart thumped under my hand.

"Xavi..."

He needed to stop. Comfort was one thing. This was bordering on another.

"I was an idiot," he said softly. "I hope one day you'll forgive me."

"I—"

I wanted to say yes. But frankly, I wasn't there yet. Still, this was helping. Standing up to my mother helped.

But one conversation wouldn't erase nearly two months of pain and anguish. Sometimes neglect was the most painful weapon of all.

His blue-eyed gaze drifted down to land on my lips. It was clear what he wanted, and I wasn't entirely certain I would stop him if he tried.

"Xavi..." I drifted off yet again.

It was the best I could manage.

"I'll always fight for you," he said solemnly. "I'll prove it. You just wait."

I bit my lip and immediately regretted it when his eyes dilated with obvious desire.

"That damn lip," he said, then released my face with a chuckle, allowing me to step away from him and gather myself.

It was then I finally checked my watch and started when I saw the time. "Crap, we are never going to get downtown in time for the appointment."

At the mention of the entire purpose for his visit, Xavier's face lit up. "Oh, yes we will, babe. Give me a second and I'll call round my car."

EIGHT

Thirty minutes and one flustered car ride across the river later, I was safely checked into the third-floor office of my OB in the East Village.

Xavier had initially tried to get me to switch to a new doctor—someone profiled in *New York Magazine* who catered to the penthouse dwellers of Manhattan. But keeping my doctor was a hard line for me. Dr. Kyler had delivered Sofia and saw both of us through her considerable complications at birth.

At the mention of that, Xavier shut right up. After all, he couldn't argue when he wasn't there in the first place.

Maybe that was why he blustered into the tiny ultrasound room with all the grace of a windstorm. He was making up for lost time.

"Jeez!" I cried, clutching for the thin paper draped over my spread legs as the sudden door opening sent a breeze through the room that would have blown it right off had I not kept it in place. "What are you doing here?"

"You didn't think I was going to sit in the waiting room, did you?" Xavier smirked through the darkened room. "It's nothing I haven't already seen, babe. And become *well* acquainted with. This place is a cupboard, isn't it?"

He peered around the tiny room, located a stool that he could sit on to my left, and proceeded to cram his over-large body onto it in a way that still made him look like he was taking up approximately half the space. His whole being vibrated with the kind of nervous energy I usually saw in children on their first day of school.

I just closed my legs and glared at him. "I told you this wasn't necessary. The tech is just going to check for the heartbeat and take a few quick measurements. The real scan isn't for several more weeks."

"And I told *you*, I'm not missing any of them," Xavier informed me as he tried and failed to make himself comfortable.

I opened my mouth to argue but found I couldn't.

The truth was, I wasn't totally disappointed he was here. Just like I wasn't mad he had showed up at my doorstep. This was the Xavier I'd been missing all summer. The one who barged in with the grace of a bull, maybe, but whose loyalty to those he loved was never in doubt.

The question was, what had changed?

And would it change again?

We sat together silently, clearly unsure of what to say to each other. Xavier was chewing on his bottom lip while he studied the bulky ultrasound machine, then gazed around the rest of the room, which had been painted dark blue. Maybe to calm terrified expectant mothers like me. Or jittery fathers-to-be like him.

Without thinking, I reached out and set a hand on his knee, which was wriggling like a toddler in a bathtub.

Immediately, Xavier froze, looked down at my hand, then back up at me. The utter vulnerability there was as vivid as a summer sky.

"It's going to be okay," I told him. "It's just a scan."

"Sure, but—" he cut himself off with a sigh. "All right. Yeah. I know."

"Thank you for what you said back there," I whispered as I drew my hand away. "To my mom, I mean."

Xavier just looked down at me, attention pulled from his obvious worries. "You don't have to thank me for that, of all things. She had it coming and a lot more."

I frowned. "Well, I'm grateful."

He blinked. "It's what I should have done all along."

Before I could respond to that, the door opened, and the doctor came in.

Wait, what?

"Dr. Kyler?" I asked as my actual OB-GYN entered the room instead of the tech I was expecting. I didn't think a doctor had performed a single one of my ultrasounds throughout my pregnancy with Sofia.

"Hello, Frankie," she said in a calm, direct voice. It was a tone of mild irritation, I thought, but also competence, which was something I valued in a healthcare provider.

"I thought—" I glanced back and forth between her and Xavier, who didn't seem the slightest bit surprised to see her. But then, why would he? "Doesn't a tech usually do this?"

"They do, yes," she agreed as she took a seat on the stool next to the ultrasound machine. "But while my time *is* expensive, Mr. Parker here was willing to pay for it and then some."

No, I definitely did not imagine the irritation this time.

"The hospital board is also very happy for your donation." Dr. Kyler's brow furrowed suddenly. "Or should it be Lord something? I'm sorry, we're not very familiar with how to address men of your, er, stature around here."

Donation?

Xavier just quirked a funny smile, assiduously avoiding my inquiring gaze. "Xavier's fine. I think we're more interested in what's going to be on that screen than titles no one cares about."

"I should think so," Dr. Kyler replied. "Well, let's get this show on the road. Frankie, if you don't mind..."

She gestured toward my legs, which were covered by the paper sheet and my tunic. Obediently, I placed my feet into the stirrups and spread my knee while she turned to the machine and applied a condom and some lubricant to a large wand.

Xavier's eyes grew about the size of hubcaps. "Is that—where is that—*what are you doing?*"

I started to giggle as Dr. Kyler moved to a seat between my legs, then sucked in a breath as she inserted the wand between them. "Yes, it's going where you think it is," I said. "And Xavi, do *not* go down there to look."

"At this point in the pregnancy, the fetus is usually too small to detect with an abdominal ultrasound, so we do the first ones transvaginally," Dr. Kyler said in a tone that told me Xavier wasn't the first man who had ever been shocked by the, well, phallic shape of the instrument. It did look like a really big dildo.

"Doesn't it—doesn't that *hurt?*" Xavier looked like he was going to keel over.

I snorted. "How do you think it felt when you put the baby in there, Xavi?"

Dr. Kyler chuckled. Xavier looked even more shocked.

"I—Christ."

"Not showing yet," the doctor remarked, nodding at my still-flat stomach as she started to move the wand around a little. "To be expected."

I flinched, watching a screen full of what looked like static. It didn't hurt exactly. But it was...intrusive.

"Is that bad?" Xavier asked, eyes now glued to the screen as well.

"Sofia was the same," I told him. "Started small too. Don't worry. In another month or two, I'm going to look like I swallowed a basketball."

"Not quite that big," Dr. Kyler said with a distracted smile. "More like a grapefruit. You didn't really pop until almost the third trimester, if I remember correctly."

"Well, my boobs certainly have. They already look like I'm breastfeeding," I joked.

Xavier's eyes darted briefly to my chest before moving back to the screen as Dr. Kyler focused more on what she was doing.

I giggled, earning another flash of humor and a crooked smirk from Xavier that warmed something deep in my chest. He still didn't smile much and hadn't at all since we broke up. It was kind of funny seeing him so tied up in his emotions, overwhelmed and in the dark, and slightly turned on all at once. It was basically how I felt around him always, so it was about time we were even.

"There we are," said Dr. Kyler, as she finally held the wand still. "Let's see...yep, there's your little peanut, growing like a weed."

She pointed a finger toward the screen, and Xavier and I both followed, riveted by the flickering image. In the middle was a black triangular area, and within that were the clear, discernible shapes of a head and body. It wasn't much, but it was moving. And almost certainly alive.

"One second..." Dr. Kyler murmured as she moved the wand around again. "Yes, there it is."

She pressed a few buttons on the machine, and a rushing sound filled the room, something like wind whispering through cattails on a windy day in Central Park. The even, hushed call of a fetal heartbeat.

Beside me, Xavier stiffened as if he'd iced over.

"You okay?" I asked quietly.

Without thinking, I offered my left hand to Xavier, which he swept between his in an iron-tight grip. I squeezed his fingers, but he didn't move his gaze from the screen as we listened to the heartbeat and watched Dr. Kyler take a few measurements.

"My God," he finally managed. "It's—there it is. It's—she's—he's —fuck, the baby is really coming, isn't it?"

I could understand his shock, if that's what you could call it. It was an intense experience, hearing the heartbeat for the first time. When I heard Sofia's, I almost fainted. It made her a fact in my life, rather than a dream. Something very real. And very scary.

"Yeah, hon, it's real," I told him with a smile. "And in about seven more months, they'll be the most beautiful thing you've ever seen in your life."

He looked down at me then. "I doubt it."

I ignored the way the warmth in my chest bloomed into a heated ember. Honestly, when Xavier Parker flashed his baby blues that way, a dead woman would have blushed. It really wasn't fair, pulling bedroom eyes on a pregnant woman pumped with hormones.

Xavier turned back to the screen, as rapt as a fortune teller looking at a crystal ball. "Can you—could you tell the sex already? Is it a boy? Is that it's—Christ, he's really packing, isn't he?"

"Oh my God," I said. "Could you be more of a man right now?"

"That's the beginning of a leg," the doctor said with the dry patience of someone who has explained that difference at least a thousand different times to a thousand different fathers. "We won't be able to determine the sex for another ten weeks or so."

Xavier offered us both a lopsided smile that made my heart squeeze. "Ah. Well, can't blame a bloke for wishful thinking, can you?"

"Do you want a boy?" I wondered, although I wasn't sure I wanted to know.

For some reason, the idea that he would prefer a son bothered me. Maybe it was the fact that as a duke working hard to protect his estate, he would need a male heir to carry on the title under the laws of primogeniture.

Of course, that would require us to be married too, which, at this point, was completely out of the question. Xavier hadn't mentioned the big pink ring once since I'd turned him down, and I'd pretended that horrible proposal hadn't even happened.

I also pretended the idea of it never happening didn't render me nauseous in a different way than morning sickness.

Xavier seemed to notice something amiss in my tone. He turned back to me, then brought my hand, still clasped between his, up to his mouth and pressed a firm kiss to my fingers.

"The only thing I want is you and the baby, healthy and happy," he said solemnly. "Boy, girl, I don't care. Whatever they are, they'll be a gift. Just like the daughter we already have."

It was a very, *very* good answer. Just like the hope that shone from his expression.

I swallowed hard.

"Heartbeat sounds good and strong," Dr. Kyler said as she clicked over the image, taking a few other measurements. "I'd say you're nine and a half weeks along, based on these measurements. Which puts conception right at the beginning of August." She turned to us triumphantly. "About what you thought?"

Xavier's gaze flickered over me, but I couldn't bring myself to meet it. I couldn't even answer her question, flooded as I was with sudden emotion. The beginning of August...well, it wasn't the start of summer, when London had felt like a magical place full of possibility and love. August was the beginning of the end for us. It was when we'd left London for Kendal. When Xavier had transformed from the handsome, impetuous chef I'd fallen in love with into the cold, reserved duke who'd broken my heart.

August meant it could have been either version of this man who had overcome such banal things like birth control pills to knock me up a second time. It might have been the one who swept me into my bedroom and promised me the world when he finally came down from his office...or it was the man who took me hard against stable walls out of frustration, anger, and passion.

God knew I loved them both.

But only one had really loved me back.

I sniffed as tears sprang to my eyes. "I—yes, um. That sounds right."

"Yeah," Xavier said quietly. "The first nights in Kendal."

He sounded so forlorn—could he have been thinking the same as me? Could he feel as hopeless and despondent over what that period meant to us then...and how it shut down our future now?

I couldn't bear to see it on his face if he were.

The doctor pressed a few more buttons, then removed the wand while the machine printed out a series of images. I pressed my legs together, suddenly feeling self-conscious.

"Everything looks good and normal," she reiterated. "But I'd like you to schedule an echocardiogram just to be safe."

Xavier and I both swung around as though we were puppets on strings. An echocardiogram was definitely not normal. I hadn't had to do that with Sofia at all.

"Why?" I asked. "Is there something wrong with the baby's heart?"

Just like that, all the lingering warmth in my chest froze into pure terror.

Xavier's hand in mine had turned to ice.

"Nothing to be alarmed about," Dr. Kyler said warmly as she shut down the machine and cleaned off the wand. "I just hear a slight murmur, so I want them to check it out. It's probably nothing. Totally normal."

There was that word again. Normal. For something that seemed to me to be very outside the norm.

"Are you sure?" Xavier asked. "We can take the truth."

"I'm sure," Dr. Kyler said, though she was facing the machine, preventing either of us from reading her face. "It's just a precaution."

"Do you hear that?" Xavier asked me. "She's fine. The baby's fine, all right? We're just going to be safe, babe. Just breathe."

He took both of my hands in his large, warm ones and held them tight until I stopped shaking. I didn't correct him on calling me babe or pull away. Right then, I didn't care about making him remember that we weren't together. I just needed to feel safe, like he said. And Xavier was the only one who could make me do that.

I followed his instructions, taking several deep breaths until my own heartbeat returned to normal.

"Okay," I replied at last with a weak smile. "We're going to be okay."

"You're brilliant," Xavier said softly.

When I met his adoring gaze, my heart nearly stopped again, but for entirely different reasons.

Dr. Kyler handed me a cloth to clean myself up, then turned to give us a moment while she flipped on the lights and shut off the ultrasound machine. I cleared my throat, sitting up and dropping my feet from the stirrups while I pulled the paper sheet back over my knees. I was grateful for something to do other than meeting the sharp blue gaze of the man next to me.

I didn't think I could bear it if I saw the same thoughts running through my mind in those eyes.

Thoughts like, *I miss you.*

I need you.

I still love you.

Dammit.

"You can take these home with you," Dr. Kyler said briskly as she handed Xavier the pictures.

Then she smiled warmly at me, as if she could see the new tension in my shoulders, though likely misreading it as a pregnant woman's natural fear rather than the fact that I was completely and utterly pining for the father of this pending baby, whom I had absolutely no business being with. Not anymore.

"They'll take care of you up front after you're dressed," she said. "We'll still need to have the radiologist look over the images, but you can schedule that echo as soon as fourteen weeks. I'll see you then for your next checkup too, and the one after that will be the big scan." She glanced at Xavier. "I assume you'll be paying for my services again, Pops?"

Xavier smarted. "Damn right, I will. Only the best for these two."

Dr. Kyler rolled her eyes and shook her head. "Well, then I'll be seeing you too. Take care, Frankie."

And with that, she left us in the tiny blue room together. Still wondering if an entire ocean of hurt lay between us, but sitting very, very close.

NINE

"I brought these for you."

Xavier had barely said five words by the time he'd paid for the ultrasound, left the office, and exited the building onto the relatively quiet street in the Village with me at his side. Which was why I was surprised when he turned to me suddenly as he opened the passenger door of the hired Audi and removed a canvas tote bag.

I took the bag and looked inside, finding a stack of nondescript black notebooks I recognized immediately—the memorandum books used by the dukes and stewards of his family for the last two hundred years or so, which I'd previously discovered on a dusty shelf in the Corbray Hall library.

I looked up with genuine shock. It was the very last thing I expected him to bring me. Most men looking to make amends would bring flowers. Jewelry, maybe. But not books.

Look who knows the bookworm, tittered Kate's snarky voice in the back of my mind.

I blinked. "Why?"

Xavier gave a shrug. "You were working on something with those.

I won't pretend to understand why you found my family's boring old journals about rain and blight and mining the slightest bit interesting, but it was important to you. Something about narrative records among the English gentry."

I couldn't help but smile. "You remembered the title."

Another shrug, but his long nose turned slightly pink with something akin to embarrassment or maybe pride. The few times we'd talked about it, Xavier had seemed so distracted by his own affairs that I hadn't even believed he could hear me, let alone remember what I was doing.

Apparently, I was dead wrong.

I was offered a lopsided smile that made my chest ache with want. "I should remember more. But I'd never forget something you need, you know." He nodded. "That was your 'something more,' right? I wasn't sure if you'd have the time to continue, but I thought I'd give you the option."

Another surprise callback to one of our first conversations upon my arrival in Kendal. My desire to be more than just an accessory to his life. The need to have something of my own.

In response, Xavier had offered me yet another library and complete access to any family secret I could find. At the time, I'd thought maybe it was his way of saying "My life is yours to share."

This felt like the same sort of token.

"I...thank you," I said honestly. "But Xavi, I can't take your family's history. Not now, right?"

"You mean since you've brutally rejected me several times over?" he said lightly.

I frowned. I didn't find it funny.

Xavier just sighed. "Just because you're not there doesn't mean you should give up your work. You wouldn't ask me to stop cooking just because we broke up, would you?"

I swallowed. "Of course not."

Xavier without a kitchen was like keeping Picasso from his paints.

The man was an artist—I'd never deprive the world of his talents or him of his passion.

"If you don't want them, I'll take them back," he said. "But if you're still interested—"

"I am," I interrupted. "Interested, I mean. I don't know when I'll get to reading them again, but I'd love to. Eventually."

He examined me for a long minute, like my response wasn't quite satisfactory. He was looking for something, but I honestly didn't know what it was.

Then he took the sack from me, put it back in the front seat, and closed the door. "Do you fancy a walk?"

I glanced at my watch. It was coming onto five o'clock, but Sofia was safe with Joni, probably having the time of her life over pizza and a giggle fest.

We had time. But what it would accomplish, I wasn't so sure.

"I—all right."

———

IT WAS A RELATIVELY balmy day for mid-October. The last vestiges of summer had disappeared weeks ago, but sunshine still speared the multi-colored leaves overhead as we zigzagged around the streets of the Village, eventually finding ourselves on the west side. The ones that had fallen still crunched underfoot before the autumn rains began in earnest. The air was crisp and chilled but not uncomfortable as the sun started to sink below the buildings around us. A perfect day for a stroll.

"I always loved this neighborhood," I said after two blocks of near silence on Perry Street. "Aside from how beautiful it is, I honestly think literally every building within a five-block radius has hosted at least one literary icon."

"Like who?" Xavier asked, almost a dare.

"Too many to count. Thomas Paine. Anaïs Nin. Dylan Thomas. Henry James. Richard Wright. Edgar Allan Poe. Shoot, literally every Beat writer. I could keep going." I shrugged, well aware I was babbling/lecturing in that way my sisters couldn't stand. He did ask, though. "It's amazing, really, to think of how many of the world's talents came to this little patch of earth to follow their dreams and make art."

I grabbed a red-streaked maple leaf from a tree we passed under and turned it back and forth while we walked. This part of Manhattan was oddly peaceful despite being only a few blocks from Washington Square Park. A few cyclists passed us, as well as a pedestrian or two, but it was far enough from the subway and the traffic of downtown or Washington Square that we didn't have to shout to be heard. Almost as quiet as Red Hook.

"Would you want to live here if you could?" Xavier wondered. "Join your writers. Follow your dreams, too?"

I snorted. "Who wouldn't want to live in a West Village brownstone? It'll only cost me, oh, a casual twenty million or so. Give or take another five or ten mil. Chump change, right?"

Xavier gave me a queer look. "How much do you think a penthouse in Mayfair costs?" He peered around us curiously. "It's a nice street. We'd get on well, although I'd miss our view."

I didn't know what to say. It almost sounded like he was serious. *We? Our?*

"We could do it, you know. Live here if you wanted."

He stopped in front of one particularly beautiful townhouse made of gleaming white stone that called back to some of the Georgian houses around Mayfair and Hyde Park. Still built like a brownstone, though—it was the perfect blend of New York and London architecture.

Now he definitely wasn't joking. There was none of the telltale humor gleaming from his blue eyes. Just eagerness, maybe. But mostly a serious question.

"You could go back to school, too," he rattled on. "Quit teaching and write the book on those journals, or whatever else you want. Isn't there a university close by?"

"NYU, yeah," I said slowly. "It's a few blocks that way. But Xavier—"

"So you study there. Or Columbia, if you'd prefer. Get your PhD, learn more about all these writers. Live your own dreams, instead of always helping littles find theirs while you pretend to inhabit someone else's story in your mind."

He gazed back up at the white house, clearly entranced by the prospect. He had a look in his eyes that I imagined was similar to the one he probably saw in mine whenever I imagined myself an Austen heroine.

"Sof could have the run of a place like this," he went on. "The little one too, once they're born. Plenty of space for everyone. No more two to a room or sleeping on old couches or landings. It'd be perfect, wouldn't it? No titles or estates or papers or mothers or anyone to interfere. Just us again. The way it's meant to be."

By the time he was done speaking, it felt like there was something very large and awkward lodged in my throat. He couldn't know how many times I had imagined something just like that. Even walked up and down this very street, long before he'd ever come back, fantasizing about exactly that sort of life for myself. Right now, I was feeling an odd sense of déjà vu, of when I was pregnant with Sofia, letting myself pretend in my weaker moments that somehow Xavier would leave his betrothed, find me again, and we'd be a family.

But it was no less a fantasy now than it was then—for one very specific reason.

"It would be lovely," I said. "If we were still together. But...we're not."

Xavier turned back to me so slowly that I thought he might be ossifying in motion. He watched me for a long time before glancing back at the house once or twice.

"Hmm," was all he said. And then turned and continued down the sidewalk.

I followed him, as confused as ever. What was going on? Had he completely forgotten that I'd turned him down? Did he even care?

I was a quiet shadow to his looming steps until we'd crossed Tenth Avenue and Hudson, then zigzagged over to a streetlight in order to cross the West Side Highway and walk to one of the lonely piers that stuck out over the river and granted a view of New Jersey. The roar of traffic now competed with the sound of water sloshing against the pilings of the pier.

But Xavier's deep voice still topped every noise when he spoke again. "So, what now?"

He turned to lean against the pier's railing, casually balanced on his elbows while he raised a brow and examined me sardonically.

I frowned. "What do you mean?" It was obvious the question was loaded, but I rambled on anyway. "Joni is meeting us at the house with Sofia in about an hour, probably. Tomorrow, more work. Four more weeks, the echocardiogram, another scan. I'll probably need to notify the school about taking maternity leave at the end of May. They won't really care—the kids are basically useless after Memorial Day anyway. After that—"

"I'm not talking about your bloody schedule, Francesca," Xavier cut in sharply.

I broke from my contemplating and sighed. "I didn't think so. But Xavi—"

"I'm talking about *us*, Ces. I'm talking about our family." He turned and gripped the rail so violently that his knuckles turned bright white. "In seven months, there's going to be another baby."

"Oh, I am *well* aware of that," I returned. "Believe me, much more than you are at this point."

"I doubt it."

"Do you, now? Well, Your Grace, let me tell you—you have *no* idea what's coming. Between not sleeping more than forty-five minutes at a time, cleaning up more bodily fluids than you can possibly imagine, and having to decipher twenty different cries for a being who won't be able to *speak* for at least a year or more, it's going to be a literal shitshow that will make you happier and more miserable than you have ever been in your life. Even I'm going to be blind-sided, and I've already done this once before."

Xavier worried his mouth a bit, taking it all in. "But this time, you won't be alone," he said stubbornly.

"I wasn't alone last time either," I cut back. "I was at Nonna's, actually. I had a whole family around me. Sisters and my grand-mother to step in when I needed them. Thank God one of us knew what we were doing."

My voice warbled at the end. For the first time, I realized I was scared to do this on my own. The way things stood, Xavier and I would likely be living in different places, but it would be months, maybe years, before he would really be able to take both kids on his own, if I was even comfortable with that. I wouldn't have Nonna's capable hands at my disposal or my sisters as impromptu babysitters, or my brother ready to pay the mortgage so I could take a little extra maternity leave.

It was just going to be me.

And I wasn't the slightest bit prepared for that.

"Well, this time, you have your baby's actual father." Xavier's voice was starting to cut, the timbre rising like a threatening tide. "Who, if you've forgotten, can give you everything you need if you just accept it instead of being so stubborn. You can do whatever you want here, babe. Take the house. Go back to school. Just give me a bloody chance."

"Xavi, I already said no—"

"And I said I don't care if we get married," he broke in. "I just want to make things right. Let me try to make things fucking right!"

"Then stop pressuring me and give me some space!" I cried. "Stop yelling at me. Stop trying to give me the world. All I ever wanted was you, Xavi!"

"I tried to give you that, but I wasn't fucking good enough, was I?" he said bitterly, as cutting as the wind on my cheek.

I swallowed. Suddenly my face hurt. "No, I—" I shook my head. I didn't know what to say.

Xavier sighed and rocked back and forth on his heels for a moment. His chest moved up and down as he took several deep breaths. When he spoke again, his voice had calmed somewhat.

"Look," he started. "Maybe I'm never going to be the man you want me to be. I can't be the dukes in those bloody novels. I don't ride a white horse. I can't sweep you off your feet. I'll never rescue you from a tower."

Part of me wanted to smile. He was so close to those things—he really had no idea. True, he had no white horse. His favorite in Kendal was brown, actually. He had never technically swept me off my feet, but he'd picked me up more times than I could count. I had no tower from which to be rescued—but in a way, he had saved me from my landing in a shabby little row house.

As if any of that mattered at all, though.

"The thing is," he continued, the South London edge of his accent sliding into his speech like a cool breeze, "that's just fiction, isn't it? They're not real. But I am, Ces. I'm here, and I'm bloody well not perfect, but I'm real, and I fucking love you and Sofia. More than this life, more than the next." He swallowed, as overcome with his emotions as I was. "But me and them fancy heroes, we got one thing in common. They never give up the chase, babe, and neither will I. I will come for you, and I will burn for you, and I will wait for you for the rest of my days if I have to. Because, Francesca Zola, we were created to love each other. I don't know much, but I know that. I'll always know that."

By the time he was done speaking, my head was swimming. I didn't know whether to kiss him or slap him. He talked so good, but every part of my brain was screaming at me to wait.

This man had hurt me more than anyone. He had proved to me over and over again that we weren't right for each other.

That he wasn't, just as he said, the man I wanted him to be.

Even if he was the man I loved.

What was I supposed to do with that?

"You can't buy me a house," I said at last, grasping for tangible things to manage. "I-I can't talk about the rest. I just—I can't. But there is no way I'm going to be able to go back to school with a three-month-old baby. It's too much."

"No, it's not." Xavier looked up from watching the river, like he really couldn't believe that's what I was choosing to focus on. "Women go back to work all the time after three months. You're just scared, and you know it."

"You're damn right, I'm scared!" I broke out. "In ways you can't possibly understand because you haven't been around. For five years, my entire life has been about one little person. And I don't care how much anyone loves their child. The truth is, you lose yourself as a new parent. Between midnight feedings, giving every extra cent to clothes and toys and diapers, being a slave to naps and finicky schedules, trying to decipher what kind of cry they are making at a particular moment, and not sleeping more than forty-five minutes at a time for potentially a year or more, you give up pretty much every semblance of independence you have for *years*. So I can't dream for myself right now, Xavi. Not when I'm about to lose that self all over again!"

"Except you won't." Xavier pushed off the railing and, before I could stop him, had captured my face between his large hands, forcing me to look up at him and see whatever earnest truth was in his dark eyes. "Listen to me. You will not lose yourself. I won't allow it. I'll be with you every step of the way. If you're lost, I will find you. I *promise*."

"Like you promised this summer?" I mumbled.

And there it was. The gap between us that he couldn't quite bridge. Not with rings. Not with fancy houses. Not with promises to be my hero and love me always.

Words couldn't cover it any more than empty promises of the future.

I honestly didn't know what would.

I wanted desperately to look away, but Xavier had me trapped.

His blue eyes reflected the darkening sky back at me, plumbing my depths with tools of sorrow.

"I didn't even know you were lost until it was too late," he said in a low voice. "And fucking hell, Francesca, I will *never* stop regretting it."

I shuddered. He couldn't know how badly I had yearned for those words for more than a month now. When his eyes dropped to my lips, I licked them as if on command. Decision took him as he bent down and kissed me.

Home. I was home again. It didn't matter that I'd run back to New York, the city of my birth, nearly six weeks earlier, intent on finding safety and refuge from the hurt the summer had caused. The reality was that for a central part of me, home was right here in this man's arms, with those sure fingers molded around my jaw and neck, these soft yet firm lips seeking entry to mine, that tongue tasting every bit of me like I was the nectar of life itself.

I moaned into the kiss, opening to him, completely and fully aware of just how my very hormonal body was reacting.

Hormonal.

Pregnant.

Oh *God*, what was I doing?

"Xavier," I gasped as he moved that wicked mouth across my jaw. "Xavi, please."

"Fuck, my love, my love," he murmured, stubbled chin causing goose bumps to pebble over my neck. "I need you, Ces, don't you understand? I need you like a tree needs a drink after a long drought. I'm dying without you. I'll die the rest of my life."

His mouth found mine again, and I couldn't quite stop my hands from slipping into the thickets of his black mane, pulling him closer, devouring him until, finally, my brain kicked in.

This wasn't real. It was hormones. One kiss didn't make every-thing he'd done disappear.

I broke the kiss, panting, then somehow managed to wrest my

hands from his hair, set them on his chest, and push him away. "Xavi, we have to stop."

His broad chest heaved as he stared at me, inky hair deliciously mussed, full lips even more swollen from the effect of our kiss. He looked somehow more edible than ever. I wanted nothing more than to consume him, body and soul.

"Why?" he demanded. "Why the fuck do we have to stop? You feel it. You love me. I know you do."

I didn't argue with him. By God, I couldn't lie like that.

"It's...complicated," I said weakly.

Lord, I could barely think when he looked at me that way. Like I really was the oasis, and he had come wandering in from the desert.

"It's not complicated," he said. "It's simple. I'm here. I came to New York."

"You came because I had a scan."

"I came for *you*," he repeated. "We have a family. Another on the way. But more importantly, *I love you*. Don't you believe even that anymore?"

In a way, it really was music to my ears—but in the same way a siren's song would pull sailors to their deaths in the sea. Xavier would pull me under all over again if I let him. And I had more to think about than just myself.

"I do believe you," I said softly. "Honestly, I do, because I...I love you too."

His shoulders relaxed a bit but tensed again once I continued speaking.

"But I also think there is still a big part of you that is figuring out just what that means. And I can't risk Sofia and myself and maybe this baby getting hurt by it again. Xavi, I'm sorry. But I just can't."

"So, I've got to prove myself all over again. Is that what you're saying?" he asked, unable to keep bitterness from lashing through his voice.

"I'm not saying anything." My speech was weak. Almost as weak as my resolve. "I'm saying we have to stop."

"Right back where we started, then."

"No," I said. "Where we started was with a future. But now we know what that future holds. We only hurt each other, and I won't do it anymore. Xavi, I love you too, but it's *over*."

He stared at me for a long time, the muscle in his jaw ticking ferociously while he clenched and released dual fists over and over again. He looked like he wanted to tear the entire pier apart. Like he could actually do it if he had a mind to.

But to my surprise, he turned to walk back down the pier in the direction we'd come from, pulling his phone out of his pocket and sending a message as he strode on.

"Where are you going?" I called as I scampered behind him. "What are you doing now?"

"I'm *trying* not to yell," he said, barely getting the words out through his teeth, though he had slowed so I might catch up. "Someone told me I was a bully a bit ago, that my temper gets in the way of things I care about."

His eyes practically cut right through me with a quick shear of a glance.

Me. I was the one who told him that.

My jaw dropped, stopping me for a half-second before I caught back up to him. By the time we had exited the pier, his car had already pulled to the curb.

"I can take the train," I said lamely, even as I allowed myself to be shepherded into the back seat.

"Don't try me right now, Ces," Xavier said as he got in beside me. "John, back to Francesca's house, all right?"

The car took off down the West Side Highway, leaving Xavier and me to sit silently, if not sullenly, in the back together.

"Xavi," I started, but he just held up a hand.

"I need a minute," he said. "Just some quiet until we get there."

I opened my mouth but decided to nod instead. This was...different. Certainly, not the hothead I typically had to deal with. Where it was coming from, I didn't know. But if he needed space, I could afford him that. Perhaps take the ride to think myself.

"But, Ces?"

I turned back to find him studying me closely.

"This discussion is *not* closed," he said.

Then he leaned in, so his stubbled jaw tickled my skin. His soft lips on my cheek sent a shiver down my neck and a flush over the rest of me while his deep voice rumbled in my ear.

"Love can't burn this hot only to flame out in a single night. I don't know much, but I do know that."

"D-do you?" I asked. My voice was barely above a whisper.

Xavier took a deep breath, inhaling deeply just over my pulse. "Just like I know that I have loved you since the day I saw you in that bloody pub. I know that we are a family, whether you want to fight it or not. I know we belong together, no matter what anyone else says. And I know, without a shadow of a doubt, in the very depths of my soul, that we are far from over."

TEN

"And he didn't say anything else? The entire ride back?"

I popped a calamari in my mouth and shrugged at Kate's questions following my debrief of the afternoon. After Xavier had dropped me back at the house, he'd offered to take Sofia for a walk to the park before the sun set completely, leaving me to share a meal with Joni and Kate, who happened to be in the neighborhood after a day of scouring estate sales for her shop.

Kate arrived with wine and takeout. Joni chose the music off her phone. And I poured out the intensity of the afternoon to my sisters' eager faces.

I grabbed another calamari but could only look longingly at the glasses of Sangiovese she and Joni were enjoying next to me on the back deck.

"Not a word," I said after I swallowed. "Other than to ask about taking Sofia to the park, that is."

"So, he stands up to Mami for you," Kate recounted. "Then practically cries when he sees his baby for the first time—"

"He didn't *cry*," I said, although there had definitely been a telltale sheen in his eyes. Tears weren't totally out of the question.

Plus, the room was really dark.

"And then he offers to buy you a mansion, kisses you on the pier—"

"Don't forget declaring his undying love for her," Kate put in while she cut herself a bit of the eggplant parm I'd picked up down the street.

"Right, right. Then he declares his undying freaking love, says you're anything but over...and gives you the silent treatment?"

Joni shoved a hand through her hair, which she had apparently tipped blond in after I'd left for work. If I hadn't been so wrapped up in my drama, I'd have been annoyed my bathroom now reeked of bleach.

"That's beyond messed up," she said. "Sounds like a whole lot of fuckboy behavior."

"Sounds like he's figuring some shit out." Kate swirled the wine in her glass and tipped her face up toward the lights strung around the deck, looking like Elizabeth Taylor with her big silk hair scarf, vintage gold earrings, and aggressive cat eye.

I shrugged, wishing with my whole heart I could partake in wine too. "Apparently. Honestly, the whole exchange was kind of weird. By the end, I could tell he wanted to yell at me. Like, really let me have it. Then take me somewhere and, well, let me *have it*, if you know what I mean. Before, that's exactly what he would have done."

"Yell and ravish," Kate translated. "Let's not pretend you didn't like it when the not-so-gentle giant lost his shit a little, Frankie. Especially the ravishing part. Especially in the alley behind his restaurant or two."

"I didn't know you had an exhibitionist streak," Joni said with a grin. "Damn, my sis is a closeted freak!"

"I never should have told you that," I informed Kate dryly.

She just shrugged. "My point stands. After all, you did let this man knock you up *again*."

I threw a calamari ring at her, which she dodged, laughing. Joni watched us with glee, happy for once not to be the naughty one in the family.

"I didn't like any of it," I told them, though everyone there, myself included, plainly knew I was lying.

It wasn't that I liked being yelled at. But Xavier's passion was another story, especially when he let it out in other ways. I'd never minded his tendency to say exactly what he was thinking. When it came to Sofia and me, he'd always shown his emotions as he felt them, even if they sometimes erupted like a thunderstorm.

It was when he had started bottling them all up that we ran into trouble.

Or when he had taken those repressed frustrations out on me in other ways.

Was his restraint today just more bottled urges? Or was he trying to change something more fundamental about himself?

"It *is* kind of satisfying to know he was willing to come to your rescue with Mami, though," Kate said. "I still can't believe she went to the *Post* about you."

"She's desperate," said Joni. "I mean, she'd have to be, right? No one would rat out their kids otherwise. Maybe we should help her or something."

Kate and I both looked at her with varying measures of pity. It was sweet, really, the way she wanted to think the best of our mother. But she was too little to remember much of the bad stuff.

"I just wish he would have stood up to his own family like that for me," I said.

"Well, maybe he's just getting started," Kate offered. "Maybe you should go back to London and see what he does now."

"Ha. Not on your life!" I reached for a tentacular calamari, only to have Joni steal it from my reach. "Hey, I wanted that. You're supposed to give pregnant ladies everything they like, you know."

"Gimps too," Joni said, gesturing toward her scarred knee, which was propped up on the only empty chair at the table, marring her otherwise perfectly svelte dancer's legs encased in cutoff shorts.

"I don't think that counts when you're six weeks post-surgery, babe," Kate informed her. "Speaking of, what's the prognosis from PT? When can we expect you back on the stage?"

An unfamiliar darkness shadowed my baby sister's face as she stuffed another calamari in her mouth and chased it with the remainder of her wine.

Kate and I just waited her out.

Eventually, Joni mumbled something under her breath.

"I'm sorry, what was that?" Kate asked. "Did you forget how to speak?"

"I *said* I tried to do a cabriole," Joni enunciated with flushed cheeks. "And then I fell. Hard."

Kate and I glanced quizzically at each other, then back at her.

Joni just huffed.

"A cabriole," she repeated as if we should know exactly what that meant. "It's a dance move. A really hard one. Where you jump and hold your top leg at a forty-five or ninety-degree angle, and then beat the bottom leg to it without losing that angle." She sighed. "It used to be only men could handle it. I was the only one in the *Chicago* cast who could do it at all, male or female."

"So, it made you a hotshot," Kate said with better comprehension.

"It got me hired," Joni corrected her. "The director told me point-blank that's why he chose me to understudy over more experienced dancers."

I nodded appreciatively. "That's awesome, Jo. Badass, really. Sounds like that PT is really paying off quickly."

"I said I tried it," she muttered. "And I fell. Like a sack of bricks." She leaned over onto the table and buried her face in her hands. "I'm finished. I can barely do a pas de bourree without feeling like my knee is twisting off. But my Equity benefits ran out, so PT is done. I'm over. Finished."

Another glance at Kate told me she didn't know what "pas de bourree" meant any more than I did, but it was clearly something that upset Joni.

"I'm sure it's not that bad," I said as I rubbed her back, lying the way only family can. "You're young, Jo. Your body is going to bounce back. It's only been, what, three months since the accident?"

"Yeah, maybe just take a little more time on your own," Kate chimed in. "Hey, why don't you visit Marie in Paris? We could probably scrape up a ticket for you."

Joni just sat back up and made a face. "And sit around in her tiny apartment while she cracks eggs and whines about her boss all day? No, thank you."

"That's right, I forgot she had a thing for one of the Lyons brothers," Kate said. "What's his name again?"

"Daniel," Joni said with relish. "And I only know that because Mimi used to write Mrs. Daniel Lyons all over her recipe notebook like she was freaking twelve. How pathetic is that?"

"So she still just likes the one?" Kate asked. "I thought there were two hot brothers running the Lyons family now."

Joni and I both looked at her in surprise.

"And how would you know that, Katie?" I asked.

She shrugged. "One of them has a stylist. She likes my shop. And she gossips."

That tracked. Kate's shop was small, but she'd grown a national following with influential stylists all over the place—to the point where she was considering getting into that line of work herself.

"Anyway, yeah, there are two," she said. "Look."

Joni and I both leaned over as Kate pulled up a picture on her phone. Two extremely handsome men looked directly into the camera outside something that appeared to be a benefit, maybe, or a very fancy award ceremony. Despite the fact that they were brothers, the resemblance between them wasn't particularly strong, and their personality differences were even clearer. One was probably my age, with dusty blond hair, blue eyes, and a bright smile. The other was older, dressed in a somber gray suit and wearing glasses. His brown hair and gray eyes were the personification of a storm cloud, and his mouth bit back a perennial scowl.

I had a feeling he and Xavier would get along very well.

"That's the one Marie is obsessed with," Joni said, pointing to the blond one.

Kate made a face. "Ew, he looks like Ryan Seacrest."

I giggled. "Oh my God, he does." It was the last type I would have expected Marie to have. She almost never wore anything but black—a lot like the stormy brother, actually.

"He's better than the other one. He's cute, but he looks like *such* a square," Joni said. "Like, get contacts, Grandpa."

"I doubt Lucas Lyons cares much about fashion," Kate said. "He's too busy running the second largest media conglomerate in the world to care. Anyway, it's the younger one whose stylist I've met. Party boy, that one."

"You can tell," I said as I handed Kate back her phone. "He looks better groomed than Nonna. I had no idea Marie liked pretty boys."

"She likes *this* pretty boy," Joni said. "Has ever since she started working for their family, remember?"

Kate and I murmured our agreement. It was a while ago, but I did remember Marie's consistently dazed expressions when she got her first after-school job as a kitchen assistant at the massive estate. "Can you imagine crushing on someone for five whole years and never making a move?" Joni wondered.

I actually could. In fact, I knew exactly what it was like to pine for someone you couldn't have for five whole years. And this boy was eons out of my mousy wallflower of a sister's league.

"Well, in that case, it's better she went to Paris," Kate said. "Maybe she'll pick up some lovers and some style while she's there."

Joni snorted. "No kidding. Ditch the nun getups. God knows she never wanted my help in the clothing department."

"That's because she doesn't want tips in her G-string, Jo," Kate said, laughing when Joni dipped her fingers in her wine and flicked them at Kate in response.

"All the more reason for you to go to Paris now and help her out,"

I joked, but before Joni could reply, we were all interrupted by a knock at the front door.

I excused myself, walked through the house, and found the downstairs tenant waiting outside.

"Hey, Pete, come on in," I said, opening the door for him.

Pete was a forty-something bachelor who worked as a gaming designer. He was quiet, preferred his computer to any kind of sex life, and had lived downstairs without a peep for the past two years. In other words, he was the perfect tenant.

"Thanks," he said, shoving a hand into his jeans. "I, uh, won't take up too much of your time."

"No worries," I said, guiding him to the back to join us. "Want a glass of wine? My sisters are here."

"No, I'm good. Got a cold one chilling in the fridge downstairs. Oh, hi ladies."

Kate and Joni both waved disinterestedly when they caught sight of our guest.

"Everything all right?" I asked. "Is the furnace acting up again? I can have Matthew send someone."

"No, no, everything's fine," he said kind of nervously while he adjusted his baseball cap over his thinning hair. "I just wanted to come tell you in person that I'm moving out when the lease is up next month. I, uh, met someone last year, and, well, we've decided to move out to New Jersey. She has a house in Paterson. Bigger space and all."

I fought not to drop my jaw. So much for having a better relationship with computers than people. When had Pete had time to date?

Probably when I was gallivanting all over England.

"Oh," I said. "Well, um, that's great. I'll let Matthew know."

"Do you have to?" Kate asked. "The house is yours now, isn't it?"

I shot her a look. "It will be, but—"

"That's great," Pete interrupted. "Congratulations. And thanks, yeah. Jen, she, uh, wanted me to come out sooner, but I told her I couldn't break the lease, you know. Couldn't leave you hanging like that...right?"

Ah, so that's what he was after.

His cheeks were ruddy, and despite the fact that I was definitely going to miss the extra income from the mother-in-law, I didn't want to be a jerk and stand in the way of love.

"Hey," I said, setting a hand on his shoulder. "It's really not a big deal. You can leave whenever you want. Just let me know when so I can start looking for a new tenant, all right?"

His wan face brightened. "Really? In that case, I'll probably be out this weekend. I, uh, already kind of started moving my stuff over there."

"Aw, Pete, you old softie," Joni said. "You got it bad, don't you?"

Pete, a man I'd never seen exhibit much in the way of emotion, blushed from head to toe. "When you know, you know, right?" he said. "Anyway, thanks again, Frankie. Been a pleasure renting from you guys."

"You too, Pete. I'll talk to Matthew about your deposit and everything."

He left, and then I resumed my seat with my sisters while they continued to gossip about our siblings and other bits and pieces of drama in their lives. I, however, was already preoccupied.

With Pete moving out, I was losing my tenant, yes, but also the last remnant of life with my brother. I had originally planned to put that money toward payments to buy the house properly from Matthew and Nina. Now I'd have to find a new tenant, which sounded horrible, especially given the fact that in a matter of months, I'd be right back on the landing again in order to give the other bedroom to the baby-to-be.

I could ask Xavier for money to cover the cost of keeping the basement to myself, but after today's events, I already knew that would come with more strings than I was willing to deal with. Kissing strings. Family strings.

In a single day, more questions were coming up than I had answers to, and I didn't like that feeling. Not one bit.

ELEVEN

"I'm sorry, Frankie. I really am. But we have to let you go."

When it rains, it really, really pours. I'm not talking buckets of rain or a silly little thundershower. I'm talking a hurricane out of nowhere.

One week after Pete gave his notice and Xavier made his explosive pronouncements on the pier, my mouth fell open, and my eyes flew up from where I'd been covertly peeling dried tempera paint from my fingertips.

"You have to what?" I asked.

Principal Stewart, better known to me as Carrie, the kindly woman with ashy-blond hair who ran staff meetings, bought everyone a round of drinks at the end of the school year and sometimes provided a place to send unruly students, just looked at me with sympathy across her desk.

"For what it's worth, we really are sad to be losing you," she said. "You're a good teacher, Frankie, and the kids will miss you. I'm happy to write you a glowing reference, no matter what you choose to do."

My brow wrinkled into a web of lines—I felt like I was lost and unable to read a map. "I don't understand. What have I done to deserve being fired in the middle of the school year?"

The teacher shortage in New York was well known. People didn't lose their jobs unless serious stuff went down, like endangering students or sexual assault.

Carrie sighed. "It's not really you, Frankie. It's...the complications you've brought with you this year." When I continued to stare like she was talking gibberish, Carrie pointed to her window. We both followed the gesture toward the spot on the other side of the school fence, where, yes, a few photographers lay in wait under a molting maple tree.

I blinked. "You're firing me for a couple of tabloid photographers?"

Carrie grimaced. "It's two now. There will be another three or four by the end of the day. You said they would lose interest—"

"And they have," I interrupted. "There were at least a dozen here the day that story broke in the *Post*."

"Yes, and since your—Mr.—er—the duke—"

"Xavier," I said. "You can just call him my daughter's father. And there was only one photographer here yesterday at this time."

"Since *he* announced this morning that he is possibly opening another restaurant in the city," Carrie continued like I hadn't said anything, "and the *Post* thought that running another feature on your mother would be a good idea, I think it's fair to say their interest isn't waning."

I swallowed back a lump newly forming in my throat. When Xavier's text from London a few days ago had told me the same news, I had initially been happy, if only because it would give him a legitimate reason to be in New York and close to Sofia before the baby was born. I knew it was only a temporary fix, but I liked the idea of not being his primary focus, given the current tension between us.

The feature on my mother, however, was something I was just trying to ignore.

"I—but—I'm not at fault here, Carrie," I said. "I haven't done anything but exist."

I hated the pity that sprang into her eyes. I hated even more that a part of me knew this was coming. It's not like I hadn't heard the whispers of staff behind my back over the last few weeks. Wondering if I was going to stay a teacher when I was getting my fifteen minutes of fame.

I'd brushed it off as jealousy. Nothing to get worked up about. Certainly not fired over.

Carrie's expression told me it was a very real issue.

"Look, if it were just some photographers, I wouldn't get so upset," she said. "But they're harassing students now. Yesterday, a few of them asked some of the kids about you and your daughter, wanting to know where you live, where she goes to school. As far as I know, no one was able to tell them anything. But one grabbed a girl's arm and yanked her against the fence. It left a bruise, and the child was very shook up." Carrie shook her head in disgust.

I swallowed. I knew about that, but really, what was I supposed to do about it?

"The district is trying to get a temporary police patrol in place," Carrie said. "One is already coming to clear out the photographers before you leave. But no matter what happens, we can't keep putting the kids at risk. And since you're not yet tenured, the union rep agreed severance is the best way to go. Even if we do love you here."

She reached across her desk and set an envelope in front of me, presumably carrying my discharge papers, or whatever they were called. I stared at it for a moment, unable to move. Was this really happening? First, my brother left, then my relationship fell apart, a surprise pregnancy, and now losing my job?

What was happening to my life?

"You'll receive salary until the end of the year, after which the district has chosen not to renew your contract," Carrie said. "But I'm afraid you'll have to leave at the end of the school day." Her hand squeezed mine like it was trying to pulse life back into it. "I'm sorry, Frankie. But your time at P.S. 058 is over."

———

I WAS STILL numb as I gathered my personal knick-knacks and belongings from my classroom and the teacher's lounge. There was surprisingly little after having taught the third grade for three years now.

Perhaps that should have clued me in on the importance of my job. So many teachers donated a variety of resources to enrich their classrooms, but I'd generally depended on the materials left to me by the prior teachers, subsidizing with parent donations when they could.

In the end, my belongings fit into a small cardboard box with room to spare.

A few books I'd donated to the classroom library.

A coffee cup with "Future Mrs. Darcy" printed on the side.

A box of my favorite English Breakfast tea and a half-empty jar of honey.

A picture of Sofia and a potted fern.

That was it. That was all I had to show for my years as a third-grade teacher at Carroll Elementary.

I'd still barely even registered that I was crossing the empty playground for the last time, ready to cart my box home, when my name was shouted behind me.

"Frankie!"

I turned at the back gate, thankfully out of view of the photographers who had been cleared from the grounds. Adam Klein was jogging after me across the playground.

I sighed and shifted my box onto one hip. This was really the last thing I needed. "Adam, what do you want?"

Since our confrontation in my classroom a few weeks earlier, Adam had wisely done as I asked and generally left me alone.

Though I'd still noticed him watching me during staff meetings and covertly following me with his gaze when we passed each other in the hallway, he hadn't so much as peeped my way beyond the occasional head nod or wave.

"Nice hello," he said once he caught up. "Good to see you, too."

I didn't answer, just gave him Nonna's patented "get it out, child" glare and waited for him to continue.

"Elaine said she saw you packing up your stuff," he said. "Did Carrie let you go?"

I swallowed hard and nodded. "Looks that way, yeah. They didn't want a paparazzi target teaching the kids and drawing bad types to the playground. I guess one of the photographers hurt a child."

Adam looked appropriately disgusted. "That's horrible. Jesus."

"Yeah," I said. "Anyway, it's effective immediately, so I guess I'll be seeing you."

I turned, wondering why I'd even offered that nicety after telling Adam I wanted him to leave me alone.

"It won't stop, you know," Adam called as I started walking away again.

I turned back. "What won't stop?"

"The press. The interest. I don't get it either, but I watched it happen for years in the UK. There's something about him. Maybe he's rotten to the core, but that doesn't curb people's fascination."

Disgust—or maybe envy—practically dripped off his vowels. I didn't have to ask to whom he was referring.

"Xavier has a lot of charisma," I agreed. "But in the UK, it's because he's the Duke of Kendal and all that. Americans don't care about that sort of thing the way the British do. All the fuss will die down, they'll get bored with my mom, and things will go back to normal."

"Is it worth it, though? Especially now that's he's out of your life?" Adam pressed.

"Who said he was out of my life? He's the father of my children and has every right to be a part of whatever I'm going to do next. Whereas you, unfortunately, do *not*. Why do I have to keep reminding you of this?"

"I saw the articles in the *Post*," Adam rattled on. "Everyone has. He's already cost you your freedom, your youth, and now your job, Frankie. How much more are you going to let him take, huh? When are you going to realize the only person Xavier Parker looks out for is himself and no one else?"

My shoulders slumped the more he spoke. The box seemed so heavy. Suddenly, the world seemed so heavy.

"Just let me go, Adam," I said. "I understand your concerns, but I can deal with all of this myself."

Just like I always had.

He watched me for a long moment, then eventually nodded and took a step back.

"I have to go," I said. "I'm meeting Xavier at Sofia's school, and then I have to get home." *To sort out the rest of my life.*

"I get it." Adam nodded, brown eyes begging me to listen. "If you ever need anyone, just know I'm here for you. Always. I meant what I said. Don't forget it."

What he'd said was that he loved me.

To some, it might have felt good. Warped, maybe, but this was a warped, lonely world. So maybe it should have been nice to know that someone else in it still felt that way about me, even if it was someone like him.

But for some reason, it just made the stone in my stomach sink even lower.

I wished I could forget Adam's revelations. I wished they had never happened at all.

———

I TRUDGED the five blocks or so up to Sofia's school like my feet were made of lead. My arms felt like rubber. That heaviness hadn't left my shoulders—in fact, it had worsened the farther I got from the school.

"Ces."

Xavier stepped out of his black Audi, looking svelte and casual in a pair of jeans and yet another hoodie.

"Hey," I said. "What are you doing here? I thought you weren't arriving until tonight."

"Got in early. Thought I'd meet you for pickup."

I swallowed as a million questions buzzed through my mind.

Was he starting that restaurant for real, or was it just an excuse to see us?

Was he here for her or for me?

Why did I want to know at all?

"Can I put these in the trunk?" I asked at last, holding up the cardboard box.

Xavier's quick blue gaze flickered over my belongings, but before he could answer, the door to the preschool unlocked, and they opened the top half to start welcoming parents.

"Sure," he said, then signaled to his driver to open the trunk while I turned to sign Sofia out of school.

————

WE RODE BACK to the house in silence while Sofia chattered about her day, talking to her daddy, a.k.a. her Favorite Person in the World, while I stared moodily out the windows, ignoring Xavier's concerned glances. I could tell he knew something was wrong but seemed to recognize I wasn't interested in discussing it in front of Sofia.

It wasn't until Sofia had had her snack and settled herself in front of the TV that he cornered me in the front foyer, where I was sorting mail.

"All right," he said. "Care to loop me in?"

I gave him a look, and he immediately pulled me outside to the front stoop, where we could talk out of Sofia's earshot.

"What is it?" he demanded. "What happened? Was Adam bothering you again? Did he do something—"

"Adam did nothing," I said quietly. "I got fired today."

Xavier's brow crinkled. "They sacked you?"

"Yes."

"But, why?"

I sighed. "Because of all the press. The paparazzi have been harassing students, and they had to let me go."

Because of you, I almost added. For whatever reason, Adam's comments about everything Xavier had cost me kept running through my mind.

"And on top of everything else," I added. "Pete's moving out this weekend, which means in addition to losing my job, I'm losing my other means of income."

My God, when was it going to stop? All the loss. All the heartache.

When was I going to be able to take care of myself?

"Ces," Xavier said. "I'm so sorry. But you're not without help, you know."

"I have child support from you, yes, which we still need to iron out with a mediator."

I rubbed my forehead. It was important, but just one more thing I had to pay for with my low funds. Not to mention the idea of mapping out money with Xavier was just depressing.

"I'm only taking what's necessary, though," I said. "I don't have a claim to your money, Xavi, nor do I want it, despite what the papers might say. I don't need to be a wealthy woman, and Sofia doesn't need to be an heiress."

For some reason, the idea of him throwing cash at the situation hurt more than everything else. Sure, accepting it might solve these stressors, but it would also just underline how transactional our relationship had become.

On my insistence, yes. But it still hurt.

"I'm not just talking about that," he said. "You've got me too."

"I don't *have* you," I said with a bit of a snap. "You live across the freaking ocean."

"I'm here now, aren't I?"

"For another weekend. For your kids. Certainly not for me."

"Says who?"

Yes, he had said he still loved me. Yes, he said he wanted us to be together. He'd offered a townhouse in the Village. He'd offered me a life.

And I'd said no to all of it.

Because I already knew that sometimes what Xavier Parker offered and what actually came to be were two different things entirely. He couldn't save me from my problems. And I needed to stop letting him.

Suddenly unable to breathe properly, I turned away and began flipping through the mail in my hands for want of something to *do*. Something to manage. Something I might be able to control.

"Oh, *fuck*," I gasped, unable to help the uncharacteristic profanity or the fact that the wind had picked up suddenly off the East River enough to yank the stack of bills from my fingers and scatter them all over the steps. "Oh, dammit!"

For some reason, the accident was enough to make me cry. The cherry on top of this horrible, horrible sundae.

"I've got it," Xavier said, jumping into action as he gathered the mail off the ground and set it on the front step under a rock to keep it in place. "See, got it all. No harm, babe. Ah, fuck."

Now that I'd started, I couldn't stop crying. Everything just seemed like *too much*. There was a new baby coming, on top of so much loss. My brother was gone. My job was no more. Even Pete was leaving. And then, of course, I'd lost Xavier.

The love of my life.

"It's okay," Xavier said, gathering me against his chest. "It's okay, babe. You don't have to be strong all the time, you know."

"Am I?" I whimpered into his chest. "God, am I strong at all? Sometimes I feel like the weakest person on the planet."

A large hand gently stroked my hair, petting away the fear and the torment. "We all feel that way sometimes. But you're one of the strongest people I've ever met."

I sniffed back another sob. "I don't know about that."

"I do. Look at what you went through as a kid, losing your parents and what. And then your grandfather. Growing up in that house with all those kids and still becoming as bloody smart as you are. Taking care of Sof all by yourself, raising the most perfect little girl on the planet."

I giggled through another sob against his chest, trying to ignore the way I basked in his warm, fresh scent. "I think you're a little biased on that count. She has half your genetics."

"Never. And when I think of how you endured this summer— the way you took everything that was thrown at you like a pro, barely even flinching every time some new surprise tried to knock you down." Xavier shook his head, chin moving against the crown of my head. "I didn't appreciate it. I was too sucked into my own fears and grief to see it then, but I see it now. You're a brick, babe. Resilient and strong and kind and loving. More than you'll ever know."

I couldn't come up with a single retort. It was exactly what I needed to hear.

"It's okay," he said as he rocked me gently there on my doorstep. "You can break with me."

Gradually, my tears ceased, though I allowed him to hold me for a few more moments until I finally pulled away.

Xavier's hands lingered on my shoulders as he examined me up and down. "All right?"

I nodded, wiping the remnants of tears out of my eyes. "All right."

"Good." Then his gaze jumped over my shoulder toward a letter he'd missed on the ground. "What's that?"

I turned as he walked around me and picked up the envelope,

which was scrawled with jagged handwritten letters. Not quite a child's, but not quite an adult's either.

"Weird," I said as I opened it up on the spot.

Then I read the note inside and thought I might faint all over again.

Xavier grabbed it from me and read it aloud:

> Frankie—
> He isn't what he seems.
> Get rid of him before I get rid of you.

He looked up again just as I was peering into the envelope, where a bunch of something that looked disturbingly like ashes lay at the bottom. He looked inside, then snatched it away.

"What are you doing?" I demanded, even as he whipped a crumpled paper bag out of his pocket and stuffed the envelope and letter inside.

"You don't know what that is," he said. "It could be anthrax."

"It's just a letter—"

"From a fucking stalker!" Xavier practically exploded, although he managed to get his murderous expression under control before turning back to me.

"A...stalker?' I whispered, unable to feel my legs all over again.

"I'm so sorry," Xavier said. "But yeah. You'd better call the cops, Ces. And make up the landing for me this evening. Because I'm not going anywhere."

TWELVE

"Without knowing who sent it, there's not really much we can do," said Derek Kingston at about six thirty that evening, just before he shoveled an extra bite of pasta into his mouth.

Upon receiving the creepy letter, Xavier's first instinct had been to call the police—preferably the chief or at least the Brooklyn DA, i.e., someone he perceived was possible to bribe. I, however, calmly took out my phone and called Derek, my brother's former investigative partner with the NYPD, best friend, and a known and trusted ally to my entire family.

And, sure, yes, someone I briefly dated.

A fact that Xavier appeared to remember the second Derek arrived, looking far too dapper in a button-down shirt and slacks, with his NYPD badge sitting on his hip next to a holstered gun.

The detective glanced around the dinner table stacked with Zola siblings and a scowling duke as if he was unsure about whom to address this comment to but seemed to settle on me.

"Derek, come on. There has to be something we can do besides sit around with our thumbs up our butts," Lea pressed as she refilled his wineglass in the practiced, automatic way she could have only learned from Nonna.

Right after I'd called Derek, I'd sent Kate a quick text about what happened. I should have known better. An hour later, she, Lea, and Joni arrived with baby Lupe and a tray of lasagna like a cavalry called to arms. The Zola clan loved nothing, if not drama, and I was serving heaps of it these days. Lea was more than happy to play family protector now that she was the de facto eldest with Matthew in Boston.

To be honest, I was more than a little annoyed with the entire situation. It was a letter. I was kind of surprised I hadn't received more, given the number of times my name had been in the papers over the summer, and right now, I had bigger things to worry about than some idiot who didn't like Xavier.

Derek, thankfully, was reasonably used to our chaos. The only thing that seemed to be making him uncomfortable was the six-foot-five duke who had been glaring blue murder for the last thirty minutes.

"I wonder if the NYPD can do anything at all," Xavier mumbled. "It might be more useful to ask a neighbor's dog to help guard the place. I think the couple across the street has a Pomeranian."

I elbowed Xavier in the stomach. His scowl disappeared for a moment when he turned to me.

"Be nice," I mouthed.

One side of that broad, full mouth rose, but the scowl resumed its position when he turned back to Derek, who was used to all measure of things much more intimidating than Xavier's smart mouth.

"Just keep track of things going on here," he told me. "Be smart, you know. Don't go out by yourself late at night, see if you notice anyone following you. That sort of thing." He must have caught my forlorn expression when he set down his fork. "Frankie, you know I care about you guys. You and Sofia are like family to me."

Beside me, Xavier's entire body tensed.

"Is there anyone you can think of who might have a motive?" Derek asked.

"Besides every woman who has seen Xavier's face in the *Post*?" Joni asked, then shrugged when she found everyone looking at her. "What?"

Lea rolled her eyes and turned back to me. "Anyone treated you weird since you came home?"

"Stuff like this usually comes from people close to you," Derek said.

I blinked, glanced up at Xavier, then back at Derek. "I—well, there is a, um, a colleague at school."

"Adam," Xavier growled. "Of course, it's him."

I winced at his obvious vitriol, then turned back to Derek and recounted the last few conversations I'd had with Adam—including his obvious obsession with Xavier.

Derek listened carefully, taking notes.

"Could be," he said. "Worth a try, anyway. I'll take the letter with me and dust for prints just to see if something comes up in the system. See if I can't get something with his prints from the school while I'm at it. But your mailbox was wiped, so I doubt anything will come up. I'm sorry. I wish I could do more."

"Don't we all," Xavier muttered, then got up from the table as if he couldn't stand to sit still one second longer.

"You should come back to Belmont," Lea said as she resumed her seat at the table and took baby Lupe back from Kate, who was at the end. "That's what you should do. Come stay at the house with Joni and Nonna when she gets back from Italy."

"Excuse me, and what if I don't want to get murdered in my bed if Frankie's stalker follows her there?" Joni demanded before seeming to realize how it made her sound. "Sorry. I just meant—"

"I know what you meant," I interrupted a little too sharply. "And don't worry, I'm not moving back to the Bronx."

"Why not?" Kate asked. "It's not like you have a job down here anymore."

"You got laid off?" Lea demanded.

"Thanks a lot," I said to Kate.

From where he stood behind her near the screen door, Xavier just shook his head and scrubbed his forehead with a fist.

Kate made a face. "Sorry."

I turned to my older sisters. "They let me go because of all the press. I don't want to get into it."

"Well, you should definitely move back to Belmont," Lea said. "There's room for you and two kids with Marie in France. You can take the attic again with the new baby, just like you did before, and then Sof can take Marie's room, and—"

"I'm not going anywhere," I argued. "Sofia's still in school. I'm not pulling her out in the middle of the year because of a single letter. I can find temp work until the baby comes, and I'll still have my salary until then anyway. We're going to be fine."

"But what are you going to do about money after that?" Lea sputtered, rocking Lupe as if to comfort herself more than me. "I'm sure Mattie would give you a few months off paying him back, but what about food? Daycare? Bills? You have the equivalent of three car payments in student loans every month!"

"Lea, I really don't need you to contingency plan for me right now!" I was almost shouting with her by this point. With every item on her list, my own anxiety rose exponentially, and the fact that I had another mouth to feed growing under my sweatshirt wasn't helping things.

"She's going to be fine," Xavier said bluntly, his deep voice shutting down the entire argument. He turned from the screen door, arms folded across his chest. "She has me."

"Oh, because you were such a help this summer?" Lea said.

Kate snorted, and Joni said, "Oooh," under her breath.

"Stop it," I hissed at her.

"I wasn't the one who left," Xavier countered in the dangerously low voice that told me he was very close to losing his temper.

"No, but you were the one to neglect her for weeks," Lea said.

"You basically pushed her on that plane, so let's not get all high and mighty now, Mr. Duke. And be real. She wouldn't be in this situation if it weren't for you. No one would be coming after her. She wouldn't have lost her job. And she wouldn't be unemployed with yet another baby on the way."

"Lea, stop," I said again, conscious of Derek's bewildered glances between all of us and the fact that Sofia was just upstairs with her cousins and could come down at any time to hear this drama.

But my sister was on a rampage. "She needs more than a fancy man with a brooding stare who lives three thousand miles away. These are real problems. What are you going to do, throw a few dollars at her and go back to your castle? She needs real support. She needs her family."

"She has a family!" Xavier seethed.

"Yes, she does!" Lea snapped right back. "We are sitting around this table, you overbearing dick. And we do not include you!"

"That's enough!" I exploded out of my chair, surprising even myself. "Lea, I appreciate your defense, but you don't get to talk to Xavier that way. Like it or not, he *is* a part of this family now, so you're going to have to deal with that. And you—"

I turned to Xavier, who was watching me with an expression like a lion facing its tamer. I found, though, there was nothing really to tame. He wasn't the one being rude. He wasn't saying anything wrong at all, actually.

I sighed and shook my head. "I don't even know what to do with you. But Lea's right. Making a fuss over things and being an inconsistent presence isn't helping either."

Every person in the room was staring at me by the time I was done, clearly astonished. I understood why. I was no pushover, but I wasn't prone to this kind of outburst. I didn't yell. I didn't shout. I kept my cool, always, because that's what I was supposed to do as a mother, middle child, teacher, everything.

I took a deep breath and stepped around my chair. "I've had all of five seconds to process the landslide my life has become over the past few weeks. None of it is going to get sorted out in the next five minutes, so I'm going to take some time to myself without any of you breathing down my neck."

Vaguely, I registered my sisters nodding while Xavier just frowned, clearly unsure of what to say or do.

"Derek, thank you for coming," I said woodenly. "I appreciate it. Really."

"No problem," Derek muttered, clearly happy to be freed, though he did have another bite of lasagna.

"As for the rest of you," I said, pointing a finger all around the room. "I'm going downstairs to think. Do not follow me."

———

I MADE my way down to the basement that, until now, Matthew and I had kept locked for the privacy of our tenant. Pete had left last week, however, and now the place was empty.

It was odd, really. I'd never actually been down here other than when Matthew had finished the kitchenette the week before Pete moved in. It was a nice space. A small, clean living room with a sliding glass door that opened onto a patio, plus a bedroom in the back and the kitchenette made for one. A good place for a single man. An even better space for a single mother who needed a room of her own.

I sighed as I walked around the living room. One day, maybe.

When Pete had told me he was leaving, I'd been scared, but then I'd considered the alternatives. I'd made enough as a teacher to handle his "rent" to Matthew, as promised. I could have turned the basement into a refuge for myself. A primary suite where I could go when the kids were asleep.

"'A woman must have money and a room of her own,'" I murmured to myself, remembering the famous essay by Virginia Woolf.

Not yet, I supposed. Not quite yet.

"What's that from, then?"

I turned from the screen door to find Xavier entering the apartment. He looked around the basement, hands shoved casually into his pockets.

I scowled and did not answer his question. "I'm sorry, did you not hear me say I needed a minute?"

"Sure, and I gave you ten. Generous, I think, since your sisters are about to eat me alive."

I chuckled in spite of myself. I could imagine that all too clearly, with Lea leading the charge.

"You can think about it all you want, Ces, but your sister is right about one thing. You and Sof can't stay here alone. Not with someone out there looking to harm you. Even if it is a soft sock, otherwise known as Adam fucking Klein."

"Well, I don't need you playing caveman with me either," I said, defensive all over again. "I realize I'm vulnerable, but I'm really not as breakable as everyone seems to think. It was an effing letter, not a death threat."

"Oh?" Xavier's black brows knit together. "You don't think saying 'before I get rid of you' is a threat?"

"I think it's child's play," I said. "I think it's not worth one iota of my energy when I have to find a new tenant, get a new job, and figure out how I'm going to raise a second baby in another several months. Honestly, I think you're all freaking out over nothing."

"It's not nothing when it's threatening my everything."

Xavier looked like he wanted to yell, but again, he took a deep breath, closed his eyes, and managed to recompose himself.

I watched curiously. He'd been doing that a lot lately. The breathing. The resetting.

"You're not on your own here," he said in a calmer voice. "That offer for the house in the Village, or really wherever else you'd want to go—it's still on the table."

"I don't need your charity," I said lamely. "Or your mansions."

"It's not charity when it's my own family. You just said it up there."

"Sofia is your daughter, yes, but I do not belong to you, Xavi. You don't need to lock me away in a fancy cupboard to keep me safe. I can figure this out on my own."

Xavier groaned loudly. "For Christ's sake, why can't you just let me give this to you?"

"Why?" I demanded. "Why would you want to do that? We aren't together, we don't live together, and while I will certainly accept some amount of child support, I'm not looking for a free ride, Xavi. So, why? Why do that?"

"BECAUSE I LOVE YOU!" he practically exploded. "Like I keep fucking saying. Stop being so dense about it, Francesca. I love Sofia, I already love the little creature you're growing, and I love you more than life itself!"

"Stop it," I croaked. "Stop saying that."

"Why?" Xavier prowled toward me. "Because you're scared? Well, I'm scared too. I am. I was frightened the day I met you. Even more when I met our daughter. And now that we've got another one on the way, I'm fucking terrified, but not in the way you think. I'm scared the mother of my children might never love me again. I'm scared I've ruined everything." He shook his head like he couldn't believe it himself. "But in the end, it doesn't matter, because I'll tell you one thing, Ces. I'm not leaving you here to deal with all of this alone."

"Oh, please," I said. "I've heard that line before. But you can't control your own life, Xavier. You have a business, a family, practically a whole kingdom to run on the other side of the pond."

"And yet my heart resides here."

"Your heart," I spat. "Please. Spare me the platitudes. When push comes to shove, we come last after all the rest of that."

"Careful, babe. That sounds awfully bitter."

"Maybe that's because I am," I said, unable to stop the tears from choking my throat. "If there's one thing I learned this summer, it's that I'm not worth any of this insanity. I'm average, completely medi-ocre, the opposite of special. There is absolutely no reason for anyone to make such a damn fuss."

It wasn't until I actually said it that I realized why it all hurt so much. Deep down, I'd always thought that maybe that was the case. Maybe that was why my mother had left us, why our father had loved alcohol more than his kids. Maybe that was why Matthew had left for Boston or no one besides very few men had ever really been inter-ested in me.

Xavier had made me believe otherwise. He'd given me hope.

Until he'd ripped it all away and proven my worst fears to be true.

I was worthless. Or, at the very least, not worth his *real* love.

"You're wrong," Xavier said, his voice hoarse. "You're so, so wrong. You're worth everything, Francesca."

And then, before I could stop him, he crossed the room and kissed me.

Warmth. The solid, warm tower of him cornered me against the glass, hands cradling my face like I was more precious than gold while his lips found mine, caressing, nipping, sucking, licking until finally I opened to him and let him feast as fully as he liked.

Oh, it felt good. *He* felt good. Tasted *so, so* good. I couldn't deny that this was what I'd been craving for months, years, really. The way he encircled me completely, blocked out the rest of the world and made me feel like I really was the center of his universe the way he proclaimed.

But I wasn't. He'd already shown me who he was, and I was determined to take Maya Angelou's advice and believe him the first time.

"Stop it!" I protested against that delicious mouth, though I wasn't sure if I was talking to him or to myself. "Stop—I can't think when you do that."

"When I do what?" Xavier asked with a sly grin against my cheek. "This?"

He kissed me again, and it almost worked. I sank into it a little more and moaned at the feel of his hands when they reached down to take a firm grip of my backside. But then I got a hold of myself.

"Yes!" I said as I placed two hands on his chest and shoved him away. "Xavi, I told you, we are *over*."

"You keep saying that, babe, but that kiss told me otherwise." He shook his head. "Not really sure I believe you now."

"Well, *believe* it!" I yelped, scampering out from under his arms and across the room into the kitchen.

"Believe what?"

We both turned to find Kate now entering the apartment.

"Bloody *great*," Xavier murmured, though he did nothing to hide his swollen lips or the remnants of my lip gloss on his cheek.

"Why doesn't he just stay here?" Kate asked as she looked around the empty apartment.

Xavier smiled. I just gawked. What in the freaking hell was my sister doing?

"Katie..." I started.

She just continued inside like I hadn't said anything. "Pete's gone. Xavier can have his place. *If* he's willing to stay, like he said. If not, maybe install a bodyguard when he's out of town again—"

"I'm not going anywhere," Xavier interrupted. "She won't need another fucking man living with her."

"Oh, yes, you are," I snapped back. "Did your family drama just evaporate when I got pregnant? Are your restaurants failing? I didn't think so."

"It'll hold," Xavier said evenly. "It'll all hold."

"Since when?" I asked. "Since when did the great dukedom of Kendal ever just 'hold' for the rest of your life? I haven't seen it happen yet."

"Since my uncle is no longer on death's bloody door, Francesca!" His voice cracked with strain, but once again, he closed his eyes immediately and took several deep breaths.

My mouth shut tightly at that. Well, that was true. And brutal.

I was a horrible person.

"Well, er, that makes it easier," Kate remarked after a few awkward moments.

I sighed. "Kate..."

"Well, it does," she said. "Listen, I'm thinking this solves your problems for the time being."

"What are you doing?" I whispered when she came close enough for Xavier not to hear.

But my sister just shrugged, then turned and leaned against the counter so she could face Xavier. "What do you think, Your Grace? Will these accommodations serve your royal requirements?"

Xavier rolled his eyes, clearly needled by the titled approach. His blue eyes, however, lasered onto me over her shoulder. "Will you come back to London?"

I bit my lip. "Absolutely not."

"And will you allow me to move you and Sofia to a more secure building?"

I bit my lip harder. That was more tempting. But little or not, this house was home. And it belonged to me. There was something to be said for that.

"No," I told him. "I might let you install a better alarm system, though. And get us a big dog."

The look on Xavier's face told me exactly how compelling he found that idea. "You don't need a dog when you have me," he said. "I'm staying. And that's final."

"Good," Kate said. "I'll tell everyone else we figured it out."

"But—"

"Don't tell me I can't protect my family, Ces," Xavier said. "It's not an option."

I stared at him for a long time, long enough for Kate to disappear up the steps, humming something that sounded oddly like the children's rhyme, "First comes love, then comes marriage..."

In the end, I didn't say anything at all. I found I couldn't argue with the truth.

"Fine," I said. "You'll stay. But *no* more kisses, Xavi. Promise."

His blue eyes narrowed, and the side of his mouth rose again with the promise of a smile that never came to be. But at last he nodded slowly.

"Fine," he said. "No kisses."

He walked back to the stairs and up to the main floor, but not before he left me with a few final words called over his shoulder:

"Until you ask for one, that is."

INTERLUDE I

Xavier

"She just makes me so fucking mad."

I yanked on my tie like it was a noose, and just like every other time I recalled Francesca insisting we were "over," I wanted to rip it off and strangle someone with it. I wanted to set something on fire. Punch a hole through a wall. Do *anything* but admit defeat.

On the other side of her office, where she sat in a Chesterfield chair bookended by a fiddle-leaf fig and a wall full of postgraduate degrees and awards, Dr. Hazelwood eyed me through a pair of thick specs, then tucked a bit of her graying brown hair behind her ear. She didn't respond right away, and it was a bit unnerving, like always. You could practically see the thoughts turning over in her mind like cogs, but whether she wanted to share them had everything to do with my reactions.

It was part of the process. I didn't get the benefit of her reactions if I couldn't deal with my own.

I still couldn't decide whether I liked it or not, that self-control.

Or the feeling that she could see right through me with a single glance.

It was the same look my mum would wear when I'd come home too late after curfew or get in trouble at school. Swear up and down it wasn't my fault, that I had nothing to do with it. But she'd know in a second.

It was the same look Elsie had given me when I'd tried to convince myself to stay in London instead of coming to New York.

Same look Ces had nearly every bloody day, actually.

Women like that have got men by the balls from the beginning. The real question is whether you're brave enough to let them take the lead. They usually know what's best anyway.

I took ten deep breaths, flexing my hands open and closed, then visualized a calming place, just the way Dr. Hazelwood had taught me. Sometimes I needed to shove my face into an ice bath to calm down, but it was getting better. Right now, images of my favorite onsen in Japan were helping. So long as I didn't imagine Francesca naked on my lap.

"I'm doing every fucking thing I can here," I went on once my blood pressure had dropped to a normal level. "I took her rejection like a cuff to the cheek. Only came round when we had appointments or I had scheduled time with Sof. And now I'm moving into a bloody shoebox to be close to her because the woman's too fucking stubborn to marry me like we both know she should."

I expelled another long breath, then took a drink of water, wishing it were something harder. Even if it was ten a.m., talking about my feelings made me want to get pissed.

"Why do you think marrying you is in her best interest, if she does not?" the doctor asked. "Do you really believe you can decide that for her?"

I scowled. "That's not what I'm saying."

"It's a bit paternalistic to assume she can't articulate her own needs. Do you want a relationship where you are, in essence, acting like her father? Do you think that's really what she needs? Or what's best for either of you?"

Arrow, that one. Right through the heart.

"She loves me," I said through my teeth. "I know she does. For one, she can't stop looking at me. Every time I turn around, she's right there, giving me them big green fuck-me eyes. Two months ago, I'd have had her on every surface of the apartment by now. She'd have called my name like I was Jesus Christ himself, and fell asleep in my arms, and felt better for it, too."

"Pardon, but that rather sounds like lust, not love."

"With me and Ces, they're bloody close," I retorted as I flopped back into the other Chesterfield chair and yanked at my tie. "Right now, she's just punishing herself. And I'm supposed to say nothing? Do nothing?" I shook my head. "Fuck, if I so much as touch her shoulder, she scampers to the other side of the room like a scared kitten."

"And why do you think she's doing that?" Dr. Hazelwood scratched out a few notes as if I wasn't glaring murder at her. "Can you think of any reasons why she might want to keep her distance right now?"

We'd been over this again and again for the past month and a half. I'd gotten into therapy mainly to figure out how to control my temper, but it was becoming clear to me that Francesca was, if not at the root of those issues, then certainly a trigger for them.

"She's scared," I admitted for what was probably the twentieth time since August. "She's scared I'm going to hurt her again. Like I did before. Even though I swear to God, I did not kiss that woman."

"Is it really about a kiss for her?"

I knew it wasn't. Dr. Hazelwood knew it wasn't. Ces said she believed that I didn't kiss Imogene Douglas, and I believed her. It hadn't come up once since we'd discussed it last.

But I'd broken her trust in a million other ways over the summer. Put a crack in the glass every fucking day until finally, the whole thing shattered. After going through nearly every interaction we'd had together, rehearsing them all right here in this office week after week, I was finally seeing what I'd done.

That's why she was keeping her distance. It wasn't just one kiss. It was too many other moments to count.

I sat forward and hung my head. "I'm not exactly a subtle man. She used to like when I was aggressive, but now I think maybe it makes her uncomfortable. But I don't have time for her to realize I'm changing."

"Don't have time, or don't have patience?"

I grimaced. See? Right fucking through me.

"Maybe it's the latter," I admitted. "Why wait when you can get what you want right away? Why waste the time, right?"

Dr. Hazelwood tapped her lips with her pencil. "Have you considered it's not just your time that matters?"

Once again, straight into the gizzard.

I sat up in my chair. "Explain."

Dr. Hazelwood said nothing, just fixed her steely gray eyes on me and waited.

Did I mention she also took me to task on day one for barking out orders? Yeah, our first session was a fun one.

I sighed. "Sorry, yeah. Would you please explain what you mean by that question, Doctor?"

Her thin lips spread in something that was almost like a smile. "Of course. Very good self-correction, there, Xavier. I didn't even have to say anything that time. You're learning."

I nodded, ignoring the warmth in my chest at the faint praise. We'd established early on that I didn't get much of that growing up— and that was one of the key things that attracted me to Francesca. Unlike my parents, she was the definition of warmth with Sofia. And when she turned that praise on me...fuck all. I was basically a pile of goo. A really happy mountain of melted Xavi.

"Time is relative to each person when it comes to emotional matters," Dr. Hazelwood said. "The amount of time it takes for you to be ready for more may not equate to her healing time."

"I know that," I said. "I *know that*. But I just don't understand why she's denying everything between us. *That's* what's so fucking frustrating. She keeps saying we're over, and anyone with two eyes can see we're not!"

More deep breaths. More onsen images.

It was like offering a pair of gloves to a man in need of a parka. It helped a little. But only just that.

"I think we've already established that you don't like being challenged," Dr. Hazelwood said. "You were punished for challenging others most of your young life, and as a result, you see any challenges to your authority as undercutting your value as a person. Control is the only way you've learned to avoid being hurt, and so you wield it like a weapon, anticipating others' attacks."

I ground my teeth together but didn't argue. That was the root of every tantrum I'd ever thrown right there and the main reason I'd continued seeing the doctor after she'd ripped me to shreds. Her ability to compact complicated patterns into a sentence or two was attractive to someone like me who valued efficiency.

In other words, someone who wasn't particularly patient.

Dr. Hazelwood tipped her head to one side as she continued. "The problem is that true partnership includes those challenges. One might say they are necessary for its growth. The fact that Francesca is asserting her own needs with your presence in ways she didn't previously could be viewed as part of that progress, if you let it. She's self-actualizing, if you will, which means, despite appearing otherwise, her confidence around you is actually increasing. Giving herself the time she needs, while drawing clear boundaries around the ways she is comfortable with you interacting in her life, and the ways she is not. If you can accept those boundaries—accept *her*—she will eventually interpret that as unconditional respect and love."

"Yes, but what about my needs?" I demanded.

"Such as?"

"*Her*."

I pictured the onsen again, but this time Francesca was in it with me. And while, yeah, I wanted to kiss her, wanted to worship that body I loved so much, really what I ached for was her simple touch. The sweet giggle when I did something funny. The warmth in her bright green eyes when she looked at me with love.

My God, I missed her so much.

"Do you need her?" the doctor prodded. "Or do you want her?"

I shook my head. I knew where this was going. Dr. Hazelwood challenged that distinction on a regular basis, warning me that at times, my relationship with Francesca bordered on codependent, which would only enable my struggle for control.

But I couldn't see it otherwise.

"It's a need," I said quietly. "Not because she props me up or makes me feel a certain way about myself. It's because she's my family. I need her just like I need to be around my daughter. Last Christmas, I walked into that party, and she was like a shining star, guiding me home when I hadn't even known I was lost. And then she opened her door, and I saw my little girl, and..." I trailed off, finding it hard to speak as my voice cracked over the memory like an egg. "Look. For the first time in my life, I've got something to really live for, you know? I've got more than just a big kitchen and piles of money. And now that I've found it, I can't let it go. It would kill me."

"Those are very strong words," Dr. Hazelwood said in a way that somehow managed not to be horribly judgmental. She had a knack for that too.

I swallowed. "Well, so are my feelings."

She thought about that for a moment, then set down her pencil. "Then I suggest you own them. But don't make her carry them for you."

I frowned at my hands. "What does that mean?"

"It means it's not her responsibility to bear the burden of your needs any more than you must bear the burdens of hers," the doctor replied. "She has invited you to stay with her, which seems to me a positive step forward. But to be her partner is to acknowledge her boundaries and respect them until she moves them on her own. If you do need her, you might take her however she comes rather than trying to force her into something you want. Do you see the difference? We all need water. But we can consume it in any number of ways even if we *want* it hot or in ice. Do you see?"

I grunted. I didn't like it, but I understood. I closed my eyes and took myself back to the onsen again. Francesca was there, but this time, I winked her away.

Practically ripped my heart out to do it. But if what Dr. Hazelwood said was right, then Ces wasn't responsible for calming my emotions. Not even in my imagination.

The doctor tapped her mouth again with her pencil as she watched me wrestle with her ideas. "I don't generally quote religious texts in session, but I am reminded of that famous bit from the Bible that's always read at weddings. Perhaps you might carry it with you to New York as a bit of a mantra."

"Oh?" I asked suspiciously. I was far from a church-going man. "And what's that?"

Dr. Hazelwood smiled. "'Love is patient. Love is kind.' I believe you can be so as well, Xavier. For yourself as well as your family."

———

"SO THAT'S IT, THEN?" Jagger asked as Ben pulled the car up to Heathrow later that afternoon. "All you're bringing is the one bag?"

It had been a busy day. After therapy, I'd spent a few hours finishing up the last reports to the board of directors for the Parker Group. Elsie and Jagger had ridden with me to the airport, reviewing a few details of the things they would manage in my stead. Elsie had been promoted from CFO to assist Jagger in his operating capacity. I'd never had a CFO—not when I had my fingers in everything about the business. But right now, I needed someone who could essentially do my job for me. Considering Jagger had been doing that for the last few months, it was time to make it official.

I'd be back, of course. London was only a flight away. But for all intents and purposes, Jagger and Elsie would be running the Parker Group while I scouted possibilities for another restaurant stateside and, more importantly, fixed things with my family.

I shrugged as I accepted the suitcase from Ben. "It's all I can fit in the wardrobe at her place. Not much room."

"I'll send more shoes if you want, boy," Elsie said. "I can't imagine you'll be satisfied with only two pairs."

"It's all right. New York's a great place to add to the collection," I replied with a cheeky grin.

I was trying to think on the bright side. And in terms of longevity. No timetable, Dr. Hazelwood said. Patience. Kindness. That would be the key to success here.

"Anything else before I'm off?" I asked them.

"No," Elsie said. "The next box of journals was shipped to Francesca last week."

I nodded. "Good."

Giving my family's personal records to Francesca, one box at a time, was becoming a ritual every time I returned to New York. If I couldn't have her kisses, I could at least have her smile every time she opened up a new package like a kid on Christmas morning.

My girl loved books of all types.

And I loved to see her happy.

"Nothing else of note," Elsie continued. "Except, well. One thing. There have been some rumblings from the Lords. This arrived today from Lord Ortham."

"Oh God," Jagger mumbled. "Let's not waste his time with that."

"Show me," I ordered. Then, remembering my session, I added, "Please."

Elsie handed me a letter.

Your Grace—

It may interest you to know certain neighbors of mine have recently submitted to the House of Lords a packet of evidence regarding a Japanese marriage license. Or lack thereof. I personally have reviewed several interviews, testaments to the absence of certain events, and I must say, it is rather alarming. You may find them worrisome as well, and I advise you to be prepared.

Yours,
Lord O

As soon as I read it, I understood why it had been sent by messenger and not electronically. As a member of the Committee of Selection in the House of Lords, Bernard Douglas, otherwise known as the Viscount of Ortham, Imogene's father, and my neighbor in Kendal, was privy to information coming out and wouldn't want a trail of this communication.

He was alerting me to a potential ambush. The question was why.

"So, what do you want to do?" Jagger asked after I was finished reading. "If you stay, you can probably make it go away. I looked it up, and more than one of the lords on the committee has dealings with the Duke of Kendal or the Parker Group. It will take some finessing, though."

"But if you go, you won't miss any of Francesca's pregnancy. And you can make sure she's not harassed by any more terrifying letters, too. Not to mention you've got a bit of work to do to get out of that basement, don't you, love?" Elsie countered.

"When you put it that way, I'm not sure if there's even a question about it," Jagger said with a sly grin. "Parliament or Francesca? Which is more important to Xav?"

Elsie just folded her arms across her chest, looking rather smug.

"Parliament can kiss its own arse," I told them, handing Jagger the letter. "Burn that. I've got to get back to my girls."

THIRTEEN

Francesca

14 June 1983

HG back from Scotland today. Shot two more stags than allowed but terribly proud as always. Ortham wanted to hang them from the walls, but I gather his fiancée won't have it. Chap doesn't seem very happy with his betrothed. Not if he's trading a honeymoon for a hunting trip.

They'll go again next month for three full weeks after the wedding. Rupert does enjoy leaving the work for others to do.

I chuckled and took another sip of sparkling water. For whatever reason, I could not get enough of Coconut-flavored La Croix these days, despite never liking it before now. Especially when drinking it with dill pickle juice.

Ah, pregnancy. Intermittent nausea, insatiable sex cravings, and really weird flavor combos. What joy.

Said joy was currently being experienced on my couch while I watched the autumn leaves fall from the dogwood in the backyard and flipped through another journal from the stack Xavier had brought me on his most recent trip back from London. Since becoming a shockingly free woman two weeks earlier, I'd been steadily making my way through most of the stewards' journals from the twentieth century and was finally getting into more recent stuff written by Henry Parker, Xavier's uncle.

Which meant I'd be getting into stuff about Xavier.

Call me curious, but I wanted to know what the estate had *really* thought of the duke secretly marrying his cook. That was the kind of scandal that drove many a Regency novel onto the bestseller lists.

Mostly, though, I was trying to make the best of my new status as a lady of leisure.

I *was* upset about losing my job. Really, I was. But maybe not as much as I had thought. So far, it wasn't bad, having my ducal chef ex-boyfriend living in my basement.

Most of our days passed pleasantly. We took turns dropping off Sofia at preschool in the mornings, then Xavier worked out of an office he'd rented in Tribeca while I pieced together income doing online tutoring. He had insisted on paying rent for the basement apartment, which I transferred directly to Matthew despite his protests otherwise.

Meanwhile, I hadn't had to refill my fridge once since Xavier moved in. The errant duke was happily cooking for Sofia and me almost every night, and I was more than happy to inhale the leftovers for lunch, with him sitting across from me occasionally, watching me enjoy every bite.

It was nice. Safe.

Almost like we were a family again. A nice platonic family.

Which I might have appreciated more if my hormones hadn't been playing awful, horrible tricks on me.

Like on this pleasant late fall day, for instance.

The birds were chirping.

The sun was shining.

And I was making myself read about the hunting patterns of the gentry in Northwest England to avoid memories of the way Xavier's perfectly round butt had looked last night while he made Sofia and me his famous cod roe udon noodles.

And the way his blue eyes had gleamed with slightly lascivious pleasure when I couldn't help but moan at the first bite.

And the way his lush, full lips had pursed every time he sucked a tender noodle between them.

The man really could...eat.

I groaned and forced myself to stare at the journal's page, reading and rereading the same sentence about red stags at least twelve more times.

This was embarrassing. Like I wasn't a grown, almost twenty-eight-year-old woman fully in control of her faculties, but in fact, a teenage boy desperate to dirty up a tube sock. It happened almost overnight, too. As soon as the baseline nausea of the first trimester faded away and that thirteen-week mark hit, it felt like clouds disappeared overhead and a bright light primarily composed of sex hormones beamed down on me from above.

Here, said God. *Having a baby out of wedlock again? Enjoy the taste of sin.*

Divine providence as sexual torture.

Now, from morning to night, all I wanted was *it.* And it didn't help that I had a walking tower of sex living in my apartment, begging to be climbed. The way he watched me, it was as though Xavier knew I was inches from breaking. The Xavier I knew couldn't wait longer than five minutes for fast food, but this one was the soul of patience. A big black-haired panther tracking its quarry, waiting for weakness so he could pounce. He was biding his time, wearing tight T-shirts and gray sweatpants, ready for me to crack under pressure.

But I couldn't go there. Not again. There were more important things to think about besides Xavier's utterly sexy mouth and the fact that my vibrator was unequal to the task.

Suddenly feeling hot, I flipped the page to finish the entry, which seemed to be about Xavier's father's hunting prowess.

> *Venison for dinner this week in honor of Father's birthday. He always did like a good roast, and now he's Duke, Rupert seems determined to be just like him. For better or worse, I suppose.*
>
> *It would be nice if he cared as much about the mines up north as his next hunting trip, though.*

Henry wasn't given to flowery prose, but he did enjoy a casual dig at his brother. Unlike some of his predecessors who penned overblown adulations of everything from blooming roses to sunrises (His Grace the ninth Duke of Kendal simply *adored* "crystalline rays of angelic light"), Henry wrote with a familiar shorthand that championed brevity. It had taken me a minute to track the abbreviations he used for common people (HG for His Grace the Duke of Kendal, i.e., his brother, VO for Viscount) and get past his tendency to write in incomplete sentences, but I soon found a good bit of wry wit inserted between dry observations.

> *21 June 1984*
>
> *VO's wedding today. HG couldn't be bothered. Morning suit for me, then. Reasonably small affair in the village. M wore a pink dress. Excellent fruit cake.*

"Well, well, well, Henry. Got a bit of a girlfriend, do we?" I murmured as I turned the page to read about the Viscount of Ortham's wedding. Whoever M was, she figured a lot in these pages. Henry apparently couldn't keep his eyes off her.

> *Lamb for dinner. Odd taste. Mrs. Colson tells me there's*

a new assistant cook—a Japanese student from town looking for summer work. I've told her the students never stay long, but she won't listen. Shan't interfere. Too many cooks in the kitchen and all that.

I sat straight up on the couch as I finished the last paragraph. There was no one else it could be—Xavier's own mother was making an appearance in the journals at last, which meant Xavier himself probably wasn't far behind. I flipped back to the date—it was a little early, since Xavier wasn't actually born until 1986.

But this was when it started. Holy crap.

As if the pages themselves called him, a door slammed downstairs, and I could hear a pair of big feet stomping over the vinyl floors.

I checked my watch. Xavier was almost never home during the day, not to mention he never used the basement entrance. And to be coming back at not quite one in the afternoon was odd, to say the least.

Determined not to pay attention to the disturbances below, I continued reading through the next several entries.

14 July 1984

Ordered new landscaping for the back pond. Looking to restock with fish for fall. HG wishes to return to uni. Post-grad work, apparently. Am rather shocked.

06 Aug 1984

HG in the garden with new cook and VO. Must say unsurprised. M is lovely. No doubt the boys are having a field day fighting over her. Would that Rup could keep his quill in the pot. We may lose another cook.

I stared at the words. They weren't exactly clear, but this was pretty obviously referencing Xavier's mother and father's relationship. If I was reading this right, it also sounded like both Rupert and the Viscount of Ortham, his next-door neighbor, might have been fighting over the girl—even more of a scandal if the newly married viscount was somehow involved.

"Masumi, you saucy minx," I murmured, searching the rest of the page for any more clues. "Are you writing with two quills, you little jezebel?"

"Quill in the pot" made Henry sound like a seventeenth-century writer, not the young twenty-something he was at the time. He probably thought he was being subtle. He probably didn't realize these would be read by an anglophile who loved historical romance more than anything in the world.

I continued to read through the rest of the journal for the next hour or so, and when I didn't find anything more, I decided to bring what I'd found down to Xavier. If anything, he might get a laugh out of it. Or maybe a smirk. He might like knowing that at one point, Masumi had not one but two noblemen wrapped around her little finger.

Or maybe you just want to see him, you horn dog, Kate's voice rang clearly through my mind.

Oh hush, I told my pretend-sister silently, even as I crept down the stairs to the basement entrance.

Before I reached the bottom, however, the conversation Xavier was apparently having on the other side stopped me.

"I don't know how much more of this I can take," Xavier's voice rumbled on the other side of the door, still open from this morning. "I'm doing everything I can, you know? Trying to be patient. Trying to be caring. But it's like *she* doesn't care. But she still loves me. I know she does. She can't hide a bloody thing on her face, you know."

"Does she know you feel that way?" A woman's voice purred through the room with an English accent.

I frowned. Who in the hell was he talking to? Oh my God, it wasn't Imogene Douglas, was it?

Terror seized my gut. Followed by outright rage.

OMG, jealous much? This time, it was Joni's singsong taunt that floated through my brain.

Not at all, I answered as I took several deep breaths.

I was not jealous. We weren't together. He could talk to whomever he wanted. Even if it was a snooty English hussy who tracked him like a bloodhound. It shouldn't matter.

Should it?

I was too busy backing away from the door to listen to whatever Xavier said next but still flustered enough that I ran right into the coatrack he had in his hallway and knocked the whole thing down with a crash.

"What the fuck?"

To my horror, Xavier's footsteps sounded. A few seconds later, the door opened, and he found me standing over a mess of jackets and the fallen rack, trying for all the world not to look like I was eavesdropping.

Which I had been. Completely.

He wore the remnants of a dark blue suit, with navy pants and a lighter blue shirt that made his eyes shine the same color, and a paisley tie to match. A business day, then, not a restaurant day—not particularly his favorite.

Instead of irritation, however, worry colored his carved features. And then, once he realized I was all right, it was replaced by humor.

"You're shit at hide and seek, Ces," he told me with a wry half-smile. "One second."

He disappeared, and I heard him sign off with his companion.

"Next week, then," he told the woman, who responded in kind before Xavier returned to where I was already picking up jackets.

"I wasn't eavesdropping," I told him resolutely now that I had picked myself off the floor, though the look on his face said he absolutely didn't believe me.

"Never said you were," he said. "Out of curiosity, though, how long were you standing there?"

"Not long." Just enough to know you're upset about a woman. "Not long at all."

He studied me for a moment, well after I was finished rehanging his jackets. One was a trench coat. The other three were varying Arsenal hoodies. A cashmere overcoat I recognized from last winter.

It was everything I could do not to lean in for a whiff of his clean, masculine scent. And then everything I could do not to rip the shirt he was wearing off his body for the same reason. Lord, his tattoo was peeking out on his forearm, and I wanted to lick it. I wanted to lick him all over, feel the smooth texture of his skin under my tongue, taste that salty residue of his skin...

And my mind was back in the dirt.

Dammit.

"Something on your mind, babe?"

That deep voice was like a direct conduit to between my legs. Even more, when I looked up and found those blue eyes watching me knowingly, a black brow perked over the left one, like he knew exactly what tawdry ideas were floating through my mind.

I shivered. "Er—I thought you might want to see this."

Xavier's gaze fell to the journal I was holding out, and he sighed.

"It was Henry's," I said. "From 1984. He—he mentions your mother."

Again, Xavier examined me, like he could sense the tension and desire underlying even those innocuous words. A mountain of questions lay between us, as always. Questions like, *Why do you even care?* and *Do you still care about me?* and *Could you care about us again?*

He cleared his throat, took the book from me, then turned on his heel and walked back into the living room, letting me follow at my leisure.

"Does this mean you're doing it?" Xavier asked as he sank onto a leather couch he'd bought two weeks ago.

I perched uneasily on a stool by the counter. Lord, I could smell him from here. Damn olfactory overdrive from the baby. And oh, he smelled good. Like brine and water and the very best liquor and smoke...

"Ces."

I blinked. "Huh?"

Xavier tipped his head, causing a black lock to fall forward. "I asked if you'd made a decision about school. Does the fact that you're reading these mean you're going back to study?"

Something in his voice made me pause. He was acting nonchalant, but I *thought* I had heard a note of excitement in his voice.

"Maybe..." I said. "I still don't want to leave New York, though."

"Of course not."

"And I don't want to leave Brooklyn either. We're not moving to some fancy townhouse in the Village just so I can be closer to Bobst Library."

There was a light chuff, but Xavier didn't argue.

I sighed. "But, um, yeah. I suppose it does. Pending my acceptance. And funding, of course. And a new renter downstairs once you leave. But if you're willing to help more with Sofia's costs, and the baby's—"

"Done," Xavier interrupted eagerly. "Honestly, Ces, it's not even a question. We'll get a nanny for the times and whatever else you need."

I looked at him, curious. "Why—why would you do that? For me or for them?"

Xavier looked irritated at the question at first, then put the book down on the table. "Mum spent her life barely scraping two pence together. And my dad was rich, but his life was all about what was expected of him. When I struck out on my own, I didn't have anyone to look at to show me how it's done." He blinked. "I don't want our children to ever doubt that they can do what they want. And I want them to know that because they watched their parents do it too."

I blinked across the room. Whatever I'd been expecting him to say, it wasn't this. All summer long, while he'd encouraged me to do what I wanted, he'd never had a real sense of what that was. He'd seemed to think I was fine being a lady of leisure, even when I said I wasn't.

This was different. He was addressing one of my actual passions. I wasn't sure what to make of it.

So I just nodded. "Several of the programs request a research plan. I could give them my old graduate work as a sample of something to expand, but I want it to be something new. Something worth working on. I do think your family's journals fulfill that brief. If you'd let me work on them."

Xavier studied me a moment more, then stood up and made his way across the room until he was standing directly in front of me, close enough that my knees brushed the sides of his thighs. Another step forward, and he'd be wedged between them. A quick lift, and I'd be sitting atop the counter, legs wrapped around his waist or maybe his head, while he devoured me the way only Xavier Parker could.

I inhaled deeply. Wrong move. That signature scent of fire and brine wrapped around me like a foggy dream.

I couldn't think. I could barely see. Right now, the only thing I could imagine was grabbing his tie and dragging him down to heaven with me.

Or maybe it was hell.

"Here." His deep voice pulled me out of my waking dream as he held out the book. "What's mine is yours."

I shivered again, and this time couldn't ignore the way his eyes latched to my lip as I took it between my teeth.

Crap. I needed some space before I lost it all completely.

"Who were you talking to?" I blurted. "Imogene?"

"What?" Xavier stiffened as I wriggled off my seat and moved around until the kitchen's peninsula counter was safely between us.

"I didn't hear much. Just that she was English."

Yes, that was better, even if the idea that Xavier was talking to Imogene made me physically ill.

When I looked up, though, he looked about the same.

"No," he said evenly. "I was not talking to Imogene Douglas. Nor would I be. I was...inmrphmpy."

I cocked one ear toward him. "Come again? I didn't quite get that."

At that, he took his own seat on the stool. "I said I was in *therapy*."

I gaped. "You have a therapist?"

Whatever I'd expected him to say, it wasn't that.

He gave me a long, morose look, not unlike a basset hound. "Yes. I've been talking to a bloody headshrinker. Happy now you find out I'm crazy?"

"Oh," I said, all sense of joking evaporated. "Oh, I don't think that at all. Xavier, I think it's great you're in therapy. I think it's *wonderful*."

"Do you?"

He looked so childlike for a moment that I forgot my intent to put space between us and rounded the counter quickly so I could take his hand in mine and squeeze it so he would feel my enthusiasm.

He didn't squeeze back, though. Not right away. His hand lay limply, its heavy weight dependent on mine to hold it atop his knee. Like he wanted my hand to stay there and keep him functioning. His scent curled back around me like a blanket, but instead of soothing, it set every nerve I had on end.

As if it was responding to the two palms meeting, my heart gave a strong thump.

Eventually, though, I had to let go. I gave his palm a friendly tap on the knuckles, then stepped away. It was like the air was made of molasses.

"I think it's great," I repeated. "Is it helpful?"

He watched me for another long second, then sighed. "It's hard. I don't like talking about my feelings, and that's all she ever seems to want to do."

I stifled a chuckle as I sat down in my own armchair. "Well, isn't that kind of the point?"

He gave me a dirty look. "The *point* is to be a better man. For you, for Sof. For that little one." He gestured toward my belly. "For my family."

I *hated* the way my heart warmed at the term. No matter how hard I tried to fight, it did seem more and more like that's what we were. A strange little family, built across an ocean and stacked between floors of this little townhouse. But a family, nonetheless.

"I hope it's not just because I told you to—"

"It's not," he said quickly. "If you must know, I started just after you left England, before Henry died."

I cocked my head. That was a surprise. "Why then?" I wasn't so arrogant to believe my sudden fleeing the country was the catalyst for that kind of growth. If anything, it should have stymied it. Right?

He looked up then, his blue eyes sparkling. "You called me a bully, remember?"

"I..." I frowned. I had, but that was months ago now. He was still caught on that?

"I don't want to be a bully," he said quietly. "I don't want my own family to be scared of me, Ces. I don't want to be like *him*."

I took it he meant his own father. Rupert Parker.

"The way you looked at me that day...and then later, running away..."

When he shrugged, his big shoulders tugging at the material of his shirt. Xavier leaned forward to balance his forearm on his knees. A lock of black hair flopped most charmingly onto his brow again. I had to lean against my hand to stop from pushing his hair back in place and stroking the furrows out of that typically smooth skin.

"I don't ever want people I care about to look at me like that again," he said softly. "When I found out you'd gone. That you'd left me in that house with *those* people, I knew it was because of that, really. I know you saw Imogene kiss me, but you didn't even want to talk anymore. You'd given up. And after I was done raging—and I *did* rage, Ces. Tore my fucking office apart, right along with your bedroom and half the library—after I was finished and I had to look at all the damage I'd done, all I could hear in my stupid head were your words, ringing like a bloody bell."

I sucked in a breath. It was only too easy to imagine that scene. Although I'd never actually had to watch Xavier unleash his full strength on anything larger than a punching bag—and maybe my brother, come to think of it—I knew he had a penchant for letting his emotions out in violent ways. His office must have been trashed. The bedroom was probably in ribbons.

"I don't want to be someone who hurts others just because I'm hurting, deep down," Xavier continued. "It was all I could hear after you left. That in the end, you couldn't trust me to put your needs above my own impulses. That you believed I'd just keep using you again and again to feel better."

He shook his head and then swiped his thumbs under his eyes to wipe something out of them.

Tears?

I held my breath. But still had no idea what to say. Or do.

Before I could figure it out, though, the alarm on my phone burst into the air.

I yanked it out of my pocket. "Crap. Time to pick up Sof."

Xavier just gave me a crooked smile in return. One of his hands rose and hovered near my cheek. But he didn't touch me. And I didn't ask.

"Great," he said. "I'll start dinner before you're back."

"Oh—okay," I said, wondering if I imagined the other promise hidden behind his words.

And then we'll talk some more.

FOURTEEN

It had been happening almost every night at the same damn time: 10:08 p.m., approximately two hours after Sofia had well and truly fallen asleep when I was thinking about nodding off myself after watching an episode of *Downton Abbey* to soothe my nerves.

I'd brush my teeth.

Pee for the four-hundredth time that day (yay, pregnancy bladder).

Settle myself into bed.

And just when I was ready to fall asleep, it would happen.

That *feeling*.

Tonight it was worse than usual. I hadn't even made it upstairs before the churning in my stomach and clenching of my thighs began. Right after Mary Crawley made a glib remark and the heavy strings of the *Downton Abbey* theme started with the credits, I found myself unable to move from the couch because I only wanted one thing, and it was definitely not upstairs.

Maybe it was the way Xavier had charmed Sofia into eating not just two bites, but *all* the spinach risotto with shrimp he'd prepared for dinner.

Maybe it was the way his tattoo had stretched over his abs when he reached up to replace a broken light bulb in the hall.

Or maybe it was because earlier that afternoon, I'd listened to him demonstrate the sexiest emotion I personally thought a man could show: remorse.

Now I lay on my couch, trying not to reach for my vibrator while the look on Xavier's face as he admitted to getting therapy flashed through my mind on replay.

No, it was more than that.

It wasn't just that he'd taken my critiques of his anger to heart, but that he was actually doing something about it. The way he'd admitted to his faults and also was taking legitimate accountability for them. The earnestness shining through those deep blue eyes was totally foreign, totally surprising, and totally alluring.

Therapy was sexy as hell. Who knew?

Apparently me, right now, staring up at the popcorn ceiling while I tried to talk myself out of taking care of business.

It wasn't right.

Not with *him* in my head. Not with the boundaries we'd drawn. I'd drawn. That he was thoughtfully respecting.

Dammit. That wasn't helping. Nor was the fact that on the screen, Lady Sybil was getting ready to run off with Branson, the hot Irish chauffeur and bookish revolutionary. They didn't care about social propriety or boundaries on *Downton Abbey* either.

I turned the TV off only to hear the muffled noises of Xavier moving about his space before bed.

It was too easy to imagine what he was doing. We'd cohabited long enough that I knew at least some of his patterns.

He was fanatical about his teeth, so he'd usually spend a solid ten minutes in the bathroom brushing, flossing, mouth-washing, spitting, and all of it before taking another ten to twenty minutes to check and recheck that all the doors, windows, and any other potential security breaches were locked up tight to protect us all. He always slept with a fresh glass of water next to his bed and would pad around in a pair of house slippers that he set out side by side next to his nightstand so he could slip into them easily come morning. He usually spent the evening in a pair of loose pajama pants and a T-shirt but typically removed both to sleep in just a pair of boxer briefs.

Right after taking them off, though, he'd often get down on the rug for ten minutes of sit-ups or calisthenics. This had almost always had the effect of pulling my attention from whatever book I was reading before sleep. I'd peek over wherever I was on the page to spy on the mass of corded muscle and writhing tattoos on the floor, which inevitably ended up with one or both of us naked and willing within minutes.

Before I knew it, I was sliding my hand down below the waistband of my pajama shorts, which were already fitting tight, thanks to the little one in there. Like clockwork, my fingers found that familiar position just over my clit and began to move in that easy, practiced way I'd gotten so good at over many years alone.

It was like a military exercise. Soothing. Automatic. Muscle memory, if you will.

I could do this. I'd done it for six years without thinking about him—at least not *all* the time, anyway. I could push that perfectly carved jaw and those stacked abs out of my mind and focus on something that would only help me relax and wouldn't break my heart. Otherwise, I'd never get to sleep. And expectant mothers needed their sleep.

Decision made. This was for the good of everyone. Not just me.

I closed my eyes, drawing up some of my favorite fantasies—the ones that always worked in the dark of night when I didn't want to risk waking everyone so I could thumb through a dirty novel.

I could be ravished in the backyard under the stars, where the neighbors could see us at any moment.

Maybe taken in the subway late at night, the only one left in the car until a stranger entered and kept me company until my stop.

Or perhaps it would be last call at a restaurant, and the maître d' would lay me out on a table like a banquet.

Apparently, I had a thing for public sex, but now wasn't the time to analyze that. Or, it occurred to me, the fact that the only man I'd ever had sex with seemed to have an exhibitionist streak himself. After all, how many times had Xavier taken me exactly where and when he wanted, without a care in the world for who might see?

No. Stop. Now was the time to take care of what my body had been screaming for all day, what it seemed to need every hour on the hour for the past several weeks.

Except.

There he was again.

Waiting for me in the garden.

Strolling onto the subway.

Sitting at the head of the table, staring between my legs like he'd just discovered the promised land.

Even in my fantasies, his eyes were as dark blue as the deepest night. Full of mischief, lust, and intensity.

Xavier.

"No!" I hissed into the dark, willing his face to disappear.

It wasn't his fault, of course. For years, I'd fantasized about a man I could never have. Because then, he'd been a phantom in my dreams, someone who was just a memory. Someone I could never have.

Fantasies were supposed to end when confronted with the harsh light of reality.

Real things like babies and family and fighting and therapy were supposed to spoil the dream.

Weren't they?

I squeezed my eyes shut even harder, trying with everything I had to imagine someone *other* than Xavier looking at me with that kind of desire.

The cute barista at Pioneer Works.

A hot professor I'd once crushed on.

I even tried Henry Cavill, my forever standby (especially when he was on *The Tudors*).

Nothing and no one else worked.

Those damn blue eyes, that sleek black hair, that broad, smirking mouth still reappeared.

"Dammit!" I shrieked, yanking my hand from my shorts and kicking out in frustration.

My foot, however, hit the plant stand at the other end of the sofa and sent the whole iron structure and the large fern it was holding to the hardwood floor with a crash.

I froze, waiting for the inevitable "Mama?" from the top of the stairs. When it didn't come, I relaxed again.

That throbbing need in my core was still there, though. I was as wide awake as ever. And more than frustrated.

"I give up," I growled, then closed my eyes, slipped my hand back between my legs, and let his face return.

You want me? I thought. *Come and have me.*

Those full lips smiled in a way he hardly ever did these days, and it was like my heart beat in response to it.

With pleasure, my love.

In my thoughts, Xavier knelt in front of me, eyes full of schemes and promise.

Francesca, he whispered as he peeled down my pants and slipped his tongue between my legs. *God, you taste so good. So fucking sweet. I could eat you all day, you dirty, dirty girl.*

I moaned lightly at the imagined words. It wasn't really Xavier saying them if it was in my head.

Right?

"Francesca?"

At the sound of my name cutting through the night, I screamed. Then, like a trapped feral cat, I flew in approximately four directions at once, tripping over the arm of the couch, then the fallen plant before finally whirling around just in time to see the basement door open and Xavier enter my living room. He was silhouetted by a stream of light coming from behind him that somehow made him look even taller than he was and made his broad shoulders seem more like actual armor.

I really could not get a break.

"Ces?" he asked again, looking around the dark room. It took a moment, but he finally located me, quivering behind the couch, before he turned on the light. "All right? It sounded like something fell, so I—oh, Christ."

Based on the fact that he was shirtless but still in a pair of black pajama pants that hung off his hips in an extremely distracting way, I guessed he had been halfway through his sit-ups or on his way to bed when I'd disturbed him. His sharp eyes, however, were wide awake as he took in the scene—the spilled plant stand, the rumpled throw blankets, my mussed clothing. Slowly, his gaze drew up my body, lingering over the untied shorts, my perked nipples, and pillow-flattened hair.

I glanced down in horror, then back up at him, immediately seeing myself through his eyes. Mussed and undone, I looked like I'd been up to absolutely no good.

"I..." Xavier's eyes darted back around the room. "Fuck. Who is he?"

Hastily, I retied my shorts. "Xavi, it's really not what you think."

"Don't patronize me. Please." One hand curled into a fist at his side. "I'm trying to be civil here. I really am. But if you're going to lie to my face about it, I think I'm allowed to be a bit upset." He checked over my shoulder. "What's he doing, hiding in the loo? Can't he come out here and face the music?"

By the end of the statement, he'd leaned around toward the hallway, cupped his other hand around his mouth, and was ready to shout toward the bathroom.

"*Shh.*" I batted his hand away. "You're going to wake Sofia."

"And you weren't?"

"No!" I protested. "I wasn't doing anything!"

Xavier's snort echoed through the room.

"What?" I said. "I *wasn't*."

"And I'm the King of England. Honestly, I'm surprised. Our daughter is sleeping one floor above you. I'm not judging but do you really want her to come down looking for her mum and find you riding some random on the couch?" He looked again toward the bathroom and braced, muscles clenched as if ready for a fight.

"Xavi, for God's sake, I wasn't screwing anyone but myself!"

"I only thought—what?" Xavier turned back toward me, irritation replaced with curiosity. "Say that again."

I sighed, my face turning bright red as I pressed my palms to my cheeks. "This is mortifying."

Xavier's arms crossed over his broad chest while he tried and failed to mask a grin. "So, you were—" He held up one hand and fluttered his fingers in a gesture that made me flush the color of a very ripe tomato—mostly because I could imagine exactly what those fingers were capable of doing.

"I was not *doing* anyone or anything," I completed for him. "There is no one in the bathroom, hiding behind a plant, or running off into the night. Do you really think I would do that with Sofia in the house? Or you, for that matter?" Then another thought occurred to me. One I found I didn't like at all. "Would *you*, even though we're not...you know?"

He blinked again at the bathroom as if to check for an intruder once more, then looked back at me. "Right below you? Absolutely fucking not."

"Well, then, do you really think I'd be that cruel?"

Xavier opened his mouth as if to argue but then shut it as the residual anger fled his posture. "I—no." He chewed on his lip. "Yeah. Sorry."

I sighed and sank down onto the arm of the couch again. "It's fine. I know what it looked like."

"So, you were just having a bit of a wank, were you?"

My face turned approximately the color of a stop sign all over again. "Shut up."

Xavier glanced at the plant with a cheeky grin that made my insides feel funny. "I gather it went, er, well, eh? Can't recall you ever knocking down plants with me."

I sighed, surveying the disaster I'd created. There was soil halfway across the rug. "That was more out of frustration than, um, completion."

It was truly annoying how quickly his mouth curved into a knowing smirk. "That so? I don't remember us struggling with that either, you know."

"You don't have to look so proud about it." I stooped down to set the plant aright. The dirt would have to be vacuumed in the morning —I didn't want to wake Sofia. When I was finished, I flopped back onto the couch, ignoring the moment Xavier joined me. And how warm his knee felt touching mine. Or how smooth the bare skin of his shoulder was in the moonlight.

"Poor, poor Ces. A bit hard up, are we?"

I glowered up at him. "It's not funny."

"I beg to differ."

"It's not." I huffed. "*You* did this to me. I'm awash with hormones, practically swimming in a different emotion every freaking hour. For three months, I wanted to puke day and night. Now puppies make me cry and every night the 'gotta get laid' light turns on—which, by the way, wasn't nearly so bad with Sofia. And just like last time, there isn't a damn thing I can do about it. Vibrators only do so much, you know. I feel like a fifteen-year-old with one thing on my idiotic lizard brain. Do you remember what it was like to be that age?"

Xavier blanched slightly. "If you were like that, you'd be making a damn mess or taking four showers a day to cover it up. Mum used to yell at me for running up the water bill."

In response, I said nothing. I had been very clean lately.

"Christ," he said. "That's no picnic. I made myself chafe. A lot."

He sounded so abjectly forlorn about it that I couldn't help but giggle.

"I feel your pain," I said with a friendly pat on his knee. "Literally." Then I sighed. He'd given me honesty. I supposed I could give him another sort. "I guess I just can't pretend on my own anymore. You screwed it all up this year."

I turned, expecting another lopsided smirk, but instead found Xavier gazing at his hands in deep contemplation.

"Maybe...I could help." He looked up, blue eyes full of cautious hope.

I cocked my head suspiciously. "What does that mean?"

"I see how you look at me when you think I don't notice. Out of the corner of your eyes. I know you say it's over, Ces, but you also said I did this to you." His glance flickered down, first landing on my slightly swollen belly, then farther to the heat already building between my thighs. "You say you can't pretend on your own. But what if you pretend with me?"

FIFTEEN

We stared at each through the dark like we were trapped in a beautiful, awe-inspiring lagoon, not sitting on my brother's old leather couch he'd salvaged off the curb in Sheepshead Bay.

Was Xavier offering what I thought he was offering?

Was that even something I could consider?

Was my baby brain getting in the way of my actual reasoning skills?

Did I even care?

"I...I don't know," I said, even as I squirmed in my seat. "We're not...it wouldn't change anything."

Lord, those hands. That mouth. It was one thing to fantasize about complete strangers or characters in a book. It was another entirely when I had the real thing most women only dreamed about right here, offering himself up on a silver platter.

"It wouldn't be like that," Xavier said, scooting a bit closer. "I promise."

"That's easy for you to say. But how—how do I know it's not just you trying to..." I couldn't bring myself to say "get me back."

It sounded absurd. Xavier wasn't the type to play games, nor was I the kind of woman to be schemed over. Not like that. But he *had* said we weren't over, hadn't he? And while he wasn't exactly known for his patience, his success over the last ten years certainly pointed to a certain amount of resilience and grit.

He was used to getting what he wanted, and I had no doubt that sometimes it meant playing dirty.

He cocked his head to the left as he cautiously scooted again so that his leg pressed fully against mine. Warm, solid muscle that I could feel through his pants and my thin sleep shorts.

"I'm a lot of things, Ces," he said in a carefully low voice that hummed with anticipation. "But never thought devious was one of them. Do you really think I'd use something like this to fool you back together?"

It was true. Subtlety was never his strong suit. Xavier was more like a bull than a serpent. He strode into whatever room he entered, took on the task at hand without any doubt, and charged at it full-throttle.

"No," I admitted. "That's not really your style. But—"

"Doesn't seem fair," he remarked as his dark gaze passed over me sympathetically. "You have to do all the work. No release. Why not let me help how I actually can?" Tentatively, he reached out a hand, which hovered just over my mouth. "Look at you. Even your lips are begging to be kissed. You look like you're ready to burst, babe."

And I felt it. My breathing had intensified. My nipples were tingling, and that sensitive place between my legs was practically throbbing just sitting next to him.

There was no use denying it. I was basically dying for him to touch me.

"I just—I don't want you to get the wrong idea," I whispered, even as he stroked a broad thumb over my cheekbone.

His fingertips tickled the nape of my neck, causing goose bumps to fly up everywhere. I shuddered, vision already hazy with want.

"It's all right." Ever so gently, he took my shoulders, then rotated me in my seat until my back was toward him. "I know it can't—I know it doesn't mean anything."

He drew me back and settled me on his chest, nestled between his long legs. While I could feel his considerable length against my lower back, there was nothing lecherous about the movements. Instead, a feeling of safety and warmth overwhelmed me. Something akin to freedom, but in a place where I was taken care of completely.

"Just let me help," he said as his hands slid around my waist, flattening them over my belly. "Anything you need."

I exhaled, then found myself sinking into his broad chest. God, he felt good, even just holding me like this, surrounding me with his clean, salty scent. So much better than a couch or a pillow. So warm and solid, but thrumming with untapped energy.

Some things really couldn't be substituted. Things like heated muscle, arms like steel, and soft lips that feathered over the top of my ear.

"What do you want?" he asked as he stroked through my thin cotton shirt. I watched as he pulled the fabric up so that his fingertips brushed my skin. "I'm at your service, babe."

"Mmmm," I hummed as his fingers started moving up my rib cage. "Oh, I..."

"Tell me," he purred, slipping his hands under the cotton even more to tickle the undersides of my breasts.

His touch was tentative, but knowing. Because he knew I liked it when he teased me with a feather-light touch, right at the beginning. Just like he knew I loved it when he kneaded them a few times right when he entered me, then pinched and pulled right when I came. The secret to good sex, I had discovered, was getting to know your partner's body at different times—not just one reaction, but all of them.

And Xavier had learned every one of mine. Maybe even better than I had.

"Ahhhh," I murmured. "Oh, do...do that."

"This?" He cupped my breasts, distinctly heavier now, in each hand, then drifted his thumbs across my nipples.

They were so sensitive, I almost came right there. When I jerked, his tongue slid around the curve of my ear before he sucked the lobe between his teeth and tugged lightly.

"What else?" His deep voice rumbled, breath warm over my dampened skin. "What else do you want?"

"Talk to me," I sighed, half lost in a dreamlike daze from the hypnotic rhythm of his fingers at my breasts. "Tell me something, Xavi. Give me something to imagine."

There was a low chuckle behind my ear. "What else would Francesca Zola want to hear but a good bedtime story?" He tugged lightly on my nipples, then slipped one hand back down my belly to linger at the waistband of my pajama shorts. "Shall I?"

I could have stopped him then. And maybe I should have. He was crossing nearly every boundary I'd set up between us.

But every cell in me was crying for his touch. At that moment, I honestly needed him more than I needed arbitrary rules designed to keep us apart. I needed him like water. Like I needed the air to breathe.

"Yes," I said. "But keep...talking."

It would help me stay out of my head and enjoy the moment now that I was apparently giving in to it.

I closed my eyes and focused on the twin sensations of the hand that continued to switch off between my breasts, tugging and playing with their sensitized tips, and the other that quietly slipped under the waistband of my shorts and the elastic of my underwear, sinking into the soft curls that beckoned him always, my entire body shuddered in his embrace.

"Once upon a time there was a man in a bar. Tall, tatted, impossibly handsome." His deep voice was the texture of velvet.

"And scowling," I added dreamily. "Don't forget scowling."

The chuckle vibrated against my neck as the hand below drifted back and forth over the most sensitive part of me, toying lightly with the delicate skin and nerve endings that seemed to be more alive than ever.

"That too. With dark blue eyes. He was very unhappy, you see. Had a life of hardship and loss. Nothing in the world had ever seemed good until that moment, when he saw her across the pub, laughing with a friend."

I tensed slightly, though his fingers were too hypnotizing not to relax me again. I knew this story. The story of the night we met. How I went from being a virgin to...not...at the sight of a brooding British man watching me in a crowded bar on the Upper West Side.

"She was a vision in red," he continued. "This tiny shirt—"

"The shirt wasn't that small—"

"Microscopic shirt," he continued like I'd said nothing at all. "And massive earrings that shone against her long dark hair. She had an arse he could fill his hands with, apple-shaped tits, and a mouth that beckoned his cock from the across the room."

"She sounds frisky," I joked, though his less-than-gentlemanly description was already making my breathing a bit heavier.

"Hush, and let me tell it," Xavier chided me with a pinch of one nipple that made me squeak. "Then she turned and smiled. And the man couldn't even remember his own name, much less all the reasons he knew he should leave her alone."

His deft fingers dove deeper, finding my clit, beginning to move with the familiar rhythm he'd seemed to know from the very beginning.

"So he bought her a drink," he continued. "And asked her to dance. She was a tiny thing, just perfect to hold as she rubbed her curves all over him, song after song. Eventually, she let him kiss her, and her mouth tasted like the sweetest candy. He knew she'd taste even better everywhere else."

My breath caught as I anticipated the next part.

The real question was whether he was going to tell it all the way.

"So what did he do?" I whispered as I tipped my chin up and to the side.

Xavier took the invitation and pressed his lips to my neck, nipping, licking, and sucking in tandem with his fingers below. "He lifted her up so they were eye to eye and asked her—begged her—if she would let him taste her everywhere. He was hard as stone and honestly afraid he might die if he couldn't."

I shivered at the memory. The way Xavier had bent down right there in the middle of the bar and lifted me by the waist so that my feet were nearly a foot off the floor. He'd swallowed me with a kiss, then asked me in a rough burr if I'd go back to his hotel with him. Called me beautiful, sweet things while he asked again and again between mind-bending kisses.

Please, you beautiful thing, you. I'm begging. Let me taste you. Let me make you feel better than you ever have before.

"She said no," he went on, truthfully.

I swallowed as his finger dipped into me, then back up to toy with my clit some more. "She was shy."

"She was fucking exquisite. Which is why the man knew if she wouldn't come with him, he'd have to show her what she'd be missing."

I gulped. Yeah, I remembered that, too. Remembered the way he'd carried me off the dance floor just like that, toward the back of the bar, then forced open a closet so we were blocked by a door at the end of the hall near the alley exit. Told me he'd stop whenever I asked but that he needed more. Begged me for more. Literally got on his knees.

And I had said yes. I couldn't stop kissing him. Not when his hands had slid under the waistband of my jeans to take lush handfuls of flesh. Not when they moved around to undo the button and slide down the zipper. Not when he'd peeled the denim around my curves and pressed his mouth to the soft skin of my upper thigh.

From the very first night, I could never say no to Xavier Parker. I'd honestly never wanted to.

"He got down on his knees for her," Xavier continued. "Right there on that dirty fucking floor—and this man, mind you, kneels for no one."

"Dukes rarely do."

I smiled as his stubbled cheek rubbed against mine. The hand at my breast joined the other below my waist, gently pushing my legs to spread wider for his probing fingers. I sucked in a harsh breath when one breached my extremely slick opening but didn't push all the way in, instead content with teasing me there while the other hand worked my clit.

"Xavi," I gasped. "*Please.*"

"When he licked her delicate cunt, it was like coming home. He couldn't believe his luck, that she was allowing him to do this, right there where anyone might see, letting him taste her sweet flesh, drive his tongue deep inside her. Salty, honeyed, utter fucking nectar. She tasted like heaven. Like the home he'd never known he could find."

The finger at my entrance pushed in farther, then was joined by another.

"Oh *God*," I murmured, the image clear in my mind as he worked. "Oh, Xavi."

"But it wasn't enough," he growled. "It wasn't fucking enough. He needed more. His cock throbbed for her, every cell in his body wanted to devour her. He needed to be inside her, needed to spill his seed deep within her womb, needed to part the gorgeous peach of her and drive home until the entire city knew the way his name sounded when she screamed it aloud."

"Ah!" I called as his teeth latched again to my throat, holding me in place as he continued to fuck me with his hand.

"But he didn't," Xavier said. "Instead, he feasted on her with his mouth until she called above the pounding music and rode his face like a pony. He vowed to give her pleasure then and take his later. Because even then he knew. This girl—this utterly perfect woman— didn't just deserve one night. She deserved forever."

"Oh!" I cried, flailing my head to one side, then the other, as my orgasm crept to the edge of a cliff I wanted to dive over. "Oh, Xavi, p-please!"

But he didn't relent. As his fingers continued their terrible onslaught, Xavier captured my mouth with his, banishing gentle touches in favor of a bruising, punishing kiss full of tongue and teeth and all the aching want he had just described with his wicked words.

"Come, then," he ordered quietly, then kissed me again as three fingers thrust inside me.

I screamed his name into his mouth as my entire body began to shake violently. He didn't stop, just kept working me with that rhythm, as insistent and vital as a heartbeat between my legs. Fucking me with his fingers, rubbing my clit until every moan had left my body to be swallowed by that full, demanding mouth.

He knew. Oh *God*, he knew how to make it last. He knew how to press and penetrate and keep me still until every muscle had flexed beyond its abilities, leaving me to melt into a pool of depleted lust and satiated woman between his legs.

Wedged against the small of my back, the length of him still throbbed. But as I came down from my orgasm, he made no move to turn me over, pin me down, or take any pleasure for himself whatsoever.

And I wanted him to. Badly. What was supposed to sate me for the night had only turned up the heat. I needed much, much more. And that was a very bad idea.

I turned in his arms to say exactly that, but he was already shaking his head as I scrambled to the other end of the couch.

"Don't say anything," he said. "Not a word."

"But—"

He laid a finger over my lips. "I said hush. Now, I just wanted to help, babe. You don't owe me a thing." Another sly smile crept across his handsome features. "Don't make it weird, eh?"

I opened my mouth to argue but found I could only grin back at him. The sweet relaxation was still passing through my limbs. I couldn't help but enjoy the ride he'd brought me on and soon found myself yawning with bliss.

Before I could stop him, he swept me up in his arms and stood.

"Xavi," I murmured, but couldn't bring myself to ask him to put me down.

Sleep was coming fast. A few more minutes, and I was liable to use his bicep as a pillow right here.

"Come on, Sleeping Beauty."

Xavier offered me another bittersweet half-smile as he carried me out of the living room and up to my bedroom, where he laid me gently under the sheets. I allowed him to pull the blankets up and tuck me in on all sides. Anything sexual had vanished from his touch, but it was still impossibly tender.

"Xavi," I murmured.

The ability to move any of my limbs was all but gone, thanks to his work downstairs.

"Just let me take care of you."

I lay still as he finished tucking me in, then watched as he sat back on the bed and looked at me blinking up at him. My eyelids felt like they were made of iron, but I couldn't stop looking back. His eyes were like stars, calling me home.

His gaze drifted to the right side of the bed. His side. The very empty side.

It took everything I had not to ask him to get in.

At last, he offered that sweet half-smile once more. "Think you can get to sleep now?"

I nodded. My limbs still felt like noodles.

I wanted more. I'd always want more, especially when it came to him. But with his gift had come an ocean of calm that had me floating toward sleep at last.

"Good." He bent down and placed a tame kiss on my forehead. "Night, Ces."

As if by their own accord, my arms rose and wrapped themselves around his neck, holding him close. His mouth hovered just an inch from mine, close enough that I could smell his fresh breath and feel its heat on my skin.

"Xavi," I whispered.

He gave a low groan but kept completely still.

God, it was hard not to do it. I wanted to kiss him more than I wanted coconut LaCroix. More than any of the weird stuff I'd been craving night and day. More than I had ever wanted *anything*.

But to my surprise, he didn't try to kiss me. He just stayed as he was, immovable. Waiting.

"I..." I stared at his mouth, feeling as parched as I was only thirty minutes ago.

"I know," he replied. "Fuck, babe, I know."

We sat there together in a standoff as each of us dared the other to make a move.

No one blinked.

And so, eventually, I pulled my arms back.

Xavier sighed.

"I'm..." I trailed off, thinking about apologizing but not really sure what for.

I wanted to kiss him again. But I knew we shouldn't. Maybe we'd just crossed a line, but for some reason, kissing in my mind seemed to go well beyond "pretend." Kissing Xavier had never been anything less than vividly real.

"Ces, relax." He grabbed my chin, thumb brushing over my lower lip, then dropped it with a rueful glance. "It's all right."

"Do you...do you want to stay? You could just sleep here."

I couldn't for the life of me tell you why I asked.

That rueful smile broadened, but to my disappointment—relief? —Xavier shook his head. "I'll be back in the morning before Sof wakes up. Seven, right? I just need to get some sleep. If I stay here, I'm going to stare at you all night in those bloody shorts."

It was then I noticed how turned on *he* still was—thick and obvious through the thin material of his pants.

My God, the poor man.

Poor *me*.

I settled back into my pillow, unsure how to decipher the emotions roiling inside me. "All right, then. Night, Xavi."

"Sweet dreams, babe," he whispered.

And then, quick as a shadow, he was gone, leaving me in my bed with my hand to my mouth, touching the spot that still seared from his touch.

SIXTEEN

"You almost ready?" Xavier called from the kitchen, where he was finishing up the remnants of breakfast dishes.

Just like every morning since moving in and the two weeks since our little midnight interlude, he had come upstairs to help and spend a bit of time with Sofia. Today had been his day to take her to school while I tutored a student in Alabama. But instead of leaving for work afterward, he had come back and made us both a healthy breakfast of rice, sautéed spinach, and scrambled eggs. Plus the prenatal vitamins he made sure I took every morning.

I honestly wasn't sure what to make of it. It was so...normal. So much like the early part of the summer before Kendal had happened.

But then, our lives had still been separate. Sofia and I had been visitors, tourists in his world while he went on basically living the way he always had. Here, he was stepping up as a partner, the kind I'd always wanted, right down to being elbows-deep in dishes instead of hiring the housekeeper we both knew he could afford.

It would have been great. Except now, with the lines blurring more than ever, it was growing even harder to put those boundaries between the two of us that I used to be certain were necessary.

I popped out of the bathroom, where I was busy pinning my hair up. "Two minutes."

The water at the sink turned off. "One. We can't be late, babe."

We were due at Beth Israel, where I was scheduled for the neonatal echocardiogram and another sonogram, this time 3D. The latter wasn't strictly necessary, but when Xavier learned that the doctor could determine the sex of the baby as soon as fourteen weeks with it, he'd insisted on paying for the extra test if only to "check on things" and make sure everything was all right.

He wouldn't admit it, but I could see he was nervous, and not just because of a simple murmur. Why, I wasn't quite sure.

"All right?" he asked as I exited the bathroom after one minute and thirty seconds. Compromise, right?

The question felt heavy. Everything felt heavy.

Since the night on the couch, he had helped me "pretend" several other times over the last two weeks and once had even stayed the rest of the night, holding me just the same way in my bed.

Always in the dark of night. Always by telling stories about us. The ones I would never let myself imagine on my own.

Last night, he'd been unable to help himself when I'd reached behind me to grab him, eager to touch his silky steel as I shook out yet another mind-bending orgasm. Our lips had nearly met, and in the meantime, he had spilled himself against the small of my back, bucking under my hand with a pained groan while his deep eyes stared into mine, unfathomably deep with hunger.

Pretend. That's all it was.

I wished I could believe it.

Still, we hadn't kissed again. Not once. I wasn't sure what we were doing or what Xavier wanted here, but I knew he was being careful.

He hadn't mentioned the possibility of getting back together—if anything, he had accepted that we were really and truly over as a couple. A nightly orgasm felt more like penance for getting me pregnant all over again. Like making me breakfast and paying for sonograms helped him atone for the fact that he had screwed things up beyond repair.

I wasn't sure how I felt about that.

Now we stood in the hallway, gawking at each other like twitterpated middle schoolers trying to figure out how to ask someone out with notes bearing checkboxes for yes, no, or maybe.

Since I no longer had to spend my days tending to third-grade art projects and dodging squirting juice boxes, I could wear slightly nicer clothing. Today I had put on a black ribbed dress that hugged my hips and legs in a way that made my new curves more apparent. And while Xavier was pretending not to pay attention to anything about my body unless I explicitly asked him, it was impossible to miss the way his gaze floated over the new cleavage and more substantial derriere this pregnancy was giving me.

"I'm fine," I said, somehow unable to look him in the eye. "You?"

He looked as gorgeous as ever in a suit and tie, though he'd shucked the jacket in favor of a leather bomber nearly as shiny as his hair. His trousers were cut in the modern way, narrow through the legs and just tight enough that I could easily imagine the size of that *part* of him I had gripped last night. Honestly, the way I was still feeling, I could climb the man like a tree many times over.

I turned away, cheeks reddened. I really was turning into an addict.

Pretending wasn't enough. Fingers weren't enough. Loath as I was to admit it, I wanted the real thing. I wanted it like a junkie wants her next hit. And it was right there, teasing me through the finest spun wool.

Before Xavier could reply, there was a knock at the door.

"Expecting someone?" he asked as he tossed the sponge into the sink.

"No."

We both frowned in that direction, but I crossed the house and opened the door to find Derek Kingston standing outside in his detective's uniform of slacks, a gray button-down, a black tie, and a jacket thrown over his arm. It was essentially what Xavier was wearing, but the difference between the two men was night and day.

Derek was an objectively good-looking guy with broad shoulders, a reasonably trim body, and a relaxed yet powerful way about him shared by a lot of Matthew's friends in law enforcement. But while that might have done it for a lot of women, it was hard not to compare them. Derek was slightly awkward in a way that reminded me of boys in high school, whereas Xavier entered a room with nothing less than control. Derek tended to fidget, leaning back and forth on a door, picking at his nails, or shoving hands in and out of pockets, while Xavier occupied any room with stillness and gravity. To any other woman, Derek might have been a snack in his own right. But I could really only see one of them, even if whatever we had right now was more pretend than anything else.

"Hey, Frankie," Derek said as he looked over my shoulder and found Xavier watching the interaction with an utterly unreadable expression while he appeared to be fixing his tie.

"Be nice," I mouthed at him but had to stifle a smile when he just shrugged. I turned back to Derek. "Hey, we were just on our way out. Everything all right?"

Derek rubbed a hand over his closely cut hair. "Uh, yeah. I was just in the neighborhood on a job—"

"What sort of job?" Xavier cut in, coming to stand next to me.

Derek gave him a look. "My job. As a police detective. That's all you need to know."

His tone was clear with subtext. As in, *you want me to help, or do you want to be an asshole?*

I reached out to touch his shoulder in what I hoped was a comforting way. "Don't pay attention to him. We're both just a little high-strung about everything going on, you know?"

Derek's gaze flickered between me and Xavier, and I waited for His Royal Broodiness beside me to make some kind of off-color comment or snap at the detective.

But to my surprise, Xavier remained civil.

"Go on," he said stiffly, if not particularly nicely. "We do have an appointment uptown, but I imagine if you're here, it's important."

"Uh, right," Derek said. "Well, I just wanted to let you know that nothing showed up on the letter you gave me, like I thought. But a squad car down the street *did* intercept a kid delivering a second letter to your box last night around two in the morning."

I glanced at Xavier, who just flickered an equally befuddled, if not tense, look my way before we both turned back to Derek.

"I think you'd better come in," Xavier said, opening the door fully.

Derek followed us back into the living room, where I made myself busy getting him a glass of water rather than sitting on the couch and stewing with sweaty palms.

"Can we see the letter?" I asked.

Derek shook his head. "It's already been entered into evidence. But I can tell you what it said." He pulled up his phone and scrolled through some notes. "This time it was printed out from a computer. 'Get him out of your house. He doesn't belong to you.'" He looked up with a bemused expression. "We got a poet, I see."

"So, who is it?" Xavier asked. "Who the fuck is tormenting my family?"

I hated the way my heart thrilled at the term "my family." Hated and also loved it a little.

Okay, maybe a lot.

"Well, the kid who delivered it is a fifteen-year-old kid name Juan Simmons who lives about four blocks that way." Derek pointed in the direction of Red Hook West, the public housing projects on the other side of Coffey Park. "He has a couple of priors. Nothing major. Shoplifting, skipping turnstiles. Things like that."

He handed us both a sheet of paper containing the kid's mug shot and a few basic facts about him. It looked like a profile that might have been printed off a database in his office.

Xavier took the sheet and looked it over with a scowl. "So, some teenager has been messing with us...why?"

I looked at the picture. "Oh, I recognize him. I've seen him at the bodega here and there. He opened the door once for me and Sof."

"Any reason he might be stalking you?" Xavier asked. "Got a thing for the cute bird down the street, maybe?"

I shook my head. "Doubtful. To a fifteen-year-old, I'm a crone."

Beside me, Xavier chuckled. "Never," he murmured, causing my cheeks to redden. "To a fifteen-year-old, I'd say you're fodder for a lot of...pretend."

The blush threatened to become an all-out fire.

"Er." Derek cleared his throat. "It might just be that he was paid to deliver. Sort of a middleman to cover up the original perpetrator. We checked security cameras all around here, and we actually got him on camera delivering the first one too, so next step is to send a squad car down to pick him up for interrogation."

"Oh, don't," I put in. "I don't want to ruin this kid's life. Can't you just ask him what you need to know in his own home? It sounds more like a harmless prank, honestly."

"Ces," Xavier argued. "Obviously it's not."

"Or maybe it is," I argued back. "What if this isn't about a jilted lover or some weird stalker, but just some kids who saw my profile in the *Post* and wanted to screw with me? He doesn't deserve to have his whole neighborhood watch him taken away in a squad car just because of some mischief."

Derek clearly did not agree with me, but it also looked like he did not particularly want to use his valuable time hunting down teenage delinquents with mean letters when there were lots of other, much more serious crimes happening in the city.

Xavier rubbed his hand over his face. "What about a private investigator?"

"That is not necessary—" I started to say before Derek cut me off.

"That sounds great," he said, looking relieved to have Xavier (and his money) on board. "Actually, I was going to suggest it."

"I'm sure you have other things to do," Xavier told him. "We appreciate you looking into this." He set the paper down on the table and held out his hand for a shake. "*I* appreciate it. Thanks, mate."

Derek examined him like he was expecting the act of gratitude to turn Xavier into a pillar of salt. When it didn't, he nodded slowly before taking his hand.

"I'll have Elsie find someone, then." Xavier was already reaching into his pocket for his cell phone.

Derek stood, then looked at me. "Walk me out?"

"Sure." I glanced at Xavier, whose blue gaze only flickered up at me and back to his phone before he tapped his watch to indicate the time.

No sign of jealousy, though. Not even a whiff.

I wasn't sure why that bothered me. Hadn't I told him to reel it in?

I accompanied Derek to the front stoop, where he turned to me while I held the door open.

"You okay?" he asked, casting another look down the hallway toward where Xavier remained on the couch. "Things seem...weird between you two. Not that the guy isn't kind of weird already, but..."

I shrugged, not really wanting to get into it. "He's just feeling protective. Maybe more than usual."

"He wasn't around for over a month, and now he's living here? I guess you guys are working it out after all, huh?"

I swallowed. "Don't take this the wrong way, but how did you know that? It's not like we talk."

Derek just shrugged. "I worry about you. But so does your brother. He asks me once a week to come by and check on you."

I huffed. "Frigging Matthew."

"He said something about you and Nina expecting around the same time?" Derek glanced down at my belly, obviously a bit doubtful since there still wasn't much to see there yet. "I was up there last weekend. She's, uh, showing a lot."

I bit my lip. Apparently, all my business was on blast. "She's a little farther along. But, yeah, Nina and I will be about a month apart."

No one had known it at the wedding, but a few weeks after Italy, Nina and Matthew had revealed to the family that they were expecting. It explained a lot—mainly why Matthew hadn't been checking in on me himself since these letters arrived. Or come to kick Xavier out of the house.

"So, you and the Brit are..."

I glanced over my shoulder at Xavier, who was staring steadfastly at the sheet of paper and pretending not to watch me and Derek. Then I turned back to the detective. "We're complicated."

Derek nodded. "I guess so."

I swore Xavier's mouth curled at the edges. It wasn't quite a smile. But it was almost there.

SEVENTEEN

"God, I'm getting fat," I muttered as I checked myself out in the wall of mirrored cabinets beside the ultrasound chair.

We'd only just arrived at the obstetrics center at Beth Israel in time for our appointment, where we were quickly ushered into a large imaging room equipped with several big screens and a much bigger ultrasound machine than the one we'd seen before.

I stuck my chin out toward myself in the mirror. "Check out these jowls. I'm going to have a double chin by Christmas, you watch. I'm already starting to look like my great aunt Valentina."

Xavier had been brooding since Derek stopped by. At least more than usual. Brooding, but not snapping. I could live with that. My instinct when things were tense was to offer a bit of levity. Call it practice from three and a half years of redirecting eight-year-old brains from imminent drama over spilled milks and lost Pokémon cards.

"I think you look bloody beautiful," Xavier said quietly from the stool on the other side of the room.

I turned at the sound of his sincerity. "I—thank you. But you're supposed to say that to a pregnant woman. I know the glow is bull-shit. It's just the sweat leftover from nausea and running about a degree above normal. I'm basically an oven cooking this little bun. You could bake a soufflé in here."

I expected at least a chuckle but got absolutely nothing. Instead, Xavier just watched me solemnly as I laid back into the ultrasound chair, my legs covered by the disposable drapes.

"You're more beautiful than I've ever seen you," he said. "And before you ask, I'm not saying it because I expect anything. It's just the truth. You're absolutely stunning."

We stared at each other for a long minute, blue eyes meeting my green with such intensity I thought fireworks really might burst right there in the room. It was so different than sexual tension. So much more than the intensity that had passed between us when we first met, or even the longing of last spring, when we'd met again.

This tension was deeper but somehow swam right under the surface of every interaction. Transparent and yet completely unreadable.

What was happening?

I cleared my throat, and Xavier looked away.

"So, have you found anything else?" he asked, obviously looking for a change of subject. "About my mum, that is? In the journals. I saw you've gone through a few more."

I smiled. I knew he was interested. "I have, yeah. But nothing more about her yet. I don't think Henry was really that interested in the new assistant cook. At least, probably not until she got involved with your dad."

He gave a grim smile. "I suppose I just wonder how it happened. In some ways, I could see the match. Mum wasn't the warmest of creatures, and Rupert, well, he was basically an ice block. I've wondered if they sort of spoke the same language, you know?"

I nodded. It would explain a lot.

"Why do you think you are the way you are, then?" I asked.

He frowned. "What do you mean?"

"You're not cold like that."

He looked genuinely surprised. "You're the first one to say that."

I chuckled. "Hot *and* cold is probably more accurate."

"Mmm. Yeah." He snorted. "Jagger once compared me to Jekyll and Hyde. My therapist didn't think that was very funny, but I did."

"What did she say?" I asked curiously. It was the first time, other than the other night, that Xavier had even brought up the fact that he was seeking therapy.

"Probably what I always knew, deep down. I struggle with attachment anxiety, apparently. Effects of not having a dad, losing Mum so young, then having every other major person in my life die on me before I'm even thirty-five. She says I 'yearn for connection but push it away out of fear.'" The last part he stated while gesturing quotation marks with his fingers. "I don't know about all that. It makes sense, but plenty of people suffer tragedies in their youth and don't turn into assholes like me. Look at you, for instance."

"Me?" I repeated.

Xavier shrugged like it was self-evident. "You lost your dad, then your mum, in a different way. And your grandfather too—he raised you, right?"

"He did," I said. "But it's not the same as everything that's happened to you..."

"It's not far off," Xavier argued. "My point is that you've lost just as much as me, but you don't chase people off with your temper."

"I don't know," I said slowly. "Maybe I do the same thing in a different way. Maybe I freak out when I sense a threat to my little world. Maybe it's why I haven't had any other relationships besides you. Like I'm too quick to write everyone off because in reality, I'm scared of being abandoned again."

By the time I was finished, my voice had slowed, words trailing off as the realization of what exactly we were both saying settled thickly over the room like a fog. We stared at each other, blinking like owls. Xavier had a crinkle between his brows, and his fingers were gripping his chair so hard his knuckles were turning white.

I cleared my throat. "Anyway. I just see you with Sofia, Elsie, Jagger. Even Frederick, when Georgina wasn't around. And with Henry, at the end." A pang of guilt strummed through me that I had missed the real end. That Xavier had been forced to deal with that on his own. Again. "While you've got a hard shell, once it's broken, you're incredibly dedicated to the people you love."

"You, too." His deep voice finally broke through the fog. "Don't forget yourself there, Ces."

I swallowed thickly. "Um..."

"What?" he asked. "You think I stopped loving you just because you don't let me in your bed anymore? It don't work like that, babe. Love doesn't care about rules or bedclothes. It just keeps going. You taught me that."

We blinked at each other across the room, and once again, I found it nearly impossible not to get up and curl into his lap. Because he was right. As much as I hated to admit it, I did still love him. I had a feeling I always would, and I wasn't really sure what that meant for my future.

Loving Xavier was never the problem. The love between us was abundant and clear.

But just because something is there doesn't mean it's good for you.

Just because I loved him didn't mean he was right for me.

Right?

Right?

Before I could say anything else, however, the door opened, and a woman with red hair and thick glasses popped in.

"Ms. Zola?" She glanced at Xavier. "And, Mister Zola?"

I shook my head. Xavier just sighed.

"I'm the only Zola," I said. "This is Xavier Parker, my, um—the baby's father."

The woman nodded politely as she entered, followed by another younger man in blue scrubs. " I'm Dr. O'Brien, the fetal cardiologist here today. This is Timothy, our tech. Thrilled to meet you both. Now, shall we take a look?"

I settled back into my chair while Xavier came to sit next to me on the other side as I drew up my hospital gown and allowed the doctor to begin her test.

It was much the same as last time, except this time, it was done with a traditional ultrasound over my belly, and the sound of the baby's heartbeat was far louder than before. Instead of a soft whisper through the trees, the heartbeat was more like a hurricane.

Images echoed all over the screens set up across the room, and the tech and the doctor took quite a bit more time to focus on the tiny creature moving on the screens.

"You hear that?" Dr. O'Brien asked.

She turned up the volume. Xavier and I were already silent, but we focused on the heartbeat, watching the pulse read across one of the monitors.

Then I heard the skip. And thought my own heart was stuck in my chest.

I snapped my head back to Xavier, whose eyes were bright blue moons as they stared at the screen. They flickered back to mine, and I saw the same fear there that was throbbing in my chest.

He grabbed my hand before I could reach out.

"It'll be all right," he told me. "It will be all right."

He didn't sound like he could believe himself.

"That right there is the murmur your OB heard," Dr. O'Brien said. She muttered something to the tech, and they proceeded to take several more measurements over the course of the next twenty minutes.

Xavier held my hand securely. And I squeezed just as hard.

"Okay," Dr. O'Brien said when she was finished. "Here's what I know. See that?" She used a laser pointer to indicate a tiny dot on one of the screens. "That's what's causing that little skip in your baby's heartbeat. Now, here's the deal. When the heart is forming, it's actually normal for there to be some tiny holes here and there. Typically, all these holes close before the baby is born, and there is nothing to worry about. However, this one is a bit larger than we would expect, which is why we want to be sure it doesn't develop into an atrial septal defect."

"I—okay," I said, unable to think of anything better. I honestly only understood about one in three words. Defect was one of them. Hole was another.

"So, the baby's all right?" Xavier wanted to know. His deep voice soothed something at the core of me. "It's fine?"

"It's something to watch," the doctor said evenly.

"And if it does turn into that atrial septum—"

"Atrial septal defect," Dr. O'Brien corrected him.

"If it turns into that," I put in, "what does that mean? Potentially."

At that, she finally looked at me with some measure of sympathy. "It can cause damage to the blood vessels. Put a person at a higher risk of murmurs, high blood pressure, strokes, heart failure. Things like that."

With every suggestion, I felt my own blood pressure rise. "Oh—oh."

"But that's not where we are now," Dr. O'Brien said. "If you'll just wait a moment, I want to have my colleagues take a look, just to be sure. I'm going to show them the imaging, and I'll be right back."

Without waiting, she and the tech swept out of the room, leaving Xavier and me surrounded by images of our child's broken heart, feeling like ours were breaking with it.

"Xavi," I whispered, unable to stop the tears from welling.

The sound seemed to jerk him into action. Immediately, he swiveled on his stool and pulled me up so I was curled toward him. He set his forehead to mine, inviting me to follow his deep breaths.

"Listen to me," he said. "Listen very hard. Are you listening?"

I swallowed, doing my best not to sob. "I'm—I'm listening."

"We're going to be okay," he told me. "We're *all* going to be okay."

I gasped as one sob snuck through. "But the baby—its heart—"

"No," he cut me off, squeezing my hand and rubbing his nose against mine. "I said listen. No matter what happens today, what news we get, or what goes on in the future, I am not leaving our family. I am here. I am this baby's father and *your* partner in this, come what may. I am whatever you need me to be, whenever you need it. Do you understand?"

His tone brooked no argument, and I found something about that settled my thrashing heart. The prick of tears subsided as I took another breath with him, then another, and another.

He was so big. So strong. But it was really his spirit that made him a rock for so many.

For me too, it seemed. If I would finally let him.

"I—I understand." I exhaled once more, then pulled away, wiping a few stray tears that had escaped. "Thank you."

He wiped away one last tear from my cheek. "No thanks needed, babe. I'm here for you. Always."

My heart fluttered again in a very different way, to the point where I was no longer able to tell the difference between excitement and fear. It was a thin line between the two when it came to Xavier Parker. Always had been.

The door opened, and Dr. O'Brien reentered with the tech.

"All right," she said cheerfully to a room deadened with silence. "Everything was confirmed with the other doctors. We'll want to do an echocardiogram in another eight weeks to follow the progress. Now for the fun part. Who wants to know the sex of the baby?"

———

WE DROVE BACK to the house in sort of a numb daze, neither of us able to converse much beyond cursory words to Xavier's driver. It was par for the course, I thought irritably as the car turned down Van Brunt Street. Most couples would be over the moon to find out that they were having a little boy.

Yes, the heart issue was scary. But now that I had time to process,

I was able to focus on the doctor's reassurances over the time frame. That it might resolve on its own.

By the time we reached the house, I was substantially calmer. Even able to crack a joke or two. Xavier, however, was basically a statue. If I was able to turn things around, what was his problem?

And so I found Xavier lingering in the living room after I put away my jacket, seemingly unwilling to retreat to the basement or particularly wanting to talk.

Well, too bad. I was done waiting.

"Tea?" I asked as I moved to the kitchen. "I don't have another tutoring session until one."

Xavier just grunted, which I took as a yes as I set the kettle on the stove. He moved to the counter, where he sat like a disgruntled bar patron waiting for his next shot.

I pulled out the basket of tea boxes from one of the drawers and set it in front of him. "Here, pick one."

Without looking, Xavier selected a box and set it on the counter. Stash Earl Grey. A tea I happened to know he thought tasted like fireplace ashes.

I frowned as I pulled out my favorite chamomile blend. Now, I knew something was really wrong. Xavier was as discerning with the things he put into his body as a dermatologist would be with skin care.

"All right," I said. "Would you like to tell me what's bothering you?"

Xavier scowled at his hands. "You were there. It is what it is. I just have to learn to deal with it."

I sighed, then pulled out some mugs and put our tea bags into them. "Look, I get it. I was freaked out too when she first told us. But I think it's important here not to get ahead of ourselves. Let's just focus on what the doctor said about how it can resolve itself before the baby's born. Things can change."

Xavier snorted. "You can't really resolve the sex of the baby, Ces."

I looked up. "What? You're upset about the sex?"

The look on his face told me everything I needed to know.

"The heart thing—yeah, it's alarming, but we'll get through it. Like you said, the doctor isn't overly worried. But the fact that he's a boy...fuck."

I could not have been more gobsmacked if he had told me the baby was going to be a unicorn with an alligator tail and chicken feet. "Why does it matter if it's a boy? I would have thought you'd be happy."

Xavier just rubbed his face and shook his head. "Not so much. God, once this gets out, I'm going to have every lord on the island congratulating me. They'll all want a piece of him, you know, just like they'll want a piece of you. Except you aren't a part of that world, nor do you want to be..." He trailed off, and that was when it occurred to me what he was really ashamed of. This whole thing was embarrassing to him. I was embarrassing to him. Our family was his personal humiliation.

I turned back around to put the tea boxes away but mostly to school my face into something that was slightly less appalled.

"Look," I said. "I know he won't be a proper heir or ever become a duke—"

"That's not it," Xavier interrupted gently.

"But honestly, that's no reason to be disappointed in him. He's just a baby, for Pete's sake—"

"There's nothing wrong with *him*, Ces, it's—"

"He can't help it if his parents can't get their crap together. And honestly, I'm sure if you really need to produce a proper heir, Imogene would be happy to step in and make that happen."

By the time I was done spewing my personal insecurities all over the counter, Xavier had simply sat up on his stool to watch me. My face was heated, and my stomach felt sick at just the thought of Xavier kissing the neighbor girl, much less marrying her and reproducing. He said he would always be here, but what did I know? Dukes had more important things to do than take care of their ex-girl-friends and illegitimate children. Not when they had estates to run and heirs to produce.

Their babies would be so beautiful, too. Tall and dark-haired, or maybe blond and blue-eyed. Regal either way. Perfect for the next generation of lords and ladies.

"Oh God," I muttered as I rubbed my hands over my face.

After a few seconds, a hand touched one of mine and gently peeled it off one eye, then did the same with the other. Xavier's blue-eyed gaze blinked at me.

"You misunderstand," he said in a calmer voice. "I'm upset because every advisor I have will encourage me to make the child legitimate in order to secure the line of succession and further erode Georgie's claims."

"Oh," I said. "But you...don't want that. I see."

"*You* don't want that," he corrected me. "You've made it clear again and again. I'm not going to force you to be with me, Ces. And it's for the best anyway, because honestly, the last thing I want is for any child of mine to inherit this fucking mess." He shook his head ruefully. "I'm not the slightest bit embarrassed by you or our family. I just don't want any child to have my life at all."

EIGHTEEN

The conversation ended when Xavier quietly told me he needed time to think and went downstairs while I threw out his tea, finished my tutoring sessions for the day, and left to pick up Sofia. When we returned, we found him in the kitchen, chopping away at something while a couple of pots bubbled merrily on the stove.

"That smells good," I said as Sofia scampered into the kitchen.

Xavier just grunted and focused more on his vegetables. His body, however, was far more relaxed than it had been just hours earlier. Cooking was more to Xavier than a job or even a passion. It had been his therapy before he ever even considered seeing an actual therapist, his means of working out whatever demons could not be held at bay.

Within an hour of chattering with Sofia, however, his fears only seemed to hang like rain clouds over me. I was still sulking on the couch while he and our daughter were having their usual grand time making dinner, which this time apparently included rice balls shaped into Sofia's favorite animals.

"What shall it be this time, babe?" Xavier asked her. "A panda or maybe a fox? I've been told I look a bit like a fox with my long nose, you know."

He wriggled said appendage in a way that made Sofia burst into giggles at the counter and made my heart skip at least two solid beats.

Shit.

I turned back to the journal I was trying to finish today, but that wasn't helping my state of mind. Despite the fact that there had still been zero mention of Xavier's mother or him, I couldn't read the damn thing without seeing Kendal—and Xavier in it.

Why did I care so much? It wasn't like *I* wanted Sofia or little no-name inside me to have the life of an illustrious duke's offspring either. One summer of that had been quite enough for all of us, right?

"Ces," Xavier called from the kitchen. "Come here and taste this. Tell me what you think."

I shook my head. "I'm all right. I'll just wait until it's done."

"No, Mama, *come!*" Sofia insisted. "We're makin' a bloody curry over here!"

I snorted at the sound of Sofia using the word "bloody," especially to describe curry. It wasn't particularly appetizing, but it sounded adorable with her slight lisp.

"Be nice to Mummy," Xavier told her. "Mum's cooking something of her own over there. She doesn't have to do anything she don't want." He swept out of the kitchen holding a wood spoon, looking adorably rumpled in a slightly stained button-down and a splotched apron tied around his trim waist.

He looked like a very happy mess.

I'd never been so attracted to anyone in my life.

"We could use a neutral third party," Xavier said as he squatted next to me and held out the spoon. "Taste it, yeah?"

Unable to take my eyes from his blues flaring with humor and pride, I obediently opened my mouth and allowed him to slip the edge of the spoon between my lips. His eyes flashed a bit darker as I sucked the golden-brown liquid off the edge.

"Good?" he asked in a voice quite a bit lower than before.

It was better than good. It was stupidly delicious, spicy sunshine in a spoon.

I couldn't help but crack a smile. "It's outstanding."

Xavier's own grin splashed across his face with the brilliance of a summer sky, and my heart gave a few extra thumps.

"Good," he said again, this time clearly satisfied. He chewed on his lower lip, almost shyly. "I like to see you happy." Without waiting for a reply, he swept back up, spoon and all, returning to the kitchen like a conquering champion. "Good news, peanut—curry's a winner!"

My heart, however, was completely at a loss.

I'd been denying it for nearly a month now, telling myself that everything between us was done for. But there was no use. With such a simple little transaction, everything that had been swimming under the surface for the last several weeks broke through with the force of a breaching humpback whale.

I was still desperately in love with Xavier Parker.

And I'd just told him yesterday that it wasn't going anywhere. I'd broken his damn heart, and now I was breaking my own.

Quickly, I ran through all the reminders of Why It Was For The Best.

There was his horrible family, who, sure, weren't exactly in the picture. For now. The way he was married to his job. Except for the fact that since he'd been here, he was back almost every night by five, often earlier. But that probably wouldn't last.

And sure, he was in therapy. Sure, he was trying. But his anger management issues couldn't fix themselves overnight, and how would I really know he was making improvement until something presented itself? How would I know the next outburst wasn't just around the corner?

I was almost convinced until I looked up and caught him grinning at Sofia all over again. He glanced at me and winked. Actually winked. Surly, never-smiling, always broody Xavier winked at me and grinned like a black-haired ray of sunshine before turning back around to stir his pot.

As if he couldn't help himself.

As if being here with us made him happy too.

And damned if I didn't love his smile just as much as he seemed to adore mine.

I was almost ready to give up and join them when the doorbell rang.

Xavier glanced toward the door, brow adorably wrinkled. "You get more visitors these days than the queen, Ces."

I snorted as I got up from the couch. "That's rich coming from a duke who was buried in courtiers last August."

"Courtiers are for court, not a bastard heir."

"What's a bastard, Dad?" Sofia asked.

"Er—" Xavier looked to me, obviously in need of help.

I sighed. "It's a mean name for someone whose parents aren't married, lovey. Daddy shouldn't use it."

Sofia turned to Xavier. "But you two aren't married."

Xavier shrugged, darted a quick look at me, then looked back at her. "No, babe. We're not."

Sofia's face scrunched as she looked between us. "Well, I'm pretty great. And I'm a bastard too."

My jaw dropped, and I slapped my hand over my mouth to keep from laughing out loud.

Xavier's scowl quivered. "No," he told her. "You are absolutely *not* a bastard. Don't ever let anyone call you that."

Sofia just mirrored his scowl back at him. "My teacher says you can turn mean words pretty with your actions. Like when Sissy Chapman called me a potato forehead, but I just grinned and made a song about it, and then everyone in my class wanted to be potato foreheads too." Sofia grinned at me. "Remember that, Mama?"

I grinned at her. "I do, baby. You made potato foreheads super cute."

"I did." Sofia reached across the counter to grab her daddy's hand. "We can make being a bastard *awesome*, Dad. We can be bastards together!"

The doorbell rang again, leaving no room for Xavier to argue.

His expression darkened, but he wasn't able to keep a completely straight face while Sofia started singing a song about "Bastard Babes" to the tune of "Twinkle, Twinkle, Little Star."

"Better see who your next admirer is, then," he grumbled.

Because I didn't want his good mood to vanish, I gave him a cheeky grin that, to my delight, made his own emerge all over again. Then I dashed for the door and opened it.

My stomach dropped when I saw who was standing there.

"Adam?"

Adam Klein, in a pair of nicely cut navy pants, a checked shirt, and a brown corduroy jacket that cast him somewhere between Brooklyn hipster and son of a British noblewoman, stood on my doorstep awkwardly holding a bouquet of flowers. He shifted uneasily back and forth on his toes as he looked over my shoulder, obviously expecting a tall, anger-prone duke behind me.

Which meant he had come here thinking he might see Xavier.

Which made me wonder why he had come at all, given the explicit threats he'd been given to stay out of my life.

"Hi," I said uneasily. "Um...don't take this the wrong way, but what in God's name are you doing here?" *After I explicitly told you to stay away from me and mine.*

I looked behind him. I don't know what I expected to see, but maybe a cavalcade? Some sort of support? Police or bobbies or *something?*

"I tried to call," he said. "But you've, um, blocked my number. I think. Or else you changed it."

I didn't respond. Yes, I'd blocked his number. He didn't need the confirmation.

"I'm..." he sighed, then pulled off his ever-present driver's cap to rub a hand through his brown hair. "Look, I came to tell you that someone contacted me recently, trying to find out where you lived. They wanted me to deliver something to you. A letter. Offered me a lot of money to do it, too."

The hairs on the back of my neck flew up. "A...letter?"

"Yeah." Adam frowned. "I don't know who they were. It was a blocked number too. This was a few weeks ago, but I don't know. Something about it seemed really off, and I couldn't get it out of my mind." He glanced around me again. "You haven't gotten anything weird in the mail, have you?"

I paused, unsure of what I should say. I didn't trust Adam so far as I could throw him, but I couldn't think of any way this conversation could be a set up. And if he did know something about the odd letters, I wanted him to talk to Derek, not me.

"Actually, yes," I said. "There have been a few odd things. Hold on a second."

I dashed back inside to grab a paper and pen, waving at Xavier and Sofia before jogging back to the door.

"This is the number of a detective friend looking into them for us," I said as I scribbled Derek's name and number onto the paper, then handed it to Adam. "He's working with a PI Xavier hired to look into this stuff. Would you mind giving him a call? Since I, um, don't have your number anymore."

If Adam was surprised by that revelation, he didn't show it. "Sure. Yeah, no problem. Are you...okay?"

If his concern was fake, he was a really good actor.

I nodded. "Yeah, I'm fine."

He looked me over. "How far along are you? Still not showing much."

I put a protective hand on my belly. "Not quite four months. I'll probably pop in another month or two."

Adam nodded, looking slightly uncomfortable. "And Xavier is..."

"Inside," I confirmed. "Making dinner with Sofia."

He didn't need more updates than that. I wasn't interested in whatever he might carry back to his mother and, therefore, Georgina.

"Are you done spying?" I asked more bitterly than I expected. Just the idea made me angry.

Adam blinked. "I wasn't..." He sighed. "I'll go. Sorry to bother you. I'll give this Derek guy a call. See you, Frankie."

He turned to leave, shoulders slumped with dejection.

"Adam, wait," I called before I could stop myself.

At the bottom of the stoop, he turned. "What's up?"

"There's one thing that's been bothering me," I said. "In England. Before I left. You said something about how you stayed in America to 'watch and wait' to see how things turned out." I cocked my head. "Did you mean me? Since you knew...about Xavier, I mean?"

He blinked through his horn-rimmed glasses, then muttered something like "shit" to himself. "I...sort of."

"What does that mean?"

He took a step toward me but was smart enough not to come all the way back up. "I knew who you were," he said. "When we started working together at Carroll Elementary."

"Yeah, I gathered," I said. "Because you'd been stalking Xavier, or whatever."

"No, it wasn't that," he said, tugging at his beard nervously. "I know it looks that way, but I honestly didn't follow Xavier beyond keeping up with Kendal and basic curiosity. But I...yeah. I recognized you from something else."

I reared. "From where?"

He sighed again. "I did my master's in teaching at Columbia. I, um, was at the bar. The night you met Xavier. Total coincidence, I swear it...but, yeah. I was there." He tipped his head, almost looking charming. "Can you blame me for not telling you? You've already accused me of stalking Xavier. Next, you'd think I was watching you like that."

I frowned. Was he lying? There was no way that could be true.

And yet, I never recalled telling him I met Xavier at a bar. Or that it was near Columbia. How would he know if he hadn't been there, for any kind of reason?

"You had on a red shirt," Adam said. "I remember thinking you were really cute, and I was about to talk to you when this other guy stepped in. The same guy who had stolen literally everything else from me my whole life." He shook his head. "I can't even tell you how pissed I was. I cross a fucking ocean to get away from the guy, and Xavier Parker *still* managed to slide in and steal the girl."

"He didn't steal me," I said. "He couldn't have stolen me if I wasn't yours to begin with." Lord, I was getting tired of men talking about me like a book on one of their shelves.

Adam just shrugged. "Anyway, I swear I didn't follow you or anyone else after that. I had no idea who you really were until you started working at Carroll Elementary. And then I remember thinking maybe my luck was changing. Maybe it was fate. You were different, of course. You'd had a kid, and you obviously weren't looking for a relationship. But I still recognized you. I figured if I waited long enough, you'd eventually be ready." He shrugged. "I was right. But again, just a little too late."

I opened my mouth to tell him he was wrong. That I wouldn't have been ready for anyone at that point. That I wasn't sure I ever would be, and he shouldn't have wasted his time.

But what good would that do now?

"One more question," I said as a last thought occurred to me. "How did you know about Sofia, then? That she was his, I mean? If you weren't, um, *following* Xavier's life?"

Again, Adam looked considerably uneasy as he worried his hat between his hands. "I'm not going to lie. I didn't know it for sure...I only suspected." He shrugged. "But when you brought her around school, I was pretty sure. She looks just like him."

I cocked my head. "So, did everyone in England know?"

He snorted. "If you're asking if I told my mother, the answer is no. But it did make me wonder if one day he would be back. I might think Xavier's an asshole, but he's also loyal. He wouldn't have abandoned his own kid. So yeah...I did sort of...watch and wait."

I thought about that for a moment. It was still kind of creepy. "Why—why didn't you ever say anything to me?"

He sighed. "Honestly? Because I really liked you. I figured I should keep tabs on you just in case it became important to the whole entail and inheritance issue. But then I got to know you. And he never came back. So I thought...maybe it could be me instead."

I honestly wasn't sure what to say about all of that. There was nothing I really *could* say to make it okay.

"Oh," I said. "I, um, I see."

I almost said I was sorry but found I really wasn't. I felt bad for him. A little. But something told me giving him a round of sympathy would lead him on. And I didn't want to do that either. Not now.

"I know it can't go anywhere. But I also want you to know I'm not a psycho. I wasn't stalking you, Frankie. And I'm really sorry for any discomfort I ever caused you." Adam shrugged, and it was almost endearing. "In the end, I was just a guy sort of in love with a pretty girl he worked with."

"In *what?*"

We both turned to find Xavier towering over me. He still held the wooden spoon in his hand and had the same charmingly disheveled appearance.

I sighed. Not again. The last thing I needed was a fistfight on my doorstep. "Xavi..."

He glanced at me with more softness than I would have expected. "Dinner's ready, Ces." Then back at Adam with a darkened expression. "What the fuck are you doing here?"

"Let me guess," Adam said, lip curling with derision. "If I don't stop talking to her, you'll knock my front teeth in. Or would you rather smash my nose a second time?" He touched the bridge of his nose, which did look crooked, now that I was looking.

Xavier's jaw tightened enough that I could actually see the muscle ticking on one side. The hand without a spoon clenched into a granite fist. He obviously wanted to take Adam up on the suggestion.

But to my surprise, he just turned back to me. "Everything all right?"

Slowly, I nodded. I was expecting an explosion, but his attention was wholly on me. With less anger, more kindness. And compassion.

It was sort of like watching a horse try to waterski. Or something equally non sequitur.

"We're good," I said.

I quickly ran through Adam's revelation about the letter, leaving out the rest, which I could tell him later if he really needed it. Xavier glanced at the paper in Adam's hand, then back at me, and nodded.

"All right, then," he said. "Adam, you need any more help with that, just call me through the restaurant. Otherwise..." He took a deep breath, exhaled, then turned to me with a half-smile. "I'll see you inside."

He landed a quick kiss to my stunned cheek, then left me to turn back to Adam, who watched Xavier's receding form with something like shock on his own face.

I cleared my throat. "I'd better get in there."

"I take it you're back together?" Adam asked. He didn't sound spiteful. Just sort of sad.

"I..." I wasn't sure how much I wanted to reveal. "I don't know what we are, to be honest. Other than expectant parents at the moment."

"But it's possible," Adam pressed.

I found myself shrugging as I answered honestly. "I suppose it's always possible with him."

"I see."

He backed off the steps, and I was distinctly reminded of the many descriptions in books of a nobleman surrendering a duel. I almost expected him to bow, but he didn't.

"Thank you for the heads-up about the letter. And, um, good luck, Adam," I told him. "With everything. Really."

He nodded, then awkwardly handed me the flowers and raised a hand in farewell. "You too, Frankie. Have a good night."

NINETEEN

Dinner was a distinctly more contemplative affair, filled mostly with Xavier's delicious curry and Sofia's chatter while her parents ruminated at the table. Occasionally, Xavier would look up and offer one of us the trademark half-smile I always wanted to turn into an all-out grin. Sometimes, he'd catch me watching him while I pushed the remains of chicken and bell peppers across my plate.

Our daughter, bless her heart, did not notice a thing while she debated the relative magic of a unicorn horn versus a fairy wand and offered the occasional rendition of "Bastard Babes." Although I came close to doubting myself when I overheard a conversation they had right before bed.

I was bringing up a load of clean towels when I found Xavier in her room, balanced on a pillow on one side of Sofia's lilac-colored table and chair set while she set the room up for an impromptu tea party.

"What about me?" Xavier was asking. "I want a crown. I can't be a princess too?"

Sofia just giggled. "No, Dad. You're the prince, I told you." She cocked her little head. "But here. I can give you wings so you can be a fairy prince."

There was some shuffling, but when I peeked in a few moments later, Xavier had somehow managed to hang Sofia's rainbow fairy wings over his massive shoulders along with a purple cape and a plastic tiara gleaming from his black waves. He calmed drank his pretend tea while Sofia put on her own costume.

Oh, my heart.

I ducked back out, stifling my own giggle, and was about to leave when I caught the next thing Xavier said.

"You know those are just movies, right, babe?" He asked her gently. "Princes don't really exist like that. And little girls don't have to wait for someone to rescue them, right?"

I tried back just to find Sofia giving him a long look I'd seen in the mirror more than once.

"You rescued Mommy."

"Did I? Not so sure about that."

The dejection in his voice made my heart sink.

"Well, the prince always makes mistakes before he makes it right. Everyone make mistakes, Dad. You just have to say you're sorry and try harder next time."

There was a long silence filled by the sounds of Sofia "pouring tea" for the other tea party attendants, which appeared to be a large Kermit the Frog, a bear she always stole from Matthew's room, and, of course, Tyrone the unicorn.

"Cheers, Dad," he told him.

"Cheers," Xavier replied. Then, a few moments of pretend sipping later: "I love you, baby girl. You know that too, right?"

"Yep, I know," Sofia said cheerily. "But what about Mama?"

"What about Mummy?"

"Don't you love her?"

There was a long pause. I should have walked away.

"Yeah." Xavier's deep voice was barely audible, but it still drifted across the room. "Yeah, babe, I love her a lot."

"Good. She loves you too."

"I'm not so sure about that one, babe. But we get on just fine."

"No, she definitely loves you," Sofia said. "Because whenever she sees your flowers, her eyes get all misty like the rain and she says, 'that damn man!' Same as when Zio lets us use his car or pays her bills. It means she loves him. She told me. So that means she loves you too."

There was a low chuckle, but no other reply.

"Just say you're sorry," Sofia told him again. "It always works for me. Then she gives me a hug and sometimes makes me hot chocolate too. The kind with the little marshmallows. They're really good."

———

WHEN I CAME BACK DOWNSTAIRS from putting Sofia to sleep, Xavier hadn't retreated to his lair but was mulling on the back porch, swirling a glass of brown liquid like he was hypnotizing himself with it. A floorboard creaked as I went out to join him, carrying a can of La Croix and a heavy wool blanket.

I scrunched my ponytail with one hand and pushed the other over my face, stifling a yawn. "She's finally down. I nearly went with her."

He was quiet while I opened the La Croix and took a seat at the little table before covering my shoulders with the blanket. I figured I'd just address the elephant in the room—or the deck—head-on.

"So, Adam," I said. "That was a surprise."

Xavier scoffed. "That he's in love with you? Not really. He tracked you like a hound all summer."

"I wasn't talking about that." I tipped my head. "More the fact that you didn't threaten to punch his teeth in, like he said. Or make an actual attempt to strangle the guy."

Another ironic snort. "Well, I was tempted." He took a long sip of his drink. "But I've been working on it, you know. Trying to remember the main reason why I don't need to toss wankers like him into the river just for looking at you wrong."

I tensed, gripping my blanket closer. "And why is that?"

He looked over to me, and there was a shocking gentleness in his eyes I'd never seen before.

"Because I trust you, Ces," he said simply.

"I—oh."

"I know," he continued carefully. "That if we were together, you wouldn't do anything like that. But since we aren't, I also know that you don't suffer fools. If someone's in your life, it's for a good reason. If you were talking to him, it was because you needed to. I don't need to question what you do if it's what you want."

I was...stunned. Flabbergasted, to say the least. Whatever I'd been expecting him to say, it wasn't this. Just when I'd been doubting any kind of growth whatsoever, here was Xavier acting more mature than most humans on the planet could manage and about someone he genuinely could not stand.

"So, is he?" he finally asked a few minutes later.

I looked up from where I'd been staring at my hands. "Is who what?"

"Adam Klein." He couldn't *quite* keep the derision out of his tone, but he was trying hard. "Is he...what you'd want?"

We eyed each other through the crisp night air. Xavier's gaze sparkled like the stars hidden by the city's corona of light. Just like this man's smile, you know they were there, even if you couldn't always see them.

"No," I admitted softly.

The blue in Xavier's eyes glimmered with something I doubt he would have even wanted to name as hope. "Then...what...who do you want?"

I gulped. My tongue felt like it was about three times bigger than normal. Unable to keep eye contact, I looked out at the darkened yard, then back at my hands, which were toying with the edges of the blanket.

Who did I want?

What did I want?

I'd been thinking of little else for months now, but every time I came up with an answer, it felt like the one I wasn't supposed to have.

Until tonight. Until now.

"I want my life in New York," I told him honestly. "Close to my friends and family. People who offer me safety and solace for Sofia and me when we need it."

Xavier nodded. "Sounds reasonable."

"I want to go back to school and become a professor," I continued. "I want to write my dissertation on those journals. I want to have a job I actually love. I want my kids to have a mother they respect, who can teach them what it means to persevere and not give up on their dreams."

Xavier watched me intensely. "I think that's fucking great. I think you should do it all. Our children are already lucky to have you as a mum, Ces. They'll be lucky to watch you grow, too."

I swallowed again, looking away as tears pricked my eyes. Why was this so hard?

I knew *exactly* why this was so hard. Because there was another truth roiling in my gut. One that had been nipping at my tongue most of the evening, thrashing to be said since the moment Xavier had chosen to walk away from the door instead of giving in to his demons.

Perhaps it was time to give up the ghost. To stop fighting the inevitability of the two of us. I had my pride, and I had my standards, but I also had needs, and none of them ever seemed to be as desperate as what I felt for him.

And if he could change, maybe I could too.

Maybe that change could start now.

"Xavi?" I said in a voice shaking with need, fear, anticipation, and so much more.

He looked back at me with sad, mournful eyes. "Yeah, babe?"

I took a deep breath. "I also want you."

Xavier stared at me for a long time. Seconds ticked by. Maybe minutes. Enough time that I wasn't sure if he understood what I'd just said.

"Xavi?" I asked. "Did you...did you hear me?"

Xavier started then, like he was pulled out of a trance. Then he frowned and stood up. "I need a moment."

And without waiting for a reply, he left the deck and disappeared into the basement.

I turned back toward the yard.

"What the hell?" I asked the night.

There was no answer, of course.

Well, that didn't mean I wasn't going to get one.

I got up and followed Xavier downstairs, where I could already hear the telltale thwacks of his fists smashing a heavy bag.

"Xavi?" I called. "Xavier!"

I landed at the bottom of the stairs and had to squint to see across the dark room, where he was, yes, punching the crap out of a heavy bag that was swinging so hard on its chain it was creaking loudly and threatening to pull out of its frame.

"Xavier!" I called after he landed one last hard punch.

He froze, then exhaled roughly. "Francesca, I asked for space."

"I know," I said as I gave him the opposite as I walked closer into the room. "But I don't understand why. Xavi, we weren't fighting. I just spilled my guts out there. I told you—I told you—"

I couldn't bring myself to say it again. Not when he was turning me down. Not when he was already pretending it hadn't happened.

"Christ." Xavier shoved a hand over his brow before muttering something under his breath.

I picked up a pillow off his couch and chucked it to the ground, wishing it were something harder. More breakable. "Care to share that with the whole house, Mr. Parker?"

"I *said*, what good is asking for space if no one will fucking give it to you?" he spat between his teeth.

He turned to the back and delivered another loud blow. Anyone could see he was struggling. That his buttons were out, dying to be pushed.

I knew it was my fault. Maybe it was because of hormones or

sentimentality, or maybe it was the fact that I'd just realized my entire soul belonged to this man, and there was nothing I could do to stop it. But whatever the reason, now I was the one who could not hold back. This time, I was the one who wouldn't stop.

"What is your problem?" I demanded as he turned away, shoulders rising and falling like waves in the ocean. "You're here. I let you stay. I let you live here. I'm basically a doormat, considering how you walk all over me, so what is it, Xavi? What do you want now that I haven't given you yet?"

"My God, it's *you!*" he roared, voice thundering enough to rattle the pictures on the walls when he whirled around to face me again. His face was red, chest heaving, every tendon and muscle standing out on his neck and face.

He really was a beast.

But I didn't shy. I didn't run. I stood there, jaw dropped, watching at this animal of a man like he had just spoken Oompa Loompa for all the sense he made.

"What?" was all I could manage in the end.

When he looked up, he was gasping like he'd just sprinted a mile.

"You," he said again, more sedately now, as if the first version had broken some mysterious seal and now he was acclimated to it. "What I need...is you."

My mouth opened, but nothing came out. I looked everywhere but at him, as if literally anything else in the room could give me some inkling of what in the world was going on here. My shoes, the ugly painting on the other side of the wall, Sofia's doll on the couch, my slightly swollen belly.

My hand rested atop the tiny bump, barely even visibly under my shirt, tight as it was. Nothing moved there—not yet—but oh, God, my heart ached.

"But you had me," I said. "Xavi, you had me more than once. And both times, you tossed me aside like I didn't matter. Like I meant little more to you than...than one of those dolls over there. And up there, I told you I still wanted you. And you—you walked away."

I couldn't help the tears that started when I said it all out loud. Like everyone else in this life I'd loved, he had left right when I'd said what mattered most.

"You say you want me again, but do you mean it? Honestly, I've been wondering if you ever did at all."

I jerked my head up. "What the hell? How could you possibly think that?"

"I'm serious," Xavier said with a face that matched his iron tone. "You've said it too, and then *you* left, Ces. You ran away, left me among the wolves, took away my daughter, broke my fucking heart in ways you can't understand."

"*I* can't understand? Of course I understand. Xavi, my heart was broken before I ever got on that plane because you broke it every time you weren't there for us! You left me to those exact wolves more times than I can count! Could you really blame me for leaving? For taking our daughter back to where I knew she and I could both be safe?"

"No." Xavier closed his eyes and appeared to take several deep breaths before he spoke again. "I can't. But Francesca..."

"Say it." My voice was cracking with the effort not to break completely. "If you don't want me like that anymore, just say it."

When his eyes finally opened again, their fathomless blue sparked through the dark room. "Don't fuck with me, Ces. Don't you dare fuck with me."

"I'm *not*," I croaked. "I wouldn't. If anything, I'm down here laying my heart on the table for you. What do you want me to do, Xavi? Do I need to get down on my knees? Do you need to know that all I have dreamed of for the last six years is that we could be a real family? That I'd be more than just the girl you knocked up—more than once, I might add? I wanted to be your wife, your partner, someone you actually trust, someone you'd think of as your equal..."

I trailed off as I finally said the things out loud I'd only barely allowed myself to imagine in the years past. By the time I was done, I was crying so hard I couldn't see clearly. I stumbled around and fell into the couch with my face in my hands. Xavier waited a moment, then quickly crossed the room and knelt in front of me, though he didn't touch me. Didn't offer any more comfort than just his nearness.

So close, and yet so far away.

It nearly killed me.

"I know I'm nothing special in the grand scheme of things," I managed in stuttering breaths through chest-wracking sobs. "I never have been. And I don't expect to be. But I never thought it was too much to ask to be special to one person, at least." Tears fell, two silent streams through my fingers. "I guess I was wrong."

"Ces."

The tenderness in his voice almost broke me as he gathered me into his chest and started to stroke my hair, cupping my head with his big hand and rocking me side to side.

Cradled by his warmth, his strength, and the solid wall of him, I was eventually able to calm. Soothed by his scent of fire, soap, and just a hint of spice from cooking, my heart slowed. My tears subsided to a mere trickle. My breath evened. Much as he had hurt me, there was still no safer place in the world to me than right here in his arms.

"Can I say something now?" His deep voice was a caress as gentle as the hand stroking my hair.

I inhaled deeply, then finally sat up with him, swiping a few more tears from my eyes. "I—all right."

Xavier reached out to dab the last tear with a broad thumb. "It will never cease to astound me that you see so little in yourself when all I see is utter fucking majesty."

I gasped, almost coughed in surprise. "You see wha-what?"

Xavier took my hands between his, holding them between us. "I look at you, and I see the only person I have ever known who is strong enough to love with her heart and soul. I don't see weakness, babe. I don't see someone broken. I see someone who makes everyone around her whole." He shook his head as if in disbelief. "It never occurred to me to fight for you because you always seemed too strong to need it."

I took a deep breath. "Well, I do need it. Not every day. Not all the time. Everyone needs to be fought for on occasion."

"I see that now. So strong to fight for others, but for yourself, why not?"

I sighed and looked away. "When everyone ignores you, treats you like you're nothing special, maybe you start to believe it."

"Who said that?"

I shrugged. "Everyone. No one."

It was hard to explain. I hadn't been called names growing up (aside from regular sibling squabbles). No one had explicitly said, "Here is Francesca, the wallflower no one cares about."

But while I had always loved my siblings, there was also the sense that when I was with them, I faded into the background. Each of them had such intense personalities. Matthew and Lea were classic Type A control freaks. Kate was a creative, Marie was the eccentric, and Joni the life of the party.

I was just Frankie. The quiet kid who liked books. The girl who taught instead of did. The lady whose only real purpose was to take care of her daughter.

No one had ever seen me for more until I'd met this man.

When I managed to turn back, Xavier's eyes were fathomless blue depths, full of sorrow, yes, but even more heartbreakingly, compassion. "Yeah," he said with a sigh. "I understand."

I thought of his parents. A mother who died young, who worked so hard to provide for him but, by his own admission, hadn't been particularly emotive. A father who at best was absent, at worst abusive. The way he had spent most of his life being labeled a misfit bastard or else the rebel chef.

Pigeonholing was the same no matter how much money you had. Just as insidious. Just as stifling.

I thought of my own parents, one dead, the other an addict trying to make a career out of shaming her own daughter to the press.

We weren't really so different, he and I.

"But Ces?"

I hummed. "Yeah?"

"Some of us can choose different," Xavier said. "If there's anything I'm learning these days, it's that."

"Oh, Xavi. Not everyone has your brand of self-confidence. Not everyone has your ability to change."

"I'll teach you," he told me, tilting my chin so I was looking at him. "I'll teach you every day until you see what I see."

By the time he was finished speaking, I could hardly breathe.

"Starting," he continued quietly, "with this."

Then, before I could say a word, he shifted so he was fully on one knee, reached into his pants pocket, and pulled out a box.

And when I saw it, I couldn't breathe.

"I should have done this right the first time," Xavier said. "But since you're giving me a second chance, I won't mess it up again."

Any woman would know this box. Small and black velvet, the kind that made no noise when he used his other hand to open it and once again reveal the most exquisite ring I'd ever seen in my life.

I stared at the setting for a long time, taking a few moments to appreciate its beauty in a way I hadn't done the first time he'd shown it to me. I'd almost forgotten the way the delicate cluster of gems, rather than a solitaire, fit together just so. They were set on a delicately filigreed white gold band, sparkling even in the dim basement light.

And they were pink. The color of the perfect blush of an ingenue's cheeks or the shade of a London sky right after the sun had set.

The color of camellias.

Of longing.

Of us.

"Francesca Zola," Xavier said in a hushed voice, barely above a whisper. "Since the day we met, you changed me. You changed me with your smile and your kindness. You changed me with the way you love our daughter and the way I know you'll love our son. You changed me with every iron-strong, quietly ruthless, breathtakingly beautiful part of your soul, and I will never be the same for it. You beg for me, babe. Well, I'm on my knees for you."

"But you don't get on your knees for anyone," I pointed out with a shy smile.

That earned me a grin that positively lit up the room.

"I'd stay on my knee forever," Xavier said just as his left dimple appeared, "if you'd answer just one question. Francesca Zola, will you marry me?"

TWENTY

Now it was my turn to stare for what seemed like minutes. I stared at the ring. I stared at him. I stared at the rest of the room like it really might evaporate and I'd be sucked back into my bedroom upstairs, ripped away from a moment that was too beautiful not to be a dream.

And yet.

Nothing faded.

Nothing disappeared.

Somehow, this moment was actually real.

Xavier Parker had just asked me to marry him.

Xavier cleared his throat. "Um, Ces?"

I blinked. "You...you love me, Xavi?"

He tipped his head as a delicate smile flirted with that generous mouth. "Haven't I just been saying as much?"

"But...but you love me? Not how I mother Sofia or how I support you or what we do in the bedroom...or..."

One of Xavier's hands gently closed over my mouth, then fell down to rest atop my knees.

"I love *you*, Ces," he said solemnly, though humor still danced in his sapphire blues. "Those other things are wonderful, and they make you even more special, but I have always been and only ever will be deeply and desperately in love with you. Your heart. Your wit. Your dreams. Your soul." He took a deep breath, glanced down at the ring in his hand, then back up at me. "So...will you? Woman, will you please fucking marry me?"

I searched his face for a long time. I know he had already answered my question, but some part of me, that shy little girl who had never quite learned that she was worth loving completely, was still looking for the lie. Some sign of insincerity.

A shifty expression. Fidgety fingers. A tremor in his voice.

But every part of Xavier remained still and steadfast.

And that part of me, small and scared, finally closed her eyes and relaxed.

"Yes," I whispered.

"Say it again."

I blinked. Xavier's eyes blazed bluer than ever and hotter than any fire. But they were focused completely on me.

"Say it again," he repeated. "I need you to say it again."

"Yes," I said louder, more confidently as he slid the ring onto my finger, laughing as he did. The joyous sound filled the room and my heart. "Yes, Xavier Sato Parker, I will marry you."

Because I couldn't hold myself back any longer, I threw my arms around him, and he caught me amidst his joy. We both toppled onto the floor, giggling and grasping for each other, like we couldn't get close enough.

It was different than before. Different than "pretending," for sure, but also different than when we had been together.

Even in England, things between us had still just been pretend, in a way. We were trying on the relationship like I might try on a dress. Neither of us was fully committed because neither of us really believed we deserved this kind of happiness. Or maybe could fully believe it was real at all.

And maybe that was the way of most relationships, but I should have known from the moment I saw him in the middle of that party, from the time he chased me onto the street, from the second he finally kissed me in that bar all those years ago...it was never going to be practice with Xavier Parker.

It was always going to be forever.

And then he kissed me. At last.

His mouth captured mine as he rolled me onto my back, carefully bracing himself over my body like a long, lean cage. His mouth tasted of brandy and adoration, and his fingers threaded through my hair with reverence. This was what I'd been waiting for over the past weeks—really, years. This kiss wasn't just passion or longing. No more nervous energy bound up in a pool of lust. Before, Xavier would devour me like a starving man, like someone who hadn't had a drink in days.

But though he was no less voracious now, there was the way his jaw relaxed slightly or how his other hand traveled up and down my spine with total reverence rather than clinging like he might fall from a cliff.

In between kisses that left both of us breathless, Xavier laughed again and again. Deep and melodious, it was one of the most beautiful sounds I'd ever heard.

It sounded like something deep inside of him had been set loose to run.

It sounded like freedom.

It sounded like trust.

"I love you," I told him honestly.

"I couldn't love anyone more," he returned with eyes as bright as stars.

Before I could say another word, he got up onto his knees, then bent down and swept me up in his arms like he really was the gallant hero from countless novels.

Except this wasn't fiction.

This was one hundred percent real.

"And I need you more than I ever fucking have," he informed me.

Well, maybe not so genteel.

I couldn't have cared less.

He carried me through the living room and into the sole bedroom that had little more than a king-sized bed, a rack bearing Xavier's clothes, and a small roller suitcase in the corner that obviously got consistent use as he flew back and forth between New York and London.

But that was it. The entire downstairs, I realized, had hardly any personal effects beyond the heavy bag. No art on the walls beyond a picture or two of Sofia and the rental-quality prints Matthew had gotten from Target. No books or magazines or any of the other bits of detritus associated with a normal human life.

"I see you really made yourself at home here," I joked.

Xavier looked around with me, apparently seeing things anew.

"It was never going to be home," he said before pressing another eager kiss to my lips. "It was just a place to bide my time until you let me return to the one I have with you."

I frowned. "You think upstairs is home with me? You've never even lived there."

Xavier just snorted. "Home would be with you even if you were still sleeping on a single bed on the landing. Under a bridge, in a field, or in a castle. It's you, babe. You're home to me."

He set my feet on the floor. Then, with hands on my shoulders, he turned me around so he could cup my face and deliver yet another deep kiss. It went on and on, slowly this time, ever so reverently as he peeled my shirt over my head, then moved to unbutton my pants.

"I can do it," I said, reaching down to help him. It was a little embarrassing how tight my normal clothes had gotten.

"Don't," he said gruffly, batting my hands away. "I want to unwrap you myself."

"Because I'm, what, a package?" I joked nervously.

"Because you're a fucking treasure."

There wasn't much to say to that. He removed all my clothes, and I did the same for him until we both stood in front of each other in little more than our underwear. Xavier sat on the edge of the mattress, then pulled me roughly onto his lap so I was straddling his waist. He reached behind my back and undid my bra, letting the simple cotton fall to the floor so that I was nearly naked, with nothing more than my hair to shelter me from his heated gaze.

"There's no going back now," he told me seriously. "I tried to give you space. I tried to give you time to figure out what the rest of us already know. But I'm not letting you go again, Francesca. Not now, not ever."

I was the one to smile now. "I know," I said. "I never left you. Not really."

I slid my hands over his shoulders, delighting in the feel of his broad shape, the silkiness of his skin golden like the color of wheat in the sun.

"You're so beautiful," I informed him.

With a smile, Xavier brushed my hair over my shoulders, baring my breasts and the slope of my stomach to him. His eyes darted all over my changing shape, like he was expecting me to morph in front of his eyes. For a moment, they rested on my lips, and he looked like he was going to kiss me again, but then they tracked down as he teased his fingertips over one aching nipple.

"God, they're beautiful," he murmured as he moved to touch the other one in turn. "Different, you know that?"

"Tell me about it. About two cup sizes different."

He grinned with a very good impression of a tiger who had just caught his prey. "Yes. But the nipples too. A bit puffier. Darker. Like perfectly ripe raspberries." He lightly brushed his thumb over the pebbled edge.

I sucked in my breath as the move sent another shock straight through my belly.

Well, that was new.

"I've wondered how it will taste," he said as he lightly pulled at the taut nub.

"You have not," I mumbled, though I was finding it hard to focus when he was toying with me that way. Even more when he bent his head to my neck and began to trail his tongue through the curve where it met my shoulder and into the sensitive hollow just above my clavicle.

He chuckled into my skin. "I'm a sick man, Ces. Especially when it comes to you." He cupped both breasts, squeezing them lightly.

"But—you fantasize about that?" I gasped even as he took one nipple into his mouth and sucked, long and hard, as if in answer.

"Any man who says he doesn't is lying through his teeth." His words were a burr against my tender skin before he moved to the other breast and performed the same intense worship. "Sweet and rich. A perfect dessert." He suckled me hard again, causing me to shiver in his arms. "Lait de Francesca."

Maybe it was the French. Or the image of this beautiful man at my breast. But if he was sick, then so was I, because something within me responded with a deep tug at my very core. I found myself wrapping my hands around his head, urging him to take more, pull all of me into him, possess my very being if it was what he really needed. His hands traveled around my back, seizing lush handfuls of my waist, my ass, my legs in rhythm with his lips.

And then the sensations changed. The embers at my core blossomed into fire. Xavier rolled my nipple between his teeth, and suddenly the friction was too much to take. I undulated my hips into him, and the sensation of his length, solid and true between my legs, with only a few scant barriers of fabric between us, was too much to take.

I came, fast and by complete surprise.

"Fuck!" I gasped as the orgasm swept through me suddenly.

Xavier kept his mouth on my breast but pulled me closer, kneading his hands into my thighs as my entire body quaked in his clutches.

"Xavi!" I cried, grasping for his hair, his shoulders, his arms—anything I could cling to while the waves of pleasure wrecked me.

His hum was low and deep against my skin, a velvet motor.

It was too much.

"Back." With two hands, I shoved him off me, forcing his mouth from my breast with an audible pop.

He fell onto his back with a cocky grin that almost had me laughing in return.

"Like that, did you?" he asked.

"Shut up," I told him as I got off his lap only long enough to help him remove the last of his clothes. When he was naked on the bed, his cock lying stiff and heavy up his stomach, I crawled back over him, watching his cheeky mischief transform into complete and utter unadulterated need.

I straddled him once more, sliding my slick center over his waiting member. Thrilling when it moved toward me of its own accord.

"Fuck," Xavier hissed as his hands clamped on to my hips again. He tried to pull me down, but I resisted him.

"No," I said. "Now it's my turn to drive you crazy."

I positioned myself at his head. It was nearly impossible not to sink down, take him fully the way I'd been dreaming of what seemed like always. My first orgasm had already faded, and my parts were practically throbbing with need for him. Had been for months.

"Please," Xavier implored. "Fucking hell, Ces. Don't make me beg."

I leaned forward and brushed my lips over his. "But I like it when you beg. I like to know you want me."

"Vixen," he whispered, breath sweet and warm. "You own me, you know that?"

"Oh, Xavi," I said before kissing him once more. "We don't own each other. But we belong to each other just the same."

When I saw that light, that freedom, cross his face again, I sat up and took him in. Just a little.

"That's it, babe," he choked out, voice guttural and strung with need. "Take me deep, Ces. Take me fucking home."

Inch by inch, I slowly lowered onto him, taking my time, adjusting to his size until finally, I was seated around him.

Xavier shuddered. "Fuck, that's right. God, you feel so fucking perfect."

"I—oh!" I gasped as he slipped a hand into the cleft of my ass and toyed one long finger over that delicate back entry.

And then I couldn't move anymore. Pleasure started to stripe through me, coming in lashes that threatened to toss me completely off the bed. I felt like I was strapped to a horse racing toward a cliff, but I had no way to steer. No way to control the horse at all.

Xavier grabbed my body and held me in place, then thrust upward from beneath me, again and again, until we both toppled off the cliff.

"Xavi!" I screamed as my second orgasm of the night pounded through me, numbing my senses to anything but the man inside me, the pleasure he brought, and the complete and utter bliss of our union.

"Ces!" Xavier's roar was harsh and strained. His entire body tensed to the point where I could see nearly every muscle, every vein popping from his considerable physique. He reached out his long arms, hands wrapping around my shoulders as he pulled me down to his chest while he continued to pummel into me from below.

"Feel it," he ordered in a harsh whisper. "Fucking feel me. Feel us!"

"I do," I whimpered into his slick skin. "Oh, God, Xavi, I do. I love you so, so, so..."

"So fucking much," he finished for me as his hips finally slowed to a gentle rock and his breaths lengthened, though his heart continued to throb beneath my cheek.

He held me in his desperate clutch, filling me with his seed and his love and so many other unnamable things.

I barely comprehended what happened after that, how we fell from such great heights into a near slumber by each other's limbs, how Xavier managed to lift me from the bed and carry me back upstairs, or how we crawled into my bed together and curled into each other in the quiet of night just across the hall from our daughter.

But I did remember the way his eyes sparked as he cupped my face in the dark. I'd never forget the softness of his lips as he pressed one last kiss to mine, as if to seal our reunion one more time.

"Say it again," he whispered just as sleep arrived to claim us both.

"Yes," I whispered, barely able to keep my eyes open. "Yes, I'll marry you."

"Again," he prodded.

I laughed.

But he didn't laugh with me, just pulled me closer, sheltering me with the broad warmth of his shape. "Say it again," Xavier murmured into my neck. "I'll always want you to say it again."

"Yes, Xavi," I told him. "The answer will always be yes."

TWENTY-ONE

We awoke with the dawn.

Or at least I did, with Xavier between my thighs, chasing me into the fourth state of pre-matrimonial bliss I'd experienced since putting his sparkling ring on my finger.

And when we were finished, I lay on his chest, oblivious to the sheen of sweat on our skin, while he stroked my back, and I tickled his tattoo and listened to his heart gradually coming down to something like normal.

I sighed, utterly spent and feeling oddly well-rested. Despite the fact that neither of us had gotten more than a few hours of sleep—it was like we migrated to each other in our dreams, waking up multiple times to consummate whatever dark fantasies had been playing while we slept—it was probably the best rest I'd gotten in years.

This was what love felt like. Real love, made of devotion as much as passion, the kind you took with you for what I knew would be life.

When I was young, I had dreamed it would be the stuff of the old sentimental novels, sculpted from angst that made you want to scream and keep you from your sleep. Where you'd obsess about the man, terrified he wouldn't reciprocate your feelings, delighting in his company but forever anticipating the inevitable heartbreak that might follow. I'd be Catherine to his Heathcliff, maybe. Charlotte Temple to the roguish soldier. Doomed to misery and ruin because of my uncontrollable passion.

I had experienced that angst with Xavier. And probably would again—at least some of it, anyway.

But this was different. Real love was nourishing. It superseded my body's needs because of the way it fed my soul rather than taking it. It made me feel safe and sated, and so, so alive.

"How shall we tell her, then?" Xavier wondered as he combed through my hair with one hand.

"Who?" I asked, arching into his touch.

"'Little Miss, of course,'" he said in a perfect imitation of Elsie.

I giggled into his chest, enjoying the way his chest rumbled along with me. God, I loved his laugh. "Right. Well, um..."

Beneath me, his big body tensed.

I rolled to the side so I could look at him from my pillow. "What's wrong?"

Xavier turned to face me as well, not quite able to hide the fear etched over his brow. "I was about to say the same thing. You, er, don't want to hide it, do you?"

The same fear lodged itself in my stomach. "Do you?"

To my relief, he shook his head. "Absolutely fucking not. Fuck me, Ces, I want to shout it to the world." My favorite smile—the curiously shy one that only just tipped up the corners of his mouth—appeared. "She's mine," he said softly. "Finally mine."

I couldn't help but smile back. "I don't want to hide it either."

The smile broadened into a grin that made my heart thump in response.

"But," I continued, "she's going to have a lot of questions. Ones we need to be able to answer."

"Right." Xavier pushed himself up to seated so that only his lap was covered by my blankets, leaving the rest of him—including his muscled chest, stepladder abs, and his wicked tattoo—gleaming for my eyes to devour.

It was very distracting.

"Er," I started, then managed to sit up myself, though I pulled the sheets to cover my chest, much to Xavier's obvious disappointment. "Stop looking at me like that. I can barely focus on you as it is. Given your behavior last night, I think I need to be covered up to have a proper conversation with you."

"Won't do a thing. I already know what's under there." His grin turned substantially sharkish, which told me a robe or something wouldn't hurt. "Well, let's figure it out. What do you think she's going to want to know?"

"Well, for one, she's going to want to know where we'll live," I said.

"She'll want to know? Or you want to know?"

I shrugged. "Both, maybe. But it's a fair question. Xavi, where will we live? I can't imagine you actually want to spend your life in this tiny townhouse."

He tried to look as if that wasn't a horrible idea but failed miserably. I could understand why. It wasn't the smallest of places by any standard in New York, but it was a shack compared to what Xavier's immense wealth could buy us.

My immense wealth.

"Oh God," I muttered. "I'm going to have to get a lawyer, aren't I?"

Xavier scowled. "Why would you need a lawyer?"

I shrugged. "Well, obviously I'll need to sign an air-tight prenup. You'd be an idiot to get married without one."

The scowl only deepened as he looked me over. "Francesca, my love, what in the fuck are you talking about?"

I huffed. "Xavi, come on, let's not be irrational."

"I'm not being irrational. I trust you."

"You don't know what might happen. Do you really, honestly believe without a shadow of a doubt that you and I will last forever?

That something horrible might not split us up one day? I don't mean to be jaded, but it's not totally out of the realm of possibility."

He didn't answer at first. And I found I wasn't afraid of what he might say. Because as much of a romantic as I was, I knew the truth. That we both came from homes built on fragments of family, not whole ones.

"No," he said. "I know the world is fucked. And I know this isn't a fairy tale, and you're not a princess, and I'm most definitely no fucking prince. But Ces?"

"Hmm?"

"I trust you."

I sighed. "What does that even mean in this situation?"

"It means..." He shook a hand through the air like he was testing for some sort of vagrant spirit. "It means that love is a choice, right? Not just a feeling." He glanced toward the door, like he was looking for someone to come in and help him. "You make that choice every day with Sof. I see you love her, even when she makes you want to scream. You two taught me that, babe."

Something deep inside me began to warm. "All right, but—"

"It means that I know I'm going to drive you bonkers sometimes too," Xavier continued. "And you're going to make me run a mile now and then. It means that there will probably be days where we both want to leave, but we won't, because we will choose each other every single one of them." He shook his head. "I made the mistake of not choosing you once, Ces. I won't ever do that again."

I was quiet for a long time. In his peculiar way, he'd struck right at the heart of the issue, hadn't he? How did I really know he wouldn't do that again?

"I could buy you things," Xavier said. "Shower you with extravagant gifts and jewelry and what, to try to make up for it. But I know you, Ces. That's not going to work."

I curled my legs tighter. "And you know what will?"

How could he answer that question when even I couldn't?

Xavier's shoulders rose and fell. "I'm learning. I'm learning what you need, Francesca, is not always what you want. So it won't be gifts... but I'm staking my fortune on choosing you. I'd stake my life if I could."

I looked down at my ring while his words settled in. The gravity of his promise. How much he was truly willing to give up if he ever betrayed me again.

And I was willing to let him. I found that when I searched deep inside...I believed I was worth it, after all.

"Okay," I said softly. "We choose each other."

"Every day."

I smiled, then leaned over to deliver a quick kiss—one that could have easily turned into more but didn't because there were still those "questions" to answer.

"Back to the matter at hand," I said with a grin at his disappointment. "Xavi, where will we live? London or New York?"

I hated that I even had to ask. But it felt like a test of sorts. Now that I had a ring on my finger, would we revert back to a time when his schedule, his life, determined everything?

I needn't have worried.

"We'll live here," he said almost immediately. "I assumed. You said that's what you wanted, right?"

I shrugged. "I did. I do. But..." I sighed. Compromise did have to go both ways. "Look, I definitely don't want to live in Kendal, but I could probably deal with London so long as I could come home regularly. Or Oxford or Cambridge, if you were willing to commute. Maybe there's a school in London I could apply to. Maybe we could get a house, I guess, instead of the big fancy flat, that way Sofia can have a little yard, and—"

"Ces."

I looked up. "What?"

Xavier's black brows were furrowed, a sure sign that he was thinking very hard. "It should be here."

Now I was the one who was confused. "Why? All your friends

are in London. Your business is there. It's not really fair of me to insist on New York when you've got so much there."

Bu Xavier just continued to shake his head. "I've got Jagger and Elsie, but that's about it for friends, babe. My life never left much room to make others, and after Luce died, I didn't want any either. As for family, you know about those treasures..."

I snorted. I couldn't help it. But I was curious about the looks on their faces when they realized their errant duke was going to marry his American baby mama.

"You have real family here," Xavier continued. "It's messy too, but you and your sisters, your brother, your gran. It's special, what you have. I don't want Sofia and this one to miss out on that kind of family. I know exactly what happens to a kid when they don't have that. It's worth more than any restaurant I could open or any title they could have." He nodded, like he had just convinced himself too. "I can fly back to London whenever I need. New York is home for us. As long as it doesn't have to involve this rubbish bed, though, babe. My back hurts, and my feet stick off the bottom when we're sleeping."

I stared at him for a long time. Then, finally, I matched his own sly smile with a grin of my own.

"You are in so much trouble," I informed him. "Nonna's going to have an entire litter of kittens. And my sisters won't know whether to throw us a party or come after you with pitchforks."

"I'll take care of them," Xavier said confidently. "Just like I took care of you."

"They'll want to set a date almost immediately. Oh, God, you're going to have to convert, you know. Nonna will never forgive me if I don't get married at Our Redeemer."

Like a stereotypical high-born Englishman, Xavier made a particular face at the idea of becoming a Catholic. "If I must. But don't expect me to believe any of it." Another thought seemed to strike him. "How long does it take? A few weeks?"

I snorted. "Try six months to a year. You're lucky you're not a kid. I had to attend confirmation classes for two years."

Xavier's expression morphed into outright horror.

"A year?" He shook his head emphatically. "Absolutely not. I'm not waiting a year to marry you. Honestly, I don't even want to wait more than a month or two. I'd do it next week if you were willing, but I figured you'd need a bit longer to plan something you'd like."

"You want to elope?" I asked. "Why? You know I'm going to weigh approximately two tons in a matter of months, right? I'm not walking down the aisle looking like the Pillsbury Doughgirl in white lace. No."

"The fuck is the Pillsbury—you know what? Never mind. Ces, I don't want to wait long, though. Please. It's important."

"But why?" I pressed. "We know we're going to get married. As far as I'm concerned, it's a done deal, whether it happens next week or in ten years. I don't know why we have to hurry. And it's my wedding day, you know? I'd like to look and feel my best. In part for you."

He looked at me tenderly. "Fuck, all right. It's only..."

"What?" I asked.

Then the answer occurred to me.

"Oh," I said. "This isn't about us at all, is it? It's..." I looked down at my stomach, then back to him. "It's about him. You want him...to be your heir. Your real heir."

The very tips of his ears pinked where they poked through the inky black of his hair as something like shame, then indignation crossed his face.

"No, Ces," he insisted. "No. I told you yesterday, I don't want either of my children to have my life. I honestly don't care if the title dies with me. I don't. Sofia and this little peanut are both my children, and they'll inherit the money and anything else that really matters."

"Then why?" I pushed a little more. "Why do you care so much that we get married quickly?"

"Because I know what it's like to grow up with people calling you a bastard," he sputtered. "And no matter what I say, they'll always throw that word around if we wait." He shook his head. "It hurt more growing up than I can explain. I acted like I didn't care. But I did."

"Oh, Xavi..." I cupped his chin, begging him to turn his face my way. "Of course you cared."

He looked at me hopefully. "Then you understand."

I wanted to say I didn't, but part of me was sympathetic. I didn't care for the suggestions about Sofia's origins in the papers when we were there. I could only imagine they would be worse with a son in tow.

"You care about it that much?" I asked.

"I only want them to have better than me," Xavier replied. "The rest is up to you. Big wedding, small. Registry office or church, I don't care. I just want you, our babies, and that's it." He swallowed. "Please, Ces. Before he's born. That's all I ask."

I tried to come up with reasons against it and found I couldn't. Not really. Not with him. Deep down, I didn't just want to be engaged to Xavier Parker. I wanted him to belong to me and me to him. I wanted to be his wife. I wanted us all to be a proper family.

"All right."

I grinned as he leaned in to kiss me.

"All right?" he repeated into my lips.

"Yeah," I said. "Let's get married now."

"You fucking got it." He practically dove to the other side of the bed to grab his phone. "I'll call Els. She'll get everything ready. Find us a planner. We'll be married by the end of the month and—"

He stopped suddenly as he looked at his phone. The glow of joy on his face had all but extinguished.

Dread lodged itself in my stomach.

"What is it?" I asked. "Xavi, what's wrong?"

"This." He tossed his phone to me, where the screen bore the text of an email.

His Grace, the fourteenth Duke of Kendal, is officially summoned to the House of Lords to attend an inquest by the Committee of Selection to address questions regarding the entail of the dukedom of Kendal and its line of succession, including but not exclusive to the potentiality of alternative heirs and accusations regarding the veracity of marriage entail between the thirteenth Duke of Kendal, His Grace Rupert Parker, Baron of Cholmondeley and peer of the realm, and one Masumi Sato....

I looked up, barely able to parse the language that never seemed to contain more than a single extremely long sentence. "What is this? What does this mean?"

"I'm summoned to Parliament," Xavier said through his teeth. "It means Georgina has succeeded in getting enough lords to question whether I am Rupert Parker's legitimate son. She's convinced them the marriage certificate is a fraud. Just like she said she would."

"Oh, shit," I muttered. "Xavi, that's horrible. How can she do that?"

"I'll have to go back for an interview with the queen herself," he said before grinding his teeth loudly. "Not to mention an inquiry with these tired old men who have been looking for ways to get rid of me since I was born."

He exhaled heavily, hard enough to disturb the covers over his waist. Even then, however, he straightened. Naked and tattooed, more warrior than chef, he still looked as noble as he ever had. As much a duke as anyone could be.

"Maybe I should just let them have it," he said.

"You can't do that," I replied. "Then Georgina would win."

"Ces." Xavier turned to me with eyes as blue as the sky. "I don't want to go back. I don't want to ruin things between us again. You and the babes are more important to me than any fucking title!"

"And you are more important to us than some stupid British bullies," I countered.

He leaned forward and buried his face in his hands. "I swear to God, I don't know what to do."

"Well, I do," I said. "This is your birthright. It's up to you what you do with it, but you can't let someone take it from you. Much less that horrible woman."

Xavier just shook his head, then keeled to the side until he could rest his head on my chest, allowing me to comfort him and stroke his hair.

"Go," I told him softly. "You have to go back. Your family needs you."

"Not without you. Because my family does need me. Right here."

I swallowed. I didn't want to go back to England. I didn't want things to be like they were before.

But he had to have learned. He swore he had.

I had to give him a chance.

"Your family will go with you," I told him. "We'll be at your side. It's called making a choice."

That light returned. Not a lot, but a little. Some glimmer of hope that warmed my belly and every other part of me.

"All right," Xavier said, sitting back up, full of resolve.

Solemnly, he lifted my hand to kiss my knuckle and the ring he'd placed there. Like the duke he was. Like so many noblemen before him.

"We'll stay in New York," he told me. "But first, you'll come with me to take care of business in Kendal."

"I will," I said with a small smile, though a bubble of dread formed in my stomach.

He kissed my hand again and smiled. "You will. But this time, you'll go as my duchess."

INTERLUDE II

Xavier

"**N**othing more from the selection committee? Or Bernard?"
I adjusted the buttonhole flower on my lapel. A pink
camellia, of course. It wouldn't be anything else. I peered
at myself in the floor-to-ceiling wardrobe mirror—one of the perks of
my suite at The Plaza was a mirror large enough for me. There was
something wrong. I couldn't put my finger on it. My hair was all right.
Not too much product, since Ces liked it soft enough to run her
fingers through. Tie straight. Cufflinks on.

I bared my teeth. Bright and white, nothing in them.

But something didn't feel right.

"Mate," Jagger asked beside me as he adjusted his tie in his reflection. "Is that really what you want to be worrying about on your
wedding day?"

Today, Jagger wasn't just my COO, but my best man, and he
looked the part.

"I don't want to be thinking about it when I'm at the altar," I said
as I combed through my hair again. A few stubborn pieces fell

forward. Normally, they would bother me, but I happened to know Ces loved the look of a floppy-haired Englishman. She had watched too many Hugh Grant movies not to. With the state of her libido these days, all I had to do was forget the wax and roll up my sleeves, and my girl would tackle me onto the bed like we were playing rugby.

I sighed and fought not to yank at my tie. Whatever was wrong, it wasn't with my appearance.

Jagger and I returned to the sitting room, where Elsie was running down the list of to-do items we'd made yesterday.

"Anything from the committee?" I asked.

She shook her head. "Nothing to me. I've been checking your mail daily. But I don't think Lord Ortham has managed to waylay them. His warning last month was the best he could give you, I'm afraid."

I scowled into another mirror near the lift, then waved away the concerns about Parliament. They could keep for another two weeks, when I was due in front of the committee. Today was for me. Ces and me. Nothing and no one else.

"What about the food?" I asked. "Was Adolfo able to find the Spanish mackerel for the starters? Or the cod roe for the udon? I heard there was a shortage."

"He found both through that new vendor you secured last week," Elsie confirmed. "The wine from Château de Colombe as well. The florist delivered all the camellias in the city to Chie, and the staff is ready and waiting. Everything is just as planned, boy. Don't worry your head."

"Like he's ever been able to stop that," Jagger remarked as he sat next to Elsie to tie his shoes.

I huffed. He might have been right. The problem with being in control all the time is that it's nearly impossible to hand things off to others when it means so much. Francesca and I had a wedding planner to manage the pseudo-elopement, but that didn't stop me from inserting myself into nearly every detail of what suddenly felt like the most important day of my life.

And why wouldn't it? We'd been through the worst, Ces and me. We'd earned this day, our bit of bliss, our twist of fate coming to be at last. I didn't want anything to ruin it.

"All right," I conceded as I checked myself in the mirror one last time.

I'd gone with a midnight blue tuxedo instead of traditional black at Kate's suggestion. Honestly, I never needed a stylist. This was more to get on the good side of at least one Zola sister. But I had to give it to her—she knew her stuff. Francesca always did love the color of my eyes, and this tux made them blaze.

"One more thing." Elsie got up, pulled a box out of her purse, and held it out.

"Els," I said, hands up. "You didn't have to do this. I'm supposed to give the guests favors, not the other way around."

"This isn't a favor. It's from your dear mum."

Something inside me froze. The hole that had been inside my heart since I was sixteen ached and widened a bit when I realized exactly what had been bothering me.

It was her. Mum. She was missing, and no amount of faffing over my appearance could fix that.

Somehow, Elsie had known. Or maybe Mum had known it would come to this one day and had asked her friend to be prepared.

Swallowing thickly, I opened the box to find a lady's brooch resting atop a black satin pocket square. Not terribly feminine—a simple, wavy gold bar cut with something that looked like scales. At the end, the bar flowered into a serpent's head with a sapphire for an eye. It was less ferocious, more beautiful. Quite fierce, really.

"Bloody..." I drifted off as I looked at it. "This was hers?"

"She gave it to me to keep for you until the right time," Elsie said. "She said it was a gift from your father."

I looked up. "*Rupert* gave her this?"

Of everything I'd ever heard of my parents' "courtship," tokens of love had never been a part of it.

Elsie sighed. "Your father did," she concurred. "I thought you might want to wear it on your special day. Keep her—and him—with you. If you don't like it, though—"

"I do," I interrupted. My throat felt like it was closing in as I picked up the pin and examined it, imagining my mother's touch on the same parts. "Thank you, Els. Help me put it on?"

Elsie preened as she took the brooch from me and easily fixed it to my lapel just below the buttonhole. To my surprise, it fit like it was meant to be worn with this suit on this day.

"Yeah, mate," Jagger said from the couch, looking it over. "You look top-notch, man. Perfect."

A real compliment coming from my flash friend.

"She'd be so proud of you, boy." Elsie clasped my face between her little palms, gray eyes shining behind round glasses. "Of the man you've become. But also of the world you've made for yourself with those girls. All she ever wanted was for you to be happy."

I swallowed hard again, then leaned down to kiss her soft cheek. "I couldn't have done it without you, Els. You've been my mum when she couldn't. Thank you."

"Oh, dear, dear. None of that." Elsie batted me away, then dabbed at her eyes with a handkerchief. "Though I will miss having you around."

I watched her fondly, wanting another way to show her my gratitude for everything she'd done in my life.

"You know you can just stay at Mayfair, Els. You don't have to keep your flat in Croydon after I move to New York for good."

Elsie was a stubborn old girl. She'd kept the same little house in South London where she and her husband had lived for the short time they'd had before he passed away. Heart attacks, man. Lethal.

"Oh, no, I don't need anything that fancy, goodness me," she said. "Can you imagine me living in that castle of yours? I'd be expected to pop over to Buckingham Palace for tea, wouldn't I?"

I chuckled. "Just say the word, Els. I don't know if we're going to sell it yet, but until then, it'll just be sitting there empty. You might as well have use of it."

"What about me?" Jagger asked. "How come I don't get an invitation to the palace too?"

I snorted. "Mate, with what I pay you, you should be able to buy Buckingham Palace if you want it."

Granted, the same applied to Elsie's salary, especially now that she was promoted to CFO of the Parker Group, but she wouldn't have wanted me to point that out, even in front of Jagger.

My friend just smirked knowingly and stroked his goatee. "True. The girlies in Camden would miss me too much if I left, anyway."

"You really don't think you'll come back again after the title is settled?" Elsie wondered. "I should imagine you'd want to keep a home in London."

I mumbled something about yes, maybe, but truthfully, I wasn't sure. We could maybe fix up the flat in Croydon or find something smaller near Hyde Park. But London was feeling less and less like home these days—probably because my real one lived on this side of the ocean. Maybe one day, I'd convince Francesca to try relocating again. But despite the fact that there wasn't a decent pub in New York and I couldn't find a good pasty if my life depended on it, I wasn't sure I cared so much about living in London anymore.

I'd finally learned the truth: that family meant more than the right food or buildings or accents or the rest. Family meant who'd be there for you no matter what, who'd show up when you needed them, every time.

I didn't have that in England. Maybe with Jagger and Els, sure. But Ces had a whole mass of them here, and therefore, so would my children. I couldn't deny them that. The Zolas were still coming round to me—I had a feeling that Matthew was itching to break my nose if he could. But I knew it was only a matter of time before they accepted me as one of their own.

Turns out, I could be patient after all.

In fact, I was looking forward to it.

"Xav," Jagger pulled me out of my thoughts as he stood and nodded toward the lift. "It's time, mate."

I straightened and adjusted my tie once more, almost like I was going into battle. At the very least, the unknown.

See, I'd been a lot of things in my life.

Son. Bastard. Heir.

Friend. Chef. CEO.

Duke. Father. Fiancé.

I'd chased them all with everything I had, poured my blood, sweat, and sometimes even tears into every label.

But husband felt like the most important title of all. And I was determined to do it right. To only hold it once.

"All right," I said. "Let's find Francesca. I'm ready to make my girl into my wife."

TWENTY-TWO

Francesca

"I don't know, Frankie. I just don't know."

Even as she was getting me ready to walk down the aisle, Lea still couldn't help voicing her misgivings.

It had been two weeks since Xavier had proposed in the dark of night in my basement. Two weeks since he'd declared he'd make me his duchess and take me back to Kendal. And in those two weeks, everything had changed.

My man had been a flurry of action that extended to the rest of our life together. Xavier had moved upstairs properly, though he had insisted on exchanging his spacious king mattress for Matthew's old double bed. I didn't argue. After all, we made good use of the space, asleep or not.

The day after we told Sofia the good news, a wedding planner had turned up at my front door, prepared to take over my life and expedite our marriage. Meanwhile, Xavier had transformed the basement into ground zero to run both his restaurant empire and prepare for his meeting with Parliament, though neither was anything he wouldn't interrupt for dinner at Nonna's or taking me out on several more dates as we continued our reunion.

Now I sat in front of the vanity in Joni's bedroom, having my hair teased out of hot rollers while the rest of my family was a bustle of activity in my grandmother's house, helping me get ready for my wedding in a thousand other ways.

"Oh my God, Lea, give it up," Kate called from across the room where she was working at a hastily set up craft table. "She's getting married to the father of her children. Xavier finally got his head out of his butt and made things right. The man even subjected himself to your soggy manicotti to apologize to our entire family for what's gone down. What more do you want from him?"

Kate was busy sewing last-minute alterations on the wedding dress she'd found for me at an auction. It wasn't easy—my quickly changing shape required new measurements every time I tried it on until, at one point, Kate had thrown up her hands and declared she would sew me into it on the big day.

"My manicotti is *not* soggy," Lea said as she gently coaxed another curl from a roller.

Both Kate and I coughed.

Lea frowned and pulled a little too hard on the next curl.

"Ow!" I reached up to lightly smack her hand. "That hurt!"

"So did the jab. That was Nonna's recipe."

"Well, it wasn't Nonna who made it," I said, earning a guffaw from Kate. "Ow! Fine, fine, your manicotti was just fine. I'm the bride here, in case you forgot. You're supposed to be nice to me."

Lea grumbled but went back to her job more gently.

Everyone in my family had a job today. Lea was in charge of hair and makeup since she had almost finished cosmetology school before she and Mike had their first. Marie, back from Paris for the weekend, was keeping track of the caterer and pastry chefs, putting her own final flourishes on the food when Xavier could not. Joni was charged with getting the party started at the reception now that she was off crutches. Nonna was providing all my special somethings. She had gifted me a new lace garter and an old pair of pearl earrings that used to be her mother's and lent me a beautiful pearl clutch she used at her own wedding, in which she had enclosed a blue handkerchief that had belonged to Nonno. Matthew, of course, was walking me down the aisle while his wife, Nina, oversaw the flower arrangements.

Xavier had told me none of the extra work was necessary. He insisted on footing every bill, and the wedding planner Elsie had found assured me money was no object. Every last detail could and would be hired out. It was as if I could flick a wand and have my will be done. But it didn't feel right, somehow, to get married without having my family contribute. Zola affairs had always been group projects.

And this wasn't only about me and Xavier. He wasn't just marrying me, but the chaotic clan that came with. For years, I'd been supported by my sisters, my grandmother, my brother. They had raised Sofia and me together. I wanted them all to have a piece of letting me go.

"What's Lea bitching about now?" Joni asked as she swanned in, wearing her choice of bridesmaid dress, blush-pink silk that still managed to look revealing and slightly too tight despite its floor length.

That really was Joni's magical power—she could inject her brand of sexy charisma into a circus tent, and people would think it was the hottest new trend. I shook my head in minor awe as I accepted the "virgin mimosa" (orange juice with seltzer) she held out to me.

"She still thinks Frankie should wait," Marie said as she followed her in, carrying a sample of foods on a tray. "Here, try these. The caterer stopped by with some samples before heading downtown."

"I do not," Lea said as she pinned a few locks together at the back of my head. "I just did her lips for the big day. And use a straw on that juice, by the way, so you don't smudge your mouth. Anyway, I wasn't talking about the marriage when I said I didn't know—it's about time Xavier made an honest woman out of her. I was talking about the hair. It should be bigger."

"I already told you, I don't want a beehive," I argued. "I'm not trying to look like Priscilla Presley."

"But you're so much shorter than him! You don't want to look like a child bride in your pictures, Frankie."

"Lea," I said in the no-nonsense teacher's tone that I'd been using more with my family over the past two weeks than any child in three and a half years. "I am not interested in looking like a nineteen sixties go-go dancer or a place where local bees might want to hibernate. Xavier is fully aware of our differences in height. Honestly, I think he likes it. And I'm fine with it too. Besides, I'll be wearing heels."

"Big ones too!" Kate called across the room.

"See," I said. "We'll be fine. Just do it like we practiced, please."

Lea grumbled something unintelligible but obediently pulled my hair apart and re-pinned it with a decidedly less hive-like appearance.

"Crap," she said, shaking an empty bottle. "I'm out of hairspray. Hold on, I'll see if Nonna has some more downstairs."

She left the room, and Marie took a seat on one of the folding chairs beside me, checking over her shoulder for Lea before offering me one of the hors d'oeuvres.

"Thank you," I said gratefully before popping a salmon puff into my mouth. "Dang, that's good. I'm starving."

"Of course you are," Kate remarked. "You're baking a baby over there."

"That was good. Let me try the other one. What is it?"

"Goat cheese mousse with shaved endive," Marie said as I chomped down. "Pasteurized, of course. Xavier's orders. I think it turned out pretty well."

"Indeed, it did," I said, reaching for the last one on the tray.

"You know, you could wait," Marie said quietly enough that Kate wouldn't hear. "On the wedding, I mean. You still have time."

I swallowed my bite and examined her. "Why would I do that?"

Marie set the tray down on the dressing table and immediately started fidgeting with the collar of her own pink dress. True to form, it was also floor length, though to my surprise, the design included a slit to the knee that showed off one of my sister's legs. It was probably the most revealing thing Marie had worn since childhood.

"Just in case," she said. "It *is* fast. If you didn't want to stay here, you could come to Paris with me. You and Sofia both. Have your own adventure without him, but stay close enough to London that you could see him when you want. Really, I have loads of space. The Lyons family gave me their apartment in St. Germain for the year, and it's really more like a house in the middle of Paris. There are about a thousand bedrooms, and—"

"Oh, Mimi," I said, dropping my hand over hers. "I so appreciate that. I really do."

It sounded truly amazing, living in one of the most vibrant districts in Paris. Two months ago, I might have jumped at the invitation.

"But I have no reservations here," I told her. "I cannot wait to marry Xavier. I cannot wait to start our life together." I tipped my head as something else occurred to me. "Marie, is everything okay out there? Is that why you're asking me?"

An odd expression crossed my sister's face—something between happiness and jealousy. It pinked her cheeks in a way I hadn't seen before, only adding to the general impression we'd all gotten yesterday when she arrived from LaGuardia, looking like a completely different person.

The waist-length, mousy hair she typically tied into a bun had been cut to her shoulders in shiny, natural waves. Her glasses had disappeared, her nails were trimmed and manicured, and the shapeless sack dresses traded for more form-fitting if still conservative clothes that revealed a delicate bone structure and tiny waist. The changes were subtle, but it was obvious that the whole was more than the sum of its parts.

Marie was quietly transforming from a bit of an ugly duckling into an elegant swan—and she was doing it on the other side of the world, away from her entire family.

I wasn't sure how I felt about that.

"It's...different over there," she admitted. "In a lot of ways. Sometimes I do miss home."

"Well, the difference looks good on you," I told her honestly. "I didn't have a chance to say anything yesterday when you arrived, but you look amazing. Paris suits you."

Marie's cheeks flushed even more as she bit back a smile. "I had to get contacts," she said. "Too many things splattered my lenses. And it was either cut my hair or net it every day. I didn't want to look like a lunch lady. Joni already teases me enough."

I grinned. "Joni can take a swim in the Hudson. It's very chic. You look like Marion Cotillard." I leaned closer. "Is any of this maybe inspired by...someone?"

"A guy, you mean?" Marie asked.

Her blush deepened even more. It made her look genuinely beautiful.

"I see," I said with a grin. "So all this *is* for a guy."

"It's not for a *guy*," Joni interrupted as she flopped into a chair next to Marie. "It's for Daniel Lyons. I told you that."

Now Marie was positively tomato red. "Shut up, Joni. It is not."

"There is zero chance you got over him in less than three months," Joni retorted. "You've been *obsessed* with him forever. Writing his name and your name with little hearts all over your recipe book. Since you were sixteen!" She turned to me. "That's like eight years."

"Nine," Marie corrected petulantly. "I'm a year older than you. Sixteen plus *nine* is twenty-five."

"I can do math," Joni sputtered, though she was clearly embarrassed by Marie's dig at her less-than-stellar arithmetic skills. "And ten months is not a year."

"Hey, hell cats. Can we not on my wedding day?" I put in.

Both sisters glared at each other but then simultaneously relaxed in a silent truce.

"I'm going to get another mimosa." Joni got up and practically danced out of the room—or at least as well as she could on her bum knee. "But don't let her lie to you. It's more than just a haircut."

Marie watched her like she'd enjoy tripping her, but when she turned back to me, she didn't meet my eye.

"Is it true?" I asked. "Is this whole transformation about your boss?"

I hadn't been around that much since Marie started working for the Lyons family at sixteen. By that point, I'd already started college and wasn't particularly interested in my baby sister's part-time job. But I knew she worked for a prominent New York family who owned about half a dozen industries based out of New England and whose sons were regulars in the *Post*. Daniel Lyons's name had been bandied about our house for years—all of us knew about Marie's crush. I just hadn't known it actually went this deep.

"No," she said quickly. "Daniel's not in Paris. He's not even in New York right now—I think he's in Los Angeles, chasing an actress or model or someone."

She looked up and flushed when she caught both Kate and me watching her. As if she knew she had just betrayed her own infatuation.

"Anyway," she continued, "if it had been to impress Daniel, I would have done it earlier, don't you think? Back when I actually saw him every now and then."

I decided not to press her too much on the matter. "Makes sense."

"But I wouldn't mind if he saw it," she admitted a moment later. "And I wouldn't mind if he liked it, too."

And there it was. Well, at least she knew it.

"Can I ask you a question?" Marie said.

I smiled and patted her hand. "Shoot."

She frowned and worked her lips in a circle while she measured her words. "Xavier's...well, he's kind of like Daniel. In the way he's good-looking, but also kind of rich—"

"I think you mean stupid rich," Kate put in sardonically from her craft table.

"And—and also a duke, so I'm guessing he could, um, well, I'm guessing lots of types of women would be interested in him, and..."

"Are you asking how someone like me ended up with someone like him?" I asked gently.

"Seriously, Mimi?" Kate wondered. "What kind of question is that on her wedding day?"

Marie sighed. "I don't mean that you're not pretty enough or worthy of him, Frankie—that's not at *all* what I'm saying—"

"I get it," I interrupted gently. "It's just unlikely. I know. Because you're right. Before me, Xavier definitely got around, usually with semi-famous, rich, very beautiful women and all of that. So why did he end up with me, someone who isn't a superstar? Someone who is just normal. Right?"

Marie nodded weakly. Maybe a little gratefully as she avoided the daggers Kate was glaring her way.

I searched for that seed of doubt that always seemed to bloom whenever thoughts exactly like that struck. It was still there, but the truth was, it had been starved more and more over the past few weeks. I barely noticed it anymore.

Because I knew who Xavier was. I knew who I wanted to be. I knew what we were together. And at this point, I didn't have reasons to doubt that anymore. Because, like he said, we were choosing each other, and we would do that every day.

So I just shook my head and decided to be honest.

"I don't know," I told her. "All of those differences should have gotten in the way. And they very nearly did, as you know. We probably shouldn't have made it. But now that we're here, all I can say is that when you find your person, the rest of the world kind of fades away. He chose me, and I chose him, and now, all that other stuff just...doesn't matter."

I shrugged. I didn't know how else to explain it other than that.

Unfortunately, it didn't seem to soothe Marie.

"Well, I know there's no chance there," Marie said. "Daniel's a Lyons. He barely knows who I am, and I've worked for his family for almost a decade. I'm just a servant who makes the asparagus soufflé he likes on Sundays. It's all right. I'll get over him sometime." She offered a weak little smile that made my heart squeeze for her. "That's what Paris is for, I think."

"All right, I got it." Lea burst in, holding a can of Aqua Net. "If this doesn't hold, nothing will."

"Well, it makes Nonna's hair into a helmet every day, so I think she'll be fine," Kate said.

I just sat still as Lea finished pinning my half-updo, which still left a good number of dark tendrils curling over my shoulder, and sprayed the hell out of it.

"Perfect," she said approvingly.

I smiled. "It really is. Nice work, sis."

"Frankie," Kate called, holding up the dress with a few pins sticking out of her mouth. "It's time."

I crossed the room and allowed Kate and Lea to help me into my wedding dress, then stood still while Kate sewed the final seams together. When she affixed the waist-length veil to my hair, I had to avoid Marie and Lea, who had grown quiet, eyes shining as they watched.

"Don't say a word," I said to them through the old mirror over the vanity. "Don't make me cry, Lea."

"Oh, Frankie." For once, my oldest sister didn't have a critical word for anyone. "You look *perfect.*"

When Kate finished, I turned to the floor-length mirror hung over the door to look myself over. And damned if Lea wasn't right.

Somehow Kate had found the dress of my dreams—the 1960s-era sleeveless gown was nothing I'd ever imagined, but also exactly what I would have chosen for myself. A row of silk flowers marked an empire waist that called back to the dress styles of Jane Austen. Kate had sewn an additional layer of delicate lace over what she said was shantung—a roughly woven type of silk that showcased irregularities in the weave. Perfectly imperfect. Just like Xavier and me.

"Oh, Katie," I said. "You did *good.*"

"Don't cry!" Lea sprang toward me, tissue in hand. "You'll ruin your eye makeup. Those cat-eyes are perfect!"

I laughed but dabbed under my eyes just the same. There was a knock on the door. When it opened, my brother poked in his handsome head. Matthew wore another dapper suit that had to be new—none of the vintage pieces he'd gotten from Kate's shop looked *quite* that polished.

It had to be nice being married to an actual heiress.

I pinched my own arm. I was about to marry a duke, for Pete's sake. Not a lot of room to criticize Matthew on that count.

"Car's here," Matthew said as he adjusted the camellia pinned to his lapel. "Nonna already left with Sof, Joni, and Nina. Lea, Mike said he'd come next for you and everyone else." Then he looked up. "Holy shit, Frankie. You look...you look fuckin' amazing."

I blushed under my brother's frank praise. "You'd better not let Sofia hear you talk like that. Fees for the swear jar have gone up since Xavier moved in, you know. We charge in pounds, not dollars."

"Tell her to put it on my tab." He held out an arm. "Ready?"

I grinned and slipped my hand around his elbow.

It was time to marry the man I loved.

TWENTY-THREE

I didn't actually know *where* I was getting married.

Don't get me wrong. I knew how it would work. Matthew would walk me down the aisle. The wedding party itself was a little uneven—Xavier's only real friend was Jagger, who was going to accompany Kate down the aisle as best man and maid of honor. Lea would walk with her husband, Mike, Joni and Marie would walk together, and then Sofia would follow, a flower girl to Tommy, my nephew, as ring bearer.

Where they were walking, though, was a complete mystery.

It was kind of strange, but Xavier had insisted it be a surprise. It was one of the few parts of the wedding planning he had actively taken part in—even more so than the food, which was being provided by the staff at Chie (where the reception would also take place). He'd been happy to share every detail he could about that, of course. But the ceremony, beyond my part in it, was still a mystery.

It wasn't until the Town Car stopped at the edge of Bryant Park that I realized where we were. And indeed, when the car pulled up in front of the familiar steps guarded by the seminal pair of stone lions, I knew there was only one place Xavier could give me in all of New York.

"He really is a beast," I murmured as Matthew got out.

"I have to say, he must know you well," my brother said as he helped me from the car. "You getting married at the New York Public Library is pretty damn perfect. Does he like books, too?"

I chuckled. "Not particularly. But he likes giving them to me. And he likes making me happy."

For the first time, Matthew nodded with what looked like approval of Xavier. "Well, at least he has that going for him."

My brother led me up the steps that had been lit with dozens of tea candles and scattered with bouquets of sweet smelling fall gardenias and camellias. He guided me through the marble archway, up the grand staircase, and through one of the outer reading rooms to the entrance of what was probably my favorite place in all of New York City: the famed Rose Main Reading Room.

I'd never told Xavier about it, but somehow, he knew. Just like he would have known how beautiful the Beaux-Arts setting would be for a wedding, with its tall arched windows, curlicued gilt-carved ceiling, and the dozen or so chandeliers that looked like upside-down wedding cakes.

Music floated through the doors as my sisters followed us into the outer reading room. The wedding was to be held through the double doors, outside of which our little wedding procession was already starting to gather.

"Mama?" Sofia turned from where she stood next to Joni and pulled at my hand.

I looked down to find my little girl staring at me with genuine awe. Dressed in her own frilly pink dress that (according to her) topped any of the costumes in her closet at home, Sofia had left long before I had finished getting ready at the house, so this was the first time she had seen me in my full wedding regalia.

"Where's your crown?" she asked, pointing to my head.

Gingerly, I touched the veil hanging over my hair. "My crown?"

"You look like a princess," she told me. "And Daddy says you're going to be a queen. So you need a crown."

My sisters chuckled.

"She has a point," said Kate. "I told you we should have sprung for a tiara."

I smiled as I bent down to look eye to eye with my daughter. "I think real royalty doesn't have to have a crown. If you're a queen, you know it in here." Gently, I touched Sofia's chest, making her giggle.

"Do you know it?" she asked me.

I glanced toward the open doors, through which I could hear the sounds of our small crowd chattering away, where my beloved waited for me at the end. "Yeah, baby. I do."

Sofia grinned as I stood up. "Good. Me too. We're gonna go get Daddy now, right?"

I grinned back and nodded. "Yep, now we get to be a real family."

But my daughter just shook her head. "We were always a family, Mama. We just had to figure it out first."

Before I could answer my wise-beyond-her-years daughter, she was ushered away by the wedding planner, who did her final check of me, handed over my bouquet of pink gardenias, then lint-rolled Matthew's shoulders before checking with her staff in the microphone.

"All right," she said into her headset. "Bride's a go."

With a wink and a nod, she opened the door to the reading room, where my brother escorted me up the red brick path that led straight to my heart's desire.

It was a small congregation for such a large room. Most of the reading desks were still in their places, filling the space the way a large number might. But we had chosen to keep things intimate. To the soft parochial tunes of a string quartet, I followed my sisters in their blush-colored dresses to the end of the aisle, where Xavier's and my collection of friends and family had gathered.

I barely saw any of them. My eyes were only on the man to the side of the officiant, standing taller than anyone else in a dark blue tuxedo that matched his bright gaze and made his black hair shine.

Xavier's eyes were stars as I made my way slowly to him. It was clear that just like I could see nothing other than his strong, shadowy form, I was the only light in the room for him.

"Who gives this woman?" asked the justice in accordance with the ceremony we'd written with him.

"I do!" Sofia shouted with glee, though she looked concerned when it caused a smattering of soft laughter from our guests.

"Me too," Nonna offered.

"And me!"

"I do!"

Eventually, all my sisters had offered their answers, eager to be a part of the joke until I was grinning so hard I could barely breathe.

"Jesus Christ," Matthew muttered, though even he couldn't hide a smile. "We all do, your honor."

The justice nodded with a smile of his own, then waited as Matthew lifted my veil and leaned down to press a brief kiss to my cheek.

"Love you, Frankie," he said. The green eyes that matched my own shone with something like tears.

"Mattie," was all I could say. "Thank you, big brother. For everything."

He knew what I meant.

Then I turned and took Xavier's arm, allowing him to guide me the rest of the way until we stood with our hands clasped in front of the justice.

His gaze trailed slowly down my dress, then back up with the blazing blue fire I had come to know was mine alone.

"You look stunning," he whispered. "Am I really this lucky?"

"You gave me another library," I whispered back with a blush. "I think you were ready for it."

Xavier's grin lit up the entire room. "You once told me there's a whole world in a single book."

My own happiness was practically splitting my face in half. "So I did."

"Well, I don't want to give you the world, Ces. I want to give you millions of them." He nodded toward the endless shelves around us. "You and Sof and the little one in there. You're *my* whole world. The only one I'll ever need. But I'll never stop trying to give you the rest."

The ceremony moved quickly. We'd opted for simple. No readings except a poem read by Kate and then our vows. By the time we were finished, Xavier looked ready to carry me out of the room over his shoulder, practically bursting at the seams to grab me.

"I now pronounce you husband and wife," said the justice. "Er, you may kiss the bride."

"About bloody time," Xavier growled as he yanked me across the aisle, lifted me off my toes, and landed a soul-searing kiss that had me very glad we weren't in a church—a priest would have been utterly scandalized.

"Me too, me too, me too!" crowed Sofia even louder than the cheers from our audience.

Xavier broke our kiss long enough to sweep Sofia up in one arm, allowing her to throw her little arms around both our necks and cackle as she pushed us together for yet another kiss.

"Mine at last," Xavier murmured before his lips met mine.

His at last, I thought, as all faculties for speech had been effectively cut off. *And ours, for always.*

———

THE PARTY MOVED SWIFTLY to Chie, which was only five blocks away in the heart of midtown. The restaurant, with its pinks and purples, was alight with flowers, its furniture completely rearranged to accommodate our guests and provide a small dance floor in the middle of the space where, eventually, Xavier and I would go through all the other milestones for a pair of newlyweds. We spent the first hour or so greeting our guests, accepting completely unnecessary envelopes from my relatives, and letting great-aunts and distant cousins kiss both of us on our cheeks and remark on how very tall "Frankie's man" was.

It wasn't until everyone was settled and we were digging into the second course of the evening, a salad of fresh mizuna and feta in a sesame vinaigrette, that Xavier and I finally had a moment to ourselves.

We hadn't stopped touching, of course. If Xavier's arm wasn't slung over my shoulders, shepherding me close to his side, his hand was toying with my hair, slipping around my waist, or reaching for my knee.

"No champagne?" I asked as Xavier took yet another sip of water.

He shrugged. "If you're not drinking, neither am I."

"You don't have to do that."

"Yes, I do," Xavier said before pressing a kiss to my lips. "We're in this together, babe. Top to bottom."

It was then I realized that more of the reception had been planned for me as well. Despite the fact that the restaurant primarily served Japanese fusion, there wasn't a piece of raw fish in sight. Nor was there anything else in the way of cured meats or raw cheeses. Nothing a pregnant woman like me couldn't enjoy.

For at least the twentieth time that night, I wanted to tackle Xavier into a back room and show him *exactly* how much I appreciated his thoughtfulness. By the look on his face, he was more than ready to accept my thanks as well.

Alas, too many guests.

There would be time for that later.

"Are you sad that more of your family didn't come?" I wondered as he played with my fingers, watching my engagement ring and its matching band gleam under the candlelight.

Xavier's side of the aisle had been woefully small. Mine was bursting with extended family, cousins, family friends from up and down Arthur Avenue, as well as a few from school. I wasn't Miss

Popularity, but it was warming to see just how many people wanted to wish me well.

Xavier's side, however, had consisted of a handful of people from his old neighborhood, a few work colleagues, Jagger, Elsie, and, to my surprise, Frederick.

Xavier was quiet for a moment but offered a shrug in response. "Everyone who matters to me is either gone or here," he said. "But you can see why I don't mind leaving. I see what you have here. I suppose maybe now I want to be a part of that too."

I nodded. "Well, you're stuck with us now. The Zolas are pretty ride or die, so hopefully you don't regret it."

He lifted my hand and pressed a reverent kiss to my knuckles. "Never."

"Might I offer my congratulations?"

Xavier and I both turned to find Frederick standing next to us.

His stepbrother was dressed like any other wealthy man might be in a dark gray suit and blue paisley tie. Even if I hadn't known him from before, I would have thought he was from out of town simply by the tilt of his head and the ramrod-straight posture.

"And best wishes, of course," he said as he leaned down to kiss my cheek. "It was a lovely ceremony. Truly."

Xavier glanced at me as if to ask, "What do you want to do?"

I shrugged. He was already here. Clearly, Xavier had invited him, and while I absolutely despised his mother, Frederick had never seemed anything but young and reasonably courteous.

Xavier pulled out Sofia's empty chair next to him (our daughter, of course, had been lost in the crowd with her cousins for a while now). Frederick took a seat and smiled when one of the servers brought over his place from where he had been seated with Jagger and Elsie.

"You know, I don't think I ever knew how prolific the Parker Group really was," Frederick said as he admired Chie's lush interior. "I remember your pub in the village, but I don't think I've ever gone to any of your spots in London. And there are more, too..."

"In Paris, Prague, Madrid, Berlin, among others," Xavier confirmed.

"So, er, how many restaurants do you actually have now?" Frederick wondered.

"This made fourteen," Xavier said somewhat cagily. "First in New York, but we've plans for more."

"Amazing," Frederick remarked, more to himself than to us.

Xavier just made a nondescript sound that I recognized as his "where have you been?" noise. I'd heard it several times whenever some random lord recognized him and acted like this big, strapping, extremely successful duke had appeared out of thin air.

"You're very lucky," Frederick went on. "I didn't realize what an empire you've built, but I'm so glad you have."

"Why's that?" I wondered.

Frederick took a sip of wine. "Because," he said eventually, "my brother here will always have something of his own. No matter what anyone might do...or take."

Xavier and I sat there for a moment. Neither of us seemed to know what to say.

"Anyway," Frederick said. "I just wanted to wish you both my best. You deserve to be happy, Xavier. Happy at last. And Francesca is wonderful. I mean that."

Without waiting for a response, he picked up his plate and glass and adjourned himself back to his table. Xavier watched him until I couldn't take the silence any longer.

"Well, that was nice of him," I said. "To say congratulations, I mean."

"That was more than congratulations, Ces," Xavier said wryly. "It was a warning."

I frowned. "A warning about what?"

He downed the rest of his water, looking very much like he wished it were something harder. "Of what's to come when the party's over."

TWENTY-FOUR

12 Oct 1985

Gardener says the camellias at the south end are dying —some sort of virus. Not sure.

The real news is from HG, back from his first session with the Lords, only to cause yet another scandal, which I have promised not to detail here, though the papers may not be so generous, despite our donations to their cause. Sufficed to say, the engagement to Lady Harwood has been called off, and it's most likely he shall have to weather the storm here in Kendal rather than resuming his place in town.

You can imagine how happy he is about that. The camellias are more cooperative, frankly.

M is pregnant.

So much for keeping promises.

Honestly, I don't know what to do.

———

"Ces? Ces, did you hear me?"

I looked up from the journal, which I'd been engrossed with ever since arriving in Kendal yesterday evening.

Xavier had surprised me yet again on our wedding night by booking not a lavish suite at The Plaza or some swanky penthouse, but instead the same room he'd occupied when we'd first met. The boutique hotel on Riverside was a far cry from a five-star place on Central Park and certainly wasn't up to Xavier's usual standards, but he teased he'd gotten used to smaller quarters after living in my basement for the last month.

Besides, tradition was tradition.

"And I want to fall in love with you all over again tonight," he pronounced as he picked me up and carried me across the threshold.

I couldn't argue with that.

The next morning, however, we went to Nonna's to kiss Sofia goodbye (she would fly to London with Elsie to give Xavier and me a few days on our own), then met up with Jagger at Teterboro and flew to Manchester, where Ben was waiting to drive us straight to Kendal while Jagger left for London.

It was quite a different entrance from the one I'd made the first time. For one, we arrived at the estate to find the entire staff waiting outside in a line, ready to welcome their duke home again.

"Is this always how they greet you?" I asked nervously as Xavier helped me out of the car.

"It is when I come home with a bride," he said with a purely piratical leer.

Then he turned to the row of people who made the estate function, pulled me in front of him, and introduced me to everyone as the new Duchess of Kendal.

The men bowed.

The women curtsied.

I felt like I was on the set of a BBC drama. And desperately in need of some etiquette lessons.

The next morning, after a long night spent rechristening our bedroom and sleeping in far too late, Xavier and I were cozied up in his office while he went over the accounts that Frederick had overseen in his absence, and I dove into another of Henry's journals.

"What's got you so interested over there?" Xavier asked from his desk. "You're making the same sounds as when you discover a new Marvis flavor."

He wasn't particularly stressed. That was good news. It meant that in spite of his stepmother's best attempts at interfering, Frederick had done right by the place while Xavier had been gone.

I paged forward, hoping that Henry would elaborate on whatever scandal was happening that ruined Rupert's impending marriage. It didn't seem to be related to Masumi's pregnancy, especially since he said point-blank that he wouldn't write down the details. But then again, wasn't that scandalous enough?

"Well, for one, you've finally made an appearance," I said. "Your mother showed up again in Henry's journals. And now she's pregnant."

"Ah." Xavier seemed oddly uninterested in the revelation.

I put the journal down. "Don't you want to know what he said?"

My husband—it was still surreal to call him that—just shrugged his big shoulders. "I already know what happened. I was there, wasn't I?"

"Well, not yet, you weren't." I picked the journal up again and re-scanned the section. "Do you know of any sort of scandal that happened in 1985? Regarding your father, I mean?"

Xavier snorted. "Besides my conception?"

My shoulders slumped. "Just listen." I read the section out loud, then looked up, expecting a remark. Maybe an elaboration. Something more than the blank look I was facing.

Xavier just shrugged again. "It sounds like he convinced himself not to describe how my father had knocked up Mum, then thought otherwise at the end. Also, sounds like Dad and I had more in common than he let on."

I frowned. "How do you mean?"

"'Yet another scandal,' didn't he say? You don't want to know how many times I was told *not* to embarrass the family. God, I wish I'd have known about this back then. Way to be a fucking hypocrite, Dad."

I sat back in my chair, somewhat disappointed with his cavalier attitude. Or maybe it was the fact that he'd undone my suspicions with a single guess.

Xavier seemed to sense my disappointment, so he set aside the ledger and flicked his finger at me. "Come here, let's have a look."

I joined him at the desk, only to be pulled unceremoniously into his lap. Henry's journal was plucked from my hand and tossed to the floor before I was thoroughly ravished.

"Put that away," he said, burying his face in my neck. "It will keep. You won't."

"Ah!" I squealed as his long nose found its way down my shirt. "I was looking at that!"

"And now you're looking at *me*."

He swiveled around, then heaved me up so I was sitting on his desk. Immediately, my mouth was captured by a kiss that made all thoughts of journals, pregnancies, dukes, and scandals evaporate completely. My hands slid into the silky softness of Xavier's hair while I lingered in his musk, enveloped in his taste.

Lord, the man could kiss. And he really was all mine.

After nearly every thought in my head had been completely obliterated, Xavier sat back in his chair and surveyed me, looking rather like a king peering over an expanse of kingdom he had just conquered.

"Wouldn't you know it?" he said with a devilish cock of his head. "I'm a bit famished."

I bit my lip. "Haven't you had enough? You only kept me up all night. And the night before. And the night before that. I haven't gotten up before noon for days."

He responded by peeling off my leggings and underwear and tossing them to the floor beside the journal.

"There's never enough Francesca," he rumbled before delivering another soul-searing kiss. "I'm addicted now, you see. *And* a newly-wed. Every few hours, I need my hit of sweet new bride. Right here on my ancestors' furniture."

I giggled but did nothing to stop him as he undid the top buttons of my shirt—which happened to be one of his, since most of my shirts were suddenly too small—and settled his mouth on one breast while sliding a hand up and over my clit.

"Oh!" I gasped as one long finger slid inside me.

Xavier's teeth bit lightly before he released my nipple and kissed me instead.

"Lie back," he ordered, pushing me down until I did as he said and lay splayed completely across the enormous mahogany surface. He spread my legs farther, then lifted them over his shoulders and pulled my hips to the edge, like he was about to attend to a feast.

Which, apparently, he was.

"Touch yourself," he ordered, pulling my hands to my breasts. "Pinch them a bit and pull. I know you like that."

I found myself obeying once again, using one hand to toy with my bared nipple and the other to take a handful of his hair while he bent to his work.

"Oh!" I gasped as his tongue slid over that most sensitive spot—more sensitive now than ever due to the raging hormones of my second trimester.

Seriously, two swipes and I was ten seconds to heaven.

My head met the desk with a thump as Xavier went to work, proving to me yet again just how much *taste* the man really had.

"I know he said that, but honestly, Gibson, it will just take a moment!"

My eyes flew open at the sound of an extremely proper, petulant, and extremely unwelcome voice in the hall. The door creaked open, and I opened my eyes just in time to see a flash of round gray eyes, fair skin, and feather-soft blond hair.

Imogene Douglas's shocked face peeked through the door and, to my surprise, didn't immediately move.

"*Fuck*, Ces."

Xavier appeared to be too lost in, well, *me* to notice our intruder. And with his other hand locked around my waist in an iron grip, I certainly wasn't going anywhere.

Unable to stop myself, I offered our voyeur a satisfied smile. She started, like my acknowledgment of her presence was akin to a jolt of lightning.

"Yessss," I hummed, gripping Xavier's hair and pulling ever so slightly.

In response, I received a most animal growl.

"Babe," Xavier hummed against my flesh, "you taste *so* fucking good."

It was the key to my undoing, audience or no. My back arched off the desk, my eyes squeezed shut, and it was everything I could do not to scream as pleasure flooded my body in hot, heavy waves. Xavier's tongue continued its magic until my body was a sponge, every drop of ecstasy squeezed out, and I was left limp, lifeless, and completely satisfied there on his desk.

A meal completely consumed.

When I opened my eyes, Imogene was gone.

"That ought to keep her away for a good while." Xavier sat back in his chair and removed a handkerchief from his pocket to dab at his mouth as if he'd just finished a particularly wonderful meal.

I sat up on my elbows. "You knew she was there?"

Xavier chuckled, then gently pulled me back up so we were nose to nose once more. "I knew, yeah. Just like I knew you didn't mind the show, you little minx."

I flushed even as I gave a half-hearted shove in response. I wanted to argue, but he was right. I hadn't. In fact, I had been more than happy to let the interfering brat see exactly what she was trying to get in the middle of. That a man like Xavier Parker wanted to get down on his knees for someone like me. That he had made me his duchess for all to see.

"Do you?" I wondered. "Mind, I mean. I suppose I used you too a little."

"Do I mind you getting a bit territorial?" he posed. "Fuck, no. It's hot, but also, it's nice not to be the only one with a jealous streak for once."

Before I could respond, he cupped my face, urging me to look at him directly. All vestiges of humor were gone, leaving only pure, earnest love in his bright blue eyes.

"You do know you're it for me, right?" he said. "That you've nothing to worry about? Not with her, not with anyone else. I know it's scary facing all this again. But it won't be forever, and in the meantime, *you* are the most important thing to me. Do you believe that?"

I watched him but nodded almost immediately and was rewarded with a smile of singular sweetness. It was an easy thing to believe. Even if it was forever. Even if we had to stay in Kendal and be gentry or even do something else completely different than either of us had ever imagined.

We had each other now. And somehow, I knew that wasn't ever going to change.

"I know," I told him. "Though I don't mind it either when you go out of your way to demonstrate it to any naysayers."

His black brow rose sardonically. "Is that right?"

A blush warmed my cheeks and neck. "Could be."

"Minx," he mouthed again before kissing me once more.

Then he stood, allowing his tall form to cast its shadow over my body, which I found was humming with anticipation all over.

"Well, if you need me to demonstrate it again, my beautiful duchess," Xavier said as he reached down to unbutton his trousers, "I've got a few things in mind."

TWENTY-FIVE

Xavier took an hour before dinner to train in the estate's gym, so I decided to go for a walk around the grounds, even dressed as I was in comfortable leggings and one of his enormous shirts belted around my waist. Apparently, men's dress shirts made perfect maternity wear. Who knew?

It occurred to me that I had generally kept my exploration of Kendal to a minimum over the summer, venturing only where Sofia was interested in going, which was mostly the sheep paddocks and the library Xavier had "given" me. But this whole place was mine now too, in a way. And one day, might belong to the little one inside me. He'd share it with his sister—I'd make sure of that. But the title, the management, all of it would be his if he made the choice to take it on.

And I *would* make sure he had a choice. Neither Xavier nor I would ever force this little lord to be anything other than what he wanted. Should he decide that washing windows was his bliss, I'd be the one to provide the very best bucket and rags.

In the meantime, I knew it was time to stop shying from the place and learn to take charge—starting with a tour of the back gardens, which I'd never really explored beyond the library patio.

I didn't get far, however. Just as I started to round a particularly tall boxwood hedge, two voices stopped me in my tracks.

"I don't know what to tell you," Frederick was saying. "He's married her. The ceremony was a bit unorthodox, but perfectly legal. It's done."

"But it *can't* be done." Imogene's voice was shrill and shaking, almost like she was crying. "She must have tricked him somehow. I'm sure of it."

"I'm very sorry to inform you, but there are no tricks involved. And you must have heard the rumors."

"Bah. What rumors?"

There was an awkward pause. "They are...expecting. Or so Mother has suggested. Don't ask me how she knows—I haven't the foggiest."

I peeked around the hedge just in time to see Imogene's jaw practically drop onto her lap where she was sitting on a bench, facing Frederick. She was too surprised to spot me, so I popped back safely behind my boxwood, shamelessly listening in. Honestly, after what she'd done, I had no qualms about a little eavesdropping.

"But there's been no announcement," she said. "And she doesn't *look* pregnant."

"Yes, but..."

"But what?" Imogene sounded for all the world like a little girl who'd been told she couldn't have ice cream before bed.

I could practically hear Frederick's nonchalant shrug in return. "Well, I was at the wedding. And the reception. And I noticed the bride failed to partake in any of the libations."

"She didn't?"

"Nor did Xavier."

"No!"

"And then, of course, there's the fact that her family isn't exactly discreet. I'm afraid there were several toasts to the bride, groom, and their, er, children. Plural. To great applause, I might add."

At that, Imogene didn't appear to have an answer at all.

I smirked to myself. *Take that, you brat.*

"My God," she said. "So she's really done it? Forced her way in and produced an heir all in one go. That is the next duke in her belly, isn't it?"

"Not if Mother has anything to do with it," Frederick remarked wryly. "It's why they're here, you know."

I made a face. Oh, we *definitely* knew. These stupid Parliamentary shenanigans were replacing my honeymoon, and I was not happy about it.

"Oh, please," Imogene argued. "Papa told me all about that, and *he* says the committee thinks it's a joke. They've only agreed to call the meeting as a ruse to please the old guard. They'll snap at him a bit, but then they'll let him go because the one thing they *really* want is for Xavier to take his father's spot in the House of Lords next year."

"Mmmph," Frederick replied.

Imogene just rattled on. "Papa said the Earl of Lonsbury, in particular, has had his eye on Xavier since your stepfather passed. One of only ninety-two hereditary peerages—they won't let him squander it. They want him to take his place, not to mention help modernize the party. Golly, can you just imagine it? Someone who looks like *Xavier* for the Tories?"

My mouth curled. I could practically taste the lust dripping off every syllable when she spoke about him. Clearly, *she* had imagined it plenty of times. With herself on his arm.

"You might want to try sounding a little less excited about the prospect. It's not polite to salivate."

I snorted. Frederick's dry tone matched the sardonic comments I'd been silently making to myself throughout the exchange.

"Did you hear that?" Imogene wondered.

"Not at all," Frederick said as I stepped farther behind my hedge.

"Are you saying you don't believe me?" she pressed. "Papa *is* on the committee, after all."

"I just wouldn't be so sure," Frederick replied. "Mama hasn't played all the cards up her sleeve. Lonsbury might want him, but there are plenty who don't. And if there is anything I've learned as Georgina Parker's son, it's *never* underestimate a Parker woman. The men are hapless dogs, but the women are wolves to the core."

Something in his final statement chilled me to the bone. Perhaps that was always what had seemed wrong about Georgina Parker. That, for all her ladylike composure, the woman really was ruthless. She had been on the hunt for me from the moment we met.

"Well, whatever she does, I believe I'll place my bets on the winning pony, Freddy. Xavier will come 'round and make the right decisions. I know he shall."

I'd had enough. I stepped out from behind the boxwood, arms crossed, ready for battle. "And which decisions would those be?"

Imogene jumped in her seat with a decidedly unladylike yowl. Frederick barely moved a muscle, only turned and greeted me with a shallow tilt of his head.

"Your Grace," he called. "Fine evening for a walk, is it not?"

"You—why you—you were listening the whole time!" Imogene screeched. "Freddy, do you believe her?"

Frederick looked as nonplussed as ever. Certainly not surprised as I approached. He only offered the same patented shrug I was starting to think was something they taught these boys at Eton. They all seemed to do it.

"Well, it is her garden now," he pointed out. "I daresay she's allowed to walk wherever she likes. Or listen to whatever she wants."

"It was very interesting," I said. "I came out here to listen to the birds and ended up hearing your squawking instead. What's the matter, Imogene? Didn't get enough of a reality check in Xavier's office?"

Her eyes blew into saucers. "I-I only—"

"You were only interfering," I finished for her. "Again."

Frederick frowned between us. "What does she mean, again?"

"Imogene likes to *watch* what goes on at Kendal, doesn't she?" I said. "Just like she really likes to have her *hands* on things. Even if they don't belong to her. Isn't that true, Imogene?"

Imogene just continued to gape at me as if I were a statue come to life.

"I suggest you stop boring Frederick with your plots and run along home," I told her. "I know my *husband* already said that you were no longer welcome. It's time to get the hell off our property."

"Your—*your* property!" Imogene stood in a rush, towering over me by at least three or four inches at her full height. "My family has been here for generations! You've been here five minutes! You are nothing but a *rude American!*"

I didn't back down, though. It helped that her eyes shifted nervously to my rings, which gleamed in the afternoon sun. But it helped more that I believed everything I said.

I didn't have to let any of these people walk over me. I had nothing to prove anymore.

"I know you love him," I told her. "And honestly, I don't blame you. He's very easy to love."

Her face started to heat visibly, while Frederick's gaze, still carefully flattened, continued to bounce between us with curiosity he couldn't quite hide.

"But if you ever touch my husband again," I said in a voice low enough that it forced her to lean down to my level, "you will learn just how rude Americans can really be. Right in that pretty nose of yours. You got me?"

It took her a second to fully comprehend that I had just made a physical threat on her person, then a second longer to figure out that I meant it. And I did. I might have been small, but I was strong. Not to mention raised in a house full of sisters and a brother who knew how to fight dirty. Catfights were something I was *very* familiar with. Pregnant or not, I would have no problem taking down someone like Imogene Douglas if it really came to that.

It didn't. Gradually, she took a step back, then another. She glanced at Frederick, then appeared to realize he wasn't coming to her proverbial rescue any time soon.

"Right," she said. "I'll just be on my way, then." She nodded to Frederick.

"I'll come 'round tomorrow," he replied.

But she was already fleeing the garden.

We both watched her go, waiting until her footsteps on the pebbled gravel were no longer audible in the deepening afternoon.

Then Fredrick turned to me and gestured that I might take her seat.

Gingerly, I did.

"I shouldn't have said that if I were you," he remarked.

"Oh?" I said.

Frederick examined his fingernails as though we were discussing the weather. "She doesn't seem that way, but in her heart, Imogene can be a vindictive little cunt."

I blinked. I didn't think I'd ever heard Frederick use such language.

"Like her mother, my mother, and all the rest of them, she is exceedingly scheming and conniving. Even better at planning her revenge." He cocked his head, like he thought he'd heard something. "She thinks I'm too young to remember what she did to Lucy."

I frowned. "Her sister?"

Frederick nodded.

I gaped. "She didn't—she wasn't the reason Lucy—"

"Died? God, no." He shook his head. "But she did cause her a fair amount of stress. I don't suppose Xavier told you about their failed engagement?"

Two months ago, something in me would have tensed immediately at the memory of his last engagement. But I found I trusted Xavier, just as he trusted me. Now, I was only full of curiosity.

"What happened?" I asked.

Frederick sighed, almost as if the entire affair bored him. "The Orthams always dreamed they might one day join their estate with the Kendal. When Xavier was announced as heir, they were over the moon about it. Mostly because he was already friendly with one of their girls."

"Just not the one he could make an heir with," I said wryly.

"No," Frederick said. "I suppose you could say they all found it rather insulting when, in the end, he got engaged to Lucy simply to spite the duke and give the girl a bit of romance before she died." He shrugged. "Rather nice of him, I'd say."

"How old was Imogene at that point, though?" I wondered. She was younger than me. She couldn't have been more than twenty.

"Old enough that she'd heard the talk of their imminent match for years." Frederick shook his head. "Imogene made Lucy's life bloody miserable there for a bit, just before things really went pear-shaped. She was so angry that he'd not only refused her but had gotten engaged to her sickly sister instead. Everyone knew Lucy wouldn't live very long—Lucy herself most of all. So to Imogene, it just felt unfair. An entire family's dream tossed to the side out of spite."

"Well, no one should have forced him to begin with," I said, feeling the need to defend Xavier. "He was already shoved into this world where he didn't belong, and suddenly everyone was pressuring him into essentially an arranged marriage. That's not fair to do to a twenty-five-year-old."

Frederick appeared to agree. "Indeed. But I still felt for the girl. She's always thought she was in love with him, waited forever for him to come back. She'd complain to me about it. It's very hard to love someone when they can never love you back, you know."

Something in his voice made me stop. It made sense then why she had come to Frederick, of all people, to act as a sounding board for her concerns.

Something else made sense too. Why else Frederick might have been listening to her nonsense at all.

"Do...*you*...love Imogene Douglas?" I wondered.

It was only a split-second, but the entirety of Frederick's blue-blooded being froze there in the garden before he resumed his typically stiff, yet nonplussed pose.

"Ah," I said. "I see."

He shot a sharp, brown-eyed glance my way. "I didn't realize you were so direct."

I shrugged. "Not always, but you people seem to bring it out in me."

Frederick seemed to relax more as he gazed in the direction Imogene had gone, as if he was envisioning the pair of them walking together. "I am four years younger than Imogene Douglas. She still thinks of me as barely out of nappies and knee socks. I can't imagine she would ever consider me as anything more than a sympathetic ear. And therefore, neither would I."

"I see," I said again. "Well, things change. She's young. You're young. Give it another few years. A four-year difference won't mean anything at all."

He seemed to think on that for several moments. Frederick, I noticed, rarely gave anything away. It was an unusual trait for someone so young.

"For what it's worth," he said at last, "I think you will be an excellent duchess. You may be exactly what this place needs."

I balked. Whatever I'd been expecting him to say, it certainly wasn't that. Ever.

"What's your deal?" I asked him. "Are you on your mother's side or not? You came to our wedding, so obviously you care about Xavier a little. But now I hear you gossiping with Imogene and practically plotting your stepbrother's demise."

"I was doing no such thing," Frederick said blandly. "I was simply conveying the different scenarios in play and the fact that my mother is a formidable woman." He looked at me pointedly. "I believe I offered the same message at your wedding."

I narrowed my eyes. "Walking a bit of a tightrope, are we?"

He just nodded, then got up from the bench. "I see you have finally learned the way things work around here, *Your Grace*, in a way my dear brother never has. Keep it in mind in the coming days. It will serve you well."

TWENTY-SIX

The next day, Xavier and I sat down for a late breakfast with my iPad in front of us while we waited for Elsie to answer her phone. According to her texts, she and Sofia were at Teterboro waiting for their flight to board for London.

A second later, my daughter's face splashed across the screen. Well, part of her face. Sofia, like most four-year-olds, was very good at giving a FaceTime camera an excellent view up her nose while she looked down at us.

"Hi, baby!" I cheered at her. "Are you ready for your flight with Elsie?"

"Yep," Sofia said. "And so is Tyrone! I gave him a really pretty pink bow for the journey."

Xavier nudged into the frame beside me, looking for Sofia's stuffed unicorn. "Show us his bow, babe. We want to see Tyrone in his Sunday best."

"It's not Sunday, Dad. Elsie says it's Tuesday. I think you might need a calendar."

I chuckled while Xavier made his amends for mixing up the days and paid Tyrone lots of compliments to scrub the disappointment off Sofia's face. Lord, she was like her father. No one got a break.

"He looks great, bug," I told her. "Have fun on your flight. Listen to Elsie, and we'll meet you in Mayfair when you get here, all right? Ben will be picking you two up right at the airport."

"Okay, Mama! Elsie, can I watch *McStuffins* yet?"

"Not until we're boarded, lovey. That's in about ten minutes." Elsie's motherly voice filled the room, followed by her face on the screen. "Everything's swimming along here. She's a pearl, as always."

"Thank you so much for taking her, Elsie," I said honestly. "Giving us a couple of days to ourselves after the wedding."

"Well, after the baby comes, you two should take a proper honeymoon. Consider me the volunteer nurse for the kiddies, all right?"

Xavier winked at me and grinned back at her. "Thanks, Els."

"See you lovebirds soon."

The call ended, and like he'd been waiting for the silence, Gibson approached, holding a tray.

"Some messages arrived for you this morning, Your Grace," he said in his patently droll manner. "And for you, Your Grace."

I almost jerked to find him looking at me with the address. I shouldn't have been surprised, but given our first interactions, it was a bit shocking that Gibson, with his familial pride and upright posture, would be the slightest bit happy to address an American interloper as his new duchess.

His face, however, bore no trace of resentment or even irritation with Xavier's or my presence. Yesterday, he'd addressed me the same, without a drop of irony either.

Gibson, the soul of tradition, was simply getting on with things.

"Sort of exciting, receiving a letter on a silver tray," I joked as I took my letter, contained in a simple white envelope. "Instead of text or email, I mean. Now I really feel like I'm in the middle of an Austen novel."

Xavier barely responded, engrossed already in the letter he'd opened with his butter knife.

"What is it?" I asked. "Good or bad."

He finished scanning the paper and set it down on the table. "It's from a member of the House of Lords. The Earl of Lonsbury, as it were."

I perked. "The one who wants you to take your father's place?"

Xavier looked up. "How did you know that?"

Quickly, I relayed the events of the previous evening to him while I forked a few pieces of kippered salmon onto my plate, along with some pickles. Xavier's eyes just grew wider and wider until I got to the end, when I'd informed Imogene of just how rude of an American I could be. Then he laughed, loud and hard.

"Fucking hell, Ces," he wheezed. "You didn't actually smack her, did you?"

I blushed and took a bite of salmon. "No. Wanted to, though."

"You're getting as bad as me. You really told her off like that, though?"

"Why, you think it's funny?"

"Not a bit," he replied with a grin. "I rather think cornering you would be like trapping a badger. They're small, but they'll scratch your eyes out if you don't take care."

I preened. I couldn't help it. "Well, she deserved it. I do feel a bit bad for her, though, after what Frederick told me later."

I continued the story with Frederick's odd remarks that I still couldn't quite make sense of.

"It does rather sound like he wants to have his cake and eat it too," Xavier agreed. "He left this morning to go back to Parkvale, where Georgina's staying. I'm honestly not sure what he's after."

"Let's be careful around him, then," I said. "Anyway, that's how I knew about Lonsbury. I gather he's a powerful man?"

"He heads the Committee of Selection and also sits on several other important ones, including horticulture, rural economy, and regulatory reform. Yes, he's bloody powerful in the Lords. And a major figure for the Tories."

He made another face that told me exactly what he thought about that—party or politics, I wasn't sure.

"So...what does he want?" I asked. "Besides you, of course."

Xavier twisted his mouth around like he'd just tasted something bitter. "He's asked me to meet him in London before the committee hearing about the title." He folded up the letter. "Can't, of course. Sof's arriving tonight."

Gibson remained standing at the far end of the room, but his eyes flickered to the folded letter like he wanted to take it away. Or perhaps help Xavier reply.

"Well, I can handle that," I said. "If you need to meet him. Maybe it would be good to see what he wants. Make sure he stays on your side of things."

"My side," Xavier repeated as he twisted his water glass back and forth. "If I knew what that was, I'd have something to bargain with, wouldn't I?" He shook his head. "No, I reckon it comes down to what Imogene said. Only I think the threat will be a bit clearer. Agree to take my seat for the conservatives, and they'll uphold my claim. Refuse, however, and they might be petty enough to strip the title using whatever Georgie's given them."

"Would they *really* do that?" I asked. "I mean, Parliament hasn't stripped a peer's title since 1917."

Xavier's mouth quirked with one of my favorite smiles—the one he bore when I knew far more about something than he would have expected.

I shrugged. "I did a little research."

"Thank God I married a bookworm." He leaned in to deliver a brief kiss. "Right, well. Technically, it wouldn't be removing the title or stripping it completely. They'd be...moving it to the rightful heir. Whoever they determine that to be."

"Frederick? Or could it actually be Adam?"

"I doubt it. Frederick is most likely, since that's what Georgie's aiming for. But honestly, I don't remember the birth order of the two cousins Georgina and her sister married and whose fathers were twins. Never really cared to know. And since Adam's father *was* disgraced, I don't think he'll factor in here." Xavier sighed and shoved his hands into his hair. "I've never wanted to be a politician. And to be honest, I haven't a clue why they even want me to join."

"Well, I do," I said as I reached for another helping of fruit. "It was all the events of the summer. You couldn't see yourself the way everyone else did. I know you were talked into going to help Frederick make the right connections, but my love, you have this habit of pulling all the attention in the room. You're like the sun with gobs of shining charisma. No one can look away."

"That's impossible. All those people hate me, Ces. Always have."

"Ever heard of the thin line between love and hate?" I asked. "I think you crossed it this summer. A couple of balls under your belt and a few good whacks with your mallet on the polo course, and suddenly everyone in the stands was drooling over you like a piece of prime rib."

Xavier frowned, clearly not liking the sound of that.

"Whether you intended it or not, you made quite the re-entrance into society. So, I have to agree with Imogene. It's obvious that everyone wants to see someone who looks and acts like you stepping in and modernizing things." I grimaced. "Trust me, I had to hear enough of them talk about it right in front of me. Including their opinions about having an unsuitable American girlfriend."

My obviously worried husband had the decency to look contrite. "I hate that they put you through that."

"It's over now," I said simply and meant it. We were moving on.

He leaned over and kissed me again, clearly not caring about the aftertaste of salmon or the lemon still lingering on my tongue. I didn't pull away. I would take as many of these humming kisses as he wanted to give.

"I don't deserve you," he said. "But I'll be damned if I let you go now, babe."

I could only grin in response as I reached for my letter, still unopened, on the table. But the second I opened it, my smile disappeared, as did most of the blood from my face.

"Ces?" Xavier put down his fork. "Babe, what is it?"

Wordlessly, I handed the letter to him.

Your marriage is a sham.
Leave him while you can.
Before I make you.

It was clearly typed, just like the last one, but was printed on a slightly different color paper. No signature. Nothing else to mark its sender other than the familiar three-line threat in curt, short prose.

"Gibson," Xavier barked. "Who delivered this letter?"

The butler's eyes popped open, and he practically jogged across the room. "I—I couldn't say, Your Grace. It was in with the rest of the mail this morning."

"And we don't have security cameras installed near the post?"

"I—no, Your Grace." Gibson looked like he believed he was solely responsible for that oversight. "The last was knocked out during a storm over the winter, and Lord Henry never thought it worth replacing, I'm afraid."

"See it's reinstalled at once," Xavier ordered, then turned back to the envelope.

"Did the PI ever come up with anything more about the last one?" I asked.

We'd been so busy planning the wedding I'd barely thought of it. But I knew Xavier had hired someone immediately after our talk with Derek.

"Nothing," Xavier said. "Your neighbor said the person who paid him called through a blocked number. He never saw him. The investigator agreed the others were likely just byproducts of the *Post* coverage."

The hair on the back of my neck flew up.

"You don't think..." I was starting to shiver. It couldn't be a coincidence.

But for someone to send them here. To find out where among all of Xavier's properties we were located, then take the time to find another local patsy to deliver the letter and make sure we would actually receive it.

This was much more than a simple prank. This was personal. And after my last conversation with Adam...there was only one person I could think of who wanted Xavier enough to try to scare me away. Someone who also knew we were here.

"You don't think it's from..."

"Imogene?" His face was grim. "It has crossed my mind."

I sighed. I didn't want to be a source of this kind of drama, but honestly, the girl had it coming if she wasn't going to step off from her little interlude last night.

"Gibson," Xavier asked. "Call the Orthams. Request that they join us for dinner this evening if the cook can accommodate."

"Certainly, Your Grace." Gibson left the room, and we continued to finish our lunch, though both of us seemed to have lost our appetites.

I'd only been in England for a few days, but suddenly I yearned for New York more than I ever had. Not because I didn't feel a sense of ownership here—I didn't over the house, but I certainly did over my husband. It was more the feeling of exhaustion. I just wanted to be done with the place. But I was starting to feel that, like a parasite, Kendal would never be done with us.

A few minutes later, Gibson returned.

"Your Grace, it appears the Orthams left this morning for Parkvale House. With Ms. Imogene."

Xavier's head snapped up. "Parkvale?"

"Yes, Your Grace."

"As in *my* Parkvale House?"

"Yes, Your Grace."

Xavier chewed on his lip a moment longer, then glanced at me. "Ces, didn't you say that Frederick meant to call round the Orthams this morning?"

I frowned. "He did say something about it to Imogene, yes."

"Christ." Xavier pushed violently back from the table, causing the ice to rattle in our water glasses and the cutlery to clatter on the plates.

"Where are you going?" I asked, though I had a feeling I already sort of knew. "What do you think is going on?"

"I think Georgina is doing her very best to turn Ortham against me. Not hard if his daughter's already feeling her worst."

I cringed. Crap, that had been partly my doing.

Xavier held out his hand and helped me up from the chair. "Don't feel bad. She had it coming, babe. And for what it's worth, I'd give anything to have seen her face when you told her where she could go."

I tried to smile, but it was hard. I honestly wasn't sure of what to say.

"Gibson," he barked. "You'll tell anyone who asks that we're still leaving for Mayfair."

"Of course, Your Grace."

"We're not going to Mayfair?" I asked as Xavier started towing me out of the room. "And we're leaving now?" We weren't supposed to meet Sofia at the house until much later.

"We are," Xavier confirmed both questions. "With a stop at Parkvale."

TWENTY-SEVEN

That was the first day I realized how quickly things moved in Xavier's world when he really wanted them to. Within fifteen minutes, he'd wolfed down the remainder of his lunch. Thirty more, and he'd left instructions for the staff in his absence, and another assistant of his had sent a helicopter to pick us up in one of the estate's paddocks, of all places. Less than two hours later, we touched down on a heliport practically a stone's throw from Mayfair just as the sun was starting to sink closer to the buildings guarding London's skyline.

Both of us were jittery with *something*. Excitement? Nerves? I honestly didn't know.

But there was a distinct feeling that both of our lives were about to change forever.

"What do you think we'll find?" Part of me wondered if this wasn't a bit too anticlimactic. Maybe we'd hurried a bit too much, rushing things without thinking. It had the feel of playing into someone else's trap.

"I don't want to give her time to scheme any longer," Xavier said as Ben pulled up outside of the Parkvale gates. "Stop here, mate.

We'll let ourselves in. Make sure you're there on time for Elsie and Sof."

"Of course," Ben said.

Xavier helped me out, then turned as the car pulled away. "I just want to be done with it. If she and the Orthams, or anyone else, are doing anything to interfere with our lives, it's got to stop. The notes, the terrorizing, all of it." He gripped me by the shoulders and touched his long nose to mine. "This is our time now, Ces."

My heart thrummed in response. Xavier going to battle for his family? Yes, please. I'd never get sick of it.

"Then let's tell the snooty jerks where to shove it," I said and allowed him to lead me up to the house's entrance, where he unlocked the massive front door and let us inside.

It was clear even then that this was certainly not a "quiet night in" for Georgina. Parkvale was by no means as large as Kendal, but it was still enormous by most standards. The labyrinth of rooms meant that in order for voices to carry through to the foyer, as they were now, there had to be quite a party assembled.

Which likely meant a lot of plotting afoot.

"Excuse me, may I help—oh! Your—Your Grace."

After Xavier had helped me remove my trench coat, I turned to find the Parkvale butler, Bledsoe, approaching at a steady clip across the parquet floors. The pencil-thin man looked a bit frazzled—I wondered if he was as surprised by the night's party as we were. Or if it was just us that had him in a tizzy.

"Hello, Jeeves," I said cheerily to the butler. "Remember me?"

Xavier snorted. "Jeeves?"

"It's our little joke," I told him before patting Bledsoe lightly on the shoulder. He looked as though I'd smeared jelly on his clothes. "Remember? That night after the Ortham Ball? I meant to apologize, Bledsoe. It was really horrible of me to treat you like that. I was...how should I say it?"

"Under the weather," Xavier advised with a rather saucy grin. If I enjoyed seeing him ride to my rescue, he seemed to enjoy me when I was acting, as he called me, like a "minx."

"Under the weather," I repeated back to the butler, who was still staring at me as though I'd just suggested he trade one of Sofia's princess dresses for his uniform. "And a bit heartsick for this one, if you know what I mean."

"Mmm," the butler managed to reply. "I see, miss."

"It's 'Your Grace' now, Bledsoe," Xavier corrected him, holding up my hand to show him my rings. "Francesca and I were married last week in New York. The staff should have been notified."

"Indeed, we were. I apologize, Your Grace."

I couldn't tell if he was speaking to me or Xavier. I got the distinct feeling he would rather address me as Ronald McDonald than admit I was the new Duchess of Kendal. Honestly, Bledsoe didn't seem to like using the phrase for Xavier either.

"Where is my stepmother?" Xavier asked as he adjusted the collar of his shirt.

"Er, your—you mean the dowager duchess?"

"Well, I only have one stepmother. I assume she's home unless the staff is having a party in the back."

Bledsoe flushed a brilliant shade of fuchsia. "Indeed, they are *not*, Your Grace."

"I didn't think so. Where is she?"

"Er—" The butler twisted his hands together before appearing to give up the ghost. "The duchess is in the drawing room. She is entertaining—"

"Thank you, Bledsoe."

"Will you be needing your rooms tonight, Your Grace?"

Xavier almost shuddered. "No. We have business with Georgina, but after that, we'll be heading home." He glanced down at me with a smile. "To Mayfair."

He didn't wait for the butler to reply, just handed him our coats, took my hand, and strode down the corridor toward the drawing room at the end.

It was exactly as we'd imagined: the beginnings of a small dinner party that included Lord and Lady Ortham and Imogene, all sitting in a row across a Louis XVI sofa. They faced Georgina, who was talking animatedly in one chair, and Frederick, looking bored as ever in the other.

All of them stopped immediately when we entered the room.

"Xavier!" Georgina exclaimed, though I didn't miss the narrow glance she shot at her son. "What in heaven's name are you doing here? I thought you'd be on your honeymoon. Or perhaps preparing for your hearing tomorrow."

She sounded almost gleeful at the prospect.

"I'm here to ask Imogene a question," Xavier said.

"Oh?" Imogene asked, far too eager for my liking.

"Yes," I put in. "We wondered if you would like to confess to harassment before we file charges."

Xavier pulled the most recent letter out of his pocket and waved it in front of her.

Imogene's face screwed up with immediate confusion. "What? I've no clue what that is. Harassment? Is she joking?"

"Francesca's received three of these," he told her. "It didn't make sense until the other day. But you've made your intentions clear with me from the start, and it's been very obvious you don't want to take no for an answer."

"Perhaps I had hoped..." Imogene looked nervously at her parents, who appeared admittedly appalled at the idea of their daughter sending creepy stalker notes. "But that doesn't mean I had anything to do with this. Honestly, Xavier, do you really think I would stoop so low?"

"I don't know what to think about you anymore," he told her honestly.

I couldn't help taking a little pleasure in the way the chill in his voice made the girl shudder.

"I say," said Lord Ortham. "Isn't that Caroline Klein's personal stationery?" He turned to his wife as if for confirmation. "I remember it, you see. She showed it to me over tea after the Troop's Cup in August. Made with a very rare weft that you can't find anywhere but from the one man in India, she said. Rupert used the same papers. Must have given her the connection. Fascinating."

I frowned. I had no idea Lord Ortham had such an eye.

"Oh, Bernard," Lady Ortham mumbled under her breath in the exact same tone Lea used whenever Mike, her husband, went off for too long about his fantasy football picks.

At that, I had to hide a smile. Maybe it, was a husband thing. Lord Ortham's love of stationery was akin to things like fake sports teams or flyfishing.

I was making a mental note to ask Xavier what esoteric hobbies he planned to cultivate when something else Lord Ortham said stuck out.

"Klein?" I asked. "As in...*Adam* Klein?"

"Why yes, that's his mother," Lord Ortham said. "And Georgina's sister, didn't you know?"

"Mother, you didn't," Frederick put in with a shake of his head.

I turned to her. "Was this from your sister? Was it from...*you?*"

For once, Georgina's sleek feathers were ruffled beyond repair. Her expression ricocheted around the room, bouncing between people like a pinball.

"Fine!" she sputtered. "But only because Carrie was so very clumsy, wasn't she? No doubt this time her hands are all over it."

"Do you think this is some kind of joke?" Xavier demanded, brandishing the letter like a sword. "Sending my wife terrifying notes? Making her feel like someone's following her? Stalking her?"

"*I* didn't think it was funny at all!" Georgina insisted in a voice that rang a bit too loudly. "It's only that Adam was so very attached to you, my dear, for God knows what reasons. And my sister simply can't stand to see her darling boy unhappy. So when you had gone back to New York and your mother was still giving those horrid interviews, Caroline was convinced this might be the nail in the coffin, so to speak, that might finally send you his way. After all, it wasn't that difficult to make you run the first time. Why not keep you going?"

My jaw dropped. "That is demented. This was all some kind of prank to free me up for your nephew?" I felt like I'd been physically shoved backward. "Did Adam know about this?"

"God, no," Georgina said. "Bloody boy scout, that one. He's been determined to rehabilitate his family's reputation since birth. Seemed to think being a do-good teacher would help. Horrible."

"It's not the worst idea, Mother," Frederick put it. "Especially if one is caught pulling such pranks on new family."

"Indeed," Imogene agreed with him. "Although it's not much worse than getting involved with *her* to begin with."

"*That's enough!*" Xavier's voice cut through the chatter, and suddenly the room was quieter than a tomb. Slowly, he rotated, turning degree by degree so that he was able to get a good look at every person sitting before us.

"Let me make one thing clear," he said. "Whatever your designs on my title, your plans to take what has never been yours, there is one thing I will not tolerate, and that is harassment of my family. Do you see this woman?"

He pointed to me, then pulled me to his side while everyone turned their cold, fishy eyes on me.

"*She* is the most important to me. Not this house or any of the others. Not the title you've been chasing or the accounts you've been using like they actually belong to you. Certainly not some stodgy position in Lords that I've got no fucking clue what to do with. Her. Our family. That's all I care about. And so any form of harassment of them *will stop.*"

By the time he finished, I was practically glowing inside.

I didn't realize how much I had needed him to say this to these people until now. Right this moment.

"Now, Georgina," he continued. "Let's not pretend that tomorrow morning, you aren't doing your very best to take away the acknowledgment I waited nineteen years to receive from my father.

This was more than a joke. It has always been about humiliation with you. Different means of casting me aside to elevate you and Frederick into positions you've always wanted, never earned." He shook his head. "Even Frederick knows the likelihood of the title reverting to him, much less Adam, is next to none. For the connection to Kendal going that far back, there would be too many potential heirs to count."

Lord Ortham chuckled to his wife. "Golly, maybe that means *I* should be the next Duke of Kendal, eh? I think our families intermarried back there at some point. Plenty of kissing cousins, you know?"

"Oh, Bernard," Lady Ortham moaned again.

"Exactly," Xavier said.

"You have *no* idea what you're talking about," Georgina spat at him. "And even if you did, it wouldn't matter. I would honestly rather see the title die with Rupert than continue with the barbaric likes of you, you little bastard. You've been a stain on this family since your birth. *That* will never change!"

"Oh, no you did *not*," I started toward her, but to my surprise, Xavier pulled me back.

"Don't," he said in a stony voice that was surprisingly calm. "She's not worth it." Then he stood taller than maybe I'd ever seen him. "Since threats don't have an effect on you, it's time for action. I'll give you this last night at Parkvale, Georgina. Time enough to get your things together." He glanced at Frederick. "You can keep the residence in Bath, Fred. If you want your mum there, that's up to you. But Georgie, after tonight, you are no longer welcome at *any* of the Kendal houses, nor will you have access to any funds beyond the trust my father left you."

"But—but that was a pittance!" she cried. "It's nearly gone now, you obviously know that. He intended for me to stay at Kendal as the dowager duchess—"

"I don't care if you're the former duchess," Xavier spat. "I don't care if you're the Queen of fucking Narnia. You whored your way into my father's bed for who knows how many years and abandoned him and his brother when they needed you most. You don't have any rights to *my* estate while I'm the duke. And even if that's only for a few more days, that's still too long for you to spread your stink on it any longer."

"Xavier," Imogene put in. "Don't you think that's a bit heartless? She's nowhere to go."

Xavier paused, and I was genuinely surprised his expression didn't turn the girl to stone.

"No," he said. "And let that be a warning for the rest of you and anyone else you'd like to tell. No one threatens my family. In any way. Ever again." Without waiting for a reply from any of them, he took my hand. "Come on, babe. Let's go home and see our girl."

"Sounds good to me," I replied.

"You'll regret this!" Georgina called from the melee that broke out immediately as we left the room. "Mark my words, you cannot make enemies in society and survive, Xavier! You'll see!"

"As if I fucking care about that anymore," Xavier muttered.

We strode through the grand hallways, accepted our coats from Bledsoe with a stiff bow and a sniff, and left nearly as quickly as we'd arrived.

"Are you all right?" I asked as the oversized door slammed behind us. Bledsoe had seemed more than happy to see us off.

Xavier sighed. "I honestly don't know what I am right now. Exhausted, maybe. Angrier than I've ever been. But mostly just relieved it's out there. They know where we stand. Now, we'll just have to let the chips fall where they may."

I grabbed his arm and gave it a thorough squeeze. "I'm proud of you. Standing up to a room full of bullies isn't easy for anyone. And you didn't even lose your temper."

For that, I received a sardonic smirk. "I didn't?"

I chuckled. "Well, not completely. Given Georgina's tantrum, you were the picture of patience."

"Well, that's progress, I suppose.

He slung his arm around my shoulders and shepherded me down to the gate, from which we could call an Uber home.

"You almost had it, you know."

Both Xavier and I froze at the bottom of the steps, collars still in our hands as we were putting on our coats. In concert, we both turned to see Georgina standing at the Parkvale entrance, clad only in the dark gray cocktail dress she'd worn to play hostess, bitterness dripping off her fine features like an over-applied glaze.

"Does she have a death wish?" I muttered to Xavier.

One corner of his mouth twitched upward—the only sign he had heard me.

"You won't win after tonight," she told us. "Not after making that scene in front of Bernard. You think he won't skip straight back to the committee and tell them everything he knows about you now?"

I really couldn't believe this woman. She sounded legitimately happy about the idea. Like she had been waiting for Xavier to bluster in tonight, specifically for this reason.

"It's true, there was a faction who enjoyed the idea of someone like *you* in the Lords," she admitted as she took a few steps down. "But the moment you stepped into this house, I knew I'd won. This time next week, we'll receive a call from Lord Lonsbury. And it *will* be good news. Frederick will become the rightful Duke of Kendal, and *you* will be just another dirty-blooded upstart bastard married to an equally gutter-born wench."

"Shut *up*!"

Before I could stop myself, I had flown back up the steps and slapped Her Grace Georgina, the Dowager Duchess of Kendal, hard across the cheek.

I knew it wasn't right. I knew it was the exact same thing I had wanted Xavier to *stop* doing months ago. Just like I also knew I was playing into her hands, acting exactly like the social cretin she had just accused me of being.

But I wasn't just anyone anymore.

I was a duchess now.

And more importantly, I was Xavier's woman. And no one could talk about my man like that.

Georgina reeled backward, clutching her cheek and gasping with shock. "Why, you little—"

"Just try me," I growled as I took a step upward that made her flinch. "You want another? I got plenty more."

"You *dare* lay a hand on Her Grace!"

To everyone's surprise, it was the butler who spoke up through the open front door.

"Her Grace does," Xavier said simply, though his eyes were blazing as he looked at me. "And considering *she* is the mistress of this house, not my former stepmother, then *Her Grace* may do as she sees fit. Particularly to those who insult her husband." Then his eyes zeroed in on the butler, who couldn't help but shudder under their terrible, quiet wrath. "Or are *you* also disloyal to this house, Bledsoe? I'm sure my wife would have some thoughts for you too."

The butler worried his mouth while Georgina continued to nurse her cheek. Neither of them, however, said a word.

"I thought so," Xavier said. "Now leave us. I expect you both to be gone from this house when I return tomorrow evening. Go. Now."

It wasn't until the door shut behind both of them that his large shoulders finally drooped with pure exhaustion.

"Come here, you fierce little thing," he said as I returned to his side and allowed him to wrap a long arm around my shoulders again. "Bloody good fighter, you are. You might be the first person in decades to shut up Georgina Parker."

I giggled. "I hope I won't be the last. She deserves to have her mouth washed out with soap."

Xavier sighed as we walked toward the street. "It's a nice thought. Right now, though, all I want is to take you home, bury myself between your thighs, and forget this night ever fucking happened." He took out his phone. "Let me see what's keeping Ben."

"That sounds like an excellent plan," I said as I took his hand in mine. "Let's go home, babe."

But before we could go any further, Xavier's phone buzzed in his pocket. He took it out, revealing a battery of missed calls, all blocked by Parkvale's less than stellar reception, and at least five missed messages.

His arm dropped from my shoulder as he turned to me. It was like I was looking at a ghost.

"What?" I asked. "Xavi, what is it? What's wrong now?"

Another note? Another article? Some other equally irritating news that would cost us more headaches over the coming days?

But it was far worse than I imagined.

"It's...it's Sofia," he said in a voice that was barely above a whisper.

And then I watched as my husband, my tall, strong tower of a man, collapsed right there on the sidewalk.

"Sofia?" I repeated, hearing my voice rising to shrill heights within a second. "Xavi, what happened to Sofia?"

"It's—she's—" He gulped and looked up at me with eyes that had morphed into whirlpools of fear. "Our daughter's been kidnapped."

TWENTY-EIGHT

Back at Mayfair, the world was still as chaotic as it felt the moment Xavier broke the news of Sofia's abduction. Maybe even more as the facts sank in.

I had been precariously balanced on one of the kitchen stools for nearly an hour while Xavier, Jagger, and Elsie were a storm of action along with the rotation of law enforcement officials who had come and gone at Xavier's bidding.

The world was spinning. I was having trouble breathing. I couldn't think straight, could barely comprehend what had happened.

Sofia was gone.

Sofia was *taken*.

My sweet, spunky, amazing little girl was not, in fact, on her way to us from the airport but had been kidnapped almost immediately after exiting customs.

It's every parent's worst nightmare, losing a child. It's completely unnatural. You're supposed to outlive them. You're supposed to help them grow, send them off into the world, meet a few grandbabies if you're lucky, and then die knowing you left them capable of caring for themselves and the people with them. Just like you did.

You are *not* supposed to lose them at almost five years old to God knows who.

Every time I thought of the fact, my breath left me all over again.

And I hadn't stopped thinking about it since we'd received the messages from Elsie and Jagger nearly two hours earlier.

Since then, Mayfair had transformed into ground zero for the entire city to locate Sofia Zola Parker, the name on her months-old passport. With Jagger's help, Xavier had called in every favor he could, making connections at every crime fighting organization in the UK and Europe, including the National Crime Agency, Interpol, even MI6.

Matthew, who was freaking out in Boston, had called his friends at the CIA and the FBI for assistance, though no one had much to offer. Even Derek had been looped in on the process in case he knew *anything* that could help.

Elsie, in her abject state of guilt, was manning the sort of communications center that had been set up in the living room, which consisted of two laptop computers, four cell phones (two of which were on hold with some agency or another), and a headset allowing her to organize the search effort. It was the least she felt she could do, considering it had been on her watch that Sofia had been abducted from the private airport just outside of the city. Elsie had been locked in a bathroom by an unknown assailant. Meanwhile, the kidnapper had swooped in and taken Sofia, somehow without a fight and without raising the suspicions of the small number of airport employees who hadn't heard Elsie's shouts until it was far too late.

Now, while we anxiously waited, Xavier was pacing the apartment like a rabid tiger, clearly wishing he could take to the streets himself in search of his daughter. In lieu of that, he was back to throwing arrows where he could.

"Where the *fuck* is she, Georgie?" Xavier's voice boomed across the entire Mayfair flat, echoing off the walls like thunder threatening to split the marbled floors in half. "Where is my daughter? If you know anything, you had better speak the fuck up."

"Well, *how* in the world should I know?" Georgina's shrill voice rang through on speaker. "Did I look like I'd gone and kidnapped the girl whilst hosting a dinner? I've been here the whole time, and well you know it."

Over the speaker of Xavier's phone, her voice sounded tinny and even more disingenuous than usual. It made me want to scream from the kitchen, feeling a bit feline myself.

"Do you think we're stupid?" I snarled as Xavier came closer. "You literally threatened us less than an hour ago, and not five minutes later, we get a call that our daughter is missing. You are the obvious prime suspect."

"Oh, love," Elsie murmured.

Maybe it was the audible crack in my voice that caused such obvious pity. I'd already broken down exactly four times since hearing the news. Number five was coming.

Xavier, on the other hand, had only one emotion running through him in perpetuity: murder.

"I swear to God, Georgina, if you're lying, I'll fucking finish you for good," he hissed. "I'll have the queen open the Tower of London just for you. Maybe retrofit the old chamber in Kendal, since you're so keen to get your hands on the place. I'll have them bring back the rack, or maybe the Scavenger's Daughter. You think the public likes pictures of me and mine? They'll devour a duchess on display."

"You're a monster," Georgina said flatly, though even I could hear the fear in her voice. "You always have been. I hope you understand these threats will not go unheard."

"It's what any sane man would do upon losing his daughter," Xavier snapped right back. "I challenge you to find one who wouldn't do the same."

"Be that as it may, it makes no sense to accuse me. I shan't stand for such insults!"

"You'll stand for whatever the fuck I say until I have my daughter back safely!" Xavier roared.

"Boy—Xavier—Your Grace—"

"Elsie, what the hell?" Xavier whirled around. "Since when have you *ever* addressed me as a duke?"

I plucked the phone from his hand and ended the call to Georgina promptly—she didn't need to hear whatever this was.

Elsie simply crumpled on the couch.

"Xavi, be nice," I said weakly. "She's feeling bad enough as it is." I turned to her for what had to be the tenth time. "It wasn't your fault she was t-taken, Elsie."

Shit. I really couldn't even say it without wanting to scream and cry myself.

But Elsie just shook her head and refused to engage with that line of thinking, though her lower lip was also trembling something fierce. "Detective Kingston has just returned our calls, sir. He's on the third line." She held up one of the cell phones.

Without another thought, I flew across the room and snatched the phone. "Derek, hey. Do you have *any* news? Anything that might help us find her?"

It was a long shot, of course, asking a New York detective to help with a London kidnapping. But he wouldn't be calling us back without something other than condolences, would he?

"Actually, maybe," Derek's friendly voice was a balm to my very soul. "And maybe not. Honestly, it doesn't make any sense to me."

And also a dart.

I sank onto the couch opposite Elsie while Xavier raced to my side, took the phone, and put it on speaker.

"Derek, it's Xavier," he said. "What is it? What did you find?"

"The prints your police found on the third letter sent over actually did match someone in the system. Frankie...shit...the fingerprints belong to Guadalupe Ortiz. It's your mom."

Xavier and I just stared at each other over the phone.

"I—*what?*" I asked, even as Xavier was turning toward the airport security footage now replaying on one of Elsie's monitors.

It was another bit of bad luck that no matter the angle, absolutely none of the cameras at the private airport had managed to capture the kidnapper's face. It certainly didn't have the same type of security as a place like Heathrow.

But now, as I watched the kidnapper for what was probably the fiftieth time usher Sofia out the front doors, I recognized the short, squat shape of my mother, wisps of her ashy blond hair sticking out from the thick cap that shielded her face.

"*That's* why she didn't fight it," I murmured, even as my heart turned to ice. "That's why the airport security didn't think anything of her leaving without Elsie." I turned to Xavier. "I don't think Sofia even knows her name. Just would have called her *abuela*, like my mom has always said, and everyone would have thought she was the perfect grandmother."

"No one would have seen it. Christ, it's the perfect crime." Xavier shook his head. "Is she really that obsessed with getting to know you?"

"It's for money," I said tightly. "It's always been for money. You know that. My mother would sell her soul for a bit of publicity and some extra cash. I'm sure there will be a heavy ransom request coming if there hasn't been already."

"As it happens..." Jagger said, holding up his phone. "One's just arrived. An email to the Parker Group addressed to the 'so-called Duke of Kendal'—the kidnapper's words, not mine, mate—requesting that you admit to falsifying marital records between the former duke and your mother in front of Parliament, thereby relinquishing your title and all parts of inheritance related to the dukedom that go with it."

Xavier blinked. "You're kidding. This is about my *title?*" His gaze raced back to me. "Georgina."

I shrugged. "Maybe." She had seemed awfully distressed on the phone.

"Plus fifty million pounds," Jagger added wryly. "Messenger fee, I reckon."

"And that's why my mother's involved," I said dryly.

"Derek?" Xavier demanded. "Did you hear all that?"

There was a sigh. "Send me the email. Maybe we can trace the IP address. Honestly, I don't know. This isn't my jurisdiction, so I'll have to be working with law enforcement over there. I don't know the legalities of everything."

"Els, send it to the other agencies too," Xavier said. "This has to be from Georgina. Has to."

"Already done, boy."

"I'm not agreeing to shit," Xavier told Jagger flatly. Until he caught my expression.

"You'll agree to whatever it takes to get Sofia back safely," I told him point-blank. "I don't care if we become paupers in the process. I don't care if you have to lie on your back and call yourself a puppy dog in front of Parliament and the queen, Xavi. You will do whatever it fucking takes to get our baby girl back!"

I wasn't going to say it out loud, but he knew it was true. None of this would have happened if he wasn't who he was. If he didn't have things my mother wanted. That Georgina or whoever else was behind this wanted.

Xavier swallowed roughly as he sank to his haunches beside me. "We'll find her before it comes to that."

"Well, that's the thing," Derek interrupted.

We both jumped, having forgotten he was on the other end of the line.

"When anyone enters the UK, you know they have to leave a forwarding address. And, well...I don't know if this was her being dumb or brilliant. But Xavier, she left yours, apparently."

Xavier frowned. "*Mine?* As in Mayfair?"

"No, I mean, your old one. In some place called Croydon. On South End road. Does that ring any bells?"

Xavier stilled as I turned to him. His blue eyes sparked with danger. And recognition.

"That's...that's my old flat," he said. "The one above my mum's restaurant. Ch-Christ. They're in *Croydon*?"

"It's probably just a practical joke," Derek said. "I really don't think she could be that dumb to provide the *actual* address where she was going."

"Then you don't know my mother," I said dryly. "She doesn't exactly think."

Then I noticed that Xavier was on the move again, prowling around the apartment. Looking for keys, apparently, which he immediately shoved into his pocket. Like he was *going* somewhere.

"Xavi," I called. "Stop. She's not there. How would she have even gotten the keys? Think, this isn't reasonable."

"Since they want you to give up your title, makes sense they'd remind you where you're from," Jagger put in. "It's a joke, Xav. Nothing more."

But Xavier was already grabbing his jacket, unwilling to listen to any of us now that he had been presented with something to *do*. "Well, there's only one way to find out. I can't just stay here anymore like a sitting fucking duck. I'm going to check for myself."

TWENTY-NINE

W hen the Range Rover pulled up to the curb in front of the little brick building in Croydon, the night wasn't exactly quiet. The sun had gone down long ago, and while some of the smaller restaurants had been closed up for the night, most of the street was still alive with the sights and sounds of people out with friends, utterly unaware of the crimes being committed in their presence.

It was flush with diversity—the variety of tiny restaurants alone told me plenty of immigrants lived here right alongside a more moneyed youth that could afford places like the minimalist boulangerie across the street. A center for troubled youth stood next to a day spa. Much like my neighborhoods back home, it was obviously coming up in the larger London ecosystem, but not so much that the business owners could afford to forego security shutters over their windows.

I might have looked around more curiously if I hadn't been flush with fear and fury. This was, after all, the place where Xavier had been raised for the first sixteen years of his life. The building where his mother's restaurant had been fit right in among the rows of little brick townhouses and apartment buildings, none of them reaching more than three or so stories high. Xavier's family's building was one of the smaller ones, constructed of worn red brick, currently housing a closed Nigerian restaurant on the bottom floor.

"Sure you want to do this?" Ben asked. "The police will be here in a few more minutes. I'd wait for them."

But Xavier was already staring hard at the second-story window just above the restaurant. "That was Mum's bedroom. No one lives there now. It's empty. Just like I kept it."

"Do you leave a light on when you aren't there?" I wondered, though I had a feeling I already knew the answer.

Xavier stared even harder at the shine of yellow peeking through the blinds. "No. I don't." Then he turned to me. "I'm going up. Ces, stay here with Ben until the coppers arrive."

It didn't escape me the way, even within minutes of arriving in his old neighborhood, his south London accent had thickened considerably.

"Absolutely not," I said. "I'm coming with you."

"Ces, no—"

"*Yes*," I hissed, not wanting to shout in front of Ben. But I was feeling immovable too. "Xavi, that is *my* little girl up there. There isn't an army in the world that could stop me from seeing her right now!"

Xavier just continued to shake his head. "It's too dangerous, Ces. You need to stay here. You and the baby need to stay safe."

"It's my mom," I argued, trying a different tack. "If she's up there, maybe I can help, all right? Talk her out of whatever idiocy she's into."

He opened his mouth to argue again but shut it almost immediately. Apparently, he could see I meant what I said.

I followed him out of the car, then around to the side door of the building, which opened easily. We walked up a set of narrow stairs to another door above the restaurant.

Xavier paused. He looked like he wanted to say something. Then he shook his head, inserted his key into the lock, and opened the door.

"I don't *want* to watch any more TV, and I don't want any of that stinky food! I WANT MY MOMMY!"

"Sofia?" I called as relief flooded through me. I had *never* been so thrilled to hear the beginnings of an all-out tantrum. Honestly, if I hadn't needed to see her safe, I might have let Sofia give whoever she was talking to what they deserved.

We stepped into a small sitting room that was, for lack of a better word, humble. Connected to a tiny kitchenette in one corner, it was barely large enough to contain a thread-bare plaid loveseat shoved against one wall, a few oak side tables that would have been at home during the late fifties, and a walnut stand that should have held a television. Faded, rose-colored carpet covered the floors, which were reasonably clean, if somewhat dusty. The walls were painted a dingy cream, including a few art prints hung here and there—one a poster of the Madonna with a Victoria and Albert logo at the bottom, another was a print that looked like Japanese block art.

This was where Xavier had grown up. I would have been entranced with every small detail had I not been completely focused on the theme song of *Daniel Tiger* that played behind a closed door across the room alongside the familiar shrieks of my five year old in the throes of an all-out tantrum.

"No, Sofia, please don't go—"

"Mamamamamamamamamama!"

The door opened, and Sofia careened out of what looked like a bedroom and straight into my arms, allowing me to pick her up and swing her onto my hip. "Where have you *been*? Abuela said Elsie got sick at the airport and told her to bring me here to wait for you."

"I—Elsie did get sick," I told her as I hugged her more tightly than I ever had, trying to make the tears that were already welling up go away. By some miracle, she seemed mostly unaware of what was going on. All I wanted to do was get her out of there before anything else changed.

"Fucking hell," Xavier said with relief as he threw his arms around both of us. "You're safe. Are you all right? Did anyone hurt you?"

"Yesmph." Sofia's response was muffled by both sets of arms squeezing her half to death, though she didn't seem to mind the effect. For a few seconds, anyway, until she was shoving at both of us to let her breathe.

"I thought you'd never get here," she told us. "Abuela told me to watch TV for hours, and I'm only allowed two shows in a row. I *told* her, but she didn't listen! Mama, why are you crying?"

I couldn't help but laugh in the middle of my tears. "Just—just happy to see you, baby. So freaking happy."

I hugged her again and probably squeezed her tighter than she liked. I couldn't help it. I couldn't get her close enough.

"This is kind of a funny house for you, Dad," Sofia was saying over my shoulder. "It's a lot smaller than your other places. It's even smaller than home. Daddy, are you crying too?"

There was a cough, and then I turned to find Xavier giving a grim smile with reddened eyes. "Not at all. Come on, we're leaving."

"No!" my mother's voice screeched through the room.

We both turned to find her standing in the doorway of the bedroom Sofia had come from, looking very tired and even more terrified.

"No, you can't leave!" she exclaimed with eyes that danced all over the room. "No, please, they'll—"

"They'll what?" I demanded. "Mom, what the hell are you doing here, anyway? How could you even consider taking Sofia like this? How did you even get here on parole? How fucking *dare* you!"

"Swear jar, Mama," Sofia whispered, though her little arms around my neck hadn't stopped squeezing.

Her face reddened even more. Her nose had that pink tinge that told me she was drinking again, and the sallow color of her skin suggested she was using something more. She'd lost a lot of weight since I'd seen her last, and under her eyes, it looked like she hadn't slept in days.

"I needed the money, Frankie," she said weakly, not even bothering to answer the question.

I supposed I could fill in the blanks.

"Who did this, then?" Xavier demanded. "Who paid you off? Tell us *now*."

"I needed the money, and you did nothing to help me," she rattled on as she stepped toward us. "What was I supposed to do?"

"How about *not* kidnap your own granddaughter for ransom?" I snapped. "How about *not* betray your own flesh and blood?" I closed my eyes and pinched my brow. "You know what? Forget that. We're not family. We're not even related as human beings. You're not worth the sympathy or even questions to answer. Xavi, let's go."

We turned to the door, Sofia's body still ensconced in my arms.

"*Mija*, you wouldn't—"

I whirled around. "Did you really just call me 'daughter'? I have *never* been your *mija*. You've never treated me or any of your kids like your actual children—just means to an end, even if it was to assuage your own conscience! Right now, my only priority is Sofia, so if you don't want us to throw the absolute *book* at you, let us go in peace."

"Why would you throw a book at her, Mama?" Sofia wondered. "She was just picking me up."

"They'll do it again!" she cried out just as we turned to the door.

Xavier stopped at the door. "Who?"

"I-I don't know the name," she admitted as she sank onto the sofa. "They never told me. I heard one of the men mention a Park House, but that's all." She bit her lip. "They promised Sofia would stay safe all right. I wouldn't have agreed to it otherwise. Even then, I refused to leave when we got here. Not without making sure she was going to be okay."

"How very generous of you to make sure my daughter's kidnapping went safely," I spat. "Jesus *Christ*, Mom."

"Kidnap?" Sofia looked at my mother with eyes wide with betrayal. "What's kidnap?"

"Something that will never happen again," I assured her. "I'll explain later."

I *hated* that I would have to do that.

"Parkvale," Xavier muttered. "Fucking Georgina."

"Swear jar, Dad," Sofia remarked automatically as she reached out to twiddle a piece of hair that had fallen over Xavier's brow.

"That *bitch*," I seethed.

"You too, Mama. Jeez." Her tone, however, sounded a bit more alarmed. Sofia rarely heard me curse.

I sighed. "Sorry, baby. But in very rare cases, that word is warranted."

Sofia simply burrowed closer into my side with her head on my shoulder. If that hadn't told her something was very wrong, nothing would.

"Wait!" my mother called to us. "If you're going to go, take me with you, please. If they come back and see that she's gone, they'll blame me and do what they did to that other woman."

"You mean Elsie?" I said. "Don't worry, she was only locked in a bathroom for two hours. If you're lucky, that's all that will happen to you."

"Frankie, please. If they come back—"

She cut herself off when the sound of men's voices filtered up the stairs through the still-open door. Xavier and I backed into the room so as not to be seen immediately, while he tucked me and Sofia behind him.

"Good God, Barnaby," said an oddly posh, familiar voice. "Can't you do anything—*oh!*"

They looked up to find a room full of people staring at them.

"Crikey," said Barnaby in a much deeper voice that sounded like the other man's but was filtered through a very strong East London accent. "What do we have here, eh?"

I was too busy staring at the first man to answer.

"Jeeves?" I asked as I peeked around Xavier's shoulder.

"Isn't that one of the butlers?" Sofia asked. "The mean one at Parkvale?"

Xavier seemed to be equally paralyzed. "Bledsoe, what are *you* doing here?"

The butler's beady-eyed gaze bounced between us, as though he wasn't convinced we were actually there.

"So it *was* Georgina," Xavier said to himself. "I knew it."

"It absolutely was not." Bledsoe finally found his voice. "The duchess had nothing to do with this little scheme gone awry, and I'll thank you to keep her out of it!"

"Yeah," said Barnaby. "It's just bad luck for you that my brother here's been in love with the duchess since he was a lad. Would do anything to please her, he would. Even get rid of a duke."

"For the last time, he's *not a duke*, Barnaby!" Bledsoe suddenly sputtered to life. "And this has never been about the duchess! It's about protecting what's sacred." He literally tipped up his nose toward us. "Never in all my years did I imagine I'd have to serve the likes of you, who aren't worth what's on the bottom of the duchess's shoes. You aren't a gentleman. And you are certainly not a proper duke. Only a bastard, born to this very hovel!"

I waited for the explosion I knew was coming. We'd already heard this once from Georgina, and right now, I had to imagine Xavier was getting tired of his birth status being thrown in his face, incorrectly or not. The fact that I'd already met my limit for those insults before him was enough of a shock. There was no way Xavier would let this go without at least a warning shot.

But to my surprise, he only smirked at the man. "I might be. And I might not. But I don't care anymore, and that was never for you to decide, you deceitful bit of scum." He turned to me. "The police should be here soon. Ces, let's go."

"Not so fast." Barnaby stepped forward as he pulled out a shiny silver handgun.

"Oh shit," I muttered.

"Mama..." Sofia's whimpers grew more hushed as she kicked her legs and dropped to the floor. "He has a gun."

"That I do, wee girl. There's the matter of payment, Your Grace," Barnaby said with a sneer. "Now, the title, I don't care about that at all. But I believe there was a sum requested for the return of your daughter."

"That's *right*," hissed Bledsoe. "Fifty million pounds, and you *will* renounce your title. I don't care what my brother says."

He jerked forward as he spoke, shoving his finger directly into Xavier's face.

Which, of course, was his fatal mistake.

With zero hesitation, Xavier grabbed the man's finger and broke it with a nasty crack. As Bledsoe squealed and fell to the floor, Xavier took advantage of the moment of surprise to swing a hard left punch over the butler and directly into his brother's face. The gun fell to the floor with a *thwack*, which I quickly picked up to unload before it could do anyone else harm. Living with Matthew, a former Marine and DA who never left the house armed, had given me at least a few skills of use here.

"Empty," I said. "My God, you two really are idiots, aren't you?"

Before they could answer, more footsteps thundered up the stairs, and we were quickly joined by several police officers as well as Xavier's driver, Ben.

"Thank God," I murmured. "It's theirs. And it was empty," I said as I handed one of them the gun and immediately pulled Sofia to my waist, keeping my girl close.

"Frankie!" my mother called as her hands were cuffed behind her back. "Frankie, *please!*"

But her cries fell on deaf ears as I huddled with my daughter.

Bledsoe was being read his rights to silence while his brother was being revived for the same purpose. Eventually, all of them were shuffled toward the door, my mother the last to leave.

"We'll need your statements, Your Grace," said one of the policemen.

But Xavier just turned to me and extended a hand. "You'll have to take them at my flat in Mayfair," he said. "I've got to get my family home safe."

THIRTY

Everyone else saw it happen on TV. Maybe through one of the many tabloids. It was like something out of *Clue* (The butler did it! By kidnapping the duke's daughter with a gun!). One of Xavier's actual mothers-in-law, a supposedly loyal staff member, plus a crooked brother committing a heinous crime in a twisted act of love and greed. There were photos of the three of them being cuffed and led from the Croydon flat by the police. Other pictures of Georgina being escorted into another police car from Parkvale House, Frederick looming behind her with a bemused expression.

We didn't read any of the headlines. I would remember my mother's cries for mercy for the rest of my life, just as I would remember ignoring them. Apparently, I had finally found my line. Xavier and I had both discovered when enough was enough—it was when you hurt our kids. When you messed with our family.

In light of the arrest of Georgina Parker and her sister, Caroline Klein, for harassment along with a surprising charge of conspiracy to kidnap a minor (according to Bledsoe's brother's confession, both women had been tacitly encouraging the butler's ideas on the matter for weeks), the House of Lords had canceled Xavier's hearing and had thrown out the entire question of his legitimacy, given that any evidence submitted by the dowager duchess was fully compromised in light of her designs against the duke.

Photographers were camped out in front of Mayfair for several days while we treated the flat like our own private bunker, recovering just the three of us in warmth and privacy. After they were reassured of Sofia's safety, my family shockingly left us alone, and Xavier's staff seemed to understand the need for space as well.

This world, composed of the three soon-to-be four of us, suddenly seemed so precious. And so we revisited the tentative home the three of us had made together earlier that year. A place that wasn't steeped in a thousand-year lineage or a shabby little house my brother had given me out of a sense of charity, but a home, luxurious as it was, that had been completely redesigned around our needs, even if for a short time.

Xavier cooked for us each night. I read in the evenings from *The Secret Garden* and basked in the delicious sound of Xavier's rare, full-throated laughter when he heard my horrible Yorkshire accent. Sofia drew pictures of unicorns, slept in her *Moana*-inspired bedroom, and received more hugs than she knew what to do with. Xavier and I visited the rooftop *onsen* more than once while our daughter slumbered (well, he got in while I dangled my feet, dreaming of when being pregnant would no longer keep me from a nice long soak). We made love next to the steamy waters and afterward whispered about futures together we'd barely hoped for in the past.

Places we'd like to visit. Dates we'd like to have. Names of our future child.

There was something about the peace that felt, if not permanent, more solid than before. As though our little trio knew we'd been through just about everything together and could survive anything else.

Including a visit from Lord Ortham nearly a week after Sofia's rescue.

"I'd say I can't believe it, but I was there," he said cheerfully after accepting a nightcap from Xavier's private store. "When she told me what she was planning for the committee, at least, I thought even that was ridiculous. But I never imagined a duchess would be taken away by the police on charges of kidnapping, of all things."

Sofia had gone to sleep long ago, and Xavier and I had just been considering going to "sleep" ourselves while a storm rolled in from the north. My husband had been pouring himself a glass of water when the concierge called up to announce Lord Ortham.

Now, we all sat in the living room around the fire crackling in the enormous grate—me curled up into Xavier's warm body on the sofa, Lord Ortham swishing his glass of port appreciatively from one of the oversized armchairs.

"And might I take the moment to offer you both my sincerest congratulations and best wishes on your marriage," he added after a healthy drink. "Not surprised you didn't want the fuss of St. Paul's. Bunch of pomp and circumstance, that. Better to keep it quiet in the family. Though I should have liked to have been there. Stand in for your father and uncle, you know."

I smiled at his genuine warmth. "Thank you."

To my surprise, I found I quite liked the viscount. We had barely interacted all summer, and most of my impressions of his family were linked to his stuffy wife and insufferable daughter. Alone, however, he wasn't stifled by their sense of propriety. Between his horsey laugh, obsession with inane historical details, and blunt sense of humor, he was almost down to earth, like an uncle I'd never had.

"I am leaving for Kendal in the morning. But I realized I couldn't go without saying something." His speech was suddenly a bit awkward as he set his glass on the coffee table. "Once I discovered what Imogene had done—" He broke off, shaking his head with obvious shame. "Appalling. Just appalling. Xavier, I really am so sorry."

"It's all right, Bernard," Xavier said as he stroked my shoulder. "It's in the past."

"No, no, it's not," he said. "For my own child to act with such impropriety—as if she had any right to you in any way, when you have a family of your own, for God's sake—horrible, just horrible. The strain it has put on our families' long friendship..."

Xavier just remained quiet as he sipped his water, while I glanced between them, somewhat confused. I understood some of this, of course. Various Orthams showed up in the Kendal journals for around two hundred years, which I gathered was about the age of the title. But Lord Ortham spoke with a lot more feeling than a simple neighbor and fellow peer.

"Rupert's death...and now Henry's..." The viscount shook his head again. "We're not supposed to show it, but it really was quite hard. We all grew up together as boys, you see. They were...family to me. And so were you, Xavier. Especially to my Lucy. Don't think I've forgotten that."

Xavier stared at the man for a long time, blue eyes icy and opaque. But his hand braced on my arm told me that he was feeling more with the man's words than he wanted to show. Only he and Lucy would ever know how and why the unlikely bond had formed between them, but I knew him well enough to see that part of it had been from common grounds of isolation and loneliness. One of many family members he'd lost too young.

Hearing her father acknowledge it must have stirred something deep within him.

I stopped myself from rolling my eyes. What was it with British men and emotions? They were even worse than the men back home.

"That's a very kind thing to say, Lord Ortham," I said when it was clear that Xavier was too overwhelmed to speak. "I know we both appreciate it."

Xavier cleared his throat. "Er—yes. I do." He blinked. "And for what it's worth, Bernard, I...considered Lucy like a sister as well. I'm sorry things never worked between Imogene and me, but you understand..."

"Of course." Lord Ortham offered me a friendly nod. "The

matchmaking was more my dear wife's endeavor. And Henry's, of course. He was so very determined to strengthen your legacy after you were named heir. More than Rupert, even. Rather like a dog with a bone."

I frowned. "Why was he so intense about it, do you think?"

Lord Ortham just shrugged. "God knows. Henry always was a bit more intense than Rupert. Quiet, but he loved Kendal. We always joked that he should have been the older brother. He was more suited to being a duke than Rupert ever was."

The viscount chuckled fondly, like he'd made his own private joke with the two men no longer living.

Xavier grunted, but I could tell he sort of agreed. He always had gotten along better with Henry, who had served as his keeper for so many years. He never said it, but I could tell he missed his uncle dearly. I hoped one day he would find the space to grieve him properly.

"You do look a great deal like him, you know," Ortham remarked, though he had started swirling his drink again, lost in some memory. "I doubt you hear it often, since you've the coloring and that hair from your mother. But it's in your shape. The shoulders, the way you hold yourself. And those eyes. There were times this year when I thought Rupert himself was looking at me."

Xavier nodded. "I remember. Henry's were the same color, too."

Ortham smiled wistfully to himself while he sloshed the remains of his port. Then he tipped it back and sat up straighter. "Well, with the absurd question of your legitimacy removed, I sincerely hope this means we'll be seeing you up at Kendal more often. I'm looking forward to when you put your mark on the place."

Xavier cast me a covert glance, then turned back to Lord Ortham. "Ah, well, that likely won't be anytime soon, I'm afraid."

"Planning to move the seat?" Ortham sniffed at the idea. "To London? Or will it be York? That would be a renegade move, to be sure. Hasn't been done since, what, 1645?"

I smiled. It was cute, actually, that he knew the history of the dukedom since well before his family had ever occupied the area.

Xavier simply made a noncommittal noise that I recognized as him having absolutely no clue and not wanting to admit it. His hand squeezed my shoulder again with some unknown message while he gazed at my belly.

"Actually, no," he said. "Makes sense for the Kendal seat to remain in Kendal. I just won't be sitting in it, so to speak. Ces and I will go back to New York for the time being."

Ortham blinked as though he hadn't heard correctly. Then, like any well-trained gentleman, he quickly schooled his features into something more nonplussed. "I see. Well, we shall miss you."

He then picked up a small paper bag he had brought with him and set it on the table. "I see now why Gibson requested that I bring these. He must have known you weren't to return any time soon."

Xavier picked up the bag, peeked inside, then handed it to me. I pulled out two more identical journals, which, upon flipping them open, I recognized as written in Henry's looping hand.

"What are they?" Ortham asked. "I'd never snoop, you know, desperate as I might be."

I looked up. "Oh, they're just Henry's steward journals about the estate. Mostly details about livestock and accounting and stuff like that. I'm planning a research project about them when I return to school."

"Ah, yes. I was told you are making a study of Kendal and its history, my dear," Ortham said with approval. "Gibson is quite proud of you, you know."

I smiled, imagining the stuffy old butler with his deep and abiding pride of Kendal—proud of the uncouth American he'd lectured on my first day there.

"Where did he find these?" I asked. "I went over the entire library making sure I hadn't missed any. Xavier said he checked Henry's room and the office too."

"Henry knew all the best hiding spots," Ortham said. "He loved a good mystery. He wouldn't have shown any of us, so Gibson probably found them whilst cleaning or something of the sort."

I smiled and set the books aside. "Thank you so much. I can't wait to dive in."

"Xavier, if you don't mind me asking, who will oversee things in your stead?" Ortham wondered.

Xavier glanced quickly at me. I nodded.

"Well, it's something I wanted to ask you," Xavier said as he sat forward. "I can handle the financial reports from wherever I am, but I'll need to hire a steward for the actual estate. And have, er, someone I can trust to make sure the steward's doing right by the land and our businesses around there."

Ortham was suddenly quiet. I recognized the game—he was like a woman waiting for a man to pop the question. Waiting out hypotheticals until the proposal was properly on the table.

"Would you consider it, Lord Ortham?" Xavier asked finally. "You know the estate and the land better than anyone else. You'd receive a share of the profits, of course, and I honestly can't ask anyone else to do it. Not even Frederick. Not after what's happened."

I recognized courtesy in the use of the title. This was a job for Lord Ortham, not just Bernard Douglas.

Lord Ortham was quiet for a moment, and then a smile, deep and genuine, spread across his kindly face.

"Why, Your Grace," he said softly, almost reverently. "Xavier. I would be honored. I shall do my very best to guard and protect what is yours until you come back to claim it."

THIRTY-ONE

Viscount Ortham finally left after another celebratory drink and our assurances that a contract for his oversight would arrive in Kendal within a few days. Xavier and I finally crawled into bed together sometime near midnight. He had been quiet all evening, even more so after Ortham had departed. My man was deep in thought, and I knew better than to try to pull him out of it.

I yawned, nuzzling into one of the down pillows, unable to hold my exhaustion at bay any longer. Though I wasn't as tired as I'd been during the first trimester, this baby was definitely taking more out of me than Sofia had. Or maybe it was just the stress surrounding his conception and everything that had happened since.

"Go to sleep, babe," Xavier said as he reached out to stroke my hair. "It's been a long day."

"It has not," I argued with a sleepy grin. "We played games with Sofia, you made the world's easiest ramen, and then we watched a movie this afternoon before Bernard dropped by. We've basically been on vacation."

"Convalescence is not the same thing as vacation. We've all been recovering. That will tire you out."

I couldn't really argue with that. Even so, sleep didn't quite come peacefully after the events of the evening.

"I'm glad she didn't get what she wanted," I said a few moments later. "Georgina, I mean. Taking away your title."

"Mmm. I suppose."

He was agreeing with me. Sort of.

Maybe not really?

"You don't sound very convincing," I pointed out.

Xavier sighed and rolled onto his back. "I *am* glad she didn't succeed. I wouldn't have like losing the title. That way, at least."

"What do you mean 'that way'?"

Xavier cast me a sidelong glance. "Can you really tell me there isn't a part of you that wouldn't like to leave it all behind us?"

I pushed myself up on one arm so I could look down at him face-to-face. "If you are suggesting for one second that I ever hoped that horrible, traitorous woman would *win*—"

"No, Ces." Xavier was oddly calm, though the dimple in his left cheek appeared. "But I do appreciate the loyalty."

I slumped back onto my pillow. "You'd better. You're stuck with it for life."

His smile warmed me to the core. "And I wouldn't have it any other way. But that's the thing, isn't it? I chose you, babe. And you chose me. 'Til death do us part, but we *chose* that vow." He shook his head. "I didn't want Georgina to rip away the title. But either way, it was out of my hands. I had no choice in the matter. No part of my future with the British aristocracy was ever up to me. Not when I was nineteen. Not now either."

"You have a choice," I insisted. "After all, no one says you absolutely have to take a seat in the House of Lords, right?"

He just stared at the ceiling. "Ah. No, not officially. But the evidence that Georgina offered them was obviously enough to warrant a hearing. Should they ever decide to, it could easily be brought up again."

"Do you really think Lonsbury or Ortham, or any of the others who have *chosen* to look the other way, would refuse a *quid pro quo?*"

We both knew the answer to that. Throwing out Georgina's absurd claims was the gentry's version of "you scratch my back, I'll scratch yours." Prior to last week, the committee had been split, and the half that had defended Xavier had done so with the presumed expectation that the errant son of Rupert Parker, His Grace the Duke of Kendal, would be taking up his father's former position as one of the remaining hereditary peers. They couldn't afford to lose positions. Any more than Xavier could now afford to displease them.

Just another day at the office.

"You could abdicate," I said, though even I knew that wasn't really a viable option. "Or whatever the term is. But you could tell them to take it away. You told me yourself the same committee has the power to do that."

"I could slap the monarchy in the face too. They who bestowed the title and the lands on my ancestors more than a thousand years ago. It would have about the same effect, I think."

I shuddered. "Please don't slap the Queen of England. That would be very, very bad."

We both lay still, ruminating under the reflections of London's lights blinking across the ceiling. I had a feeling we were thinking the same thing. If Xavier was going to be called back eventually, there was no way we could make the life in New York we wanted. An active member of the House of Lords couldn't exactly conduct Parliamentary business from Brooklyn or wherever else we ended up. I couldn't be an active duchess from New York City, either.

Xavier turned onto his side, then pulled at an errant curl tickling my cheek. "It's not too late for you and the babes, you know. We could get an annulment, Sofia can't inherit the title anyway, and the little one here could still be born out of wedlock..."

"After all that consummation?" I joked. "I don't think so. Besides, this one needs his father."

I pulled his hand down to rest atop my belly, which had only just started to poke out considerably this week, like a flower that knew it was safe to bloom.

Xavier's palm flattened over it, as if to cover the evidence of our coming child. His coming heir.

"I know you don't want to live here," he said. "And I don't want to force you and the kids into a life you didn't choose. But honestly, Ces, I don't know how I can get out of it. Hereditary positions...fuck me, it's a *life* term. Maybe after a few years they would allow me to step down and come to you, but that's years of you waiting in New York. And then there is always the possibility they'd call me back."

"I would never do that," I said automatically, even as the dream of our home in New York, surrounded by family and friends, slipped away. "If you have to stay, you have to stay, but that means we stay with you. We're a family. No matter what."

"You didn't choose this, though. Neither of us did." His entire body tensed at the thought of it, making the dragon's claw over his chest grip the skin.

"But I chose *you*, Xavi," I told him. "And you me. Yes, I want to be in New York. Yes, I would prefer to raise our family there with my siblings and my grandmother around. But *I chose you*. That means taking things as they come together. As a real team." I reached over to cup his face, urging him close so I could kiss the end of his long nose. "If you have to stay, we all have to stay. We'll work it out in the end. I know we will."

He examined me for a long time, then slipped his own hand around my head to deliver a long, bittersweet kiss. His tongue twisted around mine in a terrible, sad dance that still made my breath come up short.

God, I loved him.

Perhaps life as a duchess would be hard, but it would never hurt so much as being without him.

I knew that now.

"I am so fucking lucky to have you," he whispered against my lips. "So bloody fucking lucky."

"We make our own luck, Your Grace," I whispered back before licking the edge of his mouth with my tongue.

He laughed and kissed me again.

"Well, there's no law that says a duchess can't be a professor." He shrugged. "The upside is that I suppose every university in the country will be scratching their eyes out to have you. Might as well take advantage of the benefits, yeah?"

I tried to look hopeful. He wanted so badly to give me something to be hopeful about.

And so I kissed him again, willing myself to get lost as his big hands slid around my waist, pulling me into the shelter of his body.

Whatever the future, we'd be hopeful about it together.

———

HOPE WASN'T enough to help me sleep, though. After showing me just *how* lucky he felt to have me—twice—Xavier fell into a deep sleep, arms crossed over his chest like a carved knight atop a medieval sarcophagus. I, however, tossed and turned until finally, I padded out to the kitchen, made myself a cup of herbal tea, then sat on the couch in the hopes that Henry's journals might lull me into some kind of slumber.

"What were you hiding here, Henry?" I murmured as I pulled the first out of the bag and flipped it open.

I expected something about Rupert. Maybe complaining about his older brother's partying ways, his irresponsibility, perhaps his demeaning manner—all the things that had lurked in subtext before. Maybe I'd get lucky and discover Henry's true thoughts at last.

I had no idea.

30 March 1986

Masumi had the baby this morning. Five-fifteen. Fourteen hours of labor—she was brilliant.

I know all fathers say this, but he really is perfect.

We named him Xavier.

"Wait, *what?*" I squeaked into the night.

The apartment didn't answer. No one did, to the point where I thought I might have imagined what I'd just read.

Masumi, it said. Not M. And Henry had referred to him*self* as a father.

I read the passage again. Then read it again. And read it again. And then, finally, I kept reading.

I shouldn't be writing all of this down, I know. God knows it could ruin everything if anyone ever finds it. But I can't shake the idea that the boy may never really know who he is. That he had a father who truly loved him.

Masumi was in love with Rupert. That much was never a lie. Poor girl never had a chance, of course. She was a plaything like everyone else in his path.

In the end, it was as much my fault as it was hers. She wanted to make him jealous by taking up with his brother— she knew him well enough for that, at least. Rupert never has liked to come second in anything, even with the assistant cook.

And I took advantage. I was so desperately in love with her myself. I was willing to take scraps.

I offered to marry her when she learned she was pregnant. Of course, I did. I'm not a monster.

She refused until I brought her back to Japan, and her parents refused to take her in. She was a rebel already, having left Japan against their wishes to come to

England on her own. Even more for deciding to have the child.

Why should she settle now and marry a second son she could never love? When she has no other options for respectability, I suppose. In the end, though, I convinced her it was for the best, even if it was on paper only. Insurance for the child. And for her, though she'd never accept it.

She's already told me she regrets it. That she won't stay in Kendal.

I shan't give her the divorce she wants, though, even if she refuses to have anything to do with me.

Xavier, after all, needs a father.

Xavier. Good lord.

I have a son.

"Insurance?" I murmured. "Insurance for what?"

Eagerly, I paged forward.

The entries were shorter and further apart than the original journals. There were months between them—sometimes years—before he had anything more to say, providing a narrative that moved quickly through Xavier's life. Sometimes they lasted a while, Henry bemoaning his frustrations with Masumi's distance and the fact that she wouldn't let him see Xavier more often. Others were more like addendums to the original journals that covered the day-to-day life of Kendal, filling in the backstory of things that couldn't be recorded for public knowledge.

It was as if Henry couldn't help it—he had to add the corrections somewhere to the official record for someone's sake. For Xavier's, it appeared. It was as if he knew at some point his son would be lost in an identity crisis of his making and would need the truth more than anything else.

I read on through the night, plowing through the first journal, then the second, until the sun was starting to peek over the buildings of East London. I blinked and rubbed my eyes, feeling like I'd just passed through a hurricane.

The entire story was utterly unbelievable. It couldn't be true. It couldn't.

But it was.

And Xavier had no idea.

Just after I finished the final page, written just after Xavier's nineteenth birthday, I sprang from the couch, clutching both journals as I raced to the bedroom and jumped into bed.

"Xavi," I said, grabbing his shoulder to shake him awake. "Xavi, wake up!"

"Mmmph," he grunted and rolled onto his side.

"No, you stubborn man." I yanked harder on his arm. "Xavier, get up! You need to get up *right now!*"

"Hmm? What?" His expression opened when he caught an eyeful of my likely frazzled appearance. "Ces, is everything all right? Christ, the baby—"

"The baby's fine," I assured him. "Sofia's fine. We're all fine. But Xavi, *listen.* I couldn't sleep, so I read Henry's journals, and you're not going to believe—"

"You didn't sleep?" He pushed himself up to sitting and shoved his deliciously dark and slightly overgrown hair out of his face. "Ces, you're pregnant. You need your sleep, you and the baby both—"

"I'll nap later." I waved away his comment. "Xavi, just listen. I found out that—"

"No, *you* listen," he insisted. "You have to take care of yourself, babe. You can't just stay up all night and shout at me and forget about—"

"Xavi!" Unable to think of anything else, I scrambled onto his lap, grabbed his face, and kissed him to make him shut up.

It worked.

"Are you listening now?" I asked a few minutes later as I nuzzled my nose to his.

Blearily, he nuzzled me back and then nodded his head. "Yeah. All right."

"Good," I said before delivering another kiss. "Because I need you to hear me when I tell you that you are not Rupert Parker's son. You're Henry's."

His blue eyes were suddenly so wide I honestly thought I might fall into them. "What?"

I stroked his cheek, willing him to listen, hoping to God he would hear this for the blessing it really was. "They lied to you, Xavi. Henry Parker is your real father."

THIRTY-TWO

"So let me see if I've got it," Xavier said in a stunned voice nearly an hour later, after I'd recounted what I'd discovered and read the most important passages aloud to him. "Mum had a thing for Rupert, but Henry had a thing for her. She slept with Henry to make Rupert jealous. Didn't work, but she got knocked up. Then Henry took her back to her family, who kicked her out all over again because of the shame. So he offers to marry her, and desperate and alone, she agrees. Right?"

I nodded where I sat back on my pillows after spending the last hour going through the journals and recounting the tale I'd just read. "Right."

Xavier blew out a long, overwhelmed breath and continued.

"Then they return, and she feels she's made a mistake, but he won't give her a divorce because *he* loves her? So she leaves Kendal, refusing to be held down by a man she can't love who wants to control her. She'd rather be free and poor than trapped." Xavier shook his head. "Christ. Stubborn, wasn't she?"

"Seems like a family trait," I replied, earning a cheeky half-grin in response.

I took the humor as a good sign. If Xavier was managing even part of a smile, the news wasn't completely bowling him over.

"It's just so odd," he said. "I grew up thinking it was him. Rupert, I mean. All my life, he was the one I thought sent the money, even if I never saw him."

"Did your mother ever actually say that Rupert was your dad?" I honestly wondered how he'd gotten that impression. Or if it had just been wishful thinking on Masumi's part, given her feelings for the man.

He frowned, thinking back. "I—I think so. We'd see him on TV every now and then, right? Or maybe in the papers. He was a peer, a major leader in the country. And when she'd see him, she'd nod and tell me that was my father."

I frowned. "Was there...is there any possibility that Henry was in the pictures too? He was the steward, Rupert's right-hand man, so..."

Xavier gulped. By the look on his face, I gathered the answer was yes.

"I don't understand," he said. "Why would Rupert agree to fool everyone into thinking he was my dad and that he had actually married my mum? What was in it for him?" He frowned. "Obviously, something changed when Mum died. That's when Rupert showed up and acknowledged me as his. And then, a few years after that, the marriage certificate was found."

I poked him in the shoulder. "I'm not done with the story. But here, listen to this."

Masumi's memorial service next week. I shan't go—I won't be able to hide the absolute desolation. Everyone would know. They'd know it all. Especially the main point of going, which is to give the boy a foothold in this world.

It surprises me that Rupert would be willing to do it. Granted, I didn't give him a choice. Honestly, if he didn't want me to find him shagging the new viscount two months before his daughter was born and after rumors about them had already ruined Rupert's chances with the Harwood heiress, they shouldn't have chosen my horse's bloody stall as their rendezvous point.

But the one secret my brother doesn't want the world to know is that he loves Bernard Douglas more than anything. So it shouldn't be that much of a surprise that he would essentially become a father to protect him.

Even if it's to ensure that my own son can be the Duke of Kendal one day.

It's all I can really give him.

"Rupert didn't acknowledge you for Henry," I told Xavier after I'd finished. "He did it for Lord Ortham, don't you see? They were lovers, Xavi. The reason your fath—well, Rupert—didn't have children in the end wasn't because of an accident. It was because he was *gay*. Gay and married to a woman he probably couldn't stand." I shook my head. "He did it to protect Bernard. He didn't want to ruin what they had and blow up Lord Ortham's life either."

I closed the journal and turned to look at Xavier, watching carefully as several different emotions passed over his face. Anyone else might have seen nothing. Just another Brit keeping calm and carrying on. But I knew better. There was a flash of grief. Anger. A bit of betrayal. Maybe even some love.

"Fuck—fucking hell," he managed in the end. "So it was all a ruse...to protect me...and to protect the...*man*...my uncle...truly loved?"

I nodded. "Looks that way."

He swallowed hard. "Christ. You know, it's so odd. But now I see it. He and the viscount were such good friends. They'd go on these hunting trips together, for weeks sometimes...no one else was ever allowed to go. Lucy used to tease her father for being a bad shot because he never brought anything back." He shook his head. "I feel like an idiot now. How could they keep that a secret for so long?"

"Same as anyone else does, love," I told him. "They just kept going."

"Do you think he knows?" Xavier said. "Lord Ortham, I mean."

I shook my head. "I don't think so. He said himself he didn't read these journals, and Henry doesn't mention anything about it. If the goal was to convince the world that you were actually Rupert's son, he probably made him swear never to tell a soul. Eliminate the risk of anyone finding out, you know?"

"Mmm. I suppose."

"Plus, if he doesn't know, it explains why he likes you so much," I said. "To him, maybe you're the son he never could have had with Rupert. You're all that's left of his beloved."

"Fancy that," Xavier murmured. He rubbed his forehead, then took the journal and examined it like it was a bomb about to go off. He brushed the edge with his thumb and frowned.

"What is it?" I asked.

Xavier didn't answer, just thumbed the back edge of the journal a few more times, then slid his finger under the edge of the binding. To my surprise, he withdrew a folded sheet of paper.

My eyes popped open. "What is that?"

"Something else Henry wanted to hide." He then unfolded it. And his jaw dropped.

"What is it? What does it say?" I leaned over, but the paper, creased and spotted with age, was almost entirely in Japanese.

"It's...I think it's a marriage license," Xavier said. "It looks exactly like the one that showed my parents were actually married at some point, though the divorce papers were English. Fabricated, obviously. But this is dated November 8th, 1985, same as the original." He blinked and stared at me. "I think he forged Rupert and my mother's license based on this one. Based on *his*. And my mum's."

He picked up the journal again, examined the place where the marriage license had been stowed, then surprised us both by pulling out another folded piece of paper.

"It's a birth certificate." I gasped. "Xavier, that's *your* birth certificate."

"They said it was lost," he whispered. "Misplaced somehow when I was born. We—I—had to file for it later. With Rupert's name, of course, after Mum died."

He covered his mouth, staring with awe at the document that stated plainly his name, his mother's, and his father's—his *real* father, one Henry Merriweather Parker.

"Xavi, do you understand what all of this means?" I asked. "In terms of our situation now, with Parliament and Georgina and everything else?"

He frowned, and then, to my utter sadness, he deflated a bit. "I suppose it means I am really and truly the Duke of Kendal, doesn't it?"

It was true. Because if Rupert died without issue, Henry was the next in line. And since he was, in fact, married to Xavier's mother at the time of his birth, and Rupert ended up having no other children after marrying Georgina, that made Xavier fully legitimate.

It wasn't how I saw it, however.

"No, my love," I told him as I took his chin and turned his head. "It means *you* hold the keys to your future right here in your hands. It means for the first time, *you* have a choice."

Xavier looked down, his gaze bouncing between the documents and the journal as he processed exactly what I was saying. That just like his father before him, he held legitimate fodder over powerful men who had previously toyed with his life like a puppet's on a string. That he could decide whether to keep the truth hidden, let it out, or perhaps use some of the details to convince Lord Ortham, a powerful member of the very committee that might determine his future, to convince the others that whatever Xavier wanted for his future was in fact what was right.

The choice was his.

The choice was ours.

"So, I could be a bastard after all?" Xavier laughed, a sound of pure, booming joy that shook the room like thunder. "If I wanted....I could *choose* not to be the Duke of Kendal. Which means you, my love, would be no duchess."

I grinned so hard I thought my face might split.

"It means," I told him. "We can be whatever we want."

He dropped the papers, then pulled me across his lap and wrapped his arms about my waist.

"Whatever we want," he confirmed as he kissed me once, then again, and again. "So long as we're together."

THIRTY-THREE

"Close your eyes!"

I grinned but did no such thing. I wanted to soak it all in.

It was the kind of homemade party I had grown up with. My grandmother's house was jam-packed with Zolas, Scarrones, Ortizes, and all number of friends and neighbors who had known me since childhood and onward. The dining table was piled with potluck dishes—two platters of Nonna's lasagna, antipasti from the Vincent's, homemade pasteles and empanadas, plus bottles of wine and rum arranged across the kitchen counter that was now acting as a bar. Pink and blue streamers stretched across the ceilings of the living and dining rooms to celebrate the babies on the way—the baby who was now due in six weeks and the little girl Matthew and Nina were expecting in about two.

Right now, the stereo was blasting a playlist Joni had made by a friend of hers who electronically mixed rat pack standards with bachata and salsa beats. It made for a surprising amalgamation that satisfied all age groups in attendance—the younger kids enjoyed the beats while the elders could dance to salsa while singing along with Dean Martin.

I was resting my feet in one of Nonna's wingback chairs, just taking it all in. It was eons away from the luxe lifestyle I'd been living with Xavier for the last several months. To my surprise, I was becoming accustomed to the little benefits of being married to a man richer than God. Things like using a hot water dispenser at the sink instead of waiting for the kettle to boil. Or buying organic almond butter whenever I liked instead of saving up for my guilty pleasure. Having a car at my disposal at any time of day instead of arranging my schedule around public transportation.

These didn't ultimately matter in the grand scheme of things, and I didn't exactly mind the way it used to be. Nothing compared anyway to the comfort I felt right here, surrounded by all the people I loved.

I had two homes now, I realized.

One was here, in the house where I'd been raised, a place my siblings and I would always identify as a safe haven, no matter how old we got. And we'd passed that safety along to our kids. Sofia was scampering around with her cousins like she had all her life, and had taken Olivia, Matthew's new stepdaughter, under her wing as the other girl in the family. Nina watched her daughter with a shining face, and I knew without a doubt that their new baby girl would no more be a stranger to this group than Xavier's and my son. Our family lasted. Always.

Another part of me that yearned for the quiet home Xavier and I were building for ourselves just a little further away.

We'd stayed in London through Christmas, taking a few more months to tie up loose ends before coming home for the foreseeable future. Henry's secret journals lay safe in a vault deep inside Coutts, where the Parkers (along with half of England's aristocrats) had stowed their most valuable treasures and secrets since the sixteen hundreds. It took some time, but in the end, Xavier had decided to keep the title his *real* father had fought so hard for him to have, though he did give up his hereditary seat in the House of Lords. Should the day come when someone or other wanted to hold the matter of his legitimacy over his head, we had the evidence that would confirm his claim, even if it would potentially blow up another man's world.

Not that we worried much about it. The only other person who knew about the journals was Bernard Douglas, the Viscount of Ortham, who was now an entirely useful advocate in Parliament. Discovering that we not only knew about his past but didn't judge him for it made Lord Ortham even warmer toward Xavier. Like an uncle, maybe. Or a stepfather.

But even more important was that, for the first time in his life, Xavier's world was a matter of his own choice. Not someone else's. Not hostage to a signature or one man's recognition.

It belonged to him.

Henry had given him that, even if unwittingly.

Maybe, deep down, Henry Parker knew that every person deserved the truth. Especially since, in our case, it really did set us free.

It was in that spirit that Xavier and I had purchased a townhouse on Riverside Drive, one of the quietest parts of the Upper West Side. Initially, I had argued that we should wait to make a decision on where to live until we knew which school I was going to attend next fall. Xavier, however, was fully aware that Columbia was at the top of my list, just like it was when we first met, and wouldn't believe in anything other than my immanent acceptance.

"I'd never bet on failure," he'd told me when we toured the house right after the new year. "Not when it comes to you, babe."

And then he had proceeded, in very Xavier-like fashion, to lay out a perfectly logical argument about the centrality of the Upper West Side to all the other boroughs, no matter where I was accepted. That, combined with the fact that it was my very favorite part of the city and, of course, where we'd first met, won me over.

Xavier had always understood the unique combination of whimsy and pragmatism that enchanted the path to my heart.

"Frankie!" Lea barked from the other side of the kitchen counter. "For God's sake, Nina's cooperating. Stop being so difficult so we can freaking surprise you!"

"Better do what she says, babe," Xavier murmured. "I tried to offer advice on how to dice the onions for the sauce yesterday, and I thought your sister was going to chop my balls up instead."

I snickered, too easily imagining Lea waving a knife Xavier's way, but obeyed and shut my eyes.

"Finally," Lea breathed. "Come on, Katie. These things weigh a ton."

I squinted with one eye open in time to watch Lea and Katie walk into the room, each bearing one of the familiar sheet cakes from Gino's. One was decorated in pink for Nina's baby, the other in blue for us. Both were outlined with ribbons of thick, buttery icing, scrawled with "It's a Boy!" and "It's a Girl!" on our respective sides, along with appropriately colored rattles.

"Do you think we should tell them the tech made a mistake?" I murmured to Xavier, who just grinned. "That we have no idea what the sex really is and won't find out until the baby is born?"

"Do you think I want to tell Lea she might be wrong in front of sixty members of her closest friends and relatives?" he responded. "I'd still like to be able to make a third baby with you, Ces."

My jaw dropped. "You'd like to *what*?"

Xavier just offered me his patented shark-like grin—one of many that was appearing more and more frequently. "One day, maybe." He leaned in close so his scent of fire, salt, and man could drive the shock off my face and replace it with pure desire. "Woman, I'd make a dozen babies with you, if you were willing."

Before I could reply, he nipped my ear, then delivered a kiss to my cheek that somehow managed to be chaste enough for our family audience and still set the rest of my skin alight.

"Congratulations!" Lea and Katie said together, which prompted the rest of the crowd to offer varying iterations of the same thing in Italian, English, and Spanish as Nina and I both leaned over to blow out our candles. Then they all blew up in applause the way only people from this neighborhood, causing both Nina and me to laugh so hard we almost started crying while Xavier and Matthew looked on with the proud expressions of expectant fathers. I even caught my overprotective brother offer Xavier and handshake and a slap on the back—a far cry from a fistfight in the Mediterranean.

A bit of guilt pulled at my stomach as I watched Xavier accept this kind of love for maybe the first time in his life. Whenever we had these moments, it would hit me just how much I had taken from him the first time. The parties and celebrations, first steps or smiles, or just the opportunity to be part of a family like this. The kind of family Xavier had, in his heart, always wanted.

And then, like it always did, the feeling passed when he turned to me, blue eyes shining with love and forgiveness, and squeezed my hand. Because he knew what I was thinking. Just like he knew that while neither of us could change the mistakes of the past, we could look to the future and love each other as best we could, moving forward.

We could make that choice every day for each other.

And we did.

———

TWO SLICES of cake and several toasts later, I was watching Xavier and Matthew engaging in a rousing game of tag with the littles in the backyard when Joni came to stand next to me.

She tossed back what smelled like a very strong rum and Coke to my oversensitive nose, then leaned her forehead against the sliding glass door and heaved a great sigh that clouded half the pane of glass.

Joni was never much for subtlety.

"You okay?" I asked with a hand on her shoulder.

I'd noticed something had been off all afternoon. Usually, Joni was the life of the party, flirting with half the boys in the neighbor-hood and several of their fathers too. Today, however, she'd been pouting in the corner for a while now, giving one-word answers when approached, ignoring all five of the Ramirez boys, and casting nasty looks at Lea and Nonna every few minutes. Most likely, Lea and Nonna had vetoed an inappropriate wardrobe choice or maybe embarrassed her in front of one of her friends.

But instinct told me it was something more. Just like Joni wasn't one to avoid the spotlight, she also wasn't one to hold a grudge for longer than thirty minutes.

My baby sister sighed again. "I just got some really, *really* bad news this morning." She cast another long look at Nonna across the room. "Look at her. Laughing away like she didn't just toss me to the curb this morning like yesterday's trash."

"Nonna kicked you out?"

I frowned toward Nonna, who was in classic gossip mode with her best friend, Mrs. Castanetta. That didn't sound like my grand-mother at all. She wasn't exactly easy on us, but she'd provided a landing place our whole lives. Granted, Joni was the baby and maybe needed to be pushed out of the nest a bit, but she was still only twenty-four, and New York was expensive. Maybe I was jaded, but we'd all assumed she'd just live with our grandmother until someone put a ring on it and housed her somewhere else.

"Yep," Joni replied bitterly. "I'm officially homeless. Nonna's getting rid of the house."

My head snapped back to my sister. "She's selling the house?"

A pang of fear lodged itself deep in my gut. Even though I'd prob-ably never live here again, the thought of this place no longer being available was scarier than an act of revelation.

Joni shook her head. "Even worse. She's renting it so she has a little extra cash-o-la coming in while she frolics all over Europe like a ho."

Fear melted into annoyance. "Joni! Don't talk about Nonna like that."

"Oh, please," she snarked, tossing back another mouthful of Coke-flavored rum. "What do you think she's going there for? The good pasta? She spends three whole months there this fall, comes back for Christmas, then jets back for another three months until the shower and my downfall. She's obviously met someone. Or someones."

"Or maybe she's reconnecting with her family for the first time in decades," I said back. "She's spent most of her life taking care of kids and grandkids. It's about time she takes care of herself. You can't really hold that against her."

"But what am I supposed to do?" Joni whined. "I only just went back to work at the lounge, but they haven't even promoted me to bartender yet. I barely make enough to pay my cell phone bill, much less cover rent anywhere within two hours of the city." She snorted. "Watch me have to move to like Buffalo or something just to survive."

"What about dance?" I asked. "I thought that's what you were working toward. You've been out of surgery for six months now. Are you still doing your PT exercises at home and everything?"

Joni shook her head. "I—I just can't risk it. It's not going to happen for me anymore."

I bit my lip, concerned. This was worse than I'd thought. The last we'd spoken about her injury—which admittedly hadn't been for several months—I got the impression that Joni was on the road to recovering her once-burgeoning dance career.

Now she'd given up completely on the one thing she'd ever been proud of.

"Wow, Jo. Gosh, I'm so sorry."

She slumped against the window. "It's fine. I'm dealing with it." Then she tossed back the rest of her drink and stared at the empty cup. "Looks like I'm due for a refill." She turned around, clearly looking for the bar full of drinks. "Looks like Johnny Ramirez is still pouring cocktails. Maybe if I flirt with him enough, he'll convince his parents to give me the spare room in their attic."

It was a joke. Or I thought. But something in her voice truly broke my heart. My little sister was in the process of losing, well, if not her innocence, then some kind of faith in the world. The belief that no matter what happens, everything will turn out all right in the end.

It's a sad realization that everyone has to have when they truly grow up.

Happy endings come to those who make them, not those who wait for them.

"Joni," I said again, reaching out to keep her from doing something stupid.

But she shook me off.

"Don't," Joni replied too sharply to be a product of alcohol. "Don't pity me like that unless you're willing to help, Frankie."

Without waiting for a reaction, she weaved her way through the party to where the Ramirez brothers were waiting, both eager as always to bask in the attention of Belmont's biggest flirt.

I sighed. There wasn't much I could do. Some things Joni was just going to have to learn on her own.

"All right?"

The screen door opened behind me, and Xavier wrapped his arms around my shoulders and pulled me against his chest.

I nuzzled into his forearm and sighed with contentment. "I'm fine. Joni, though..."

I told him about our conversation. By the end, Xavier was frowning compassionately.

"Poor girl," he said. "It's rough, being tossed out on your own for the first time. I don't care what the circumstances are." Then his eyes blinked open a bit wider. "She's not going to ask to live with us, is she? Seriously, we don't have that much room with the construction."

I'd personally thought the new house was fine as-is, but Xavier had insisted on opening up two full floors to accommodate the needs of a world-class kitchen and a primary suite on the floor below the kids for our...privacy. When I asked why, Xavier only said it was his right as my husband to make me scream as loud as he liked.

I wasn't about to argue with that.

Right now, however, we were confined to a kitchenette in the attic and three small bedrooms.

As if in answer to new uncle's question, Lea's youngest opened her mouth and delivered a world-class shriek. Across the room, Joni visibly shuddered.

"I doubt it," I told him. "There's a reason she never wanted to live with Lea's family either, even after they inherited Mike's parents' place and had five bedrooms. If anything, she'll try to bum off Kate."

Xavier thought for a moment. "Should we offer the Red Hook house? It's not too late to back out of the lease. We could talk to your brother."

Matthew, ever the protective eldest Zola kid, still insisted my name remain on the deed of the house, even after Xavier and I had gotten married. I really didn't need it anymore, but we were now co-owners of yet another safety net.

"Just in case," he'd said with a cryptic look at my husband, whom I had a feeling Matthew would always want to punch a little. And judging from Xavier's glare in return, it was a feeling that went both ways.

I also had a feeling I knew what Matthew would say to that proposition—exactly what I was thinking when it came to Joni.

"I don't think so," I said. "I think maybe Joni needs to figure this one out on her own first. Or at least try."

"I'm surprised," Xavier said. "You and I both know how hard it can be out there on your own. Why make it worse for her than it has to be?"

I thought about that for a moment. "I mean, I'd never leave her homeless or anything. And part of me wants to help more. But it's not like Joni has a baby to support or is incapable or anything. She's just a twenty-four-year-old who needs to learn to be on her own."

I turned in his arms to look at him. Even with my belly putting a bit more space between us than we liked, Xavier was big enough that his hands still caught my waist with ease.

"You have to understand. Ever since she was a baby, Joni's had everyone doing everything for her. She didn't learn to walk until she was maybe fifteen months because we carried her everywhere. Never had to do homework on her own because we'd step in and help her. She didn't even learn to tie her shoes until she was maybe twelve because someone would always give in and do it to get us out the door." I shrugged. "If Nonna's kicking her out, I think it's for a good reason. She probably knows the same thing—Joni's got to grow up. We shouldn't stand in the way of that."

Xavier didn't argue, just smiled at me. "Look at my smart wife. God, you're a good mum, Ces."

I grinned. "Even to my baby sister?"

He pressed a kiss to my forehead. "To anyone who needs it. But especially our babies."

Automatically, I set a hand atop my belly, imagining the little one within. Who they might be. What they might look like. Life was about to change drastically for our family, but instead of being afraid of those changes, I honestly couldn't wait.

I wanted to see the look on Xavier's face when he held the little creature for the first time. What songs he would sing when he rocked them to sleep. How he'd feel the first time they'd take their first steps or say "Dada" out loud.

If there was anything Xavier and I were supposed to be together, it was a family. Of that, I had no doubt. Adding to that family would only add joy.

"I've got a surprise for you," Xavier said after delivering a kiss that left me breathless.

I chuckled. "You're not really making sex jokes in the middle of our baby shower, are you?"

He snorted. "No. Although I wouldn't mind dirtying up your childhood bedroom while the party goes on. No, it's this. Arrived in the mail this morning. I snagged it on our way out."

He pulled an envelope out of his back pocket and handed it to me. Immediately, I spotted the return address in the top left corner: Columbia University.

All my breath left me as I took the letter, then looked up at Xavier as terror skittered up my arms and into my chest.

"Oh, fuck," I murmured.

Xavier chuffed. "Better not let Sof hear you. I know you're afraid if you're using that word."

"Open it." I thrust the letter at him. "Please, Xavi. I'm too scared..."

He opened his mouth to say no, then tipped his head as he seemed to sense something on my face that shouldn't be pressed too far. "All right."

I shifted between the balls of my feet as he ripped open the envelope and read the letter silently to himself.

It took forever.

"Come on," I demanded impatiently. "Xavi! What does it say?"

"Hold on, I'm reading all of it." He seemed determined to torture me as he continued, forcing me to wait far longer than necessary.

"Xavi!"

Finally, Xavier looked up from the letter with a sly grin, blue eyes dancing. "Does this mean I'll get to call you Professor Parker when we're in bed, my love?"

I grinned, pinked with pleasure at both the ideas of my husband's moves and being addressed that way by anyone. "Give me that."

There it was. The official words I'd been dying to see for the last three months—really the last six years, ever since I'd been a master's student at CUNY, hanging out on Amsterdam Avenue and studying at the Morningside campus, dreaming of the days when I could be a part of the most venerated institution in the city of my birth.

Dear Ms. Zola,

We are pleased to offer you admission to the PhD program in English Literature at Columbia University...

The rest of the words of my acceptance letter faded away as other visions took their place.

I could see it now.

Lecture halls full of students. Mountains of papers to grade. Presentations at MLA. Tenure meetings. Being part of a community of scholars as passionate about literature as I'd always been.

Heck, maybe I'd even get a corduroy blazer with patches on the elbows. I wondered if Xavier would mind if I ever needed glasses. Knowing him, he'd probably make me wear them in bed with nothing else on. Give a whole new meaning to being "hot for teacher."

I looked up at that strong, talented, mercurial, impossibly beautiful husband of mine. Hope and happiness glittered in his sapphire blue eyes, and I knew mine radiated the same emotions right back at him.

"Happy?" he asked as he leaned down to press his lips to mine.

I nodded. "So happy."

And I meant it.

Because whatever the future held, as duke and duchess, chef and professor, or husband and wife, we'd face it together.

And I, for one, couldn't wait.

EPILOGUE

Giovanna Emilia Zola—known to her family and friends as Joni—stood outside of the Ambassador Theatre in the heart of New York's Broadway district. It was only eight o'clock—nowhere near late enough for her sister and brother's co-baby shower to be winding down back in Belmont. Italians and Puerto Ricans knew how to get down. More than likely, the celebration would still be going by the time she got home, well after anyone expecting babies or older than eighty decided to retire for the night.

Normally, Joni wasn't the type to skip out on any kind of party. She was more the dance-on-tables, sing-karaoke-'til-three, make-out-on-the-terrace-'til-five type. The one-everyone-stuck-around-to-see-what-she-would-do type.

Normally, she thrived on that kind of attention. Tonight, though, she just couldn't stand it.

Yes, part of it was finding out literally the morning before the guests started arriving that her grandmother was moving to Italy for a year and renting out the house while she was gone, giving Joni exactly two weeks to pack up her world of twenty-four years in that house and find somewhere to live.

But it wasn't just that.

It was the joy on her sister's face when her giant hulk of a husband fed her a forkful of the too-sweet cake from Gino's.

It was the way her brother grinned, giddy with excitement, at Nina's giant belly whenever he thought she wasn't watching him.

It was the fact that even Nonna, an almost eighty-year-old widow who hadn't traveled so far as Yonkers in the last fifty years, was stepping out for an adventure of her own and probably getting laid to boot.

Everyone had something.

And Joni had nothing but a bum knee, a GED, and a body most men liked to look at but had never once talked about marrying.

She found herself standing outside the Ambassador Theatre, tall and brown with the banners for *Chicago* toppling down its sides, displaying its dancers with their fish-netted legs and red lips and sexpot looks for days. The choreography was famous, just like almost any show done by the great Bob Fosse. You couldn't watch these dancers with their sultry, sinuous moves and not want to be them.

And she'd almost done it. God, she'd been so close. Two days from accomplishing the dream she'd had since she was seven years old and her second-grade class got to see *Cats* right before it left Broadway. It was a bonkers musical, just one random song after another while these people dressed up like freaking kitties had danced all over the stage, hung like acrobats, even swayed their way up and down the aisles. She hadn't had the slightest idea what was happening. All she knew was that she wanted to be right there. On that stage. With those people.

And everyone's eyes on her.

At the time, she'd been a mediocre student in a weekly ballet class at the Belmont community center. But from that point onward, she became the star, to the point where Ms. Velasquez told Nonna within a year that Joni had real promise and helped get her a scholarship to a serious dance studio downtown.

Dance was the only thing she'd ever been able to focus on. It was there when she couldn't pass the tenth grade. It was there when she couldn't hold on to any other jobs. It was there always, the only dream she'd ever had, existing right here on these very streets, in theaters like this, giving her hope she could really be something in this life.

Until it all ended just six months ago, days before she was supposed to dance on Broadway right here. In this very show.

They'd taken her name and pictures off the outside display the day after she'd screwed up her knee. She only knew because Kayla, the company member who was taking her place, had posted a picture of it on her Instagram stories with a bunch of heart emojis and the words *OMG MY BROADWAY DEBUT!!!* in giant red letters that matched the *Chicago* logo.

Joni turned, but instead of walking in the direction of Times Square, toward lights and people and, most importantly, the subway stations that would carry her back home to the Bronx, she walked west toward Hell's Kitchen, until she found herself on Eighth Avenue, where cars rushed past the odd, twenty-four-hour mix of theaters, tourist shops, and the last remnants of the peepshows and strip clubs that used to take up most of this part of town well before she'd been born.

"Hey, sweetheart! Need a lift?" shouted a guy from a beat-up Acura zooming past while it blared old-school Run-DMC from the stereo.

The others with him hooted and whistled, like she was no better than the sex workers who used to walk this corner back in the day.

"To your mother's house!" she called, swinging a hand toward the car like she wanted to give the guy the finger. It was the same half-gesture she'd learned from her grandmother and her aunties and however many other women all over the Bronx who did the exact same thing to any no-good asshole who yelled things at strange women on a Saturday night.

But the car had long disappeared with the flow of traffic under the city lights. And when Joni stopped staring in the direction it had gone, she turned and found herself looking up at a sign, lit up just like one of the marquees on Broadway, except this one had silhouettes of naked girls and a cat wearing a top hat on the front holding a stack of dollar bills.

Funny what a difference a block makes.

One of the doors swung open, making way for clouds of stale alcohol, screeches of eighties hair bands, and men hooting at the dancers collecting cash in their G-strings.

Maybe this was where she belonged. She knew enough girls in this business who swore up and down you could make some real money if you were any good. Joni already knew men liked her—had known since she was far too young. Why not put that to use? She was naked all the time in her bedroom—was there really much difference doing it in front of strangers who wanted to give her their money for the pleasure?

She bit her lip and almost reached for the door. But it opened again as another man left, and again, the scent of stale alcohol followed along with cheap cigars and bad sex.

Not here, at least. Not now. There had to be other ways to find rent for a place to live that wouldn't make her siblings give her *that* look of shame every time they saw her—the one she'd been avoiding all her life.

Joni turned on her heel and walked on, until she had reached her final destination in Hell's Kitchen.

"Hey, Winston," she said to the bouncer, who waved her into Opal without a word.

The bar was quiet for a Saturday night, but it was still early. It didn't really fill until almost midnight anyway, when the girls got on their platforms and Tom, the owner, turned up the bass. It was early enough that Tom himself was still manning the bar until the main staff arrived.

Joni took a chance.

"Hey, kid," said Tom as she approached. "You're not working tonight. Unless you changed your mind about that spot again..."

Joni glanced nervously at the empty platforms built into the wall over the bar. The second one from the right used to be hers—the prime spot everyone saw the second they walked in the door. It wasn't Broadway, but it was still an audience. An audience she almost missed...

But Joni shook her head. "No, I still can't dance. But I wanted to know if we could start training tonight instead of next week. I just found out my living situation is changing, and—"

"I'm sorry, kiddo," Tom said. "I don't got the time, and we're expecting a rush after *Chicago* gets out. I'm already out a bartender as it is until the ten o'clock shift starts."

"Then tonight is perfect!" Joni cried. "I'll be your apprentice. I'll even work for free tonight, Tom—do whatever you want, help however I can, do what you do so I can take over when you're ready. *Please*, Tom. Just until Conrad or Liz get here. I can do it, I know I can."

The older man gave her a long look. "You think you can really do this? You can't be messing up my cash flow, Joni. I know you ain't so good with numbers."

Joni bit her lip. It always came back to that, didn't it? So what if she barely passed her GED and flunked out of college? Twice. Dancing was supposed to be her exit from that world, but it wasn't like bartending was rocket science.

"I'm better now than when I was a shot girl," she lied completely. "I won't mess up any of the tabs. Please, Tom, I'm desperate. I—I really need this."

Something in her voice broke, but that seemed to do it for her boss. Tom just pulled at his mustache and shook his graying brown head.

"Shit," he muttered. "Don't go crying on me now. You're lucky you're so cute, you know that, honey?"

"Thank you!" Joni squealed as she practically leaped over the bar and threw her arms around Tom's neck.

"Easy," said the barman, though he was laughing as he did. "Now, go in the back and get yourself an apron, all right? You're gonna need it until you get your bearings."

All smiles, Joni practically skipped through the bar to follow Billy's commands. Maybe it wasn't a job on Wall Street, but if she could get her shit together, she might convince Billy to give her this shift and start making some real tips. Maybe then she could afford at least a room with a few other people—Hoboken, maybe, or Riverdale, near Kate.

Her dreams of living in Manhattan and dancing on Broadway were long gone, but maybe one day, she could find what her siblings had in partners and jobs and kids and all that. But for now, she could start small. A job today. A place to live next week.

One step at a time.

Almost like a dance.

————

Francesca

"I wonder where Joni went," I said as I got ready for bed later that evening.

Xavier and I had left the party in time to get Sofia down for bed, though it was still in full swing when we'd said our goodbyes.

My husband looked like a particularly delicious rake this evening, sitting shirtless in nothing but a pair of silk pajama pants that pooled around his hips. His winding tattoo climbed up from the waistband, wrapping around his torso and left arm, which he tucked over my shoulder. He was reviewing menus from prospective chefs for the gastropub he was planning in Brooklyn. His forehead crinkled with an adorably pensive expression as he made notes on each one, frowning over the words in a way that caused a divot to appear between his brows.

"Was she here?" he murmured as he penciled a note that looked like it said "mushroom fiesta," but was probably something else.

"Of course not," I said as I combed out my hair in front of the full-length mirror set up next to our shared closet.

The room was small for the two of us. A guestroom we were using while our primary suite downstairs was being finished. I didn't mind. I was used to cozy enclaves, and considering I had been sleeping at the top of a staircase until about nine months ago, this was still pretty damn luxurious to me.

Plus, I sort of liked cuddling up together every night. I had no plans to stop once we were back in a king-size bed.

"She disappeared about an hour before we left. You didn't notice?"

Xavi looked down his long nose at me in a way that said both "you ridiculous woman" and "I love you to pieces" at the same time. It was one of my favorite expressions.

"Considering I spent most of my evening eating far too much of your grandmother's pasta and trying to stop your brother from making jokes about punching me again, I can't say I noticed when one of your four sisters left a crowd of two hundred."

"Fifty-five, maybe, but I see your point," I said as I turned back to the mirror. "And I don't think my siblings will ever get over that joke, so you'd better get used to it."

"They'd better get used to me," Xavier mumbled as he went back to his menus. "Bloody prat."

I smiled to myself. While I doubted that Matthew and Xavier were ever going to be best friends, a grudging respect had grown between the two after the story of our last months in London had gotten around. The fact that Xavier had essentially given up an entire dukedom to raise his kids near my family definitely earned him a bunch of points. Likewise, the insults that Xavier accorded my brother had been downgrading steadily. Calling Matthew a "bloody prat" was practically asking him out for beers in Xavier-speak.

So maybe they weren't bosom buddies yet. But I had faith.

A pair of arms wrapped around my waist as Xavier's chin appeared over my shoulder in the mirror's reflection. His hands curved over my stomach, which was roughly the size of a basketball pressing through the fabric of my nightie.

"Sometimes I think you will *never* be as beautiful as you look right now," Xavier murmured before nipping lightly at my ear. "But the next day, you blow me away all over again."

I purred like a kitten as his big hands rubbed over my bump, then slid up to cup my breasts, which were full and increasingly tender. Every inch of my skin was set alight when Xavier touched me.

He said the same thing nearly every day as my pregnancy progressed, and miraculously, it seemed like he meant it. As I'd started to show, I'd worried that Xavier might be repelled by my changing body—a true hardship given the fact that my increased libido showed no signs of letting up. But every day, this beautiful man found ways to show me how desired I was, how treasured in his eyes. We took the concept of choice seriously in our house—and every day, we both chose each other.

I drifted my hands over his forearms, wrapping my ribcage, reveling in the muscles that somehow managed to be powerful and graceful at the same time. I trailed a finger over the whirling designs over his left wrist, then threaded my fingers with his and leaned back into his chest, content to rest there for a moment, looking at the two of us—no, *three* of us here together.

We had circled around and around for weeks when it came to names, especially now that we knew we had to be prepared with two options.

"What about Masumi or Henry?" I'd offered at first, but that was quickly batted away.

"Let sleeping dogs lie," Xavier had said. "My parents made enough trouble in their own lives. I'd rather let them rest now."

There was one person he wanted to honor, however—the only other person who had ever loved Xavier for exactly who he was, no questions asked, no expectations, no other requirements.

In the end, Lucia or Luciano had meant the same thing as their namesake, Lucy: light. That was what she had been to Xavier. And that was what we were to each other now.

At first, I'd been sad when the radiologist told us he thought the first 3D ultrasounds had been read incorrectly. I'd really believed I was having a little boy. I'd imagined the way he'd look—button-nosed and blue-eyed like his sister and father, but maybe with slightly darker skin and a bow-shaped mouth like mine. Sofia was a tiny thing, but I thought maybe her brother would be tall like their dad. And loved by both of us for anything he wanted to be. So, so loved.

But standing there, I realized it didn't matter whether the baby was a boy or a girl, what features they might have from either of us. The last part of my dreams were never going to change. This treasure would be adored just like their sister. We'd worship this little creature with everything we had. Give them everything we could.

I imagined myself their parent, holding the baby, cooing to their face, kissing their dimples. And I smiled because it was going to happen, no matter what. It really felt like our *family* was going to happen no matter what. We were meant to meet that night in the bar. I was meant to have Xavier's baby, just like he was meant to run into me years later. No matter how many times we tried to stay apart, fate kept throwing us back together.

Just like it had again with this little one inside me.

"Babe. *Babe.*" Xavier's fingers guided my face back up to meet his, those blue eyes sparking with curiosity and love. "I know that look, Ces. What book are you living in now?"

My smile widened. My husband knew me well. But he didn't know this.

"Just me."

I pulled him down for a kiss. Then another. And another and

another until Xavier's grin lit up the room and his growl stirred my deepest desires.

"Just Francesca Zola Parker," I said against his lips, sighing with more contentment than I ever thought possible. "My story has such a happy ending, it's the only one I need."

———

THE END

THANK you so much for reading the Silver Spoon Trilogy!

WANT MORE XAVIER AND FRANKIE?

Get your extended epilogue here or copy and paste www.nicolefrenchromance.com/silverspoonepilogue into your web browser.

———

LOOKING FOR JONI'S STORY?

Her roommates-to-lovers, grumpy-sunshine romance with a billionaire doctor is coming 2024! Keep reading for a sneak peek or **preorder here: www.nicolefrenchromance.com/ jonisstory**

———

NEED MORE BILLIONAIRE ROMANCE?

She's a prickly law intern who hates rich people. He's her billionaire boss who won't take no for an answer.

Read Legally Yours now in Kindle Unlimited at www.nicolefrenchromance.com/legallyyours or keep reading for a free excerpt.

———

WANT **Matthew and Nina's story?**

You can read their prequel, The Scarlet Night, FREE via my website. **Get your copy here: www.nicolefrenchromance. com/thescarletnight**

ACKNOWLEDGMENTS

I am absolutely blown away by the love readers have shown Frankie and Xavier. Thank you all so much for enjoying and supporting their story from the beginning. Readers are the end-all, be-all, the absolutely reason for being of this industry. I could not do it without any of you, forever and always.

There are, of course, other people who must be thanked for their help in making this book happen. The usual suspects, of course, in Patricia, Dawn, Kymberly, and Lacie. Your cheerleading and critical feedback keep me writing every day. Another massive thanks to Michaela, who was ever-willing to correct my British slang and point out when Frankie needed to stand up for herself.

Loads of gratitude to Danielle Leigh, my assistant, who is always available to manage my ARC team (thank you to them as well!) and pinch-hit on a variety of other tasks whenever I need her. To Dani Sanchez of Wildfire Marketing, who has stepped up as my agent as well and is always willing to brainstorm marketing, blurbs, or any other part of the business at any time. To my editorial team in Emily Hainsworth and Marla Esposito, who always make sure I don't overuse the words "really," "open mouth" or "sharks" (among many others). You are all gems in a world of coal.

And of course to my people. To Laura, Kate, Jane, Claudia, and Parker, who assuage all amounts of crying on my part with their wit, humor, and compassion. You are treasures. And, of course, my very own broody lord—Mr. French, whom I love more than any of these words, and the family we've created together. I love you all more than any of these words could ever say.

xo,

Nic